WHEN YOUR LIFE BECOMES CONSUMED WITH HUNTING MONSTERS, CAN YOU REMEMBER WHAT IT MEANS TO BE HUMAN…?

"The horror of the werewolf is not truly in his claws and fangs, but in his heart. There is a reason why werewolves are drawn first and foremost to hunt the ones whom they love when in human form. Ultimately, the curse draws them not to gain animalistic urges, so much as to lose their humanity. Do you see the difference?"

"I think so," I said, but the immensity of that was hard to wrap my head around.

"Do not ever mistake a werewolf for an animal, Detective," he said. "They are not animals—they are *monsters*…" He stared off into the night again. "And the tragedy of it is that every last one of them ultimately *wishes* to be such a monster…"

Also by Kevin Wright

The Danse Trilogy:

THE KNIGHT OF CUPS

THE QUEEN OF PENTACLES

THE KING OF SWORDS

THE QUEEN OF PENTACLES

— The Danse, Book Two —

Kevin Wright

Dedicated to

Wendy, Megan, and Alex, for their encouragement, support, and love

and to

Dad, Mom, Lindsay, Craig, and my whole family, for their inspiration

and to

Richard, Randy, Cliff, Bill, and the FCC family for making this happen
(especially Jim, for encouraging this and lending it a special poignancy)

Table of Contents

Preface

Okay, I guess that I should probably start out by apologizing for lying to you the last time. But then again, when you think about it, I wasn't *really* lying, so I guess that I shouldn't feel too guilty. I mean, the last thing I said was that I never saw Durant again… and that was true, at the time that I'd written it. I really did figure that I'd never run across him again, and that life would more or less settle back down to normal after all of that fiasco with Lord Ruthven and the gang war cooled off. Go figure.

Of course, that was all a while back, and before everything that went down around Roscoe Village with Sydor and Lyn, before that trip into the dark tunnels of Mkogisos and the Lost Children, and before I learned firsthand about the war between *La Société des Dragonistes* and the *Synod of Crows*. And before the Grail was—

Nope, I'm doing it again. I'm getting ahead of myself, and I promised her I wouldn't do that. Nothing that I'm writing here is going to mean what it *should* mean unless I put it in its proper context, and I owe everyone involved the honor of at least trying my best to make it mean what it *should* mean.

Think about it—if I didn't do this right, how would anyone accept that the same sort of crap could happen to the same cop twice? You'd laugh it off as an impossible coincidence, when in this case, coincidence obviously had absolutely nothing to do with any of it.

So just read it, and hopefully you'll see what I mean. But let me warn you right now, before you begin—this story does not end nicely…

Chapter 1
The Body in the Alleyway

So, this winter, Tony de Tullio and I were chasing Terrance "Sticky Ike" Eisenhower down an alley in Roscoe Village. Now, before you say anything too snarky, yes, Tony was actually running. He wasn't very good at it, mind you, but what he lacked in athletic ability, he more than made up for in determination. So while I was catching up with Ike, Tony was painfully but determinedly huffing and puffing not that far behind me. I figured that he'd have to down at least two cans of Coke when this was all over to make up for the effort.

But maybe I ought to back up a little bit, since not everyone reading this will have read my previous book. Okay, let's be honest here—almost no one read my previous book. My wife, Joanna, did, but that's because she's nice and she loves me and because she's good at fixing all of my spelling errors for me. My mom read it, but that's because *she's my mom*, and it's in the "mom contract" somewhere that reading your kid's book belongs in the same category as going to all of the football games, plays, recitals, track meets, etc., to give them that all-important "attaboy" to keep them feeling good about themselves. Tony said that he'd started to read it, got bored, and gave up on it. In all, I figure that maybe—*maybe*—seven people on the planet read the stupid thing, and that includes the editor who published it.

So why did I write it? Well, certainly not because I have any gift at writing, obviously. But I'm still happy that, officially, the truth is out there. Every night, parents tell their children that there's no boogeyman in the closet or monster under the bed, and they're probably right. And they're completely right to try to alleviate the kids' fears. But the truth is, there really are things out there that go "bump" in the night, and not every horror story is entirely fiction. I've seen some pretty terrible things in the past two years perpetrated by some pretty unbelievable creatures—but I also know that they're not the only things out there in the night. The things that stalk the rest of us are being hunted by something even scarier than they are, and they know it... and that's how I sleep well each night.

Then again, I've seen some pretty terrible things over the years being perpetrated by regular, honest-to-goodness human beings, too. To give you some context for that night in Roscoe Village, Tony and I were on loan to the department's joint task force, working with the FBI on the clean-up after this year's Operation Cross Country, the national sweep targeting child prostitution and human trafficking. More than 100 kids were rescued and more than 150 people were arrested in the span of three days—and that was just *this* year's sweep—so that should tell you something about how much is going on out there.

Now, whenever I start talking about human trafficking, people always seem to think about mail-order Russian brides, or about girls being shipped off to Thailand, but the truth is, slavery is alive and well right here in the United States too. Oh, it's illegal—and it *is* worse in other countries—but that doesn't mean that it can't or doesn't happen here. We found one teenaged girl chained by her ankle to a bedpost in a nice-looking house in a middle-class, northern suburb. They'd gotten her addicted to heroin as a control mechanism, and then forced her to service multiple johns a day, or else they'd cut off her supply and refuse to give her any food. You'd think that the neighbors would've noticed the lines of guys that came by the house every evening when the day shift let out, but I guess as long as you mow your lawn and trim your hedges, people don't really tend to care about what's going on inside your home.

The fact is, human trafficking of one kind or another is the fastest-growing crime in our world today, whether or not we want to admit it, for the same reason that media piracy is so rampant. You can only sell a bag of cocaine once, to one buyer or another, but you can copy the same movie or pimp out the body of the same prostitute multiple times, to multiple consumers, and still retain your original product at the end of the day. There's a good reason why the consistently highest-grossing genre of movie in America isn't comedy or science fiction, but pornography—because every economist knows that low overhead plus high consumption equals massive profit. Worldwide, the average slave only costs about $2,000 to buy, and yet brings in more than $2,500 in net, ongoing, *monthly* income for their owner. That's a 1500% profit in the first year alone. And whether that slave works his fingers to the bone in a bean field in California or works on her back in a bordello in Houston—or the suburbs of Chicago—it doesn't change the fact that the slavery *exists.*

Anyway, so Tony and I were working with the Feds, as well as with a couple of detectives from Area 3, along the lakefront—which is what had brought us over here to Roscoe Village. I know that I've said it before, but I have to admit that I've always had a weird sort of vibe whenever I'm in the Village. It always feels like I've stepped into someplace *else*, like it isn't really Chicago anymore, like it's an older world or something. It's a dumb feeling—I mean, North Center's a great area, and Tony says he's never felt that way at all—but I can't help that it just makes me feel like something's a half-step off whenever I cross under those Metra tracks into Roscoe Village. I felt the same way that day.

Of course, it also doesn't help that it's Insane Deuces territory, and they're none too fond of Tony and me since that gang war that *almost* happened a couple of years back. They tend not to like cops in general, but they really hold a grudge against cops who were involved with the killings of some of their most popular gang members. When we'd investigated the murder of an ID enforcer named Hector Flórez, I ended up killing (okay, *re*-killing) another one named Mojo, and Durant killed a well-liked guy that they'd known as Billy "the Kid" Rivers—who actually turned out to be a vampire named Ruthven, who'd been around for centuries. Yeah, it was that level of weirdness. And if you don't already know who Durant is, this isn't really the time for me to explain him to you. I'll have to get to him later on.

So we were working with an Area 3 detective named Emilio Santos, following up a lead on a murder that we were trying to tie to an Isador Postyshev, a member of the *Solntsevskaya Bratva*—the Russian mafia— and a key figure in the underage sex trade on the north side. The Russians have always been big on things like wire fraud, cybercrime, and identity theft, but lately, they'd been muscling in on the Chechens and human trafficking. I'd always thought that the Chicago gangs were tough, but the Russians and Chechens made them seem like pussycats in comparison. I'd never even *heard* of some of the methods of torture that I've seen over the past year, coming from these guys.

Sources suggested that "Sticky Ike" was a material witness to this murder, as well as being a well-known snitch for the police, so we went to his apartment building in the Village to have a talk with him. We figured that we could probably get something from him if we flashed him some cash, but we also figured that there was also a good chance that he'd try to bolt, rather than rat out anyone from the *Bratva* who'd be willing to skin him alive just for talking with the cops. So that evening, Santos and I climbed the stairs to the third floor, while Tony stayed out front, just in case Ike might try to get past us.

Tony also doesn't like stairs. Now, part of me doesn't blame him— he weighs about as much as me carrying my five-year-old daughter, Chelsea, *and* my toddling twins on my back. I couldn't imagine going through life with that much extra baggage with every step. Then again, the multiple cigarettes he'd smoked every day hadn't helped much, either. He used to claim that his hatred of stairs was because of back problems, but lately, he'd been complaining that his left elbow hurts whenever he tried to climb stairs.

"I think I got elbow cancer," he'd say, rubbing his arm.

"There's no such thing as elbow cancer," I'd tell him.

"The 'Big C' goes wherever it *wants* ta go!" he'd reply, pointing to his elbow. "Yer gonna be real sorry fer laughin' if the doc comes back an' says I'm gonna die from elbow cancer…" Santos basically thought we were nuts for even having these sorts of conversations, and I have to admit that he's got a point—anyone who would demand that his doctor test him for elbow cancer has got to have more than a few screws loose somewhere.

So Tony lit himself another cigarette and watched from the street level as Santos and I went up the stairs. Come to think of it, Ike's building wasn't that far from the apartment rented by Frank Sydor a couple of years ago back, when Durant was last in town. Anyway, the building was more than just a bit run-down, and the walls must have been paper-thin, since we could hear someone coughing in his room on the second floor as we passed and music coming from the third floor as we approached… which turned out to be coming from just the apartment that we were looking for. We also heard voices inside—a male and a female voice, having some sort of heated argument, though we couldn't make out any distinct words. I knocked on the door, and the voices abruptly stopped. Then I stepped back and let Santos take the lead, since this was his town.

"Ike?" Santos called through the door. "This is the police. Please open the door."

In response, a shotgun blast ripped through the door and blew a meaty hole in Santos' chest. I don't know who looked more shocked— Santos or me. Ike was a low-life scum, but as far as either of us had ever heard prior to that moment, he'd never even fired a weapon before, much less at a cop. Now, any time you're on the job, you need to be aware that you're *always* in a dangerous situation, but it never seriously occurred to us that he'd respond this way, so neither of us was wearing a vest. Either we had totally misjudged Ike, or he was absolutely terrified to open that door.

I drew my pistol and double-checked on Santos, but it was obvious that he'd been dead before he'd even hit the floor. I heard Tony start to come up the stairs in response to the gunshot, so I yelled that Santos was down, but that he should stay down there and call for back-up. I really hoped that he was carrying his phone on him, like he'd promised. Inside the room, I heard the woman screaming something in Spanish, and I heard a commotion, followed by the sound of crashing glass. I figured that Ike wasn't wanting to have a stand-off against a bunch of cops, so he was probably trying to get away by going down the fire escape.

The door was half-open now anyway, so I darted my head in for a moment to get a quick lay of the apartment. The place was a pig sty, and a skinny Latina was standing in the middle of the main room wearing panties and a tee shirt, screaming hysterically. Some kind of *norteño* music was playing loudly, and I could see Ike's foot as it passed out of a smashed-open window in the kitchen in the back.

"He's coming down to you!" I yelled down to Tony. "Down the fire escape!"

"Gotcha!" Tony yelled back.

I kicked in the rest of the door and swung inside, spinning to my right to make sure that no one else was there. I figured that if Ike had been in here listening to music and arguing with his half-dressed girlfriend, they were probably alone, but it never hurts to be overly-cautious. All there was to the right was a ratty old couch, but the shotgun lay in the middle of the floor. There was a small bathroom off to the side, and what looked like a bedroom in the back. The bathroom was obviously clear, and I took a chance that the bedroom was as well— I wasn't going to let Ike get away.

"Tranquilízate!" I shouted at the girl as I passed her, kicked the shotgun away from her, and moved to the kitchen, keeping my pistol pointed in the direction of that open bedroom door. She quieted down a bit and nodded, sobbing, and trying to cover herself. "Hay alguien más aquí?" I asked, poking my head around the refrigerator, just to make sure no one else was in the kitchen. She just stood there, trembling in shock. "Mujer!" I called out to her louder, "Hay alguien más aquí? Anyone else here?" She shook her head, and she looked too messed up at that moment to lie to me.

"Estancia aquí!" I told her as I moved to the broken window. I poked my head out for a second, and there was Ike, clambering down the fire escape. The lightest snowfall was just beginning against the night sky as I jumped out of the window to follow him.

"Ike!" I yelled down. "Stop now!" If he heard me, he gave no indication of it. He just kept climbing down to the street as fast as he could. I stuffed my pistol in its holster and slid down the metal ladder, not even touching the rungs. When I got to the second floor, he was already on the street, so I called out to Tony to get his butt into the alley and join us. I jumped the last half-floor's worth of ladder to try to catch up.

Now, Ike was no great athlete—fortunately for us—but he *was* desperate. He was about halfway down the alley by the time that I hit the ground and Tony turned the corner. I pointed toward Ike as I drew my pistol again and Tony nodded, and both of us took off running after him. I shouted again down the alley for him to stop, but Ike didn't even break stride.

It's a funny thing to run in the cold when you're not used to it. You stiffen up faster than you'd think, and your lungs start to burn, even within the first few seconds. All of that work on the treadmill seems like it did no good at all. Ike was already starting to slow down by the time we got to the end of the alley and into the next street, so I was able to close the gap. I heard Tony wheezing behind me, and I was pleasantly surprised at how he was sticking with it. Then again, I suppose that momentum was on his side, seeing as how we were all running in a straight line.

Ike stopped for a second to catch his bearings, then darted across the street and to the right. Luckily, there were no cars coming, and I didn't even have to slow down to follow him. He ducked down into another alleyway between two storefronts, and I was right there with him. He knocked down a crate as he ran past, and I had to dodge it, but I was still close behind him when he reached the end of that next alley as well. He stopped again at the street to figure out where to go next—he glanced left, and was about to glance right, when something happened. It all happened so fast…

I wasn't more than ten feet from him when I saw a great, gray blur swoop in from the right with a roar that sounded like thunder. There was a ripping noise, and Ike let out a high-pitched scream that sounded like a little girl would make, but it was cut short suddenly. My first thought was that Durant must have been back in town—he's about the only thing I've ever seen move that fast before. But when I saw that Ike had been raggedly ripped in half, I thought differently. Whatever it was that did this to him, it wasn't Durant. We never did find his lower half, but his upper torso seemed to hang in mid-air for a second, and then fell to the ground with a wet slap, like raw meat. He lived for another several seconds, flopping around on the ground like a fish out of water, gurgling. In those last few moments, he looked right up into my eyes and reached out toward me with a bloody hand. More than anything else, he looked surprised… and then he died.

I glanced down the street in both directions, but I didn't see anything. In the dark, I couldn't even make out any trail of blood to see where the killer went. I knew that the CSI guys would almost certainly have to be able to find something later on with some better light, but whatever it was that killed Terrance Eisenhower, there was no way of chasing it down at that moment.

Tony eventually came up behind me, coughing and puffing in the cold night air, but he got real quiet when he saw Ike's body.

"What the—?" he started, but that's as far as he got. Five minutes earlier, Detective Emilio Santos and I were climbing the stairs to talk with an informant. Now, both Santos and that informant were dead, and I had a much bigger mystery on my hands than whether or not we could prove that Isador Postyshev was a murderer.

The sad, funny thing is, one thought kept reverberating in the back of my mind: *Why do these things always seem to happen in alleyways?*

Background
From *Of Ghosts and Spirits Walking by Night* (Lewes Lavanter, 1572)

from *Chapter XVII*

*That it is no hard thing for the Devil to appear in diverse
shapes, and to bring to pass strange things.*

It is no difficult matter for the Devil to appear in diverse shapes, not only of those which are alive, but also of dead men (whereof I spoke also before, when I entreated of Samuel's appearing),[1] yea, and (which is a lesser matter) in the form of beasts and birds, etc., as to appear in the likeness of a black Dog, a Horse, an Owl, and also to bring incredible things to pass, it is a thing most manifest: for he may through long and great experience, understand the effects and force of natural things, as of herbs, stones, etc., and by means hereof work marvelous matters. And then he is a subtle and quick spirit, which can readily take things in hand, which in each thing is of no small weight. By his quickness, and by his knowledge in natural things, he may easily deceive the eyesight, and other senses of man, and hide those things which are before our face, and convey other things into their places. Whereof the holy Scriptures, and histories, and continual experience bear record. How did the wicked spirit handle Iob?[2] What did he not bring to pass in short space? What strange works of an evil spirit did Bileam[3] bring to pass? Did he not purchase a famous name by his Magical arts? What wonderful great miracles did Pharaoh's Sorcerers?[4] Did not Simon Magus[5] so bewitch

---

[1]   *Earlier, Lavanter had argued that the appearance of the spirit of the prophet Samuel, resurrected by the witch of Endor (as recorded in the Biblical* I Samuel, xxviii) *was actually a manifestation of the Devil.*

[2]   *That is, Job (from the* Book of Job*), where God allowed Satan to torment Job and his family to demonstrate the man's unswerving faith (see the* Book of Job, i, 6-12).

[3]   *That is, the prophet Balaam (from the* Book of Numbers, xxii)

[4]   *In reference to the works of the sorcerers and magicians of Pharaoh Rameses II (1303-1213 BC), as recorded in the* Book of Exodus, vii, 8-13.

[5]   *As described in the* Acts of the Apostles, viii

the Samaritans with his unlawful Arts, that he would say he was the great virtue of God? Touching this conjurer, the old Fathers write many things, as Iereneus[6] in his first book and tenth chapter, and Eusebius[7] in his second book & thirteenth chapter. Egesippus[8] writes in his third book and second chapter of the destruction of Hierusalem,[9] that this Symon *[sic]* came to Rome, and there set himself against Peter, boasting that he could fly up into Heaven, and that he came at the day appointed unto the Mount Capitoline,[10] where leaping from the rock, he flew a good while not without the great admiration of the people, who now began to credit his words, but suddenly he fell down and broke his leg, and after being carried unto Aritia, there died.[11]

Iohannes Tritenhemius,[12] Abbot of Spanheimium, writes in his *Chronicles*[13] concerning the Monastery of Hirsgraue[14] of the order of St. Bennett, in the year of our Lord, 970, that Peter and Baianus,[15] the two Sons of one Simon,[16] a Monk, ruled over the Bulgarians, whereof the one, namely Baianus, was thoroughly seen in the Art of Necromancy,[17] and thereby wrought many miracles, He changed himself into a Wolf as often as he list, or into the likeness of another beast, or in such sort as he could not be discerned of any man, and many other strange things he could do, and did, whereby he brought men into great admiration.[18]

And after, in the year 876, he writes, that there was a certain Jew named Sedechias,[19] sometimes philosopher and physician to Lewes the Emperor,[20] who being very cunning in sorcery, did strange miracles and

---

[6]   *Lavanter refers here to Irenaeus and his book,* Adversus Hæreses *(c. 180)*

[7]   *Eusebius Pamphili's* Historia Ecclesiastica *(c. 324)*

[8]   *Or Hegesippus, who wrote the* Hypomnemata *(c. 180)*

[9]   *That is, Jerusalem.*

[10]   *That is, the Clivus Capitolinus, which led up to the Campus Martius in Rome.*

[11]   *As is recounted in full in the* Acts of Peter and Paul *(4ᵗʰ century)— discounting the earlier assertion by Hippolytus in* Refutatio Omnium Hæresium *(c. 220) that Simon survived his fall to commit even more heinous blasphemies later on.*

[12]   *Johannes Trithemius or Johann Heidenberg, the writer of the* Steganographia *(1499)—a book whose reading was prohibited by the Catholic Church until 1900.*

[13]   *Heidenberg's* Annales Hirsaugiensis *(1514)*

[14]   *A misspelled reference to the monastery of Hirsgau, in Swabia.*

[15]   *That is, Bajan (or Benjamin)*

[16]   *King Symeon I (or Simeon the Great—864-927)*

[17]   *Sorcery via communication with the dead.*

[18]   *See also Nicolas Rémy's book,* Daemonolatreiae Libri Tres *(1595), for more on this story.*

[19]   *That is, Zedekiah*

[20]   *Actually, Zedekiah was the beloved physician and confidant not to Louis the Pious (778-840), but rather to his son, Charles the Bald (823-877), who*

wonderful sleights before the Princes, and before all other men. For he brought it to pass by his cunning, that he seemed to devour an armed man with his horse, and all his harness, and also a cart laden with hay, together with the horse and carter. He cut off men's heads, their hands and feet, which he set in a basin before all the lookers on to behold, with the blood running about the basin: which, by and by, he would put again upon the places whence they seemed to have been cut off, without any hurt to the parties. He was seen and heard of all men to exercise hunting and running, and such like things in the air and clouds, as men are accustomed to exercise upon the earth. He practised so many and diverse deceits, that all men marveled and were astonished out of measure.

---

ruled as Holy Roman Emperor for the final three years of his life. Interestingly, many scholars believe that it was actually Zedekiah who ultimately poisoned Charles on his trip across the Alps back home to Gaul (see The Universal Chronology, *1825, by M. St. Martin and Henry Boyle;* Mémoires de Bertrand Barère, *1844, etc.).*

Chapter 2
Strays

"So, is this gonna be one o' them 'stick' cases?" Tony asked me.

That was what he was calling the crazy cases that we'd been running across over the past few years, ever since Durant had blown into town and turned my understanding of the world upside-down. He called them "stick" cases in reference to the staff that Durant gave to me, the *Matteh ha Shelomoh*—the Staff of Solomon. Durant said that it had been used by the real, honest-to-goodness King Solomon to get rid of a bunch of nasties that were off-shoots of some sort of ancient Assyrian pseudo-vampires called the *Lilitu*, but that he himself had picked it up, like, 400 years ago in Devonshire from a friend of his. Whatever. All I know is that the thing had a cat's head carved at the top of it, and it was crazy impressive against monsters. No matter what we used it against—revenants, vampires in the gang war, that snake-thing that we found in the sewers last year, you name it—the staff just smashed through them like they were made out of peanut butter. Bullets may or may not even slow these creatures down, but a 3000-year-old wooden stick seemed to be poison to them.

So, yeah—it seemed like probably a "stick" case to me, too.

We called it in, and I stayed with Ike's body until the CSI guys got there while Tony went back to the apartment building to secure the crime scene—and our witness—until they could get there, too. The more I looked at Ike's corpse, the more creeped out I became. Like I said, he hadn't been sliced in half—he'd been *ripped* in half. Something very strong and very fast literally took him apart right in front of me, and there was nothing I could've done to stop it. Stick or no stick, I knew that if I ever came up against that thing in a dark alley myself, I'd be a dead man. But on top of that, I had to wonder about the motivation behind the killing. *Why* do it *this* way? To a detective, the "what," "when," and "how" are always important, of course, but you really need to understand the "why" in order to get to the "who" in a case.

Let's say that this creature was just a wild animal—then why just take Ike's lower half? I mean, if the thing was wanting to feed, Ike's upper half was where all of the meat was, and it would've been the more natural half to grab anyway. For that matter, why not just take the whole body—why only half? Or, if you really want to get down to it, if this thing was as powerful as it *appeared* to have been, then why not kill me, too? Why hide from more potential prey? Was it just that it heard Tony coming up behind me, and it didn't know how many more people were going to show up? But I sat there alone with Ike's corpse for almost half an hour, and it never came back for me. Does that mean that this thing is furtive by nature? Or that there's something about the lower half of Ike's body in particular that it needed? I wasn't going to figure it out sitting there on that sidewalk, waiting for the CSI guys, but it's the way my mind works.

As for Ike's girlfriend, Trinnie Moreno had only known him for a few weeks, so she expressed to Tony that she'd be more than happy to cooperate with the police, rather than be implicated in anything that he'd been up to. Unfortunately, she didn't know anything about any Russian mafia, or anyone named Isador Postyshev.

*   *   *

By the time that the Soviet Union broke up in 1991, the government had held absolute power over its populace for almost 70 years—no one other than the oldest Soviet citizens could even *remember* any other way of life. The government controlled the media, they controlled the schools, and they did everything that they could to control the very thought-lives of the Soviet people through fear and propaganda. Dissidents were rounded up and placed in gulags by the thousands. Gone were the foundations of the traditional social structures of family and religion—instead, the State was the sole, dread authority from which all benefits, punishments, and value structures derived. After several generations of this, fear of the State had become absolutely entrenched in the minds of the Soviet peoples, and the basis for all of their morality, activity, and productivity. So what happens when all of that suddenly goes away?

Prices, debt, alcoholism, absenteeism, etc., all skyrocketed overnight. Russia lost 50% of their gross domestic product over the next few years, the birth rate dropped, the death rate grew, and almost half of the former Soviet peoples found themselves in a state of utter poverty. The gulags were suddenly emptied of prisoners who had spent *generations* being incarcerated, creating their own worlds of clans and tribes within the brutal penal system. Is it any wonder, then, in the midst of all of this chaos, brutality, and inevitable corruption, that organized crime would flourish? Over the last couple of decades, various mobs— the *Solntsevskaya Bratva,* the *Dolgoprudninskaya* group, the *Chechenskaya* mafia, the assorted Romanian clans, etc.—have exploded across the former Soviet republics, thriving on the vacuum of both moral conscience and governmental authority. Prostitution, drugs, slavery, gambling (you name it) have risen to epic proportions—far worse than things *ever* were in Chicago, even under Capone's watch. And much like Capone, the current head of the Russian mafia—Semion Mogilevich, who had risen through the ranks of the *Lyuberetskaja Bratva*—now lives and operates out in the open in Moscow.

To try to combat all of this, the Russian Federation even tried inviting Christian and Muslim missionaries to come in and preach their religions in public schools to try to instill a moral foundation in the upcoming generation of citizens. Ironic that after years of forcibly keeping missionaries *out* of Russia, the government was actually paying to ship them *into* its public schools—and at the same time that the United States was taking steps to remove religion from its own.

So beyond all of the horrors that domestic American human traffickers inflict upon our fellow Americans, the CIA recently reported that an estimated 45,000 to 50,000 women and children are being brought into the United States every year as part of foreign human trafficking rings. The Chicago Outfit has tried to keep them out of here for years—and, to be honest, they've probably done a better job of it than we have as a police force—but it was inevitable that their operations would grow to touch just about every large city in America. And now, our own, home-grown gangs have gotten in on the action, recruiting and turning out their own prostitutes as well. Girls as young as 12-14 years old, turning up to 50 tricks a week, sometimes even getting literally, physically branded by the gang as their property—it's a horror show that most of the girls see no way to escape from. It's a brand new spin on the oldest of crimes, and one that we're only just starting to get a handle on.

Enter the FBI.

For the past several years, the Feds have been trying to organize the various police forces in the nation to work together on sweeps like Operation Cross Country. At first, it was like herding cats, and we spent most of our time in interdepartmental squabbles and angry toe-stepping. But it's eventually evolved over the years into a fairly well-oiled machine, and we're starting to really make a difference on the streets in the area of human trafficking. Of course, saving 100 people is a bit of a "tip of the iceberg" thing, if you believe the CIA's number of 45,000 new victims emigrating into the U.S. every year—but hey, I'd rather start chipping away at the iceberg than just resign myself to letting it grow bigger and bigger.

Besides, it makes all the difference in the world to those 100 people that we save.

In our District, the lead investigators were Nate Kingery, his new partner Leah Wheaton, Tony, and me. We liaised closely with the FBI, and the two agents that Tony and I were attached to in all of this were Special Agent Ben Bucher and Special Agent Carolyn Davidge.

Now, Ben Bucher was a bit of a cipher. He had that close-cropped hair and dark suit that so many FBI guys cultivate—the austere professional who could be a cop, a Secret Service agent, or a very stern stock broker. He was trying to be non-descript, but there were still some little clues here and there that gave me some insight into what kind of a man he was. He was middle-aged and yet still quite fit, and he moved with a military bearing, so I was guessing that he'd been in the Army or the Marines at some point, though he carefully never talked about his background. As a matter of fact, he never talked about much of anything outside of the case files. But then, I noticed the scar from a pierced ear on one of his lobes, which seemed more than just a little bit out of character with the rest of him. Since the FBI frowned on that sort of thing in its male agents—and since he was *so* careful never to talk about his background—I figured that he'd probably been undercover until some point fairly recently (which opened up a number of interesting questions in my mind, not the least of which was why he'd changed up to go plainclothes now). He was efficient and effective, and I didn't mind working with him any more than I minded working with a good computer—he was a machine, and even if he was a closed book, he was still a good investigator.

By comparison, I saw Carolyn Davidge as an open book. Her dirt-colored hair was cut at shoulder-length with an eye more for ease of upkeep than for aesthetic appeal—just long enough to be pulled up tight into a little bun half of the time. Her conservative pantsuits were simple, and none were fitted to conform to her trim build—maybe a swimmer, but I'd guess more likely a runner, from the way that she moved. She applied just enough makeup to look professional, but showed no interest in trying to soften her angular, often angry-looking face. She tended to speak in clipped, terse bursts—commanding, and yet coming across all the more anxious and needy in her attempt to seem like she was in charge. In short, she gave every indication of being a woman who was uncomfortable in her own skin—who, with every movement and every syllable, appeared to be trying to prove that she was more than capable of handling herself in a world that she apparently saw as incompatible with femininity. When you think about it, that alone probably perpetually kept her feeling inferior to the men around her, and thus perpetuated her conscious austerity, which then compounded the problem, etc., in a vicious cycle.

As a side note, it's been my experience that people who try to prove themselves to others rarely succeed in doing so. Then again, maybe she was just trying to prove herself to *herself*…

"What happened?" she barked, barging into the office. I looked up from my computer, and she looked exactly the way that I expected her to look—tight, insecure, and accusatory.

"I'm writing up the report now," I said, pointing to my computer.

"Not good enough," she replied, and Tony rolled his eyes, stirring some sugar into his coffee. Bucher just hung behind, quietly watching all of it. "Eisenhower was a lead that we desperately needed to get leverage on Postyshev, and you lost him."

"No," I corrected her, turning back to my typing. "I only lost *half* of him…" Tony chuckled, but Bucher's expression didn't change one bit. Now, if I'd have taken the time to think it through, I probably wouldn't have said that. Yes, it made me feel a little better about being chewed out when I'd done nothing wrong, but it's never wise to publicly undermine an insecure authority figure. That just tends to make them stomp on you harder in order to make themselves feel all the more in charge.

"Do you think that this is funny, Detective?" she snapped back. And yes, commingled with the frustration I heard in her voice was just a little nervousness.

"Of course not," I replied, turning back to face her. "Two men died tonight—one of them, a good cop. That's never a joke. But none of that was our fault, and I don't really appreciate your attitude on this. Neither Tony nor I—"

"Appear to be as committed or as competent as we need you to be!" she interrupted. Her arms were crossed tightly in front of her. That's a defensive posture, not an aggressive one. She was mad, but more than that, she was feeling overwhelmed. That's when I realized that I was fighting the wrong kind of battle here, and I found myself letting out a nearly Durant-ish sigh. Tony sat up and started to respond, but I motioned for him to hold up.

"Listen," I said, leaning forward onto my desk and trying to measure my tone of voice carefully. "This has been a long and hard night for all of us, and we don't need to be chewing one another up over this. I'll be honest with you. The fact is, none of this went down they way we expected it to, and it's throwing all of us for a loop."

"Your witness was torn in half," Bucher said quietly from behind his partner. Yes, I'd had to put that in the report, though the last couple of years have taught us how to fudge enough here and there when writing up the reports so that people didn't hear "monster" when we submitted them. Of course, it helped that the Russians that we were after were fond of mutilating people to begin with…

"Yes, he was," I replied calmly, not taking his bait.

"An' we also lost one o' th' righteous in Emilio Santos tonight," Tony growled. "But *that* don't seem to bother *you* none!"

"Tony…" I sighed again. Then I turned back to the agents. "The department doesn't usually feel too bad when a cop-killer gets himself killed, but that doesn't mean that this is over. The fact is, we had a witness that could finger Postyshev, and someone took him out. That's actually a good sign, in some ways. It means that they're scared of our investigation, and that they know that they're not invulnerable. We'll just have to keep going and dig up some more evidence against them. 'Sticky Ike' just can't be the only one out there who knew something."

At that, Carolyn Davidge let her arms unclench, and she put her hands on her hips. Upset, but no longer so defensive.

"But after what happened to Eisenhower, do you really think that any of them will come forward?" she asked, I think more exasperated than angry.

"They might," I said, "if we spin it that this is the way that the *Bratva* treats their business associates, and that Ike would still be alive today if he'd worked with us instead of trying to hide from them." That seemed to strike a responsive chord in her, and she visibly relaxed. She turned back to Bucher, who gave her an all-but-imperceptible nod. Then she turned back to me.

"Can you get that word out on the street?" she asked.

"Tony's already on it," I answered, and Tony smiled as he lifted his coffee cup. "That's exactly what we're letting people know. Someone will come forward."

"Let's hope so," she said, leaning against Kingery's desk, across from mine. "But the word is, this isn't strictly the *Bratva* that we're dealing with."

"Whussat?" Tony asked, slurping his cup.

"Isador Postyshev is apparently a member of a splinter group of the *Solntsevskaya Bratva,* calling themselves the *'Obshchestvo Drakonisty',*" Bucher clarified. "They're a more radical faction, developing a presence here in Chicago, in Grand Rapids, Detroit, and other places."

"If they're so radical," I asked, directed to his partner, hoping to relieve more tension by helping her feel more a part of the conversation, "then won't the *Bratva* deal with them themselves? I mean, they tend to keep their own houses pretty clean, if you know what I mean. They can't want a bunch of crazies running things here in the States any more than we would."

"Apparently," she replied, "even the *Bratva's Avtoritetami* are intimidated by this group."

"That's nuts," I said, shaking my head. "The *Bratva's* not afraid of anyone."

"Even the *Bratva's Avtori-what?*" Tony asked, backing up a step.

"The leaders—the *capos* of the *Bratva,*" Bucher interjected. "From what we can tell, none of them likes the idea of this *Obshchestvo*

Drakonisty splinter group, or the idea of picking fights with the Chechens by muscling in on their human trafficking operations. But for some reason, the *Avtoritetami* stutter-step when it comes to blocking them."

"They're more afraid o' these *Drakonisty* guys than they are o' the *Chechens*?" Tony asked, just about choking on his coffee.

"That's what we're hearing," Bucher replied. "It makes you wonder, doesn't it?"

"Then who *are* these guys?" I asked.

"We don't really know. All we do know is that their operations go at least as far back as the 1980s and Evsei Agron in New York. They would use his connections with Erich Thonios and his Greek shipping lines to move slaves and other commodities in and out of the country."

"I thought Thonios was legit," Tony commented.

"The current Thonios is," Bucher said, "so far as we know. I'm talking about Thonios II, the father."

"Word is," she clarified, "Thonios III got his millions in part from shady deals his father made with Russian and Romanian gangsters in the 70s and 80s, using operating capital and connections that his grandfather had built up from working with the S.S. during World War II. The current Thonios appears to have cleaned up all of the family operations, but you can never totally erase your past."

"But with enough money, you sure can polish it up nice and pretty," I added. "I never realized that one of the world's richest men owed his money to the Nazis…"

"*Several* of the world's richest men owe their money to the Nazis…" Bucher offered, and that was pretty much the end of that conversation.

*   *   *

I got home fairly late—or really, really early, depending on how you look at it. The only one up when I walked in was Flubber, and he attacked me. But that's nothing new.

You have to understand, Flubber was a stray dog that we'd rescued from off the street one night in the early Spring. He was gaunt and shivering in the rain, with no collar, and he was obviously not very healthy. The first time we'd seen him, he was trying to find some food in a garbage can. When I'd tried to approach him, he whimpered and ran off, limping on his back left leg. He'd obviously been through a lot in his life, and I felt sorry for the little guy.

The next time I saw him was in that rain storm the next night. He was lying under a bush, trying to get out from under the raindrops, and when I approached him again, he was too weak to run away this time.

I'd seen him from our window, so I had thought to bring a package of ground beef with me when I came out. I tossed a small chunk to him, and he leaned out to sniff it, then gobble it up. After that, I tossed the next chunk a little in front of him, so that he'd have to come out from under the bush to get it. I left the remaining chunk in front of me, and then I sat down in the rain and waited.

After a minute or so, the dog crawled out from under the bush and sniffed at the second chunk, eyeing me the whole time. With his wet fur plastered against his body, I could see just how emaciated he really was. He grabbed the second chunk and ate it, crawling the whole time. The poor thing was too weak to move much more than that. After that, he looked longingly at that third chunk, then at me, and then whimpered some more. Without getting up, I tore another small chunk off of the third piece and tossed it to him. He ate it—and instinctively, his tail wagged, just for a second.

Then I picked up the third piece and crawled on the ground toward him. I didn't want to stand up, because I figured that it would spook him. But I set the chunk in front of him and then lay there with my face right next to it. I wanted to show him that it was my meat, but that I was letting him have it… but that he'd have to come close to my face to get it. He whimpered for a bit again, but then crawled forward to start nibbling on it. While he did, I reached out and gently stroked his neck. He growled quietly at that, but then I growled back at him and kept doing it, so he shut up.

Now, I'm abbreviating this story quite a bit. The whole process took about half an hour, out there in the rain. At the end of it, I lay next to him on the ground for a bit, until he seemed comfortable with my presence there. Then I gently picked him up and carried him to my car. He wasn't happy about that, mind you, but he was so weak that he couldn't fight me too hard. I drove him to a nearby animal hospital that I knew about, and the rest is history.

He was just a little mutt, and we couldn't find his owner, but we didn't want to take him to a shelter. So when he was strong enough, we brought him home to live with us. For the first several months, he was incredibly skittish—every loud noise would send him scampering across the room, and he never felt comfortable falling asleep unless it was behind a couch or under a bed. But even within the first few days, he seemed to fall in love with our family, especially Chelsea and the twins. He would jump around them, knocking them over and licking them, and he would get so excited any time one of us came home from somewhere that he'd bounce off the walls. In fact, he bounced around so much that the kids started calling him "Flubber," and the name stuck.

I still remember one turning point in my relationship with the dog. He seemed to like me, but was still instinctively scared of me. Maybe it was just that he saw me as the "alpha male" of our pack, or maybe it was that some other man had abused him in the past—who knows? But he tended to shrink back when I reached for him, and he never wanted to sit next to me, like he had come to do with Joanna and the kids.

But then, one night, I heard him whimpering in his dog bed. I got up and went over to him, and saw that he was dreaming and shaking in his sleep. I squatted down next to him and started stroking his fur, telling him that everything was okay, and that we were all right here at home with him. He didn't wake up, but he did seem to calm down. After a while, I gave him one last, little scratch behind the ears, and then went back to bed.

Within a minute, I heard the telltale skitter-scratching of his claws against the floor as he trotted down the hallway and into our bedroom. He jumped right up in our bed and crawled into the crook of my knee, curling up and nestling in with a snort between the two of us. And that's where he slept for the rest of the night.

The funny thing is, that's where he sleeps *most* nights, now. He never starts off there—he still has his dog bed—but 'round about 2:00 in the morning, he usually likes to come up and curl up next to my leg. Apparently, he's realized that the "alpha dog" is the scariest dog in the house… but that I'm on *his* side, so that scariness ends up being a good thing. Instead of being frightened of me, he's decided that I'm the best protection that he could have, and the very fear of me that once kept him away now draws him close. Ironically, that means that he's often more upset with me for coming home late than Joanna is these days.

So when I came home around 5:00, Flubber was right there at the door to greet me. He let out one sharp bark, then jumped up into my arms like he always does when I come home, licking my face and wagging his tail. I tell you, it's really hard to stay in a dark mood when your dog loves you and is that happy to see you come home, no matter how your day had gone.

Then again, that was before I got the call about Sherri Angelo…

Background
From *Daemonolatreiae Libri Tres* (Nicolas Rémy,[1] 1595, trans. M. Summers)

from *Book I, Chapter I*

*The Inducements by which Men may fist be led astray by
Demons, and so falling become Dealers in Magic.*

Experience itself, to our own great loss and bane, affords us sad proof that Satan seizes as many opportunities of deceiving and destroying mankind as there are different moods and affections natural to the human character. For such as are given over to their lusts and to love he wins by offering them the hope of gaining their desires: or if they are bowed under the load of daily poverty, he allures them by some large and ample promise of riches: or he tempts them by showing them the means of avenging themselves when they have been angered by some injury or hurt received: in short, by whatever other corruption or luxury they have been depraved, he draws them into his power and holds them as if they were bound to him. But it is not our purpose to discuss here what are those blind passions and desires by which men may be led into sin; for it would be a waste of time and an abuse of learning to involve ourselves in the much-worn controversy between Prométhée and Épiméthée,[2] reason and appetite. That we pass by, and say that Satan assails mankind not only through their secret and domestic affections

---

[1] *Nicolas Rémy (1530-1616)— sometimes known as "Remigius"—was a Catholic Judge in France who became famous for his witch-hunting (the first of whom was in 1582—an elderly beggar woman who had cursed Rémy's son, leading to the youth's death in a street accident). He claimed to have personally put to death over 900 witches in his career.*

[2] *Two of the sons of the Titans Iapetus and Clymene in Greek mythology. Prometheus (whose name, "Προμηθεύς," literally means "fore-thinker") represented the careful planner and forward thinker, whereas Epimetheus (whose name, "Ἐπιμηθεύς," literally means "after-thinker") represented the fool who only considered the repercussions of his actions or inactions after he had performed them.*

and (if I may so express it) by burrowing into their very hearts, but also openly and in declared warfare, as it is called. For he openly addresses them by word of mouth, and appears in visible person to converse with them, as he did when he contended with the Saviour in the wilderness.[3] But this he does the more easily when he finds a man weakened by the hardships and cares of life; for then he suggests to the man that he is grieved at his misfortunes and is willing to come to help him. But not even so can he aid and assist any man unless that man has broken his baptismal pledge and agreed to transfer his allegiance to him and acknowledge him as his Master. But if he cannot gain his object in this way by mere persuasion, then Satan employs those allurements and temptations which I have already mentioned: he fabricates some fair and delectable body and offers it for a man's enjoyment: or he can do much by means of a false display of riches: or by providing drugs to poison those upon whom a man wishes to be avenged, or to heal those to whom a man owes a debt of gratitude: often, indeed, the Demons forcibly drive and compel men into compliance by fierce threats and revilings, or by the fear of the lash or prison. For men may just as easily be led by violence to practise sorcery as by coaxing and blandishment, though I shall not here adduce examples to substantiate this statement, since this matter will be considered more fully in its due place: for the present I am content to say that I have found it to be the rarer case for a sorcerer to be driven by force into his abominable practices.

    This truth is that, when Satan cannot move a man by fair words, he compels him by fear and threats of danger. When Claude Morèle, who was convicted of witchcraft at Serre (5th Dec., 1586), was asked what was the chief inducement that had first led him to give himself to the Demon, he answered that he had withstood the temptation of all the Demon's fair words, and had only yielded when Satan had threatened to kill his wife and children. At Guermingen, 19th Dec., 1589, Antoine Welch no longer dared to oppose the Demon in anything after he had threatened to twist his neck unless he obeyed his commands, for he seemed on the very point of fulfilling his threat. At Harecourt, 10th Nov., 1586, when he could by no promises persuade Alexée Driget to dedicate herself to him, the Demon at last threatened to destroy the house in which she lived: and this misfortune indeed befell her not long afterwards; but it will be more convenient to discuss elsewhere whether he was the actual cause of it, or whether he merely foresaw that it would happen. Certainly there are many examples in the pagan histories of houses being cast down, the destruction of the crops, chasms in the earth, fiery blasts and other such disastrous tempests stirred up by Demons for

---

[3]   *"Then was Jesus led up of the Spirit into the wilderness to be tempted of the devil..." from the* Gospel of St. Matthew, *iv, 1 ff.*

the destruction of men for no other purpose than to bind their minds to the observance of some new cult and to establish their mastery more and more firmly over them.

Therefore we may first conclude that it is no mere fable that witches meet and converse with Demons in very person. Secondly, it is clear that Demons use the two most powerful weapons of persuasion against the feeble wills of mortals, namely, hope and fear, desire and terror; for they well know how to induce and inspire such emotions.

Background
From *The Book of Werewolves* (Sabine Baring-Gould, 1865)

from *Chapter VIII: Folk-lore Relating to Were-wolves*

Joseph Acosta[1] relates that the ruler of a city in Mexico, who was sent for by the predecessor of Montezuma, transformed himself, before the eyes of those who were sent to seize him, into an eagle, a tiger, and an enormous serpent. He yielded at last, and was condemned to death. No longer in his own house, he was unable to work miracles so as to save his life. The Bishop of Chiapa, a province of Guatemala, in a writing published in 1702, ascribes the same power to the Naguals, or national priests,[2] who laboured to bring back to the religion of their ancestors, the children brought up as Christians by the government.[3] After various ceremonies, when the child instructed advanced to embrace him, the Nagual suddenly assumed a frightful aspect, and under the form of a lion or tiger, appeared chained to the young Christian convert.[4]

Among the North American Indians, the belief in transformation is very prevalent. The following story closely resembles one very prevalent all over the world.

"One Indian fixed his residence on the borders of the Great Bear lake, taking with him only a dog big with young. In due time, this dog brought forth eight pups. Whenever the Indian went out to fish, he tied

---

[1] *José de Acosta, a Spanish Jesuit missionary to Latin America, in his* Historia Natural y Moral de las Indias *(1590).*

[2] *Actually, the Naguals (or Nahuals or Nawals) were not just national priests, but shape-shifting magic-users—precursors of the later "skinwalkers" (see Nutini and Roberts' excellent book,* Bloodsucking Witchcraft: An Epistemological Study of Anthropomorphic Supernaturalism in Rural Tlaxcala, *1993).*

[3] *A "re-paganization" attested to in the Stratmeyers' study, "The Jacaltec Nawal and the Soul Bearer in Concepcion Huista," in* Cognitive Studies of Southern Mesoamerica *(1977).*

[4] *As recounted in* Recueil de Voyages et de Mémoires publié de la Société de Geographie, Tom Deuxième ("Collection of Voyages and Published Memoirs of the Society of Geography, Book Two") *published in 1835.*

up the pups, to prevent the straying of the litter. Several times, as he approached his tent, he heard noises proceeding from it, which sounded like the talking, the laughing, the crying, the wail, and the merriment of children; but, on entering it, he only perceived the pups tied up as usual. His curiosity being excited by the noises he had heard, he determined to watch and learn whence these sounds proceeded, and what they were. One day he pretended to go out to fish, but, instead of doing so, he concealed himself in a convenient place. In a short time he again heard voices, and, rushing suddenly into the tent, beheld some beautiful children sporting and laughing, with the dog-skins lying by their side. He threw the dog-skins into the fire, and the children, retaining their proper forms, grew up, and were the ancestors of the dog-rib nation."[5]

---

[5] *Baring-Gould quotes here from* Traditions of the North American Indians *(J. A. Jones, 1830).*

Chapter 3
Beasts

Sherri Angelo was fifteen years old. On a Saturday morning this December, her mother drove her to the Atrium Mall at the Jim Thompson Center to spend time with her friends. Two more weeks, and she would have turned sixteen, gotten her license, and driven herself. As her mother went off to do some banking—and to pick up a last-minute birthday gift for her daughter—the group of girls made the usual rounds of the stores, getting pampered at Fashion Nails and Spa, trying on shoes at Payless that they would never end up buying, drooling over earrings at Momadou's, etc. Around 11:45, they decided to hit the crowded food court, but each of the girls wanted something different to eat. Sherri wanted a chai latte and a potato and cheese quiche from the Bonjour Café, so she stepped away from the other girls for a few minutes, planning to meet them back at the food court so that they could eat together. It was no big deal—they'd done the very same thing a hundred times over, she had her cell phone with her, and the mall just isn't that large in the first place.

But the staff at the Bonjour Café never saw her. No one ever saw her again.

Sherri's friends started off frustrated with her for abandoning them, but soon became frantic when they realized that *no one* knew where she was. They started running all over the mall, looking for her, and eventually found her mother. Calls to Sherri's phone went unanswered at first, but by mid-afternoon, they just went straight to voicemail. She was scrupulous about charging her phone every night when she went to bed, so it hadn't run out of a charge—someone had simply turned it off.

When Mrs. Angelo called the police that evening, they did exactly what they are supposed to do—they told her to relax and wait for her daughter. Teenagers are notorious for going off and doing their own thing without telling anyone else, especially their mothers. I know that it's a terrifying situation for those parents like the Angelos who know their children well enough to know that something must be wrong, and yet hear that the police are not going to do anything about it, but if we jumped to investigate every time that a teenager hadn't called home for a few hours or wandered off to buy herself a funnel cake at a fair, then that's all we'd be doing as a police force. And, quite frankly, we wouldn't be prepared to help families when something *really has* gone wrong.

But something had indeed gone horribly, tragically wrong for Sherri Angelo. When she didn't return the next day, the Angelos went down to the police station and demanded action. The department began to look into it, and sure enough, it became clear that something bad had happened. Sherri simply wasn't the kind of girl to up and disappear. She was even missing a special lunch the next day that she'd been looking forward to for weeks.

That's when the case got bumped up to us. Strictly speaking, it got bumped up to Kingery and Wheaton, since we were still working on the Postyshev/Eisenhower thing. But as they investigated, they found something disturbing, and that's when it came to us.

On that Saturday, the only suspicious detail that anyone at the mall could remember was the presence of a tall, broad-shouldered man with a thick moustache and just as thick an accent. When they started describing tattoos on his hands and neck, Kingery immediately pegged him as a member of the *Bratva*.

See, when Stalin threw all of those dissidents into gulags, they developed their own, unique, prison sub-cultures. Tattoos became shorthand for what kind of a person you were, how long you'd been in prison, what crimes you were guilty of, whether you were a *Vor*—a "made man" in organized crime—etc. For instance, stars on your shoulders indicate that you're one of the *Vory* and that you adhere to the *Vor v Zakone*, the internal code of the *Bratva*. A spade would indicate that you're a thief, and a beetle that you're specifically a pickpocket. A crucifix shows that you're a leader within the organization, maybe even an *Avtoritet*. The list goes on.

Kingery pulled up the mall's security videos, and though he was never able to find Sherri or what had happened to her after she left her friends, he was able to find the man being described by witnesses, hovering around the entrance of the mall. He was tall, with short-cropped hair and a bushy moustache, and the tattoos were unmistakable. He had a tiger tattooed on his neck, and a scorpion on the back of his left hand—a drug-using cop-killer. Wheaton recognized him right away from the mug shots she'd seen in briefings with their own FBI counterparts. The man's name was Nikodim Georgiyevich Bunin, and rumor had it that he was not only a procurer of children for the *Bratva*— and now, I guess, for the *Obshchestvo Drakonisty*—but also a known associate of both Terrance Eisenhower and Isador Vissarionovich Postyshev.

So Kingery and Wheaton passed the case on to us, thinking that this might be exactly the kind of link to Postyshev that we were looking for. I was only able to get a few hours of sleep before I had to come back into the office and go over the new paperwork with Tony and the Feds. Ben Bucher was his usual, cold, disconnected self… but Carolyn Davidge had a decidedly emotional reaction. It only lasted for a couple of seconds, but I couldn't help but think that it was significant.

She looked at the photographs of Sherri Angelo in the file—the school pictures, the candids with her friends, the one of her in her cheerleading uniform, etc.—and then looked at the mug shot of Bunin. Around his collarbone, under the tiger, was another tattoo that read, "*Не верь, не бойся, не проси*" ("Do not trust, do not be afraid, do not ask"). His eyes were coal-black, and the man just looked like hatred personified. Looking into those eyes, she gritted her teeth and instinctively pulled back, which surprised me. We'd investigated several cases very similar to this one, and she'd always kept her cool, maintained her objectivity about the investigation. Then again, as I said before, her personal insecurities had always been there, just under the surface, bubbling out in small ways here and there. Tony tended to dismiss them as being a "woman" thing, but he was also a racist blowhard, so I tended to dismiss Tony's prejudices. This had nothing to do with anything like that. I realized that maybe Carolyn Davidge had been even more emotionally fragile than I'd originally thought.

But I watched her. She pulled her arms in tight to her sides and clenched her jaw. Every muscle in her body went rigid. Her eyes were a mixture of anger and, what? Fear? I looked back down at the photo of Bunin, then back at her. Something about him—about all of this— obviously reminded her of someone who had hurt her in the past, and hurt her badly enough that it could come up and still mess with her today. Maybe that's why she went into the FBI in the first place, why she was drawn to investigating violence against children, maybe even why she took up running. Who knows? But I looked more carefully at Sherri's pictures. Brown hair, slim build, slender face. Looking closer at her facial structure, I suppose that Carolyn Davidge might have looked a lot like that when she was a teenager. Years on the job, years of marksmanship practice, hand-to-hand combat training, investigation of crime scenes, arrests of scum like Bunin, etc., and all it takes is the wrong combination of photographs on the wrong day to bring all of those feelings back up to the surface and make her feel like a scared little girl again, if only for a moment. I thought of Chelsea, and a loud part of me really wanted to find the man who'd hurt this FBI agent and beat him to a bloody pulp.

I decided to settle for Nikodim Bunin.

Interestingly, I noticed Bucher noticing all of this as well. His facial expression didn't change, but he never took his eyes off of her. I couldn't tell if he was concerned about her as a person, concerned about her performance as an investigating agent, or just plain surprised. But he certainly was cold about the whole thing. Like I said, the whole incident only lasted a couple of seconds, but it still spoke volumes to me about both of these agents.

"Carolyn," I said, gently. I wanted to put my hand on her shoulder to assure her that a friendly colleague was nearby, but I'd seen enough of this kind of thing over the years to know better than to do that. When a woman is remembering this level of trauma, the last thing that helps her feel safe is having a man put his hands on her. "Agent Davidge...?"

Immediately, she pulled herself up straight, snuffed once, and barked, "What?"

"We have an address for this guy, and I think that we have probable cause," I said, stepping back a bit to give her some space. "Let's get the State's Attorney to get us a warrant."

"I'll get on it," said Bucher, without hesitation. He bolted up from the chair and yanked his phone out of his jacket pocket in one fluid motion. Carolyn Davidge shook herself a bit and started sliding the paperwork back into their file folders.

"We'll get him, Carolyn," I said, trying to reassure her. "And we'll get the girl back."

She immediately stopped what she was doing, locked her fierce green eyes on mine, and said, "We don't know *anything* yet, about *anything,* Detective. Don't make promises you can't keep." And then she went back to shuffling the pages, consciously avoiding any other conversation.

She was absolutely right, of course. We didn't even know for sure that Bunin had anything to do with Sherri's disappearance. It's always best to stay objective and not to jump to conclusions or to raise anyone's hopes up. I knew that. I don't know why I had lapsed into being so unprofessional at that moment, but it just seemed like the thing to say at the time. But I really did hope that we'd be able to save Sherri before something would happen to her that would scar her as badly as Carolyn Davidge had obviously been scarred.

*   *   *

The Assistant State's Attorney tried to get our warrant from the Circuit Court—and when I heard who the judge was that he'd tried to work with, I knew immediately why it had fallen through. Judge Henry Delacroix was a dumpy little old man who, from the outside, seemed like he belonged more in Mayberry or something... but you'd never want to end up on his bad side.

Rumor had it that he'd originally practiced law down in his native

Louisiana, and then he had to *re*-learn everything once he and his daughter had moved up north. Ever noticed how in commercials, they often say something like, "Except in Louisiana…" at the end? That's because 49 of the United States do law one way, and Louisiana does it their own way. When I was a kid, I'd heard that it was because their legal system was based on the Napoleonic Code, but that's not really accurate. But both the Napoleonic Code and Louisiana State Law were actually based on the same history of Roman law in Europe, and the laws for the rest of the United States were based on English Common law. Now, I'm not really sure what all the differences are between the two, but I know that they're apparently different enough that you can't switch back and forth too easily. The fact that Delacroix was solid enough in both versions to be a judge in Illinois meant that he was a lot smarter than I was. He might have seemed like a nice little old guy, but he was hard as nails underneath that pudgy exterior.

I remember sitting in his court one time, watching this flashy, fast-talking defense attorney pull some sort of complicated legal maneuver that left the prosecutor looking like a deer caught in the headlights, and old Delacroix just cleared his throat and called both attorneys to the bench. I couldn't hear many of the words, but I heard the judge's low, slow drawl (with just that hint of French in the background), and when they came back to their chairs, the defense attorney was red-faced and sheepish, like a kid who just came back from the principal's office. I had kinda liked Delacroix after that, but not if he wasn't going to give me my warrant to search Bunin's house.

And he wasn't. What we'd seen as probable cause, Delacroix declared to be circumstantial at best, and not worthy of a warrant. Apparently, it's not that he thought Bunin was an upstanding citizen or anything—just that we had no right to infringe on his civil rights without more evidence.

So here's where things get all "gray" when you're on the job. We knew without a doubt that this guy was rotten to the core, and there was decent reason to believe that he was guilty of abducting a teenaged girl, and here we are, in the process of working with the FBI on just exactly this sort of case, but now the circuit court judge says that we need more evidence before he can issue a warrant to search the slimeball's home. So what do you do?

Well, you dig for more evidence. And that's what we did for most of the day. First, we went to Polnoluniye, Ltd.—the import company where Bunin supposedly worked. His boss, Jānis Sychkov, gushed about him being a great worker, but then he started getting a little fuzzy when we began asking him for details about what exactly Bunin did for the company. No, he didn't work on the warehouse floor, but no, he didn't have an office, etc. The place—and Bunin's employment there—was obviously a front for the *Bratva*, but it was going to involve hours of sifting through paperwork before we could make that case to a judge.

So we decided to tempt fate. I really did think that we had probable cause, and that it's usually easier to apologize later than to wait until you've checked off enough boxes so that sticklers like Delacroix feel that their legal and political butts are covered. A known criminal who's suspected of child abductions was seen at the scene of the abduction of a child. That really should be enough, I would've thought. So that evening, we went to Bunin's place to look around. We figured that having both a Chicago cop and an FBI agent on the scene would spread the blame across enough jurisdictions to cover our actions, so while Tony and Bucher were following up on known associations and regular hangouts, Carolyn and I hit his home.

The house itself was in Little India, just off of Devon, surrounded by older homes in a relatively nice neighborhood. It's not like it was the Hilton, but it was certainly nothing like what you'd stereotypically think of as a place where street slime like Bunin would live. At that moment, Tony and Bucher were actually just down the block, checking out a grocery store or something on Devon where Bunin had been known to frequent. In fact, I remembered that there used to be a really good delicatessen nearby with spectacular dark breads and some of my favorite sprats in town, but I guess that they'd gone out of business since the last time I was there.

We knocked on the door and waited. There was no car in the driveway, but we knocked again, identified ourselves, and waited again. Then I tried the door, but it was locked. We were going to go around to the back to see if there were any doors that weren't locked, and that's when we heard the sound of something moving around inside. It could've been anything—it could've been the guy's dog, jumping off of the sofa—but what it *was* was probable cause again. Someone appeared to be inside the home of a known criminal who was suspected of a major crime, and whoever it was, they weren't opening the door for the police.

I drew my sidearm from its holster, and Carolyn drew hers. She texted Bucher that we were going in, and that we could use some backup. I looked at her, silently mouthed a silent countdown from three, and then kicked in the door.

Inside, the front hallway was dark. To the left was a small dining room with no table, but littered with cardboard boxes on the floor and a clutter of wrappers, newspapers, and other junk scattered around. To the right was a living room with a couch facing a hi-def TV mounted on the wall. We left the door behind us open for Tony and Bucher, and we continued inside. A stairway led upstairs, but the hallway we were in led toward the back of the house. Now, in my experience, perps rarely try to hide on a second floor, and kidnappers usually keep their victims in a back room or a basement. Either way, it made more sense to keep going down the hallway, heading deeper into the house, than to climb the stairs. Actually, it made more sense to cover the front and the back of the house and wait for the backup that we were sure would be there in just a few minutes, but that's when we heard movement in front of us, coming from the end of the hallway.

"Nikodim Bunin?" I called out, pulling out my flashlight. "This is the police and the Federal Bureau of Investigation. Come forward with your hands up." The moment that I clicked on my flashlight, there was a sudden flurry of motion.

I saw a great, gray shape coming down the hallway toward us. It was moving so fast that it was a blur, and I couldn't see any details. But the roar that was coming from it filled the house and stopped me in my tracks—it was the same horrible sound that I'd heard the night that "Sticky Ike" had been murdered. I immediately started firing, and so did Carolyn, but I think that I only hit the thing maybe twice before it was on top of us.

With one, back-handed motion, it slapped me aside and into the living room. I must've been thrown at least a good ten feet, and I crashed into the TV mounted on the wall. I could hear growling and screaming, but it all sounded like it was in a tunnel, and a world away. For a moment, I just looked at the ceiling and heard the blood rushing in my own ears, not knowing quite where I was. It was like time stood still, and I was just floating there. Then, a sharp, piercing pain in my side brought me back to my senses and I tried to sit up.

I recognized that pain all too well. I'd had broken ribs before, and this thing had just re-broken one of them again. Even more than the pain, the whole principle of the thing made me angry. It had taken me *forever* to heal the last time, and my side *still* ached whenever it got really damp outside. Now, I was going to have to go through all of that, all over again.

But that's when I also noticed the blood. I was bleeding from my right hand, and I had no idea where my pistol had flown off to. But I was also bleeding from three long slashes to my gut. Bizarrely, my hand hurt, and my rib hurt, but these huge slashes across my abdomen didn't hurt at all—shock does funny things to the human body.

I reached down to try to hold myself together, and I felt myself starting to get woozy from the blood loss. I looked up into the hallway, and in the moonlight, I could finally get a good look at what had attacked us, since it had stopped moving. It was big—*really* big— broad-chested and tall, even while hunched over, and it was covered in shaggy, gray fur. It stood on its hind legs with its back to me, and held Carolyn's body with long, clawed fingers as it chewed on her midsection. Her face, covered in blood, was turned towards me, and she was trying to talk, but no sounds were coming out of her mouth. At last, the thing stopped for a moment and turned to look at me as well, licking the blood from its muzzle. I don't know how to explain it, but I would swear that I could see the light of intelligence in its eyes.

But when it came down to it, for all the world, it looked to me like a huge, gray wolf…

Background
From *Daemonolatreiae Libri Tres* (Nicolas Rémy, 1595, trans. M. Summers)

from *Book I, Chapter V*

That the much-talked-of Examples of Metamorphosis, both in Ancient and Recent Times, were true in Appearance only, but not in Fact; for the Eyes are deceived by the Glamorous Art of the Demons which cause such Appearances. And although these False Appearances are accompanied by Actions which are found to be perfectly Genuine, this does not prove the Truth of such Metamorphoses; for it is agreed that such Actions are performed by the Demons which control the whole Matter; they being by Nature able very quickly to bring their Designs to Effect.

It is not my intention here to bring the Ass of Apuleius[1] again on to the stage, or to adduce fresh examples to support the old tales of the poets of men being changed into beasts; but only to bring forward such instances as are attested by the evidence of many witnesses and are proved by actual experience. The witches of Dieuze, Vergaville, and Forbach, and nearly all who have hitherto been tried for this crime in the kingdom of Austria, and whose confessions have come into my hands, have maintained that they changed themselves from men into cats[2] as often as they wished to enter another man's house secretly in order to plant their poison there at night. These statements are borne out and substantiated by the evidence of many who have reported that they have

---

[1] *Rémy here alludes to the* Metamorphoses, *written by Lucius Apuleius in the mid- to later second century* AD. *In the novel, the main character (also named Lucius) is magically turned into an ass by meddling with spells which he tragically only barely understands.*

[2] *See also Bartolomeo Spina's* Questio de Strigibus *(1523), Cap. XIX ("Experientiae apparentis conversionis strigum in catos"), and Henri Boguet's* An Examen of Witches *(1602).*

been attacked by witches in such shape; and the evidence has tallied in all respects with regard to the fact itself, the place, the persons, the time, and every circumstance and detail which could be required to establish complete proof. The case of Barbeline Rayel (Blainville, Jan., 1587) is quite recent. She confessed that she had transmuted herself into a cat, so that in that shape she might the more easily enter, and the more safely prowl about the house of Joannes Ludovicus: and that when she had done this, she found his two-year-old child and killed it by sprinkling over it a poison powder which she was carrying in her paw.

Whenever (as so easily happens among neighbours and fellows) Petrone of Armentières (Dalheim, 1581), of whom I spoke a little while ago, was moved with hatred or envy against the herdsmen of neighbouring flocks, he used to utter certain words by which he was changed into a wolf; and being, in such disguise, safe from all suspicion of ill doing, he would then fall upon and rend in pieces every beast of the herd that he could find. Joannes Malrisius acknowledged that he had done the same thing when he was keeping the flocks at Sulz-Bad across the woods…   And not long ago the Dolonais[3] witnessed the public execution of two werewolves who had been condemned to death by their Supreme Court.

To this class belongs the story which I heard myself from the Illustrious Count Paul à Salm, Prefect of the Sacred Chamber in the realm of Lorraine. I was expressing to him my doubts as to whether it was an illusion when a man appeared to take the form of a beast, or whether there was really any truth in such things; when he told me the following story. He held a signiory at Pettelange, where, following their ancient custom, the inhabitants used to pay a yearly tribute of free service to him and his family. One year they had thus brought their cart-loads of fuelling, and were receiving a gift of food in return, when (as often happens) a fight began in the castle hall among the dogs that had come with them; and one bitch hid itself in an oven for heating the baths. As the rest of the dogs kept up a violent barking at this one, one of the men looked in the oven and, seeing that the bitch was far more hideous to look at than all the others, began to suspect the truth (for that district is reported to be infested with witches),[4] and gave it a deep wound in the

---

3   *Boguet (in his 1602 work,* An Examen of Witches, *XLVII) records that in 1521 were executed Michael Udon of Plane, Philibert Montot, and Gros Pierre, who confessed that they had changed themselves into wolves, and in that form killed and eaten several people. In 1573 Gilles Garnier was burned alive at Dôle for the abominable crime of lycanthropy.*

4   *A common perception. According to Michel-Paul d'Amboise (*Tractatus Artibus Diabolicis, *1453), the* consilium corvórum *("raven council")—the largest convocation of witches in medieval Europe—once numbered in the thousands.*

face with a weapon that he was wearing. Upon this the bitch at once rushed out at the door, or at any rate she was no more seen there. Shortly afterwards a rumour spread all over town that there was an old woman lying in bed with a wound, and that it was not known where she received it. Everyone then began to suspect the truth, namely, that she was that rabid bitch which had been wounded in the castle hall; and this, added to her former evil reputation, caused her to be taken and thrown into prison. Finally, on being minutely questioned, she freely confessed all as it has here been told, at the same time acknowledging many other acts of witchcraft.

Here I should relate also what I heard from a credible source to have happened not long ago in Hither Burgundy: how a certain hostess came among her guests at supper in the form of a cat and spitefully attacked them; and when one of them cut off one of her paws, she was found the next day to have a hand missing. But because my informant told me this only in passing and I cannot fully verify the facts, I have thought good to say no more about it. But one more instance I will give, which I heard from the renowned Lady Diana of Dommartin, the wife of the illustrious Prince Charles Philippe Croy, Marquis of Haurech,[5] my very kind patron, to whose good graces I owe such advancements in fortune as I have enjoyed.

She told me that there was not long ago in Thiecourt, a village on their lands, a woman addicted to witchcraft whom the Demon had endowed with this power of assuming different shapes. She had contracted an immoderate hatred of a shepherd of that village, and, wishing by any means to procure his heavy punishment, sprang in the form of a wolf upon his sheep as they were grazing. But he ran up and threw an axe at her and wounded her in the thigh, so that she was disabled and was forced to take refuge behind the nearest bush, where she was found by the pursuing shepherd, binding her wound with strips torn from her clothing to stanch the blood which was flowing freely. On this evidence she was taken up, confessed everything as I have related it, and paid the penalty of her crimes in the fire.

The common opinion about such monstrous transformations is no new thing; for it was the belief of the ancients from time immemorial, as is proved by more than one reference in their written works. Pliny[6] (VII, 22) tells us that. Euanthes, an author of great reputation, quotes from the

---

[5] *Lady Diane de Dommartin was a beautiful and influential widow who had been quickly married to the successful general, Charles Philippe de Croÿ (named Prince of the Holy Roman Empire a year before the publication of this book) after her first husband had died at the Battle of Moncontour in 1569. She was a patron of the arts—and famous for her numerous rumored affairs with artists, writers, and handsome young courtiers of the day.*

[6] *In his* Naturalis Historia, *published in 77 AD.*

Annals of Arcadia[7] to the effect that there was a family of the tribe of Anthaeus whose destiny it was that each year one of them must be chosen by lot and led to a pool over which, having undressed, he must swim; and then he was immediately changed from a man into a beast. And if, after nine years, he had not in the meanwhile tasted human blood, he might again assume his former shape.   Herodotus (*Melpomene*)[8] and Solinus[9] (*Polyhist.* Cap. 20) tell that Neuri, who live by the Dnieper, are once every year changed into wolves for a few days, and after the allotted period regain their former appearance.   And Agrippas, the author of the *Olympionica*,[10] left record that one Demænetus was changed into a wolf because he had tasted the entrails of a child whom the Arcadians had sacrificed to Jupiter Lycaeus.   The same thing happened, as Pausanias[11] tells, to Lycaon the son of Pelasgus, when he sprinkled the altar of Jupiter Lycaeus with the blood of his slaughtered son.[12]

Let no one ascribe such stories to the ignorance of heathen blindness, on the ground that they refer only to those times when men lived without the light of the Christian truth. For it is said (*Sigibert. in Chronic. Luith.* III, 8)[13] that Bajanus, the son of Symeon who was Prince of Bulgaria, could by his evil spells change himself whenever he wished into a wolf or any other beast.[14] And Torquemada[15] in his *Hexameron*,

---

[7]   *As quoted in the aforementioned section of Pliny's* Naturalis Historia.

[8]   *One of the nine sections—each named after one of the Muses of Greek myth (Clio, Thalia, Erato, Euterpe, Polyhymnia, Calliope, Terpsichore, Urania, and Melpomene)—of Herodotus' classic 5th century BC work,* Ἡροδότου Ἁλικαρνησσέος ἱστορίης. *Melpomene was the muse of music and singing, but since many of the popular Greek operas were structured as morality plays about the downfall of great men, she also became the de facto muse of tragedy. The tale of the cursed Neuri fall into that category of drama.*

[9]   *That is, Gaius Julius Solinus, in his 3rd century work,* De Mirabilibus Mundi—*also known as* Collectanea Rerum Memorabilium *and, as in this case,* Polyhistor.

[10]   *Again, as quoted in Pliny's* Naturalis Historia

[11]   *In his classic 10-volume, 2nd century work,* Ἑλλάδος Περιήγησις, *volume 8.*

[12]   *see also Ovid's 1st century classic,* Metamorphoseon Libri (*aka* "The Metamorphoses").

[13]   *Here, Rémy cites the late 11th century work,* Chronicon sive Chronographia, *begun by Benedictine monk Sigebert of Gembloux (whom Rémy appears to know by the Latinized version of his name—Sigibertus Gemblacensis) and completed by his protégé, Anselm of Gembloux.*

[14]   *As was also attested to in Lewes Lavanter's nearly contemporary book,* Of Ghosts and Spirits Walking by Night (1572).

[15]   *That is, Antonio de Torquemada of León, and not the infamous Grand Inquisitor Tomás de Torquemada of Valladolid, who actually died nine years before Antonio was born.*

VI,[16] relates that when a certain Russian chieftain heard that there was in his Principality a man who could assume any shape he pleased, he caused the man to be brought before him in chains, and ordered him immediately to give a sample of his skill. The man answered that he would willingly do so if he might retire into the next room by himself for a little. This was granted him; and he at once came out in the natural form of a wolf, but still in his chains, to the great wonder of all who beheld him; but two very fierce dogs which the Prince had concealed for that purpose, fell upon the wretched man and tore him in pieces; nor was he helped at all by his wolfish body, which at all other times had stood him in good stead...

But there is another far stronger argument which might appear to prove the actuality of these transformations. It is not only the external physical shape that appears to be changed; the witch is also endowed with all the natural qualities and powers of the animal into which she is seemingly changed. For she acquires fleetness of foot; bodily strength; ravenous ferocity; the lust of howling; the faculty of breaking into places, and of silent movement; and other such animal characteristics, which are far beyond human strength or ability. For it is a matter of daily experience that Satan does actually so empower them. Thus they easily kill even the biggest cattle in the fields, and even devour their raw flesh, when they descend upon them as swiftly as any wolf or other ferocious beast; and they enter locked houses at night like cats; and in every way imitate the nature and habits of the animals whose shape and appearance they assume. Now this cannot be explained away as a mere glamour or prestige by which our senses are deceived... for they leave behind them concrete traces of their activities. For example, they are sometimes caught in the very act; and failing that, there is the evidence of their flight, pursuit and wounding, and of the loss and damage which they have inflicted.

---

[16] *Rémy cites Antonio de Torquemada's popular 16th century work,* Hexameron, ou Six journées contenans plusieurs doctes discours sus aucuns poincts difficiles en diverses sciences, avec maintes histoires notables et non encores ouyes *(1584), chronicling the strange and mysterious things of this world (including supernatural creatures, monsters, demons, witches, and more). It was published in English in 1600 by Ferdinando Walker—who, for some bizarre reason, retitled the book,* "The Spanish Mandevile of Miracles, or the Garden of Curious Flowers" *for his English readers.*

Chapter 4
Predators of Various Shapes

I kept slipping in and out of consciousness. I was trying to get up, to help somehow, but every time I tried, I'd black out for a second and find myself flat on my back again. I also kept trying to look around the room to find my pistol, but it was so dark in there, and the world kept spinning.

The strange thing was that Carolyn was still alive, at least for a few more moments. The thing had torn her to shreds, but she was still hanging on, somehow. I realized that I needed to rescind what I had decided earlier—she was apparently a lot stronger than I'd given her credit for. Then again, it was almost, I dunno, like the thing *wanted* her alive.

I mean, it could've killed her outright—it could've come over and killed *me* outright—but it didn't. It was more like it was toying with us. It kept looking over at me with those pale, blue, wolf eyes. Was it seeing if I was still there? Where would I go? Was it making sure I wasn't going to attack it? It sure didn't seem like its backward glances were worried at all. What was it expecting from me?

At one point, I found myself on my back again, and I could hear someone shouting. It sounded like Tony, so I figured that I must've been delirious. I tried to prop myself up again, but my eyes were too bleary to make much out. But it looked like Bucher and Tony were in the hallway, too. Bucher was crouching over Carolyn's body, shooting at the thing, and Tony was waving the *Matteh ha Shelomoh* at it. To be honest, he was the one who usually carried it with him, since, quite frankly, he was better with it than I was. But the thing was moving so fast that Tony couldn't make contact with it.

And yet, it wasn't returning the attack or running away, either. It was just hovering there, snarling, and avoiding the staff. Then it glanced back over my way again, making eye contact. If wolves can smile, I swear that I saw the thing smile. With that, it scampered off down the hallway, howling, with Tony running after it as fast as he could. I could hear the smash as it crashed through a back door, and I knew that there was no way that Tony was going to ever catch up to it.

Bucher was doing something with Carolyn's body, but I couldn't tell what. The world started spinning again, and everything went dark.

*   *   *

Is it weird that the first thing I was aware of after that was the smell of Joanna's hand lotion? Before I even opened my eyes, before I realized that it was her voice speaking, I could smell that hand lotion… and my first, muddled thought was to wonder why my wife was putting on hand lotion in Nikodim Bunin's living room.

I heard her voice talking to someone, but I couldn't make out the words. When I opened my eyes, the bright light all but blinded me. I must've winced or said something, because Joanna grabbed my hand and started telling me that everything was okay. I heard Tony say something like, "Welcome back," but it was all still so garbled and foreign. I fell back asleep.

*   *   *

I opened my eyes again, and the room seemed a bit dimmer this time. I realized that I was strapped into a hospital bed, with tubes everywhere. They'd taped my side up, and there was a bandage across my belly, and my right hand was wrapped in gauze. I reached up with my left hand to scratch my cheek, but there was a bandage there, too. Joanna was at the door of the room, keeping her voice low as she spoke to a nurse. But things were quiet enough in the room that I could hear them saying words like, "lucky," and "miracle," and then something about my internal organs. I really wanted to hear more about that last bit.

"What about…?" I started to ask, but my throat was so dry that the words hurt to try to get out. Joanna turned and smiled, and ran over to the bedside. She took hold of my left hand and started thanking God.

"Internal…?" I tried again, but that was as far as I could get. The nurse came over and dabbed a little sponge in some water and let me suck it off.

"We were so worried, Tom," Joanna said, leaning over to give me a kiss on the forehead. I could smell the hand lotion again, and it made me smile. "But the doctors say that you were very, very lucky."

"Internal… organs…?" I asked again. The water from the sponge helped immensely.

"You received some deep lacerations, Detective Chapel," the nurse explained. "But somehow, none of your internal organs were damaged. You lost a lot of blood, but the wounds are essentially just superficial."

"Broke… rib…" I tried, but then a cough wracked my body with pain. Joanna squeezed my hand harder, and I focused on that instead of my side.

"Actually," the nurse replied, swabbing my mouth with the sponge again, "it's just a small, hairline fracture. It must hurt a great deal, though…"

I must've been more out of it at Bunin's house than I'd realized. I've had cracked ribs before, and I've had broken ribs before, and I know the difference. But you can't argue with an x-ray—especially when it tells you that you're not as bad off as you'd *thought* that you were. I wondered about what happened after I had blacked out in that living room, but at that moment, I just felt like sleeping some more. Which I did.

*   *   *

The next day—I assumed it was the next day, since Joanna had changed her clothes—I was feeling a great deal better. I was sipping water and chewing on ice chips, and Joanna was filling me in on the children and Flubber when Leah Wheaton came through the door. Joanna got up and gave her a hug, and Wheaton smiled when she saw how much I was improving.

"You had us all worried there," she said. Then she handed me a card from the guys down at the office that said, "Get well soon—crime just isn't the same without you." Everybody had signed it, including Ben Bucher.

"How is Agent Davidge doing?" Joanna asked her, and Wheaton's face went downcast. To be honest, I never thought to ask that, because I had just assumed that she was dead.

"She's… not going to make it," Wheaton said. "They're doing all that they can, but she was…" She glanced at me, then back at Joanna. I could tell that she was censoring herself for the civilian. "She was pretty messed up when they brought her in."

"What happened?" I asked, and Wheaton turned to Joanna.

"Would you be sweet enough to see if they have any coffee out there?" she asked her. "I haven't had any all day, and I could really use some."

Joanna smiled. "Or you could just say, 'Joanna, please leave the room so that we can talk cop stuff without you hearing it,' Leah." Wheaton looked a little sheepish, but Joanna leaned over, gave me a little kiss, and told me that she'd be back in a few minutes. She gave Wheaton another hug and said something about grabbing lunch sometime soon. When she was gone, Wheaton pulled up the chair.

"Why don't *you* tell *me* what happened?" she said, sitting down. "If we'd known you'd get attacked by a pack of wolves, we never would've tossed the case your way. That should've been Nate and me in that house, not you guys."

I assured her that it wasn't their fault, and then asked about the wolves. I said that I didn't remember much of anything—which was accurate, if not entirely true.

"Tony and Agent Bucher said that they came on the scene to find you and Agent Davidge being mauled by a pack of wolves," she said. "I wouldn't have been surprised to find that a *boyevik* like Bunin might have a Rottweiler or a pit bull guarding his house, but I never would've expected wolves. I mean, who keeps wolves?"

"Bad guys," I replied.

"Apparently," she chuckled. "Anyway, they were able to chase the wolves away and call in an ambulance for you guys."

"They ever find these wolves?"

"Not yet. But I mean, how long can it take Animal Care and Control to find a bunch of wolves in the middle of Little India? They'll get them and put them down, don't worry."

Somehow, I doubted that they would.

"What about the house?" I asked. "The girl?" Her expression got dark again.

"The basement had been extensively remodeled. There were four soundproofed cells down there, as well as a large room that we can only guess was the wolves' den. We found... remains... and the dental records checked out. Some of them came from Sherri Angelo."

"*Some* of them?" I asked. "How many bodies did you find down there?"

"We didn't find any bodies," she replied. "We found... *bits*... bones, shreds of clothes. It's really hard to determine how many parts of how many different people they'd fed to those wolves, but Bill Saunders down at the coroner's office figured that it was at least a dozen."

I could only imagine the horrors that they found down in that basement. Normal human trafficking is bad enough, but how many people had been locked in those little cells, not knowing why they were there, not knowing what was going to happen to them? How had Sherri Angelo felt, taken from an upscale mall to a dingy little cell in a basement in Little India? I kept picturing Carolyn Davidge, being torn apart by that thing in the hallway.

"It doesn't make much sense, though," she continued. "If these guys are human traffickers, then why waste all that time kidnapping people, just to end up feeding them to your wolves? I mean, you don't make any money off of your slaves that way. This is your livelihood, literally being thrown to the dogs."

Unless that was the point of the kidnappings in the first place. Maybe Nikodim Bunin wasn't just a human trafficker—maybe he was a *hunter...*

"On the plus side," she said, trying to lighten the mood a bit, "we were able to find some documents that we're hoping will help us nail these scumbags."

"Like what?"

"Well, it's mostly in Russian, so we're having them translated, but it looks like some shipping schedules, manifests, a ledger, some personal notes, etc. Oh, and we found something really creepy in one of the upstairs rooms."

"Creepier than the basement?"

"Well, no," she admitted. "But creepy enough. The rooms upstairs were mostly normal—a bedroom, a bathroom, some kind of office, whatever, but there was one little room that had all sorts of weird stuff painted all over the place in blood—crosses, pentagrams, funky symbols that I'd never seen before. It seems that this Bunin guy must be some sort of Satanist or something. There was this big, old Russian Bible on a pedestal in the center of the room next to a little gold statue of a woman. And nailed to one of the walls were—get this—thirteen crows, lined up like a cross."

"Was the cross upside-down?" I asked.

"No, why?"

"Because Satanists usually use them upside-down. But that's nothing conclusive. Anything else?"

"Yeah. The words, '*Синод Вороны*'"—she wrote the words out on a slip of paper, since she had no idea how to pronounce them—"were painted around the crows."

"What does that mean?"

"Do I look Russian?"

I thanked her for the card, slid the paper inside of it, then asked where Tony was. She said that he'd poked his head into the hospital a few times to see me, but that he'd been acting really strange for the past few days. "And not his *usual* strange," she clarified. He'd been quiet, and that in and of itself was strange for Tony. I wondered if he had just been worried about me, or if going toe-to-toe with that thing in the hallway had actually done more of a whammy on him than it did on me. I'd have to talk with him about that the next time I saw him. I asked where Bucher was, and she said that he had spent most of the past couple of days in Carolyn's room.

*   *   *

That night, as I lay in my hospital bed, I had the strangest sensation—that feeling that you're being watched. People talk about that as if it's some sort of supernatural, sixth sense, but it really isn't.

It's just your brain processing subtle input from all of your other, natural senses, but at such a low, subconscious level that you can't put your finger on just what it is that you're picking up on. Maybe it's some small movement or strange shape out of the corner of your eye—nothing major, nothing so noticeable that you'd even consciously be aware of it, but strange enough that your brain makes a little note. Add that to the birds around you suddenly getting quieter—again, maybe nothing that you'd ever notice on its own. Mix in a subtle smell that wasn't there before, or the faint sound of someone breathing where no one was supposed to be—again, anything that, by itself, means nothing. But your brain takes all of these little "nothings" and mixes them together into a picture that it quantifies as being stalked. We may have spent the past couple of centuries at relative peace with nature, but there's still that part of our brain that remembers what it was like to be more prey than predator.

The room was dark, but not so dark that I couldn't see that there was no one in it. I strained to hear anything, but all I could hear were the sounds of the various machines, the drip of my IV, and a doctor and nurse talking about another patient out in the hallway. Okay, I could also hear the heat kick on in my room, and someone's television was on next door, but nothing out of the ordinary.

And yet, I had the distinct impression that someone, somewhere, was watching me. I lay there for a while, trying to wrap my head around it. I couldn't see anything wrong, I couldn't hear anything wrong. I cleared my head and took in a long, deep breath through my nose. Suddenly, just for an instant, I smelled the very, very slightest hint of the scent of almonds... and then it was gone—and so was the feeling of being watched.

*   *   *

The doctors said that I'd made a great recovery, and that I was doing well enough to go home, so long as I came back for some physical rehab the next week. Joanna was delighted, and I called Tony to let him know. The call went straight to his voicemail. I would've gotten frustrated with that, but it's just a minor miracle that Tony had even set up voicemail in the first place, technophobe that he was.

The nurse brought in a wheelchair for me, but the truth is, I didn't really need it. I know that they have to do that sort of thing for insurance purposes, but you always feel silly riding in a wheelchair when you can walk just fine. I almost felt guilty. I mean, I wasn't even in pain any more, but here I was, sitting in my pointless wheelchair and nursing a Styrofoam cup of orange juice, while Carolyn was still in intensive care. That just didn't seem fair.

Joanna double-checked the room to make sure that we hadn't forgotten anything, and we drove home. The whole time, I couldn't stop thinking about how pointless and unfair it all was. The thing that attacked us was still out there—the CACC will never find their pack of wolves—and we couldn't save the Angelo girl. Carolyn was right—I really shouldn't make promises that I can't keep.

So how do we find Bunin now? Where would we even start looking? He'd gone to ground somewhere, and I was lucky to have survived against his guard dog. Or was that, somehow, Bunin himself, transformed? All I knew was that the last two times I'd gone to the door of a person of interest, I'd almost died. I had little desire to go for a hat trick. I couldn't just depend on Tony and the Matteh ha Shelomoh to save me next time—we desperately needed an edge.

Ironically, that's exactly what I was thinking as we pulled into our driveway. I say, "ironically," because standing at my door was literally the last person in the world that I expected to see, and yet the answer to all of my problems...

Pieter Durant...

Background
From *The Book of Were-Wolves* (Sabine Baring-Gould, 1865)

from *Chapter V: The Were-wolf in the Middle-Ages*

Stories from Olaus Magnus of Livonian Were-wolves—
Story from Bishop Majolus—...

Olaus Magnus[1] relates that—"In Prussia, Livonia, and Lithuania, although the inhabitants suffer considerably from the rapacity of wolves throughout the year, in that these animals rend their cattle, which are scattered in great numbers through the woods, whenever they stray in the very least, yet this is not regarded by them as such a serious matter as what they endure from men turned into wolves.

"On the feast of the Nativity of Christ, at night, such a multitude of wolves transformed from men gather together in a certain spot, arranged among themselves, and then spread to rage with wondrous ferocity against human beings, and those animals which are not wild, that the natives of these regions suffer more detriment from these, than they do from true and natural wolves; for when a human habitation has been detected by them isolated in the woods, they besiege it with atrocity, striving to break in the doors, and in the event of their doing so, they devour all the human beings, and every animal which is found within. They burst into the beer-cellars, and there they empty the tuns of beer or mead, and pile up the empty casks one above another in the middle of the cellar, thus showing their difference from natural and genuine wolves... Between Lithuania, Livonia, and Courland are the walls of a certain old ruined castle. At this spot congregate thousands, on a fixed occasion, and try their agility in jumping. Those who are unable to bound over the wall, as is often the case with the fattest, are fallen upon with scourges by the captains and slain." Olaus relates also in c. xlvii. the story of a certain nobleman who was travelling through a large forest with some peasants in his retinue who dabbled in the black art. They found no house where they could lodge for the night, and were well-nigh

---

[1]   *In his* Historia de Gentibus Septentrionalibus *(1555).*

famished. Then one of the peasants offered, if all the rest would hold their tongues as to what he should do, that he would bring them a lamb from a distant flock.

He thereupon retired into the depths of the forest and changed his form into that of a wolf, fell upon the flock, and brought a lamb to his companions in his mouth. They received it with gratitude. Then he retired once more into the thicket, and transformed himself back again into his human shape.

The wife of a nobleman in Livonia expressed her doubts to one of her slaves whether it were possible for man or woman thus to change shape. The servant at once volunteered to give her evidence of the possibility. He left the room, and in another moment a wolf was observed running over the country. The dogs followed him, and notwithstanding his resistance, tore out one of his eyes. Next day the slave appeared before his mistress blind of an eye.[2]

Bp. Majolus[3] and Caspar Peucer[4] relate the following circumstances of the Livonians:—

At Christmas, a boy lame of a leg goes round the country summoning the devil's followers, who are countless, to a general conclave. Whoever remains behind, or goes reluctantly, is scourged by another with an iron whip till the blood flows, and his traces are left in blood. The human form vanishes, and the whole multitude become wolves. Many thousands assemble. Foremost goes the leader armed with an iron whip, and the troop follow, "firmly convinced in their imaginations that they are transformed into wolves." They fall upon herds of cattle and flocks of sheep, but they have no power to slay men. When they come to a river, the leader smites the water with his scourge, and it divides, leaving a dry path through the midst, by which the pack may go. The transformation lasts during twelve days, at the expiration of which period the wolf-skin vanishes, and the human form reappears. This superstition was expressly forbidden by the church... In like

---

[2]   *It is interesting to note that a century after Olaus Magnus'* Historia *was published, an 80-year-old convicted Livonian werewolf named Theiss would claim at his 1692 trial in Jürgensburg that he used his lycanthropy on Heaven's behalf (as a "hound of God"), in an ongoing battle between werewolves and witches. For more information on Theiss, see Ginzburg's* I Benandanti: Stregoneria e Culti Agrari tra Cinquecento e Seicento *(1966), and Duerr's* Traumzeit: Über die Grenze zwischen Wildnis und Zivilisation *(1978).*

[3]   *Simone Majoli, bishop of Volturara and Montecorvino, in his* Dies Caniculares *(1612).*

[4]   *Professor of both mathematics and medicine at Wittenberg and an important figure within the Reformation, in his* Commentarius de Praecipuis Divinationum Generibus *(1553).*

manner did S. Boniface[5] preach against those who believed superstitiously in "*strigas et fictos lupos.*"[6]

---

[5] *8th century missionary to the Franks, famous for chopping down the "Donar Oak" at which the Germanic peoples worshipped the god, Donar (aka Thor). Originally christened "Winfrið" in Wessex, he was given the name "Bonifatius" ("Good Fate") by Pope Gregory II, after the popular (but completely fictitious) 4th century martyr, Boniface of Tarsus.*

[6] *"Witches and those made into wolves [i.e.; 'werewolves']." Note: whether or not Boniface ever preached such a sermon is debatable, since the first collection of his sermons (Collectio Veterum Scriptorum) wasn't published until Edmond Martene and Ursin Durand did so in 1733—a thousand years after his death.*

Background
From *The Vampire, His Kith and Kin* (Montague Summers, 1928)

from *Chapter V: The Traits and Practice of Vampirism*

Schernitzius[1] will have [lycanthropy] common in Livonia. They lie hid most part all day, and go abroad in the night, barking, howling, at graves and deserts; they have usually hollow eyes, scabbed legs and thighs, very dry and pale (*Ulcerata crura, sitis ipsis adest immodica, pallidi, lingua sicca*)[2] saith Altomarus (Cap. 9, Art. *Hydrophobia*);[3] he gives a reason there of all the symptoms, and sets down a brief cure of them. It is remarkable that most of these features are found in the vampire, especially the unquenchable thirst, "*sitis immodica*"[4] which is emphasized by the famous physician Antonio Donato Altomari, who was one of the most learned authorities of his day. It is also remarkable that the malady is reported as being very prevalent in Bohemia, Hungary, and Livonia, countries in which the vampire is most frequently found. There is in fact a very close connexion between the werewolf and the vampire, and the lycanthropist is liable to become a vampire when he dies.

---

[1] *Sigismund Scheretzius, in his* Libellus Consolatorius de Spectris *(1621).*

[2] *That is, "an excessive amount of leg sores; pale faces; dry tongues."*

[3] *Donato Antonio Altomare, in his* De Medendis Humani Corporis Malis ars Medica *(1553), specifically referring to his article on "Hydrophobia" ("ὑδροφοβία," now known as "rabies"). Donato actually referred to the disease as a "μελανχολία" ("melancholia"), due to the prevailing wisdom that such problems were caused by an overabundance of black bile in the body—"μέλας" (black) + "χολή" (bile). Interestingly, the name of the shapeshifting god, Þōden or Woðen (the Germanic counterpart to the Norse god, Óðinn, who frequently changed into the form of a wolf to travel the world unrecognized) was derived from the root word "wōð-," the Old Germanic name for "a wild fury," or "rabies," thus indicating another early perceived connection between lycanthropy and rabies.*

[4] *Meaning, "excessive thirst."*

Chapter 5
An Interlude with an Old Friend

My Dad used to say that there are three kinds of human beings in this world—those who follow the rules, those who break the rules, and those who change the rules entirely. Pieter Durant was definitely that third kind of person.

If you don't already know who I'm talking about, how do I describe Pieter Durant to you in such a way that I don't sound either crazy or stupid? He's a knight—he's *the* knight, the *Grail* knight. His name was Peredur (or Percival, or however you're most familiar with the story), a knight of King Arthur's Round Table, and the keeper of the Holy Grail for the past 1,500 years. And if I haven't lost you already, he's the guy who makes sure that the things that go bump in the night don't climb out from under your bed and eat you.

He's like the reverse boogey-man.

Seriously, he's the guy who gives vampires and monsters nightmares and cold sweats. I don't really know how he got started in the monster-hunter business, but he uses the strength and speed and healing that the Grail has built up in him over the centuries to hunt the things that hunt the rest of us. Nobody knows that he's out there—because, quite frankly, almost no one read my first book about him—but he actually likes it better that way. "Anonymity is the best camouflage," he once told me. I don't know if that's so that the bad guys don't see him coming, or so that the good guys don't freak out when they see him coming. Either way, I can see his point.

So there he was at my front door, in all of his fashion-plate glory. A three-piece, pale gray Hugo Boss suit, a black shirt with a thread-count in the triple digits, a black Roberto Cavalli tie, and a big, black, Burberry overcoat that skimmed the floor as he walked. How a man can simultaneously be at the pinnacle of modern fashion and still give the overall impression that he just walked out of the 19th century is beyond me, but somehow, he pulls it off.

"Durant!" I exclaimed as I got out of the car.

"What?" he asked in response, and when Joanna saw who it was, she ran over to him and gave him a huge hug. He looked decidedly uncomfortable with the display of familiarity.

"Pieter," she exclaimed. "It's so good to see you!"

"And you, Madame," he replied. He didn't return the hug, but he was far too much of a gentleman to try to wriggle out of it.

"I never expected to see you here," I said, catching up to them.

"Of course you would not," he said. "Why the devil should you?" I gave up and shook my head. I had forgotten how much social etiquette Durant had forgotten in the past millennium or so. I decided to try a different approach.

"So why *are* you here?" I asked. "Seeing you walking into a room is a little like seeing storm clouds on the horizon and hearing a tornado siren going off." He was about to answer when Joanna inserted herself back into the conversation.

"Don't you listen to him, Pieter!" she said, turning and glaring at me. "You know that we're always happy to see you, and you're always welcome around here."

"I didn't mean that he wasn't welcome," I jumped in, defending myself. "I mean, if there really is a tornado coming, I kinda like that the siren goes off. I'm just saying that—"

"You're staying for dinner," she continued, turning back to him.

"No, I've no desire to be a bother," he said. "I've places to be, and I cannot remain with you for that long."

"Fine, then it's settled," she finished. "I know that I have some steaks in the fridge, and that asparagus. I'll make some mac and cheese for the kids…" She started counting things off on her fingers as she pulled her keys out to unlock the front door.

"Tenacious woman," Durant said.

"You have no idea," I replied. He looked at me strangely, cocking his head.

"You've… changed…" he commented quizzically.

"Is that in reference to the fact that some of us actually do *age*, or the fact that I'm coming home from the hospital after being attacked by a monster?" Of course, that last bit immediately got me thinking. "Is that what brought you back to Chicago?"

"Hmm?" he asked, obviously only barely listening to what I was saying. "Oh, no. I had no idea that you were even in hospital until now."

"Then why *are* you here?" I asked.

"An interesting question," he replied. "If you shall recall, I left you nearly two years ago in order to track down the Queen of the Vampyri. I realized that I had not been to Central Africa since helping that rumble-voiced Frenchman, Roaché, and the SDECE during their *Opération Barracuda* against Emperor Jean-Bédel Bokassa in 1979. The last time that I saw Roaché was in New York roughly fifteen years ago, after he had dealt with some sort of lizard problem…"

"What does any of that have to do with Africa or with why you're here now?" I asked, trying to steer him back on course as Joanna opened the door.

"Oh, of course," he continued, back on his original track. "Whilst in Africa, I combed through the ruins of the silent city of vampires in the hills of the dead near Kôr, looking for signs of Lamashtu. Finding that she had long-abandoned that place, I followed her trail to Europe, and then to the Goth rock scene in San Francisco, and then to the back streets of Berlin. As it happens—"

And that's when Flubber attacked.

Now, having said that, you have to understand that the dog is the absolute, quintessential, dictionary definition of "all bark, no bite." So it's not like he pounced on us or anything. But when he realized that "Mommy" and I were coming inside, he bounded out of the front door to leap into my arms and lick me to death. But when he saw me standing there next to Durant, he pulled back and started barking at us.

The absolute absurdity of this little mutt actually trying to intimidate Pieter Durant with his barking made me start to laugh. I started to tell Durant that it was okay, that Flubber would get used to him over time if he came inside, but Durant—being Durant—acted before I could say anything. He quietly got down on his haunches and looked at the dog, right there in the snow-dusted front yard—not trying to intimidate, not trying to overpower, but just sitting there, looking at him. Flubber stopped his barking and looked right back at him, growling a little in confusion. But Durant stayed right where he was, simply looking at him. After a little while, Flubber ceased his growling and tilted his head to the side, as if tying to understand something. For several more moments, they just sat there, I guess sizing one another up. Then, with a loud snort, Flubber concluded that Durant was okay, and trotted right up to him, wagging his tail. In fact, he curled up against his leg and leaned his furry head into Durant's hand to be petted, as if he'd known Durant for years, as if Durant were just part of the family—which, I suppose, in a way, he was.

"Good dog…" his deep voice whispered as he scratched inside Flubber's ears. How Durant knew that that was his favorite place to be scratched, I'll never know, but the dog loved him after that. In fact, he didn't even come over to say hello to me—he was just enthralled with Durant.

*   *   *

After dinner with the family, the two of us sat down in the living room, with Flubber curled up next to Durant's leg.

"So where all have you been for the past couple of years?" I asked him, breaking the ice to get into more serious conversation.

"Most recently?" he replied, scratching Flubber's neck as he spoke. "On a short trip to Singapore to deal with a rogue *singa-laut*, but that is of little consequence to you—and 'small talk' is of little interest to me. You said something about being attacked...?"

To the point, as usual. I cleared my throat and told him about our investigation of the *Bratva's Obshchestvo Drakonisty* and about the attack on Carolyn and me at Bunin's house.

"This *Obshchestvo Drakonisty* is only the most recent incarnation of the *Orden Drakona*—the Order of the Dragon," he said, "which is far older than this modern Russian thuggery. In its guise as *La Société des Dragonistes,* it has long made use of werewolves in its ranks."

"You're kidding me," I said reflexively. I shouldn't have said it. I know that I shouldn't have said it. But it just came out.

"Yes," he said with a sigh. "I am joking. The creature which attacked you was obviously a ten-year-old ruffian with an extraordinarily impressive Hallowe'en costume. Shame on you for taking his playful romp so seriously..."

"All right, all right. I believe you," I said. And I guess that I believed him. But the word *werewolf* still sounded so silly to say out loud. "So have you ever seen a real werewolf?"

"Indeed—several times," he replied. "In fact, before I even found the Grail, there was a poor unfortunate knight in Arthur's court at Caer Mallot who was cursed by his own unfaithful shrew of a wife. His name was Sir Melion, and his wife was an Irish princess—I believe her name was Bhfeallaire, but I do not recall for certain."

"What happened?"

"She used a magical ring to transform him so that she could run away with her lover back to Ireland. Being touched with the white stone in the ring would change him into a wolf, whilst being touched with the crimson stone would return him to human form. This she neglected to do."

"I thought that you had to get bitten by a werewolf to change into one," I said.

"And you learnt this from motion pictures, yes?"

"Well..."

"The last motion picture I viewed was *Catherine the Great*, in 1934," he said with a snort. "It was so rife with historical inaccuracies that I've not been able to bring myself to watch another since then. You must not trust what you have seen on celluloid, Detective."

"Okay, but this thing at Bunin's house," I began up again. "It wasn't really a wolf. It was, you know, a wolf-*man* sort of thing."

"Thus the name, *were*-wolf, Detective."

"Yes, but you're saying that werewolves are basically just guys turned into actual wolves, like that guy you once told me about in Spain?"

"Esteban de Navarra?"

"Yeah."

"Not at all," he answered, and his tone of voice continued to make me feel like an ignorant child. "And Esteban was cursed in France, not Spain. The truth is, there are as many forms of werewolves as there are forms of the vampyri. Some transform completely into otherwise natural-seeming wolves, while others remain essentially human in form—albeit significantly more hirsute and deadly. Others transform into a tall, lean, lupine form while remaining primarily bipedal, whereas I once heard of a case in London of a quadropedal werewolf who was so broad-chested that he appeared nearly *ursine* in form."

"How come?" I asked.

"What do you mean?" he asked in return.

"I mean, why so many different kinds? What exactly *is* a werewolf?"

"You have heard of Lamashtu and her Lilitu, yes?"

"Sumerian pseudo-vampires, right?" I offered, remembering the research that I did after the last time he was in town. "Created by the demon-goddess Ishtar."

"Very good," he replied, looking rather surprised. "Though Ishtar was not a demon but rather an Osiran, created by her mentor, the Tchagal thing Tiamat"—distinctions which, I confess, are completely lost on me—"But nonetheless, though the lethal combination of King Ubara-tutu's purge and the coming of the Great Flood all but wiped out the Lilitu, their genetic strain remained. A later Osiran called Zeus infected an Arcadian king name Lycaon with a mutated derivative of it—"

"I thought that Zeus was a *Greek* god," I interrupted.

"There is but one God," he sighed. "The Olympians were simply an offshoot of the Tchagal Osirans. May I continue in answering your original question?" he asked, exasperated, as if all of that explained anything any better. I nodded and tried to keep my mouth shut.

"Zeus infected King Lycaon, altering his DNA with what has since become known as the 'Lycaon virus,' which changes a man's outward form to mirror his inward, bestial nature. In Lycaon's case, that form was the shape and attributes of a wolf, but there are many different mutations of the virus in existence today, and far more numerous attempts to counterfeit the virus' effects by magicians and shaman the world 'round. The Norse *seiðmenn*, the Navajo *yee naaldlooshii*, the Filipino *asuwangs*, etc.—all are examples of human beings attempting to replicate the Lycaon effect, to differing degrees of success.

"Thus, for instance, Richard Verstegen and I discovered British sorcerers who wrapped themselves in a wide girdle of wolfskin and painted themselves with a special salve to achieve the desired results. In doing this, they embodied the strength and shape of wolves, feeling empowered to go and perpetrate all manners of horror onto their world."

"Kind of like those berserkers you told me about," I ventured tentatively.

"Yes, the *úlfhéðnar* of King Haraldr hárfagri," he replied. "Very good, detective. I had no idea that you were actually listening to that story, much less that you might recall it…"

"I'm a detective, Durant," I said. "I try to remember everything."

"Indeed," he said, and nodded. "But it need not be wolfskins or bearskins that one uses in this manner. I once knew a man in England named Guye of Giselburn, who wore a suit made of horse-hide in an attempt to channel the strength and stamina of a horse."

"Did that work?"

"Not at all—Guye was a fool who presented himself as a knight," Durant replied, snorting. Flubber snorted in response. "His attempts to be perceived as powerful made him all the more comical instead. But I separated his head from his body when I killed him nonetheless, just to be certain. In point of fact, it was for the killing of that Yorkshire imbecile that the local sheriff, Gerard de Athies, had me imprisoned in that damnable oubliette of his, though my prison companion told the tale quite differently to any in the ale-houses who would listen to him."

"So that's how you kill them? By chopping off their heads?" I asked. "I thought that was for vampires and silver bullets were for werewolves."

"Again, we are cursed by the inaccuracies and limitations of the motion picture…" he said, sighing again. "Nearly every form of creature on this earth may be destroyed by the removal or destruction of the head—save the thing that was *Knygathin Zhaum*, but that is another matter entirely. Whether it be vampire or werewolf or water witch or common murderer that one is combating, decapitation—or complete immolation—is a wise move for one to make in order to be certain.

"In the same way, not every werewolf requires silver to destroy it, Detective," he continued. "But silver is fairly universally effective against most forms of lycanthropes. Legend has it that silver is anathema to the monsters because of its purity, or perhaps it is because of its elemental similarity to orichalcum, or because it poisons them much as arsenic or mercury might poison a human, or because silver is a natural antibiotic. Who knows? But you must remember that the Lycaon virus is as *spiritual* as it is *physical*—it infects the soul as well as the body. It is a curse, and not simply an affliction."

"So what does that mean?"

"It means that true lycanthropy cannot be cured by medicines or transfusions or simply resting in one's bed. It is an unholy thing of teeth and fur and hunger and hatred, a twisting of both man and beast into something unclean that lives only to sate its own lusts, which grow ever stronger with each passing day."

"Then how *do* you cure a werewolf?"

"You do not," he said quite gravely. "You *destroy* it."

"But they're still human," I pressed. "They're not like vampires or revenants. You can't just give up on them."

"They are the worst parts of our human souls, given a beast's form and power," he replied. "I do not 'give up on them' so much as realize that for some unfortunates, there is no returning from the abyss into which they have peered. They have given themselves over to evil, and it has consumed them from the inside-out. This is why some werewolves are destroyed only through elements of spiritual purification—through the use of silver, or fire, or holy water. Others may only be killed by acts of justice, such as by hanging or suicide. Of course, still others may be killed by much the same means as any large predator may be destroyed—any firearm with sufficient power would suffice. Much of that depends on the nature of the curse with which the person has been afflicted."

"So you're saying that I should try to shoot one in the head with silver-plated buckshot."

"Not an altogether unwise suggestion," he said, scratching Flubber again. I was going to press the issue again, when I saw Chelsea in the doorway, listening to our conversation as she sipped a bright green-colored milk-shake-looking thing that the babysitter had made for her.

"Little ears…" I said, pointing her out to Durant.

"Good Lord!" Durant exclaimed, quickly changing the subject when he saw what she was drinking. "What is that concoction?"

"It'th a Green Cow," she said, smiling. She had just lost the second of her two front teeth the week before, and she was very proud of looking so much like a hockey player. In fact, she liked to stick her straw through the large opening, just like she was doing at that moment.

"It's like a root beer float," I explained to him, "but instead of root beer, you use a Green River. Chelsea calls it a 'Green Cow,' after some ridiculous radio show hero from the 1940s."

"Indeed," he said. "I remember the program…" Chelsea smiled at that, and pointed to her mouth and the gap between her teeth. "Yes, I saw that earlier, child," he said, turning back to me.

"Um, Uncle Pieter?" Chelsea asked, stepping forward and gently tugging on his sleeve.

"I am not your uncle, little one," he replied—but gently, not angrily.

"Um, okay, but…" she continued, undaunted, "Uncle Pieter, can I tell you a joke?" Durant sighed and turned to give her his full attention.

"Yes, child…" By this time, the twins had toddled up behind her and were listening in the doorway. So Chelsea looked around the room for something to tell a joke about. That's the thing with a five-year-old—they often know what they want to do long before they have any idea how they want to do it. She knew that she wanted to tell a joke. Now it was just a matter of figuring out a good joke to make up. Her eyes finally looked out through the window and settled on my snow-covered car outside.

"What did the car thay to the—" then she stopped herself as the joke finally coalesced in her mind. "I mean, what did the *thnow* thay to the car?"

"I have no idea," he said, sighing. "What did the snow say to the car?"

"It thaid," (and note, at this point, she began snickering almost uncontrollably) "'Let me in there! I'm freething cold!'" The twins started cracking up at this, too, but mostly because their sister was laughing, and they didn't want to feel left out. That's pretty much when Joanna came and collected the kids, apologizing for the interruption.

"Not at all," Durant said—and his sincerity surprised me. "It was a welcome one. There is no better ointment to the burdened soul than to hear the laughter of loving children…" He reached out and gently touched the top of Chelsea's head, and she giggled again.

*   *   *

We said "good night" to the children, and Durant explained to us that he really did need to go and follow up on some other business. But as he was putting on his coat to leave, he pulled me aside again and spoke to me in hushed but serious tones.

"Were you alone when you were attacked?" he asked me. "And—this is crucially important—were you *bitten*?"

"No, and no," I said. "I was with an FBI agent—Carolyn Davidge. The thing just threw me across the room while it chomped on her."

"So she was killed?" he asked again, nodding.

"No," I answered. "But she's… she's not going to make it much longer. She's in intensive care."

He just stood there for a moment, those gray eyes burrowing into mine from under those dark brows. And then he looked down and scratched his chin under his beard.

"This could be… unfortunate…" he said at last.

"It's already pretty stinking unfortunate, if you ask me!" I replied.

"And things could soon grow to become much, much worse," he snapped back. "Watch her carefully, Detective. And pray that she dies soon… and *peacefully*…"

Background
From *The Book of Were-Wolves* (Sabine Baring-Gould, 1865)

from *Chapter VI: A Chamber of Horrors*

Pierre Bourgot and Michel Verdung—
The Hermit of S. Bonnot—...

In December, 1521, the Inquisitor-General for the diocese of Besançon, Boin by name, heard a case of a sufficiently terrible nature to produce a profound sensation of alarm in the neighbourhood. Two men were under accusation of witchcraft and cannibalism. Their names were Pierre Bourgot, or Peter the Great, as the people had nicknamed him from his stature, and Michel Verdung.[1] Peter had not been long under trial, before he volunteered a full confession of his crimes. It amounted to this:—

About nineteen years before, on the occasion of a New Year's market at Poligny, a terrible storm had broken over the country, and among other mischiefs done by it, was the scattering of Pierre's flock. "In vain," said the prisoner, "did I labour, in company with other peasants, to find the sheep and bring them together. I went everywhere in search of them.

"Then there rode up three black horsemen, and the last said to me: 'Whither away? You seem to be in trouble?'

"I related to him my misfortune with my flock. He bade me pluck up my spirits, and promised that his master would henceforth take charge of and protect my flock, if I would only rely upon him. He told me, as well, that I should find my strayed sheep very shortly, and he promised to provide me with money. We agreed to meet again in four or five days. My flock I soon found collected together. At my second meeting I learned of the stranger that he was a servant of the devil. I forswore God and our Lady and all saints and dwellers in Paradise. I renounced Christianity, kissed his left hand, which was black and ice-

---

[1]   *Boguet (in his 1602 work,* An Examen of Witches, *XLVII) names them "Gros Pierre" (i.e.; "Peter the Great") and Michael Udon.*

cold as that of a corpse. Then I fell on my knees and gave in my allegiance to Satan. I remained in the service of the devil for two years, and never entered a church before the end of mass, or at all events till the holy water had been sprinkled, according to the desire of my master, whose name I afterwards learned was Moyset.

"All anxiety about my flock was removed, for the devil had undertaken to protect it and to keep off the wolves.

"This freedom from care, however, made me begin to tire of the devil's service, and I recommenced my attendance at church, till I was brought back into obedience to the evil one by Michel Verdung, when I renewed my compact on the understanding that I should be supplied with money.

"In a wood near Chastel Charnon we met with many others whom I did not recognize; we danced, and each had in his or her hand a green taper with a blue flame. Still under the delusion that I should obtain money, Michel persuaded me to move with the greatest celerity, and in order to do this, after I had stripped myself, he smeared me with a salve, and I believed myself then to be transformed into a wolf. I was at first somewhat horrified at my four wolf's feet, and the fur with which I was covered all at once, but I found that I could now travel with the speed of the wind. This could not have taken place without the help of our powerful master, who was present during our excursion, though I did not perceive him till I had recovered my human form. Michel did the same as myself.

"When we had been one or two hours in this condition of metamorphosis, Michel smeared us again, and quick as thought we resumed our human forms. The salve was given us by our masters; to me it was given by Moyset, to Michel by his own master, Guillemin."

Pierre declared that he felt no exhaustion after his excursions, though the judge inquired particularly whether he felt that prostration after his unusual exertion, of which witches usually complained. Indeed the exhaustion consequent on a were-wolf raid was so great that the lycanthropist was often confined to his bed for days, and could hardly move hand or foot, much in the same way as the *berserkir*[2] and *ham rammir*[3] in the North were utterly prostrated after their fit had left them.

---

[2] *Literally, one who wears a bearskin shirt—from "ber" (bear) and "serkr" (shirt). Like the* úlfhéðnar *(who wore wolfskins into battle),* the berserkir *believed that they were able to channel the strength and ferocity of the animal by wrapping themselves in their skins, and were thus renowned as being most savage and powerful combatants. That one could access the attributes of an animal by wearing its skin was a common belief in ancient magic traditions. The 7th century Anglo-Saxon Christian poet, Cædmon, echoed this sentiment when he wrote that Satan wished "þät he mid feðerhomon fleôgan meahte, windan on wolkne" ("that he with a feather-*

In one of his were-wolf runs, Pierre fell upon a boy of six or seven years old, with his teeth, intending to rend and devour him, but the lad screamed so loud that he was obliged to beat a retreat to his clothes, and smear himself again, in order to recover his form and escape detection. He and Michel, however, one day tore to pieces a woman as she was gathering peas; and a M. de Chusnée, who came to her rescue, was attacked by them and killed.

On another occasion they fell upon a little girl of four years old, and ate her up, with the exception of one arm. Michel thought the flesh most delicious.

Another girl was strangled by them, and her blood lapped up. Of a third they ate merely a portion of the stomach. One evening at dusk, Pierre leaped over a garden wall, and came upon a little maiden of nine years old, engaged upon the weeding of the garden beds. She fell on her knees and entreated Pierre to spare her; but he snapped the neck, and left her a corpse, lying among her flowers. On this occasion he does not seem to have been in his wolf's shape. He fell upon a goat which he found in the field of Pierre Lerugen, and bit it in the throat, but he killed it with a knife.

Michel was transformed in his clothes into a wolf, but Pierre was obliged to strip, and the metamorphosis could not take place with him unless he were stark naked.

He was unable to account for the manner in which the hair vanished when he recovered his natural condition.

The statements of Pierre Bourgot were fully corroborated by Michel Verdung.

Towards the close of the autumn of 1573, the peasants of the neighbourhood of Dôle, in Franche-Comté, were authorized by the Court of Parliament at Dôle, to hunt down the were-wolves which infested the country. The authorization was as follows:— "According to the advertisement made to the sovereign Court of Parliament at Dôle, that, in the territories of Espagny, Salvange, Courchapon, and the neighbouring

---

cloak might fly, walking on the wind"—see his Anglo-Saxon paraphrase of the Biblical book of Genesis *in the* Codex Junius, *line 417), much like the* fjaðr-hamr *("feather-garment") of the Norse goddess, Freyja, which would turn its wearer into a falcon (see the* Þrymskviða *in the 13th century* Poetic Edda*).*

3 *A form of shape-shifting performed by the practitioners of* seiðr—*a shamanistic magic of the ancient Norse peoples (in particular, those shaman who worshipped the all-father god, Óðinn, who was able to change his shape at will. The seiðmann who practiced shapeshifting was said to be "hamrammr" or "shape-strong," perceiving the wearing of a garment made from an animal's skin—a "hamr" in Norse—as synonymous with wearing the animal's shape and attributes.*

villages, has often been seen and met, for some time past, a were-wolf, who, it is said, has already seized and carried off several little children, so that they have not been seen since, and since he has attacked and done injury in the country to some horsemen, who kept him off only with great difficulty and danger to their persons: the said Court, desiring to prevent any greater danger, has permitted, and does permit, those who are abiding or dwelling in the said places and others, notwithstanding all edicts concerning the chase, to assemble with pikes, halberts, arquebuses, and sticks, to chase and to pursue the said were-wolf in every place where they may find or seize him; to tie and to kill, without incurring any pains or penalties... Given at the meeting of the said Court, on the thirteenth day of the month September, 1573." It was some time, however, before the *loup-garou*[4] was caught.

In a retired spot near Amanges, half shrouded in trees, stood a small hovel of the rudest construction; its roof was of turf, and its walls were blotched with lichen. The garden to this cot was run to waste, and the fence round it broken through. As the hovel was far from any road, and was only reached by a path over moorland and through forest, it was seldom visited, and the couple who lived in it were not such as would make many friends. The man, Gilles Garnier, was a sombre, ill-looking fellow, who walked in a stooping attitude, and whose pale face, livid complexion, and deep-set eyes under a pair of coarse and bushy brows, which met across the forehead, were sufficient to repel any one from seeking his acquaintance. Gilles seldom spoke, and when he did it was in the broadest patois of his country. His long grey beard and retiring habits procured for him the name of the Hermit of St. Bonnot, though no one for a moment attributed to him any extraordinary amount of sanctity.

The hermit does not seem to have been suspected for some time, but one day, as some of the peasants of Chastenoy were returning home from their work, through the forest, the screams of a child and the deep baying of a wolf, attracted their notice, and on running in the direction whence the cries sounded, they found a little girl defending herself against a monstrous creature, which was attacking her tooth and nail, and had already wounded her severely in five places. As the peasants came up, the creature fled on all fours into the gloom of the thicket; it was so dark that it could not be identified with certainty, and whilst some affirmed that it was a wolf, others thought they had recognized the features of the hermit. This took place on the 8th November.

On the 14th a little boy of ten years old was missing, who had been last seen at a short distance from the gates of Dôle.

---

[4]   *Literally, "wolf-man"*

The hermit of S. Bonnot was now seized and brought to trial at Dôle, when the following evidence was extracted from him and his wife, and substantiated in many particulars by witnesses.

On the last day of Michaelmas, under the form of a wolf, at a mile from Dôle, in the farm of Gorge, a vineyard belonging to Chastenoy, near the wood of La Serre, Gilles Gamier had attacked a little maiden of ten or twelve years old, and had slain her with his teeth and claws; he had then drawn her into the wood, stripped her, gnawed the flesh from her legs and arms, and had enjoyed his meal so much, that, inspired with conjugal affection, he had brought some of the flesh home for his wife Apolline.[5]

Eight days after the feast of All Saints, again in the form of a were-wolf, he had seized another girl, near the meadow land of La Pouppe, on the territory of Athume and Chastenoy, and was on the point of slaying and devouring her, when three persons came up, and he was compelled to escape. On the fourteenth day after All Saints, also as a wolf, he had attacked a boy of ten years old, a mile from Dôle, between Gredisans and Menoté, and had strangled him. On that occasion he had eaten all the flesh off his legs and arms, and had also devoured a great part of the belly; one of the legs he had rent completely from the trunk with his fangs.

On the Friday before the last feast of S. Bartholomew, he had seized a boy of twelve or thirteen, under a large pear-trees near the wood of the village Perrouze, and had drawn him into the thicket and killed him, intending to eat him as he had eaten the other children, but the approach of men hindered him from fulfilling his intention. The boy was, however, quite dead, and the men who came up declared that Gilles appeared as a man and not as a wolf. The hermit of S. Bonnot was sentenced to be dragged to the place of public execution, and there to be burned alive, a sentence which was rigorously carried out.

---

[5] *In point of fact, his marriage appears to have been one of the major contributing factors to the murders. With the addition of his wife, he was too poor to provide food for both people in the household, so he confessed at his trial that—after having received a visitation from a ghostly figure who gave him a special ointment that allowed him to transform into a wolf—he would stalk and kill children in order to take their flesh back home to help feed his new wife.*

Chapter 6
Change Is In the Air

The next morning, I sat outside in my back yard, sipping a cup of coffee and holding it between my hands to keep me warm. But it wasn't really that cold out that morning—most of the snow from the day before had melted off with the sunrise. And that's not right.

You know, for years, Tony's been convinced that there's no such thing as global warming. Sure, he might admit—under duress—that temperatures might be warming across the globe, but that doesn't point to any "global warming" phenomenon, does it? He adamantly believed that it's just the earth going through a natural climactic phase, just like it's done since the dawn of time.

Whatever.

My point here is that when I was a kid, it used to snow in Chicago in the winter. Oh, Chelsea and the twins will tell you that it still snows nowadays, but all that they're used to nowadays is this crazy blizzard/thaw/blizzard/thaw/blizzard/thaw cycle throughout December and January that we see now. That's not winter—that's just winter *stuttering*. When I was a kid, it would snow in November (or even October), and you wouldn't see grass again until late February (or even March). I remember having to wear a sweatshirt under my Hallowe'en costumes because it was so cold. More to the point, I remember a snow drift one year that was so big that it went from the roof of our house down to the neighbor's driveway. My brother and I dragged our sled all the way up that thing, climbed onto the roof, then rode that sled all the way down into the neighbor's yard, across their driveway, and then into the huge snow pile on the other side. There were roughly a dozen ways that I figure that it could've ended in serious injury or property damage—and yes, we got into major trouble with my Dad—but it was *winter*. Today, my kids are lucky if they can rush to build a snowman that lasts for more than a couple of days before it melts.

Sitting there with my coffee, it just seemed like so much that I knew, so much that I was used to and that had meant something to me over the years, had changed… and somehow, I'd been too oblivious, too busy growing up and doing things, to notice until it was gone. So many things that you took for granted in life—like that the snow that fell yesterday would still be there to play in tomorrow—all seemed so up in the air, inconstant, undependable. You wouldn't think that snow was something that you'd depend on, but it was when I was a kid—I just didn't realize it at the time. It's hard to put into words, but that realization was like suddenly finding out that gravity didn't work the way that you always thought it did, and that you'd have to watch your step from now on.

When you were a kid, you played wiffle ball with your buddies in the back yard. Mom made pumpkin pie at Thanksgiving. It actually snowed in the winter. And there were no such things as vampires and werewolves.

No—scratch that. Worse than that, there *were* vampires and werewolves, but they were just cliché movie monsters that you watched in those black-and-white movies that came on WGN when they had to fill some time in the schedule, or on *Son of Svengoolie*. I mean, it's just Lon Chaney, Jr. with some hair stuck to his face, right? The guy didn't even unbutton his shirt when he transformed, for crying out loud. It was so obviously unreal that you couldn't really be scared.

And yet, I remember being scared. I remember checking under my bed before I went to sleep to make sure that there wasn't a wolf-man or a mummy or something under there. But somehow, it was a gentler, more innocent kind of scared. Like I knew that it wasn't real, that there wasn't any blood on the movie screen, that there wasn't really going to be a wolf-man under my bed. It was all just scary because it was *supposed* to be scary, and not because it actually *was* scary. It was like a little game that you played within your own mind, a little dance between you and Frankenstein's monster. Kind of like that stage of life when you finally realized that you were supposed to like girls, but you still had no idea *why*.

Somewhere along the way, we decided to make our monster movies scarier, more realistic. That's probably when they started losing my interest, since I've seen enough realistic horror on the streets every day. And yet, people still know deep down that they're all just latex masks, fake blood, and computer-generated effects on the big screen. You don't go home after watching a horror movie and expect that a giant ape might really stomp on your house that night.

I took another sip of coffee and breathed in the morning air. It still smelled like December used to smell when I was a kid, but it looked like any other day from October to February nowadays—chilly, a little overcast, with a lot of dead-looking trees. The magic and the wonder of winter just seemed to be gone. The innocence of it.

The truth is, I knew that I needed to get back to work. Yes, I'd go to rehab like the doctor wanted me to, but with a thing like this...

creature… out there, how could I just leave it all to Tony? He'd left me a text on my phone that the CSI guys had come up with some things at the scene of "Sticky Ike's" death, and that I should meet him in Roscoe Village, if I was up to it. I don't know if I'd have gone so far as to say that I was "up to it," but I really was feeling better, and as long as I took it easy, I knew that I'd be okay. But I also knew that the first stop I needed to make on the way into the office was to drop by the hospital and check on Carolyn Davidge.

And that sucked all the joy out of the morning. I mean, I'd planned on checking in on her later in the day anyway, but now… Now, I wasn't going to be checking on her to be a good partner—I was checking on her to make sure that she was dead, safe and sound. And that rips your heart out, lemme tell ya.

He didn't have to go into details the night before—I knew what Durant meant at the end there. Lycanthropy is like a virus. It passes from one person to another in all sorts of ways. *Were you bitten? Watch her carefully…* He didn't have to draw me a roadmap, because I could see where he was going with all of that. If Carolyn died, then we would all mourn her, because it would be a tragedy. If she didn't die, then there was a chance that she now carried that "Lycaon virus" infection, and that would end up being even worse.

How screwed up is being a grown-up when you find yourself praying for a tragedy?

*   *   *

So she was in the ICU at the Swedish Covenant Hospital on California. It's a really good place, started by a church way back in 1886. I guess they had twelve beds back then—now, they have more than twenty times that many. They even have something that they call their "Healing Garden," complete with a running stream, footpaths, and lots of greenery. I mean, if you're going to be attacked by a werewolf, that's pretty much the place to get sent to.

I was fairly familiar with the place by that time, so I went straight to her room, expecting to find Ben Bucher by her side. The nurses were flitting back and forth, dealing with some sort of emergency here or there, but to tell you the truth, I didn't really pay that much attention. I just walked up to the door of the room, took a deep breath, and then stepped inside.

The room was empty, and the bed had been stripped.

To be honest, I didn't know how to feel. I mean, I was sad, of course—any time that a colleague dies, it kind of takes a chunk of you along with them. But a large part of me really didn't know how I was going to react if I'd found her sitting up in bed and chatting with Bucher, when the day before, she'd been on a respirator and sliding downhill fast.   Would that have been a good thing?   Under any other circumstances, I would've called that a miracle, but given the situation as it was, I think that it would've been chilling.

I stepped back over to the nurses' station and got the attention of the nearest one.

"When did Agent Davidge pass away" I asked.

"I'm sorry, sir," she replied, glancing up at me for maybe a second before she went back to whatever paperwork it was that she'd been doing. "But unless you're a family member, I can't release any patient information."   I took out my badge and then asked her the question again.   She looked annoyed, and then clicked a few buttons on her computer.   Obviously, this was not what she wanted to be doing, first thing in the morning. But then her face lit up and she smiled at me.

"Actually, Detective," she said at last. "You'll be happy to hear that she was checked out about half an hour ago, right before I came on shift."

My heart sunk. And then I felt horribly guilty about it sinking.

"Do you mean that she was moved to another room?" I asked.

"No, sir," she replied.   "She apparently had such a remarkable recovery overnight that she's actually been released from the hospital. I don't think that I've ever seen that happen like that before—they usually require that you at least stay for tests and monitoring, though it's not like we can really keep her here against her will.   But isn't that some great news to start off your morning?"

*   *   *

Neither Carolyn Davidge nor Ben Bucher was answering their cell phones, which I didn't take for a good sign.   Actually, none of it was good, and I couldn't even find the doctor who had signed her out to ask him what on earth he was thinking.   So I left a note for him at the nurses' station to contact me, got into my car, and drove the 15 minutes or so down Western that it took to get to Roscoe Village.   Tony said that he'd meet me at the crime scene, and I texted him that I'd be there in a few.   I didn't hear back from him, but that's nothing new.   I'd already gotten more cell phone usage out of him in the past week alone than I'd had in the six months prior to that combined.

As I passed by Miska's Deli on Belmont, I remembered that deli on Devon that had closed, and I decided to make a quick stop first.   They'd just opened for the day, but I was in the mood for some corned beef, and I remembered that theirs was pretty good.   Yes, you can eat corned beef at 9:30 in the morning—don't judge me.

Miska's is a quirky little store, one of those places that just looks like a big, concrete block sitting on the corner. If you were just driving past, you'd assume that it was just a liquor store—and it mostly is, really—but they also have turkey bacon clubs as big as your head, and a really good corned beef melt. For that matter, they also have a little bar in the back that's basically just for the locals. When others might blow into town on the weekends to hit the Hungry Brain or risk those stairs at Matilda's, the local Villagers often just hang out at Miska's, shooting pool and listening to the MP3 jukebox.

Anyway, I turned my car around and made my pit stop at Miska's. I decided to grab something for Tony, too, since he'd probably be hungry… because, let's face it, he was *always* hungry. I walked through the door, and the girl at the counter flashed me a pleasant, genuine smile. I ordered an orange juice with my sandwich and got that turkey bacon club for Tony, and then I just stood there for a second, drinking in the smells of the deli. No, it wasn't the greatest deli in Chicago, but it sure smelled great to a hungry man. You could smell the corned beef, and the cheese as it melted, and the bread as it warmed, and it was glorious.

But then, for a split second, I also got a slight whiff of almonds.

I wasn't expecting that, so it took me off-guard. I didn't see any nuts around there—it wasn't like the girl was roasting any somewhere— and it only lasted a second. The whole thing was unsettling, though I really didn't understand why at the time. Of course, today, I don't really like almonds any more because of the association, but I'm getting ahead of myself.

An old woman shuffled up to the counter next to me, and when I say an old woman, I mean a really, really old woman. She had perfectly snowy-white hair, and wrinkles on top of her wrinkles. He skin was the color of terracotta, and she was wearing layers and layers of different kinds of clothing—a shawl over a coat over a dress over jeans. She waited patiently for the girl, but she was busy making the sandwiches and didn't seem to notice the woman standing there. Then again, the woman was so short that her head barely reached above the countertop, so maybe the girl couldn't even see her.

"It is very cold," the woman said to me. Her voice was low and croaky, and it was a little difficult at first to understand her.

"It was colder yesterday," I replied, but then I added respectfully, "But yes, it's still cold. The wind just cuts through you." She nodded, and we stood there for a few more moments in silence.

"You are getting two sandwiches?" she asked, smiling. "You must be a hungry young man."

"No, no," I chuckled. "One is for my partner. He's waiting for me a couple of blocks away. In fact, I should probably get him a coffee, now that I think of it…"

"Your partner…" she muttered, so quietly that it seemed more like a rumble than like words. "Are you a policeman?" I thought at first that that was kind of an odd leap for her to make, but I guess that it made a certain amount of sense.

"Yes, ma'am," I replied.

"Oh, so polite you are," she said, smiling again. "There was a killing here a few nights ago, a horrible killing. Are you investigating that?" Her smile didn't waver, like she was asking me the sweetest question about my job. *Oh, do you get to play with a siren? Did you see that mutilated corpse the other night? That's so nice...*

"Yes, ma'am, we are," I said. "But I can't really disclose any details about an ongoing investigation at this time."

"Oh, that's all right, young man," she said. "I already know who made this killing..." She smiled and continued waiting for the girl to finish with my sandwiches.

"Excuse me?" I asked.

"It was the Manetôwa," she replied, shaking her hand in the air.

"The what?"

"The Nenemehkiwaki—the thunder beings—have always made war against the Manetôwaki—the serpent beings," she croaked, nodding to herself. "True people know this." Now it was my turn to smile.

"Yes, ma'am," I said, and decided to let sleeping dogs lie. There's little to be gained by arguing with some crazy old lady in a deli at 9:30 in the morning about thunder beings and serpent beings. Besides, my sandwiches were almost ready.

"My white teachers called me Rebecca," she said quietly, "but my mother called me her Manômini. This is the name of my heart. We Meshkwahkihaki are few today, but we need to remember the old ways."

"So you're Native American?" I asked.

"I am Meshkwahkihaki," she corrected me. "My brother flew in the air in the war in Europe." She smiled at me again. "He threw fire down upon the Germans, because they were Manetôwaki."

"I see..."

"When Wisaka the Châki-ôtha created the world," she continued, folding her arms across her chest, "he sent his crows, Mehkwênemêwa and Mehkwitêhêwa, across the waters. Thought and memory imposed order on the chaos of greed and hunger, and the Manetôwaki were afraid. Serpents are creatures of chaos and hunger, and they did not like the Châki-ôtha's order. So they hid themselves in the dark waters and dark caves and dark woods, and they made war against the Nenemehkiwaki, and against anyone who would shape nature into an order that accomplished something."

"Against any kind of technology, civilization, that sort of thing?" I asked, mildly bemused. "But I thought that the Germans were all about creating their own order."

"You do not understand," she grumbled, shaking her head. "The time of the wheel is a young time, but the time of medicine is the old time. The serpent beings fear any kind of medicine that changes their chaos into order. This is why they fear the sky, and the light that comes from the sky. This is why they slither in the dark and work their foul deeds on the world."

"Okay," I said. I really wanted my sandwiches and drinks soon.

"You will hunt down the Mahwêwithowa," the old woman said, nodding and smiling again. "I know this. You will hunt them into their dens and you will save the children." She got my attention with that last part.

"Excuse me," I said again, suddenly more interested. "What did you just say?"

"The children," she repeated. "They hunt the children and take them back into their dens, these mahwêwaki, and they devour them. They treat the people as if they were prey, but we are not prey. The children are ours, not theirs. The Kâkâkiwithowa have fought them since the beginning, and we will continue to fight them."

"How do you know about the children?" I asked. "Have you seen something or heard something about missing children in this area?"

"I have heard the *wind*," she replied, as if that should have been obvious to me.

"Ma'am, I really need you to tell me if you have any information that could be helpful in this investigation. Who are these 'mahwêwaki' people? If you could just—"

She interrupted me by patting me on the hand and saying, "Shhh…" Her palms were rough, like sandpaper, and her touch actually hurt a little bit.

"You will do this with the other man," she said. "The kîshekwi man. Or you will fall and be killed. This is the truth." And then she smiled again.

The girl came back to the counter with my order, and I asked her how much I owed her. When I turned back to talk with the old woman, she was gone.

And the whole place suddenly reeked of almonds…

Background
From *The Popol Vuh: The Mythic and Heroic Sagas of the Kichés of Central America* (Lewis Spence, 1908)

The cosmogony of the "Popol Vuh"[1] exhibits many signs of Christian influence, but it would be quite erroneous to infer that such influence was of a direct nature; that is, that the native compiler deliberately infused into the original narrative those outstanding features of the Christian cosmogony, which were undoubtedly quite familiar to him...[2] A native Guatemalan, nurtured in the Christian faith, could, in fact, quite be expected to produce an incongruous blending of Christian and pagan cosmogony such as is here dealt with.

Under the veneer of Biblical cosmogony, the original myth would appear to be the sum of more than one native creation-story. We have here a number of beings, each of whom appear in some manner to exercise the function of a creator, and it might be gathered from this that the account now before us was produced by the fusion and reconciliation of more than one legend connected with the creation-a reconciliation of early rival faiths. We have to guide us in this the proved facts of a composite Peruvian cosmogony. The ruling Inca caste skillfully welded together no less than four early creation-myths, reserving for their own divine ancestors the headship of the heavens. And it is not unreasonable to believe that the diverse ethnological elements of which the Maya-

---

[1] *Literally, "The Book of the People," the* Popol Vuh *(or Popol Wuj) is a pre-Columbian collection of classic Maya myths, including accounts of their creation mythologies. It was first written down for Europeans in 1715 by Father Francisco Ximénez as part of his* Empiezan las Historias del Origen de los Indios de esta Provincia de Guatemala *("Beginning of the Histories of the Origin of the Indians of this Province of Guatemala")*

[2] *Pavón's* Nuevos Descubrimientos en la Historia de los Mayas *("New Finds in Mayan History," 1994) has argued persuasively that the pre-Columbian Maya were heavily influenced by earlier European travelers such as Madog ab Owain Gwynedd and St. Brendan of Clonfert, and were thus undoubtedly familiar with Christian thought. See also Oviedo's* General y Natural Historia de las Indias *("General and Natural History of the Indies," 1526), and the work of Barry Fell, critiqued by Kelley in* The Review of Archaeology *(Spring 1990).*

Kiché[3] people were undoubtedly composed possessed divergent cosmogonies, which were reconciled to one another in the later traditional versions of the "Popol Vuh."

This would lead to the further supposition that the "Popol Vuh" is a monument of very considerable antiquity. The fusion of religious beliefs is, even with savages, a work of many generations. It would be rash to attempt to discover any approximate date for the original conception of the "Popol Vuh." The only version which we possess is that now under review, and as the lack of an earlier version makes comparison impossible, we are thus without the guidance with which the criteria of philology would undoubtedly furnish us. That the Mayan civilisation was of very considerable antiquity is possible, although no adequate proof exists for the assumption. This much is certain: that at the period of the Conquest written language was still in a state of transition from the pictographic to the phonetic-ideographic stage, and that therefore no version of the "Popol Vuh" which had been fixed by its receiving literary form could have long existed. It is much more probable that it existed for many generations by being handed down from mouth to mouth—a manner of literary preservation exceedingly common with the American peoples. The memories of the natives of America were and still are matter for astonishment for all who come into contact with them. The Conquistadores were astounded at the ease with which the Mexicans could recite poems and orations of stupendous length, and numerous instances of Indian feats of mnemonics are on record.

It is worthy of notice that the Kiché myth embodies the general aboriginal idea of creation which prevailed in the New World. In many of them the central idea of creation is supplied by the brooding of a great bird over the dark primeval waste of waters.[4] Thus the Athapascans thought that a mighty raven, with eyes of fire and wings whose clapping was as the thunder, descended to the ocean and raised the earth to its surface.[5] The Muscokis believed that a couple of pigeons, skimming the surface of the deep, espied a blade of grass upon its surface, which

---

[3]   *The Kiché (or the Spanish Quiché)—literally meaning "many trees"—are a Native America people and part of the Maya civilization that thrived in Central and South America from the 27th century* BC *until the Spanish conquests of the 16th century* AD. *The word "Kiché" also refers to their language.*

[4]   *A common conflict in most Native American myths—the Thunderbird ("Cigwe'") representing order and light, and the water monster ("Mji-Mnito" or "Great Serpent;" also "michipeshu" or "apotamkin") representing chaos and darkness (see* Ophiolatreia: An Account of the Rites and Mysteries Connected with the Origin, Rise, and Development of Serpent Worship in Parts of the World, *1889, for parallels in other cultures).*

[5]   *see* A General History of the Fur Trade from Canada to the North-west *(Mackenzie, 1801)*

slowly evolved into the dry land.[6] The Zuñis imagined that Awonawilona, the All-father, so impregnated the waters that a scum appeared upon their surface which became the earth and sky.[7] The Iroquois said that their female ancestor, expelled from heaven by her angry spouse, landed upon the sea, from which mud at once arose.[8] The Mixtecs imagined that two winds—those of the Nine Serpents and the Nine Caverns—under the guise of a bird and a winged serpent respectively, caused the waters to subside and the land to appear.[9] The Costa Rican Guaymis related, according to Melendez,[10] that Noncomala waded into the water and met the water-nymph Rutbe, who bore him twins, the sun and moon. In all these accounts, from widely divergent nations, it is surprising to note such unanimity of belief.

---

[6]   *see* The Indian Tribes of the United States: Their History, Antiquities, Customs, Religion, Arts, Language, Traditions, Oral Legends, and Myths *(Schoolcraft, 1884)*

[7]   *see* Outlines of Zuñi Creation Myths *(Cushing, 1896)*

[8]   *see* Iroquois Creation Myth *(Norton, 1816)*

[9]   *see* Latin American Mythology *(Alexander, 1920)*

[10]   *see his 1682 work,* Tesoros Verdaderos De Las Yndias En la Historia de la gran Provincia De San Juan Bautista Del Peru De el Orden de Predicadores *("True Treasures of The Indies in the History of the Great Province of San Juan Bautista, Peru, from the Order of Preachers")*

Chapter 7
Wolves in the Morning Light

When I got to the crime scene, Tony was already there, leaning against the wall of a building and scratching his chin with the three fingers of his left hand. He always seemed to have a perpetual 5:00 shadow on his face, so his fingernails made a discernible scritch-scratching noise when he did it. That usually meant that he was worried about something, so I was surprised that he wasn't reflexively lighting up a cigarette. I didn't see any recent butts on the ground near him, either.

"Whassup?" I asked as I walked up to him. He looked up, and frowned when he saw me.

"I didn't think ya'd show," he said. "Yer supposed ta be restin', right?"

"What, and miss all this fun...?" I ducked under the tape and looked at the remnants of dried blood on the ground. "You said that the CSI guys had found something new?"

He nodded as he dug a candy bar out of his pocket. I held up the bags that I'd gotten from Miska's and told him that I'd brought him a sandwich.

"I'll eat that too, in a minute," he said, shoving the whole candy bar into his mouth and tossing the wrapper onto the sidewalk.

"That's littering," I said.

"So call a cop," he replied, his mouth full of chocolate. A breeze picked up, so I set the bags down and snatched the wrapper before the wind could blow it away. There was a dumpster not thirty feet from us, where a bunch of cops were gathered, so I walked over to throw it away. On my way there, Leah Wheaton broke from the pack and started walking my way, looking more than just a bit frustrated.

"G'morning," I greeted her as she approached.

"It *was*..." she grumbled, shaking her head.

"What?" I asked. She stopped, looked at me as if she was going to answer, and then shook her head again and kept on walking past me, toward Tony. The other cops were laughing and seemed to be in a good mood, so I shrugged my shoulders and went over to the dumpster, crumpling the wrapper into a ball and throwing it in. But I'll tell you, getting this close to that dumpster was disgusting—it was easily the worst-smelling one that I'd ever been around. I almost gagged on the stench of rotting garbage, so I stepped away as fast as I could to see what the cops were talking about.

There in the middle of them stood Carolyn Davidge.

*   *   *

At some point in her life, my wife Joanna decided that the different words we use for attractiveness should each mean something quantifiably different. She's always hated it when people used "pretty" and "beautiful" as if they were synonymous. So—and, bear in mind, I'm still not sure that I quite get all of the distinctions myself—someone who is "cute" may or may not be "beautiful" as well, but she certainly wouldn't end up being "gorgeous," in Joanna's estimation. It's not like one word pointed to more attractiveness than another, really, but rather that they indicated different *kinds* of attractiveness. As near as I could figure it, "pretty" would indicate a *simple* kind of beauty—one achieved without much ornamentation and decoration, like a rose just naturally is—and "cute" would be like a subset of that, reserved for innocent and youthful creatures like children and puppies. "Gorgeous" would be the exact opposite of that—someone who was attractive because of an artful use of complexities like makeup or jewelry or well-done hairstyles. So Ginger would be "gorgeous," but Mary Ann was "pretty" (or, arguably, "cute," depending on the episode). I guess that "beautiful" was somewhere in-between those, since Joanna has always seemed to reserve it for more of a clean, classic kind of look, like Audrey Hepburn or Kate Beckinsale. The growing plethora of Hollywood starlets and music video vixens who try so hard to make men drool over them apparently fall into a broad, dismissive category labeled "hot"—the use of which was almost invariably accompanied by Joanna rolling her eyes with disdain. Beyond that, I can't remember any other categories, though I'm sure that she'd thought plenty more of them out.

The reason that I bring all of this up is that Carolyn Davidge had always been actively plain—not *ugly*, by any means, but she'd always taken great pains to downplay her looks. The FBI agent standing in front of me was beautiful—not pretty in a simple way, and not gorgeous in a made-up way, but just drop-dead, phenomenally sexy beautiful. And she smelled so good that I couldn't even smell the dumpster any more.

A large part of her allure was due to how she was dressed and how she moved. Gone was the frumpy business suit. She was now dressed in a fitted purple blouse that she'd unbuttoned maybe one button more than she should've to have been entirely professional, a stretchy black pencil skirt that hit her above her knees, and black knee-high boots. She also had a black jacket, but she'd it slung over her left arm instead of wearing it, even though it was still a bit chilly out—obviously to show the athletic body that, up until that point, she'd always tried to hide. Her hair was wavy and blowing in the breeze, and she'd applied her makeup in such a way that her face looked softer, smoother, and amazing.

But most of all, she *held* herself completely differently. She'd always been tight, awkward, uncomfortable with her own body. But now, she was swaying back and forth, making eye contact with and smiling at each of the guys as she addressed them, cocking her hips, and laughing. The most surprising detail—and, to me, probably the most quietly unsettling one—was that she made it a point to reach out and touch each guy when she was talking with him. Nothing major, nothing inappropriate, but a light resting of her hand on one guy's forearm when she mentioned something, or a light tap on another guy's chest when he said something witty, that sort of thing. It was all gently flirty, and it was working.

"Carolyn?" I called to her, more than just a little shocked. She turned and noticed me, and her face lit up.

"Oh, Tom!" she called, and her voice was musical. She all but ran over to me and threw her right arm around my neck, giving me a quick—but not quite quick enough—peck on the cheek. Up close, her scent was intoxicating. "My hero..." she cooed, her warm, green eyes locked onto mine.

"Excuse me?" I asked, feeling more than just a little uncomfortable. She stepped back, but made sure to keep herself inside my left arm as she turned back to face the group. I couldn't help but notice the warmth of her body against me.

"I was just telling the guys how you tried to save me," she said, leaning in tightly against me, with her own arm around the small of my back. "Here he was," she told them, "thrown across the room, torn and bleeding, and he still kept trying to get up to help."

At first, I couldn't tell if she was being sarcastic or not, since I didn't really do anything but watch her being gnawed upon. But as she continued her story, I could hear that she was being sincere, and she kept holding me tightly. Of course, even then, I realized that she was always in motion—she was always moving her hand, or her hips, or her legs. It made everyone around continually conscious of every move of her body, and for a moment, I completely forgot what I'd gone to the hospital that morning to check on. Her hair smelled like strawberries...

But let me stop here for a second and tell you that I've been whammied before, and by the best in the business. So, this was kind of a "been there, done that" sort of thing. Yeah, for a moment, I was as drawn in by Carolyn's charms as the next guy, but it was only for a moment. Very quickly, the rational, moral side of my brain kicked in, and I was far more creeped out than I was turned on.

Out of the corner of my eye, I saw Leah Wheaton on the corner, talking with Tony. The look on her face was so disgusted that I felt dirty, just standing next to Carolyn—or "Lyn," as she was asking all of the guys to call her now. I pulled myself away from her, peeling her arm off of me in the process. She pouted a bit, but somehow, it still came off as flirty.

Personally, I'd been mentally prepared to be terrified if I'd have seen Carolyn sitting up in a hospital bed, feeling better. I hadn't even considered a situation like this. I'd seen victims of abuse become hyper-sexualized as a means of coping with their trauma, but not this kind of turnaround, not overnight. She was obviously changed—*changing*—and she had certainly healed a lot faster than anyone who'd gone through the kind of the mauling that she'd gone through had any right to have. It had to be the Lycaon virus in her system, transforming her—not only physically, but apparently mentally as well. This was not a good thing.

"This…" I started, not exactly knowing where I was going with that sentence. "This isn't *you*, Carolyn…"

One of the guys muttered something under his breath that I didn't catch, but a couple of other cops laughed in response. I looked at them, and I was struck by the leer in their eyes. These weren't animals or savages—they were fellow cops, decent guys. But here they were, hovering around a sexy woman like a pack of hyenas circling fresh meat. I mean, that's kind of creepy, in and of itself. But when you realize that this woman had *never* been like this around any of us, that she had been on a respirator the night before, *and that it had never even appeared to dawn on any of them to ask her about any of that*, then I guess I could see why Wheaton was so upset.

But why were all of the guys *so* turned on, so… animalistic? And was Leah Wheaton just offended by her colleagues' conduct, or was there something more going on? Everyone's emotions just seemed to be ratcheted into high gear all of the sudden. Lyn's scent wafted in the breeze, and I almost lost myself to it again—and that got me thinking. I remembered reading about how most animals other than humans use pheromones to attract and repel other animals. If Lyn really was in the process of transforming into something… else… then maybe she was pumping out pheromones into the air—attracting all of the males and repulsing all of the females. If so, then it was certainly working pretty well. I don't know what a pheromone smells like, but I'll bet that it would smell like Carolyn Davidge did that morning.

"We've got to talk, Carolyn," I told her sternly.

"We *are* talking, Tom," she said, with a bit of an edge to her voice.

"And call me 'Lyn'…"

"Okay, Lyn," I continued. "What happened last night? Doesn't it concern you that you've healed so… miraculously?" Then I noticed something that I should have noticed right away (I really, really hate being whammied). "And where's Agent Bucher?"

"Oh, he's around," she giggled. Then she turned back to the crowd of cops and added derisively, "He's always following me around somewhere or another." The rest of the guys laughed at that, but I found myself disgusted with the disrespect that she was showing her partner—Bucher obviously cared about her, but here she was, treating him like dirt. Was that for our benefit, or was it a power play to make herself feel superior?

"We're not done yet!" I said, grabbing her arm and turning her back to face me. The scent suddenly changed to something harsh, and her eyes flashed at me in anger. The rest of the guys stiffened and immediately started to get angry, too, stepping toward me to defend her. As one guy brushed against her, the jacket over her arm shifted slightly, and for a split second, I saw something on her palm, before she quickly covered her hand back up. At first, I thought that she'd cut herself, but then I realized that it was upraised, more like a pink welt or even a brand… in the shape of a circle, with a five-pointed star inside of it.

"Tom!" I heard Tony call from behind me, and I heard him trotting up to us. "Got a sec?"

I looked at Caro—at *Lyn*—and then at the pack of guys that she'd gathered around her. I realized that I wasn't going to be able to get any more information from her right then without this getting really ugly, really quickly.

"We'll talk more about this later," I told her, and she just smiled in response. But the scent didn't change.

"Whatever…" she cooed, and she turned back toward the group again.

*   *   *

Tony wanted me to drive him back to the department right away, but he wouldn't talk with me until we got into the car. So we scooped up our deli food and started walking. As I came up to Wheaton, I asked her if she'd keep an eye on Lyn for me. She swore under her breath, but when I reminded her that Carolyn had been through a huge trauma and wasn't acting like herself—when I reminded her that this was exactly when even the most strong, confident women were at their most vulnerable point—she grudgingly relented and agreed to do it. "Under no circumstances is she to go off alone," I told her. "You call us if she's on the move somewhere…"

When we got into the car, Tony smacked me on the head.

"Man, you was this close ta gettin' yer stupid head blowed off!" he growled at me.

"What?" I asked.

"Them guys wasn't thinkin' right," he said, pulling our sandwiches out of the bag. He told me that Lyn had arrived just before I had, and that once the guys started acting so strangely, he'd been trying to figure out what to do about it when I got there. Apparently, while I was talking with Lyn, Wheaton just swore at him and told him that her father had always complained about "that kind of woman," but that she was pleasantly surprised when she saw that I didn't fall prey to the same whammy that everyone else had. I told Tony that I was proud of him for resisting Lyn as well.

"Not in the mood," he grumbled and took a big bite of turkey bacon club.

As we drove, I asked him about what the CSI guys had found, and he told me that there had been traces of wolf DNA in Sticky Ike's wounds—like that's a shocker there—so the running theory was that he'd been killed by that pack of Bunin's wolves that Tony and Bucher had lied about being there that night. I asked him about Bucher, but he said that he hadn't seen him—that *no* one had seen him in the past twelve hours.

On top of the DNA, they'd found some bloody partial footprints from the "wolves" along the sidewalk. But the shape was wrong—too human, Tony said—and they were too far apart. And then they just disappeared. I wished I could tell them that they were so far apart because the thing was running so fast, but no natural wolf runs as fast as this werewolf seemed to be able to. I wondered if even *Durant* could move as fast as this thing could.

But the kicker was that, right where they lost the trail of their "wolf pack"—about two blocks down—that's where they found the bottom half of Sticky Ike. His body hadn't even been chewed on at all. There was no reason for the werewolf to have killed him except that, for some reason, it had wanted him dead. I had always heard that werewolves were basically just, you know, monsters. They were perpetually hungry, and attacked and ate whatever they found. But that didn't seem to be the case here. I thought again about Carolyn, and how the thing had chewed on her, but didn't *eat* her—at least, not much. In fact, for as fast as the thing was, it sure seemed to stay in that hallway for a long time, doing a whole lot of not much, until Tony came in with his staff and scared it off.

I thanked him again for that, and told him that I missed him at the hospital. He seemed like he was about to say something about that, but that's when I realized that we had driven right past Pieter Durant, who was talking with a couple of Insane Deuces outside of the Four Treys on

Damen. Tony just about spilled his coffee when I slammed on the brakes and screeched into a parking spot on the side of the road.

We jumped out of the car and started running back along the sidewalk to talk with him. As we approached, he noticed us, and I overheard him tell the two guys to "Run along now…" which they seemed to do very happily and very quickly. Durant had the remarkable ability to make anyone feel intimidated, no matter how tough they thought they were.

"Where have you been?" I asked him when we got to him.

"Around," he replied. When he saw Tony coming up behind me, he called out, "Detective de Tullio…" and greeted him coldly with a slight nod.

"Durant…" Tony responded in kind.

"You've some sort of mustard on your jacket," Durant continued, pointing.

"Savin' it fer later," Tony replied.

"Nice shades," I said to Durant, pointing to his sunglasses, trying to break the tension between the two men. "Oliver Peoples. Those cost, like, $400-500…"

"I would not know," he said, taking them off and sliding them into his jacket pocket. "They were a gift from an operative friend who had liked the style so much that he thought that I would appreciate them as well. I had introduced him to the CIA in 1992 after his Ranger unit and a Navy SEAL team assisted me in saving Lech Wałęsa at Kraków from a dragon sent by the Tchagal thing, Czarnobóg. His great-uncle was an evil wretch whose demon-possessed corpse had to be destroyed on Venus in the 1940s, but Michael himself is quite a resourceful young man…"

"A dragon?" Tony snorted. "Venus? This guy is so full o' crap…"

Durant sighed.

"So you were talking to some IDs, huh?" I asked him, trying to break the tension that I'd inadvertently continued with my last tension-breaking attempt.

"I have found that, when stalking game, it can often be helpful to acquaint one's self with one's quarry's competition," he said. "Since your werewolf problem seems to be related to the *Bratva*, I thought it best to have a chat with some of the indigenous toughs as well."

"That's… That's actually very clever," I said, a little surprised. "I never saw you as much of an investigator, really."

"*I… founded… Interpol…*" he replied deliberately. Tony snorted and said something more than just a little foul under his breath.

"So…" I tried again, "what did they have to say?"

By this point, he wasn't in much of a mood to talk with us, but he told us—briefly—that, according to what he'd been able to scare various

IDs into telling him, the *Obshchestvo Drakonisty* was not only growing in power within the *Bratva*, but they were also gearing up for some sort of big gang war. But from what they could tell, they weren't rattling their sabers against the Deuces or the Latin Kings or any other Chicago gang—it was some other, rival European group that had also moved into town, though none of us had ever heard anything about it, not even its name. But so long as it was one out-of-town gang fighting another out-of-town gang, the Chicago gangbangers weren't losing a lot of sleep over any of it. *None* of them wanted the Russians in town anyway.

"And what of your colleague?" he asked me when he was done with his information. "Did she expire in the hospital, or will we have another problem?"

"What's that supposed ta mean?" Tony asked.

"Tony…" I said, waving my hand at him to calm him down. "It's… complicated." Then I turned back and looked at Durant. "She had the most miraculous recovery the hospital had ever seen, and they released her this morning." I thought about the reaction of the cops by the dumpster, and I realized that it wouldn't have taken much of that same pheromone cocktail on the ICU doctor to make him sign the release forms.

"So the creature is at large?" he asked.

"Hey," Tony interjected. "She ain't a *creature*—she's a *person!*"

"Not for much longer…" Durant replied.

"Yes, she's out," I added. "But she's under surveillance. Detective Wheaton is watching her, so we know where she is, if we need to pick her up."

"'*If* we need to *pick* her *up*'?" Durant repeated angrily. "Do you still not understand? Why are you handling this with such nonchalance? Do you have any idea what will happen to your Detective Wheaton if this woman begins to change? Do you wish *another* death at these fiends' claws?"

"No," I replied. "But, what was I supposed to do? She was standing there in broad daylight, surrounded by cops. Was I supposed to shoot her?"

"With that weapon?" he asked, pointing to my sidearm. "Scant good that should have done."

"That's right," Tony grumbled. "I shoulda hit 'er with th' stick…"

"Good Lord," Durant said, turning to Tony. "Does this orangutan still wield the Matteh ha Shelomoh? Do you allow your children to play with kerosene as well?"

"Okay, okay…" I said, literally stepping between the two of them. "The point is, she hasn't changed, and she's under surveillance. She's not going anywhere without us knowing about it." And then I added a question that had been bouncing around in my mind all morning. "She's not going to change until the night of the next full moon, right?"

Durant raised one of his eyebrows slightly—the Durant version of the shoulder shrug.

"Impossible to tell," he replied. "That depends entirely upon the type of werewolf involved. Did you notice anything unusual about her?"

Unusual? Where to start…? We began walking back to the car, and I told him about the way she looked, the way she acted. I told him about the reaction of the other cops, and about the effect she even had on me for a second. He nodded and said that it sounded relatively common for cases of lycanthropy.

"The virus brings the beast out in the victim," he said. "The darkest, most hidden parts of a person are drawn to the surface and given free reign."

"That makes sense," I said. "It looks like she may even be getting into the same sort of dark magic or Satanism that Bunin was apparently into."

"Why do you say that, Detective?"

"Because it looks like maybe she branded herself or something with a pentagram…"

Hearing that stopped Durant in his tracks. "A pentagram?" he asked. "Or a pentacle?"

"What's the dif?" Tony asked.

"A pentagram is a five-pointed star," Durant replied, "but a pentacle is a pentagram, bounded within a circle. Which was it, Detective?"

"A pentacle, then," I clarified. "On her left hand."

Durant's eyes went wide.

"And you let her *live*…?"

Background
From *To Dream of Wolves* (unpublished doctoral dissertation by Eric Cord, 1992)

Though the psychological disorder of clinical lycanthropy is well-documented,[1] though quite rare, there has also been a clear and consistent belief in the existence of actual, physical lycanthropy for centuries—whether it is known as "shape-shifting," "skin-changing," "skin-walking," or some other shamanistic label.[2] To dismiss the possibility of such an actual, physical metamorphosis of an individual is simply the hubris of a modern sensibility. One cannot conclude that centuries of cultural experience and scholarly acceptance are nonsense, simply because they do not conform to our own, recent, personal experience on the matter. Note that until the 20th century, most Westerners thought that the indigenous peoples' stories about an "African unicorn"—the okapi—were mere fiction... until scholars were finally able to confirm their existence themselves.[3] Does this later confirmation justify our modern scholarly tendency toward remaining dubious in the face of countless centuries of cultural corroboration, or condemn it?

As Punt (1551)[4] wrote, "Manye a sorceryer contorteth theyre boddies by all meens of Devillish magicks into the shaypes of divvers animales." Until modern science decided that actual lycanthropy was, on a *prima facie* basis, ridiculous, it was accepted not only as a superstition by the common people, but as scientific fact by scholars...

Though there are multiple—and often wildly conflicting—accounts

---

[1] *See, for a recent example, Keck, et al,* "Lycanthropy: Alive and Well in the Twentieth Century" *in* Psychological Medicine *(1988).*

[2] *The existence of such shapeshifters was universally accepted throughout history—see Herodotus (in his* Ἡροδότου Ἀλικαρνησσέος ἱστορίης, *5th century BC), Pliny (in his* Naturalis Historia, *1st century AD), Giraldus (in his* Topographia Hibernica, *1188), the Norse* Völsungasaga *(13th century),* Bourke *(in his* Witch-Songs of the Navajo Medicine Chiefs, *1887), etc.*

[3] *See Glanville's* In Search of the Okapi *(1903) and Walker's* Mammals of the World *(1964).*

[4] *William Punt, in his* A Cataloge of Secret Abhominations *(1551).*

of werewolves throughout history, several patterns of description and behavior emerge. According to legends, werewolves are impervious to harm from conventional weapons, and may only be destroyed by silver, fire, suicide, or at the hands of another werewolf.[5] The reasons for this belief are debatable, but it appears that it has something to do with the nature of the affliction itself.

For instance, several legends speak of the lycanthrope seeing a pentacle[6] appear somewhere either on its own body, or on the body of its next intended victim, immediately preceding its transformation into a wolf.[7] There is no good, physiological reason for this sort of manifestation, of course, which suggests that lycanthropy must be more than simply a physical infection or abnormality, but rather must have some sort of mystical or supernatural attributes as well. It is for good reason that, for centuries, lycanthropy was treated by science as a *curse*, and not just an illness. The victim is tormented not only by the physical changes which they endure, but also by the natural horror at the knowledge of being forced to perpetrate such depredations on their fellow human beings, through no fault of their own. It was thus not uncommon for werewolves to seek out the help of clergy or holy men to help them deal with their situation.[8]

Many ancients believed that werewolves could be cured physically, by means of simply exhausting the victim; medically, by applying salves or medicines made with wolfsbane; or spiritually, through conversion to Christianity or by reciting specific devotions to particular saints.[9] But none of these means is truly effective for the werewolf. At best, they can only prevent a specific change on a temporary basis. So far as I can tell, the only true cure for the werewolf is to kill the head of the pack's bloodline. As with natural wolves,[10] werewolves align themselves into packs, with an "Alpha," or head of the bloodline that created the rest. If

---

[5] *Note that one of the several reasons why Cord's dissertation was ultimately rejected by its thesis committee was because this section contained far too few proper, scholarly citations.*

[6] *Contrary to modern common belief, the pentagram and pentacle (⊛) were not originally necessarily associated with Satanic rites. On the contrary, the symbols were often used as wards against demonic forces—see Agrippa's* Quarto Libro de Occulta Philosophia *(1565), or the 18^(th) century text on magic,* The Sixth Book of Moses.

[7] *See Walker's* The Women's Encyclopedia of Myths and Secrets *(1983).*

[8] *Again, see Giraldus'* Topographia Hibernica *(1188)*

[9] *See Woodward's* The Werewolf Delusion *(1979).*

[10] *See Schenkel's* Ausdrucks-Studien an Wölfen *(1947), and Mech's* The Wolf *(1970). Note, however, that since the writing of this thesis, the theory of the "Alpha" has been discredited by most scholars—including no less than Mech himself (see his 1999* "Alpha Status, Dominance, and Division of Labor in Wolf Packs".)

a werewolf truly desires to be rid of his curse, he has to discover who that Alpha is and destroy him, severing the bloodline at its source.

That being said, there are always those werewolves who grow to appreciate the changes that their curse has inflicted on their bodies and souls.[11] They enjoy the feeling of power and control that they feel, and after a time, they begin to revel in the horror of the hunt. Once that happens—once the lycanthrope has given himself over to the excitement and the thrill of hunting and devouring his fellow human beings—then it is impossible for him to be cured because, in his heart of hearts, he no longer *desires* to be cured. In effect, he has become a wolf that masquerades as a man, instead of a man who becomes a wolf.

---

[11]   *Such as Petronius' traveling companion in his* Satyricon Liber *(1ˢᵗ century).*

Background
From *Satyricon Liber* (Gaius Petronius Arbiter, 1st century AD, trans. A. Allinson)

When I was still a slave, we lived in a narrow street; the house is Gavilla's now. There, as the gods would have it, I fell in love with the wife of Terentius, the tavern-keeper;—you all knew Melissa from Tarentum, the prettiest of pretty wenches! Not that I courted her carnally or for venery, but more because she was such a good sort. Nothing I asked did she ever refuse; if she made a penny, I got a halfpenny; whatever I saved, I put in her purse, and she never choused[1] me. Well! her husband died when they were at a country house. So I moved heaven and earth to get to her;—true friends, you know, are proved in adversity.

It so happened my master had gone to Capua, to attend to various trifles of business. So seizing the opportunity, I persuaded our lodger to accompany me as far as the fifth milestone. He was a soldier, as bold as Hell. We got under way about first cockcrow, with the moon shining as bright as day. We arrived at the tombs; my man lingered behind among the gravestones, whilst I sat down singing, and started counting the gravestones. Presently I looked back for my comrade;—he had stripped off all his clothes and laid them down by the wayside. My heart was in my mouth;—and there I stood feeling like a dead man. Then he made water all 'round the clothes, and in an instant changed into a wolf. Don't imagine I'm joking; I would not tell a lie for the finest fortune ever man had.

However, as I was telling you, directly he was turned into a wolf, he set up a howl, and away to the woods. At first I didn't know where I was, but presently I went forward to gather up his clothes;—but lo and behold! they were turned into stone. If ever a man was like to die of terror, I was that man! Still I drew my sword and let out at every shadow on the road 'till I arrived at my sweetheart's house. I rushed in looking like a ghost, soul and body barely sticking together. The sweat was pouring down between my legs, my eyes were set, my wits gone

---

[1] *That is, "cheated"*

almost past recovery. Melissa was astounded at my plight, wondering why ever I was abroad so late. "Had you come a little sooner," she said, "you might have given us a hand;—a wolf broke into the farm and has slaughtered all the cattle, just as if a butcher had bled them. Still he didn't altogether have the laugh on us, though he did escape; for one of the laborers ran him through the neck with a pike."

After hearing this, I could not close an eye, but directly it was broad daylight, I started off for our good Gaius's house, like a peddler whose pack's been stolen;—and coming to the spot where the clothes had been turned into stone, I found nothing whatever but a pool of blood. When eventually I got home, there lay my soldier a-bed like a great ox, while a surgeon was dressing his neck. I saw at once he was a werewolf and I could never afterwards eat bread with him, no! not if you'd killed me. Other people may think what they please; but as for me, if I'm telling you a lie, may your guardian spirits confound me!

Chapter 8
The Synod of Crows

I decided that this sort of conversation should probably be continued someplace a little more private than a busy sidewalk, so we went across the street and a half block down to Kitsch'n on Roscoe. It's more of a family place, and I would've preferred to take Durant to a fancy place like Volo, but they didn't open for another several hours. Amazingly, Tony actually pulled out a menu and debated about getting their Hangover Brunch, even after eating that huge sandwich from Miska's. I just got some ice water, and Durant looked uncomfortable to even be sitting there.

"Okay, talk," I said, once the waitress had left us alone.

"The pentacle is a sign," Durant explained, resting his hands on the table. "It means that she will soon turn."

"Soon being...?"

"In an hour?" Durant ventured. "Or five minutes from now, or— owing to the fact that this would almost certainly be her first transformation—more probably, sometime this evening."

"But you don't know..."

"Of course not," he said. "This is a dark art, not a science. Was the pentacle bleeding?"

"Bleeding?"

"Yes, in some rare cases, the pentacle will become engorged with blood, crack open at the points of the star, and begin to bleed, immediately prior to the transformation."

"No," I told him. "It was just a little pink and puffy."

"Right. Then we probably safely have until this evening to destroy her..."

At that, Tony exploded again.

"So it's all '*kill* her,' an' '*destroy* her,' huh?" he growled. "There ain't no way that ya can see ta, I dunno, actually try an' *help* her, I guess?"

Durant hung his head and sighed. "Would you please attempt to calm your monkey associate, Detective? Histrionics are less than helpful at this stage of the operation..."

"I'm sorry, Durant," I replied. "I have to agree with Tony here. Surely there's some way for us to help her. I mean, she hasn't done anything yet. We couldn't even legally *arrest* her, much less put a bullet in her." He took a deep breath and looked back at me.

"As I have already told you, there *is* no 'cure' for her. Are there a thousand possible means by which we might be able to partially ameliorate the curse? Certainly. Are any of them guaranteed to succeed? Not at all. And which several hundred traditional remedies were you wishing to try out between now and sunset? Shall we have her eat a live frog? Shall we ask her to recite the Lord's Prayer a dozen times? Shall we force her to drink silver shavings in red wine, or apply a poultice of wolfsbane, or pull her fingernails out? For which of these classic remedies are you willing to wager someone else's life tonight in order to test its efficacy?"

I have to admit, I was feeling pretty torn at that moment. Yes, I trusted Durant's years of experience, and no, I didn't want to risk Carol—*Lyn*—turning into a monster that night and hurting someone. But how could we preemptively kill a colleague whose only crime was that she'd been attacked while on the job... and *lived*...? It didn't seem right. Again, I found myself caught in that familiar pinch between thinking like a cop and thinking like a soldier. Durant just saw these monsters as things, as enemies to destroy. The moment Lyn was bitten, he would've written her off as a casualty, like a doctor trying to quarantine a plague victim to protect everyone else.

I've heard that Israel has a similar perspective on hostages of terrorists. Instead of our perspective, where we try to negotiate with a perp and get the hostages back, Israel immediately considers the hostages to be collateral damage, and is willing to shoot through old women and children to make sure that none of the terrorists get out of there alive. Any hostages that they *are* somehow able to save—and yes, they do *try*—they consider to be an unexpected bonus. Now, the first time that I heard about that, I thought that it was a horrible way of viewing the situation, since it went 180 degrees from everything that we were taught as police officers. But the more I thought about it, the more I understood why they did that. If you were a law enforcement officer in a country that was surrounded by the nations most commonly associated with terrorism, and you knew that your country was universally hated by all of your neighbors, then you'd have to be willing to be pretty Spartan in order to protect your citizens. For instance, I can't imagine there being too many *second* hostage situations in Israel when the terrorist knows that it's a one-way ticket to the grave. Suicide bombers? Sure. Hostage-takers? Not so much.

So if you're Pieter Durant, and you've spent over a millennium fighting these things, I can see how you might begin to adopt that same

sort of mentality. There's only little Israel, surrounded by enemies…
and there's only Pieter Durant, surrounded by monsters. Everything in
his existence had taught him not to get close to any individuals, since he
was guaranteed to outlive them. He could care about humanity, but he'd
buried too many friends and family over too many centuries to let
himself care about specific *people* any more. So to him, Carolyn
Davidge was dead already, and we just needed to make sure that she
didn't take anyone else down with her.

But to be honest, I really didn't think that I could do it. I *know* that
Tony couldn't have done it.

"You didn't kill Esteban," I said at last, quietly. Durant met my
gaze and held it there, his gray eyes burning cold fire under those bushy
brows.

"Who's Esteban?" Tony asked. Durant's expression didn't change.

"He was an old friend of Durant's," I answered, still looking at
Durant. "He was a werewolf in France, wasn't he?"

"France, huh?" Tony said. "Lotta werewolves in France, are there?"

"In point of fact, France was fairly teeming with werewolves at one
time," Durant replied, still glaring at me. A couple of years ago, that
glare would've terrified me—but now, it just made me really, really
scared. "I once hunted down another werewolf in Lozère for King Louis
XV, though the region was known as 'Gévaudan' at the time," he
continued, obviously trying to diffuse the discussion by moving it in
another direction.

"After that fool of a wolf-hunter, d'Enneval, could neither find nor
stop the beast, the King implored me to help the people of the region,
and lent me a borrowed name and authority as Musket-Bearer to the
King. D'Enneval had nearly depleted the countryside of wolves—a
tactic which had not been the least bit effective five hundred years earlier
against Esteban, nor was it this time, either—and still the attacks
continued by what the idiot had come to call a 'wolf-leopard devourer of
virgins,' a beast with no discernable lair and no pack to hide amongst. I
took over the pursuit of the creature, with borrowed credentials as Gun-
Bearer to the King and Lieutenant of the Hunt, and quickly realized that
this was no mere wolf we stalked. After three long months of hunting,
my local guide, Jean Chastel, and I shot and killed the creature with
silver in…" He stopped and thought for a moment, reaching for the date
in his memory. "That would have been in September of 1765."

"Congratulations," I said, less than enthusiastic.

"In death," he continued, "the creature returned to its human shape,
so François Antoine fabricated a suitable monster to display at court.
Unfortunately…" and here, his voice went low and somber, "I later
learned—to my personal chagrin, and after the deaths of at least a dozen
more souls—that the beast had already infected another innocent with its

toxic bite by the time that I had destroyed it, who then went on to commit still more foul murders. But by that bloody December, when the second beast began its attacks in the region, I had unfortunately left for Paris, to consult with George Louis Leclerc de Buffon at the Académie Française about findings recently published in his *Histoire Naturelle* regarding what he was calling a 'vampire bat,' found in the New World. That, of course, turned out to be a needless exercise on my part—as none of the family *Desmodontinae* has anything whatsoever to do with the vampyri—but as a result, I heard nothing about the appearance of this second beast until the dreadful business was over and done with. And my friend—the poor Jean Chastel, who had taught me the countryside around Gévaudan and guided me through the Margeride Mountains on several lonely hunts—was ultimately forced to deal with what I had incompetently left unfinished."

"At least he got to be the hero," I offered.

"That is one interpretation, I suppose," he sighed. "Jean melted down his silver medal of the Blessed Virgin to forge the bullet which killed the second werewolf—his only son, Antoine—to save the people of Gévaudan... only later to be accused of training and controlling the beast himself."

"But why would they think that?"

"Because no one could understand why, *only that one time*, the beast had paused before pouncing on its prey, giving Jean the chance to aim and hit his mark with that single, blessed bullet. And Jean refused to sully his son's memory by explaining to the people how, due to being such a newly turned werewolf, his loving son could not easily bring himself to murder his own father. Jean had killed his son—but he could not bring himself to kill his *memory* of him." Durant lowered his eyes and seemed for a moment to be very far away, and I could see the grief of centuries bearing down on him. Even Tony was quiet while Durant composed himself.

"My incompetence..." he said at last. "My lack of follow-through forced a good man to hunt down and kill his own child, and then to live the rest of his life under the accusation of evil himself. I would have given much to have been able to have avoided that mistake at the time, to have ended the bloodline before that tragedy hurt a decent, Christian family for whom I had cared a great deal. Tell me, Detective—what would you be willing to give or to do in order to avoid the same sort of tragedy tonight?"

So we made a deal. I know that Durant thought it was naïve of us, but we agreed to take Lyn into our own, personal custody before the sun went down, and to be fully prepared to kill her if she began to change. We're cops, and that means that even if we *know* that someone is dirty, we have to wait and apprehend them in the act of committing their crime. That might annoy someone who thinks in such black-and-white terms as Pieter Durant, but if we would uphold the rights of an everyday perp, how could we do any less for Lyn? He sounded exasperated and frustrated as we gave him the terms—in fact, I half expected him to get up and go kill her himself right then and there—but in the end, he relented and said that he would abide by our decision. At the time, I had no idea why he did.

But in the meantime, we decided to follow up with the *Bratva* angle and see if we could follow the trail back to Bunin. I knew that Kingery and his FBI counterparts were investigating the Russians, too, but they were looking for evidence of human trafficking, not evidence of werewolves. Besides, I was hoping to see if we could dig up a little more information on that brewing gang war, if we could.

Without Sticky Ike available, I had to borrow one of Kingery and Wheaton's stool pidgeons to get some info—a short, stocky Russian book-maker named Georgiy Chernomyrdin. He was just a little fish, only tangentially associated with the *Bratva*, so we let him operate in exchange for the occasional tidbit of info on what was going down with the sharks he swarm near. I asked Durant if he could speak Russian, and he looked at me like I was an idiot. *Of course* he could speak Russian. That popped a lightbulb on in my head, and I pulled out the slip of paper that Wheaton had scribbled on in the hospital and asked him if he had any idea what the "*Синод Вороны*" was, and what it might have to do with Bunin or the *Obshchestvo Drakonisty*.

"Ah, of course," he said, reading it. "The *Sinod Vorony*—the Synod of Crows…"

"Which is…?" asked Tony.

"An international convocation of the covens of witches," he answered. "The Synod of Crows have been the mortal enemies of the werewolves for centuries. The Order of the Dragon have hunted them across Europe, and now, they must have fled here as well."

"The 'Order of the Dragon'…" I repeated. "The *Obshchestvo Drakonisty?*"

"Indeed, Detective. An Order dating back to the Library of Alexandria, with which I am more familiar as *La Société des Dragonistes.*"

"I'm guessin' these witches they hunt ain't th' pointy-hat an' broom variety," Tony ventured.

"No," Durant replied. "The nature of witchcraft—whether it be European, or African, or Cherokee, or Malayan—is to seek out powers beyond one's self in an effort to affect and ultimately control the natural world. Though some practitioners fool themselves into thinking that there exists a 'white' magic alongside the 'black,' all magicks ultimately arise from surrendering one's spiritual self to a greater and darker power, and thus all are dangerous with which to intrigue one's self."

"Not everything bigger than you and me is automatically evil," I suggested.

"Agreed," he answered. "But when you seek *spiritual* power, there are only two sources from which to choose—that which comes from the Creator of all power, and that which comes from those who would pervert that power to their own ends. It is inherently dangerous to seek spiritual power from a bastardized source that places itself at odds with the Divine. The danger is exponentially greater when one is seeking that power for one's own personal gain."

"Like, them Ouija boards either work 'cuz yer really talkin' ta spooks, or they're a total crock that people jus' psych 'emselves out with," Tony added. "I dunno which is creepier..."

"Just so, Detective de Tullio," he said. "Like all crows—if I may borrow a line from an opera which I attended at the Lincoln's Inn Fields Theatre long ago—a witch 'steals what he was never made to enjoy, for the sake of hiding it' for his own benefit. They are hoarders of power, and they gorge themselves upon it, even as it feeds upon their very souls."

"Okay, if I remember correctly," I said, trying to get us back on track with the case, "there are supposed to be thirteen witches in a given coven, right? And there were thirteen crows that Bunin had nailed to his wall in his house, with the name, 'Synod of Crows' written next to them. That can't be a coincidence there. So was that supposed to be some sort of sympathetic magic that he was using, like he was cursing them?"

"Or I got this buddy who's a boxer," Tony added. "He always puts a photo of th' guy he's fightin' next, like, on his bathroom mirror or his fridge or somethin' so's he can look at 'im every day an' remember ta hate 'im..." Durant looked shocked.

"I should think that it would be much the same with Bunin," he said. "Warrior cults have often used depictions of their enemies in rites to prepare themselves for battle. In a manner of speaking, they sacrifice their opponents in effigy before they engage them in physical combat. Thus, in their minds, victory becomes a foregone conclusion. An afterthought, if you will."

"Gotta be a heckuva morale booster on th' battlefield," Tony said.

"Indeed," Durant answered. I sat there and just watched the two of them as they kept talking about the psychology of beating the snot out of other people, and how fighters mentally pump themselves up to do it. It was the longest and most civil conversation they'd ever had with one another, and I had to think that it was some kind of bonding moment for them. I hated to break up their little party, but we needed to get moving, so I got us up and headed out of the restaurant.

"By the by," Durant told me, pulling me slightly to the side while

Tony paid for his second breakfast of the day. "Earlier, you commented that I did not kill Esteban, and you were correct. I did not do so because by the time that I had caught up with him, he had already extricated himself and his beloved from their curse."

"Right," I said. "You said that before."

"But," he added, "had he not freed them by the time that I later found him, rest assured—I would have put both of them down without a second thought…"

*   *   *

I'd heard that Chernomyrdin liked to hang out at Little Bucharest down on Elston. The place was just a ten minute drive down Addison, so we got in the car and made our way there. As I pulled out, I mentioned that Durant could probably make it there ten times faster on foot than we could by car.

"These shoes are John Lobb," he said, as if that should mean something to us. "I shan't skitter around in them unless it should prove absolutely necessary."

"Who's John Lobb?" asked Tony.

"My bootmakers for the past century," he explained. "At No. 9, St. James' Street, just down the Strand from my favorite tailor. Or at least they were until Thresher & Glenny moved to their *new* location…" He sounded freshly frustrated, as if that change had just happened recently. I looked it up later—Thresher & Glenny moved over 80 years ago.

"So why crows?" Tony asked, careening off topic.

"Pardon me?"

"Why is it a Synod of *Crows*? Why nail *crows* to the wall?"

"I see," Durant replied, nodding. "Crows have long been the familiars of those who would dabble in the black arts, both here and across the pond in Europe. The demon, Odin, for instance, kept two at his side at all times. The Irish witch-queen, the *Morrígan*, ruled the crows and often took the form of one to travel. There was even a knight at Arthur's own table—Owain mab Urien, the son of Morgan le Fay— who used magical enchantments to control crows as his own private army."

"I'm sure that helped Arthur… somehow…" I said.

"Actually, he used them *against* Arthur's soldiers at Badon Hill, but that is another story—and a frequently ill-told one at that. But the witches often use their crows as messengers to converse with their vampire masters from a safe distance."

"No trust among monsters…?" Tony asked.

"Indeed," he said. "And yet, as the korrigan Rhiannon was servant to both Gilles de Retz and Lord Ruthven, so many of the covens serve at the whims of the undead. This is, of course, only one small part of why *La Société des Dragonistes* so despise them."

"So werewolves hate both witches *and* vampires, huh?" Tony asked again.

"With a passion and a hatred that is more than returned by the vampyri, I assure you. The species perceive themselves as utter antitheses, you see—opposite ends of the spectrum. A vampire is a corpse, animated by the infestation of a demon, whereas the werewolves see themselves as the very pinnacle of life and virility. To the werewolf, the vampire is a grave-haunting parasite—while to the vampire, the werewolf is a lolloping beast."

"I always kinda figured that vampires used werewolves like, I dunno, shock troops," Tony said. "Like fer when they didn't wanna dirty their lily-white hands on a real fight."

"That's what revenants are for," I said. It just popped out of my mouth before I even realized that I'd said it, like I was becoming some sort of expert on this sort of crazy stuff.

"Precisely," Durant agreed. "The vampyri have nothing but contempt for werewolves. Think of it this way: the vampire has many supernatural powers, including the ability to change its shape into that of a wolf—and many other shapes as well. Thus, the vampyri tend to believe the werewolf to be something of a weak, slow-witted cousin."

"Yer basic one-trick pony," Tony ventured.

"Just so," he replied with a nod. "But the undead do so to their own detriment. He may not match the vampyri in subtlety or ability, but nothing in all of Nature can compare to the sheer ferocity of a strong, mature werewolf. Whereas the vampire may take on the shape of a wolf, the werewolf wraps himself in the creature's very *soul*—its darkest and most vicious essence." Something about the intensity, the utter seriousness of his tone made me shudder. "Thus, the answer to which creature is more powerful is very much a matter of the situation."

"Like crocs and sharks..." I muttered, mostly to myself.

"What was that?" he asked.

"Oh, a college buddy of mine is a marine biologist now, working at Shedd," I told him, happy to be able to actually add something to the discussion. "We were talking about how tough sharks were, and he asked me who I thought would win in a throwdown between a Great White and a saltwater crocodile. To me, it seemed like a gimme—the shark would totally kill the croc. I figured that since it's, like, two times the size of a croc and it could actually breathe underwater, there's no chance. And it's a *Great White*, for crying out loud."

"And yet, this was not the case?"

"Not so much. Apparently, a croc is much faster and more agile in the water than a shark, and it has armor, and its bite strength is roughly twice as strong as the Great White's. Since the croc can hold its breath for a couple of hours under water, the real question of who would win in a fight really comes down to how long the croc had already been under—and which monster got the drop on the other one first. If the croc has just gone under, or if it gets the first bite in, then the shark is history. But if the croc's been under for a while, and if the Great White can get its jaws around the croc first and hold onto it until it drowns, then the croc's toast. So it's a context thing."

All of that came tumbling out quite easily, but the moment I said it, I had the sudden mental picture of a vampire and a werewolf going toe-to-toe, and it was a terrifying image. I decided that I would never want to be standing anywhere near a fight like that.

I drove up Sawyer so that we could come down and park on Spaulding. Little Bucharest had only just opened up for the day, but Chernomyrdin supposedly liked to get there right away for his late afternoon lunch, early dinner thing. I told the guys to let me do the talking, at least at first, and I opened my car door.

The moment I did, that's when I got the call from Leah Wheaton…

Background

From *A Cataloge of Secret Abhominations* (William Punt, 1551, modern trans. R. Kerr)[1]

As the overabundance of witches which populate our world surely testifies, the Church, though ever the stalwart bastion of Truth and Light for those whose faith has remained pure and unwavering in this benighted age, has not sufficed in its defence of the chosen of God. In an effort to rectify this, over the centuries have arisen several orders of warriors of Virtue for whom the dedicating of one's life to the support and edification of the righteous seemed both mete and appropriate. Some of these orders, such as the *Paup. Comm. Christi Templi.,*[2] developed as good Christian knights took up arms against the Moor and the Pagan in defense of the Cross of Christ and the truth of our Lord and saw the wisdom of continuing that defence by banding together in Christian community. Taking a very different course, the *Soc. Draco.*[3]

---

[1] *Note: The most complete edition of this volume was actually printed in Amsterdam in 1840 by Wed Loveringh en Allart, though it added many additional details obviously not included in the original London edition published by William Hill and William Seres in 1551, including extended sections on British regions such as Depewatch Priory and the supposedly haunted mansion and grounds of Sir Boswell Chase.*

[2] *"Pauperes commilitones Christi Templique Salomonici" or "The Poor Fellow-Soldiers of Christ and of the Temple of Solomon" (AKA the Knights Templar)—who, contrary to the name of their order, were arguably the wealthiest military order in Europe (see Barber's* The New Knighthood: A History of the Order of the Temple, *1994), originally based in Jerusalem for the expressed purpose of defending the Christian pilgrims who visited the Temple mount in the wake of the early Crusades. Bernard of Clairvaux was an early advocate and supporter, as were Popes Innocent II, Celestine II, and Eugene III, whose papal bulls afforded the order an unprecedented level of power and authority.*

[3] *"Societas Draconistrarum" or "The Society of Draconists" (AKA "The Order of the Dragon"), founded in 1408 by Zsigmond of Luxemburg, King of Hungary and 17th Emperor of the Holy Roman Empire, to combat the enemies of Christendom (and their spiritual head, the "Great Dragon," Satan). They modeled themselves after Georgios (i.e.; S. George), the 3rd*

did find their roots in traditions of righteousness far older than Christianity itself, though they too have found themselves drawn to the Light of God in these latter days.

It was in the waning days of the empire of Alexander Magnus[4] that he constructed his famed *Βιβλιοθήκη*[5] in Alexandria as a repository of the collected *scientia* of the ages, including Plato's lost *Ερμοκράτης*[6] and the famed *Τέχνη της Ρητορικής*[7] of Isocrates; the greatest scholar of all time. As the fame and the holdings of the immense *Βιβλιοθήκη* grew, the *βιβλιοθηκάριοι*[8] expanded their mandate under Euergetes[9] to collect all of the eccentricities of power in the ancient world, including the original orichalcum light which had first illuminated the great *Pharos*.[10] At this time, the *βιβλιοθηκάριος* Yahuda[11] divided the holdings into scholarly works and culturally significant artifacts which were to be held in the *Βιβλιοθήκη*, and eccentricities of power and potentially perilous relics which were to be held in a separate facility known as the *Αποθήκη*.[12]

When Caesar lit his ships afire to defend the harbour of Alexandria

---

century Palestinian Christian soldier who, according to legend, had slain a dragon in Libya. Over the centuries, the oft-retold story of "St. George" transformed him into the quintessential Anglo-Saxon knight of the Cross.

[4] *That is, Alexander the Great (4th century BC), king of Macedon and conqueror of much of the known world.*

[5] *That is, the Library of Alexandria. Contrary to common thought, it was not built by Alexander, but by one of his generals, who succeeded him as King Ptolemy I Soter of Egypt.*

[6] *The* Hermocrates, *the third dialogue in a trilogy that began with the* Timaeus *and the* Critias. *According to legend, the* Hermocrates *(written in the 4th century BC) detailed Solon's account of the history of the fall of the ancient kingdom of Atlantis, which sunk into the sea as the result of a great and catastrophic war.*

[7] *The Art of Rhetoric (5th century BC). Isocrates was generally considered by his contemporaries as being the wisest and most well-educated of all of the Greek philosophers. Unfortunately, very few of his works have survived.*

[8] *That is, the librarians. It is uncertain why Punt expresses this in Greek as if "librarian" were a specific title, rather than simply a descriptive one.*

[9] *King Ptolemy III Euergetes ("The Benefactor"), 3rd century BC king of Egypt, who expanded the Ptolemaic Empire throughout Asia Minor, controlling much of the Eastern Mediterranean.*

[10] *The Lighthouse of Alexandria, constructed by Ptolemy I Soter. It stood as one of the Seven Wonders of the Ancient World until it was damaged by a series of earthquakes from 956 to 1323, and finally demolished by Sultan Al-Ashraf Sayf ad-Din Qa'it Bay in 1480 in order to build a fortress to guard the harbour.*

[11] *Most likely a reference to Baruch ben Judah, a famous Jewish scholar of the day.*

[12] *That is, the Storehouse.*

against *Philop.*,[13] he without intention burned as well the Βιβλιοθήκη, to the point at which the entire collection of documents and artifacts were by necessity moved to the nearby Μουσείον,[14] and the contents of the Αποθήκη were by necessity moved to the Σεραπεῖον.[15] The power of the Βιβλιοθήκη and the Αποθήκη continued to grow[16] until, under the withering attack of Aurelius[17] in his greed to conquer the East, [18] he razed Alexandria and destroyed both facilities completely.[19] Fortune favored the βιβλιοθηκάριοι, however, as Yahuda[20] had recently moved the entire collection to the catacombs of the *Kom al-Shoqafa*[21] for protection from the invading Romans,[22] and it was thus spared from

---

[13] *King Ptolemy XIII Theos Philopator of Egypt, who was engaged in civil war against his sister, Cleopatra VII, and her ally, the Roman Julius Caesar. See Aulus Gettius' account in his 2nd century collection of oddities,* Noctes Atticae.

[14] *The Museaum of Alexandria, a campus which at its zenith housed more than a thousand of the world's finest minds. Here, Punt's history fails, as the Library had* always *been housed in the Museaum. Scholars debate whether the fire even damaged the Library at all—if so, it only required the collection to be moved to a separate section of the campus.*

[15] *The Serapeum ("The Temple of Serapsis"), built two centuries earlier by King Ptolemy III Euergetes. Serapsis was a synchronistic god who combined elements of Greek and Egyptian mythology into a single "god of the deep," or "god of the underworld," who also symbolized the acquisition of knowledge.*

[16] *Actually, their popularity had begun to wane even by the time of Julius Caesar, as scholars soon realized how often Alexandria had become the focal point of invasions and sieges (see Meyboom's* The Nile Mosaic of Palestrina: Early Evidence of Egyptian Religion in Italy, *1995). In fact, the* Αποθήκη *had been moved to Europe for safekeeping by Caesar Augustus in the first year of his rule, in 27 BC (see Fischer's* The Early Empire: The Reign of Augustus, *1999).*

[17] *Punt means Aurelian—or Lucius Domitius Aurelianus Augustus, emperor of Rome in the 3rd century AD.*

[18] *Actually, Aurelian was attempting to quell the recent rebellion by Queen Zenobia of Palmyra, which had resulted in a schism within the Roman Empire and the creation of the fledgling "Palmyrene Empire"—a military action which brought Aurelian the title "Restitutor Orientis" ("Restorer of the East").*

[19] *See Phillips' article, "The Great Library of Alexandria?" in* Library Philosophy and Practice *(2010).*

[20] *Obviously a later "Yahuda" than Baruch ben Judah, who would have been dead for three centuries by this time.*

[21] *"The Mound of Potsherds," located at the ancient Egyptian site of Ra-Qedil near Alexandria.*

[22] *Note: the last time that a Roman emperor had visited the city (in 215), the Emperor Caracalla had been so offended by a satirical dramatic piece that he had ordered every young man in Alexandria to be executed, in order to*

destruction.

As a result of potentially disastrous attacks such as these, the βιβλιοθηκάριοι experienced a schism within their own ranks, between those who perceived their roles as scholars and caretakers of *scientia* and those who saw themselves as defenders and seekers of *scientia*. The latter group took the name Αδελφότητα του Φιδιού (*Frat. Serp.*)[23] in reference to our First Parents' compact with the Great Serpent to eat of the Tree of Knowledge and thus to grow in wisdom.[24] In like manner, the *Frat. Serp.* took it upon themselves to grow in wisdom by devouring knowledge, in all of its myriad forms, and using it for the betterment of all, and making use of the eccentricities of power to develop their skills as fierce warriors. Taking root in Byzantium (now called Constantinople),[25] they established themselves as the king's feared Τάγμα των Βαράγγων,[26] who were famous throughout the world for their

---

stave off what he saw as a brewing rebellion. Arguably, it was this action which actually served to precipitate the subsequent rebellion.

[23] *"Fraternitatis Serpentis" ("Brotherhood of the Snake").*

[24] *A decidedly skewed interpretation of the account in the* Book of Genesis, *ii-iii, wherein Satan—disguised as a serpent—convinces Eve to break God's commandment and eat of the "tree of the knowledge of good and evil," arguing that "your eyes shall be opened: and you shall be as gods, knowing good and evil" (see* Genesis *iii, 5)—see also the widespread association of serpent-gods with the acquisition of knowledge in* Ophiolatreia: An Account of the Rites and Mysteries Connected with the Origin, Rise, and Development of Serpent Worship in Parts of the World *(1889). Note that contemporary John Foxe had little respect for Punt as either an historian or a human being, writing, "William Punt, is and hath been a great writer of devilish and erroneous books of certain men's doings; and doth convey them over, and causeth them there to be imprinted, to the great hurt of ignorant people"—see* Actes and Monuments of these Latter and Perillous Days, Touching Matters of the Church *(AKA Foxe's Book of Martyrs), 1563.*

[25] *Modern İstanbul.*

[26] *"Varangian Guard." These troops were established in 988 by Emperor Basil II Porphyrogenitus ("Born to the Purple"), and were originally Vikings (AKA "Varyags") imported as part of a peace treaty with King Vladimir the Great of Kiev. There is no clear, historical connection between the Varangian Guard and the Fraternitatis Serpentis whatsoever. Punt appears to have been confused by the fact that the Varangians carried the banner of the* δράκωνάριοι *(the "drakonarioi" or "dragon-warriors" of the later Roman Empire). As Rome weakened internally, they routinely hired foreign mercenaries to man their legions—often Northern barbarians. The dragon had long been a powerful symbol for the Northern Vikings, often carving their ships' bows and sterns to resemble dragons (see Crumlin-Pedersen's excellent* Viking Age Ships and Shipbuilding in Hedeby/Haithabu and Schleswig, *1997), and thus, had become one of the many animal-themed standards used by the later, barbarian-dominated Roman military.*

cunning and strength, having never lost a battle,[27] as their inexhaustible faith and deadly skill with a sword became legendary.[28]

From these Βαράγγοι[29] came another offshoot; the *Univ. Soc. Frat. Milit. Sancti Georgii Ins.*,[30] which was formed during the furor of the First Crusade in Jerusalem[31] in order to search the world over for hidden eccentricities of power so that they as *défenseurs de la foi*[32] might better combat the enemies of the Faith. In this, they would be repeatedly undermined in their holy work by the remnants of their ancient adversaries, the βιβλιοθηκάριοι; but by God's grace, they would not be deterred, and the greatest houses in all of Europe have now been brought together under the banner of the *Soc. Draco.* of Sigmund of Hungary;[33] now serving the cause of Christ, but still committed to the quest for Truth and Power begun in earnest centuries before by its ancestor, the Αδελφότητα του Φιδιού. The illustrious membership has included the

---

[27] *Again, Punt's knowledge of history is somewhat faulty. Though the Varangians were, indeed, well-respected and rightly so, they were involved in significant losses against both the Normans in the West and the Seljuq Turks in the East.*

[28] *The Varangians—being comprised primarily of Norse Vikings and Anglo-Saxon húskarlar (housecarls)—were actually famed for their use of large, Danish axes, and rarely used swords. In fact, they were far more often referred to by contemporary Byzantine writers as the* πελεκυφοροι βάρβαροι *("axe-wielding barbarians") than by their official title, "Varangians" (see Turnbull's* The Walls of Constantinople, *2004).*

[29] *That is, the Varangians.*

[30] *"Universitas Societatis Fraternalis Militiae Sancti Georgii Insigniti" ("The Community of the Fraternal Society of Knighthood of the Notable Saint George,"* AKA *"The Order of S. George").*

[31] *In point of fact, though several chivalric orders arose during the early Crusades, the Order of S. George was actually formed in Višegrad in 1326 by King Károly Róbert of Hungary. It is possible that this is another example of Punt's poor facility with history—perhaps having confused the order with L'Orde de Sant Jordi d'Alfama ("The Order of Saint George of Alfama"), established in 1201 before the Fourth Crusade by King Pedro II de Aragón—but it is equally possible that he is knowingly extending the background of the order so that it might appear to be more legitimate. Note that today, the Order of S. George is the highest military honor awarded in the Russian Federation, as well as the highest honor awarded for the United States Army's mounted forces.*

[32] *That is, "defenders of the faith."*

[33] *That is, Zsigmond of Luxemburg, who was declared king of Hungary and later Holy Roman Emperor. Note: the popular 18th century European courtier, the Comte de Saint Germain, claimed to have been the legitimate heir to the throne of the Holy Roman Empire, declaring himself to be a direct descendent of Zsigmond of Luxemburg.*

great houses of Stephen the Tall of Serbia;[34] Vlad of Wallachia;[35] Hermann of Celje;[36] and Nicholas of Hungary.[37]   It was by the prompting of Hermann that the *Soc. Draco.* began its fervent and righteous ministry of bringing to light and punishing those who practiced the vile art of witchcraft.[38] So it is that the *Soc. Draco.* today operates by the official sanction of both Emperor Charles[39] and the Church[40] against the *Consil. Corv.*[41] and all true enemies of the Cross.[42]

---

[34] *Stefan Lazarević, Prince—and later, Despot—of Serbia.*

[35] *Vlad II, voivode of Wallachia who founded the House of Drăculeşti, derived from Vlad's cognomen of "Dracul" (i.e.; "The Dragon"). His son, Vlad III Drăculea, became known as "Vlad Ţepeş" ("The Impaler"), derived from his favorite form of torture.*

[36] *Hermann II, Count of Celje, who had saved the life of Zsigmond of Luxemburg in battle, and was thus given both a title and land to rule. He later married off his daughter, Borbála, to Zsigmond, making her Empress of the Holy Roman Empire (and himself the father-in-law to the Emperor and founder of their order).*

[37] *Garai Miklós II, who married Hermann II's other daughter, Anna. His granddaughter was married to King Matthias Corvinus of Hungary (AKA "Matthias the Just"). Another, later member of the order was Cardinal András Báthory of Transylvania (who not only ruled that land, but also served as Grand Master of the order), whose great grand-niece was the infamous Erzsébet Báthory—the "Blood Countess" who murdered over 600 young women in Trencsén in an attempt to gain immortality and eternal beauty.*

[38] *When Hermann's son, Friderik, divorced his wife (the wealthy and politically powerful Erzsébet of Frangepán), to marry a minor noble (Veronika of Desinić), Hermann had his new daughter-in-law tried and drowned as a witch.*

[39] *Karel V of the House of Hapsburg and 20th Emperor of the Holy Roman Empire.*

[40] *Specifically, Pope Julius III, who reigned not from the Lateran Palace (nor, for that matter, the then-dilapidated Vatican Palace), but from a lavish estate, known as the Villa Giulia, which he had constructed on the edge of Rome.*

[41] *"Consilium Corvórum" (the "Raven Council"), a loose confederation of witches' covens throughout Europe. According to d'Amboise (see* Tractatus Artibus Diabolicis, *1453), its membership was once quite large and influential.*

[42] *This war against witches found its zenith in the work of 16th century French witchfinder and magistrate Nicolas Rémy, who claimed to have personally put to death more than 900 witches. He referred to his branch of the Order of the Dragon as* La Société des Dragonistes. *Another notable member of this branch was English self-proclaimed "Witchfinder General," Matthew Hopkins, who tortured and killed more than 300 women in less than two years.*

Chapter 9
Pieter Durant Is a Very Scary Guy...

Lyn Davidge was gone.

Wheaton had totally been on her, watching her walk down the street with some beefy beat cop that she didn't recognize. They'd stopped on the corner of Damen and Roscoe, where Lyn leaned up against a wall, playing coy, smiling, touching the guy's arm when he flexed a muscle for her, etc. Wheaton said that she looked away for a few seconds—tops—to park her car, and when she looked back to the intersection, they were gone. She jumped out and ran to look down both Roscoe and Damen, but didn't see them anywhere. She said that she'd checked inside the Riverview Tavern, Robey's Pizza, even next door at the vintage shop, but nothing. Unless they were buying a muffler across the street, they were gone.

I'll tell you, I can't remember the last time that I got that angry. Not only was I mad at Wheaton for messing up the one job that we'd given her, but losing her meant leaving Lyn at risk for this evening, as well as putting someone else's life in danger—maybe even that beat cop that she'd been with. On top of that, Durant was standing right next to me. I was going to have to explain to him that our soft-heartedness—that we'd convinced him to agree to, against his better judgment—was now the reason that *another* potential werewolf was now at large. I used words on the phone that I haven't used since I started going back to church with Joanna these past couple of years. Even Tony seemed uncomfortable with that.

"She screwed up, Tom," he said. "Ease off."

"She's an idiot!" I growled.

"No, she ain't!" he shouted back at me. "She's a good cop, an' she just screwed up! *You* screw up too, sometimes, if ya recall, an' I don't bust yer chops like this! So *let... it... go...!*" I was about to yell back, but Durant stepped in between us.

"Gentlemen," he said quietly—but he said it so intensely that both Tony and I shut up immediately. "We've business inside this establishment, and then we can follow up on this matter later on this afternoon. Yes?"

I grudgingly backed down, but Wheaton could tell how mad I was. She wasn't very happy with herself, either—or with me, now, for that matter—but she promised to canvass the neighborhood. I told her to check out the Guesthouse down the street, just to make sure that they hadn't rented a room, and she assured me that she'd already thought of that. It didn't make me feel any better.

Little Bucharest Bistro was in a funky, brown, triangle-shaped building, and had been a neighborhood restaurant in Irving Park for over thirty years. It had gone through a lot of different owners and directions, but the current owner, Branko Podrumedic, seems like a great guy who knows what he's doing. The last time that I was there, when I was done with my *mititei*—my sausages and potatoes—he came by the table and offered to bless me with "holy water." He smiled so big and seemed so sincere that Joanna told me that I had to let him, so he proceeded to pull a canteen from behind his back and pour ice-cold vodka into my mouth until it dribbled down my chin. Everybody but me thought it was hilarious—I just thought that the vodka was really, *really* strong.

When we went inside, the place had just opened, so there weren't many customers yet. That's probably why Georgiy Chernomyrdin liked to come at that time of day. Sure enough, there he was, in all of his chubby little glory, slurping up a bowl of *ciorbe de burta*. Tony—astoundingly—said that it looked good, until Durant leaned over and whispered to him that it was tripe soup.

"Georgiy Chernomyrdin?" I said, walking up to his table.

"Who wants to know?" he asked, taking another slurp. I showed him my badge.

"I do…" I said again, and he set his spoon down.

"I didn't do nothing," he started in. He'd been in the States for a while, so he had very little accent left. "I'm just sitting here, eating my *ciorbe*, minding my own business."

"We know that, Georgiy," Tony said. "We jus' got us a few questions, an' then ya can go back ta gaggin' down yer tripe." Durant sighed and crossed his arms.

"We're looking for either Nikodim Bunin or Isador Postyshev," I said to him. "Even if you can give us a regular hangout, that will help."

"I dunno…" he said, going back to his soup. "That's asking a lot. I mean, these are not good people, you know?" I let him slurp a little more before I stepped in to respond. I could tell that it wasn't that he was really that afraid to give us a little information—it's that he was waiting for a bribe. But I could tell that both Tony and Durant were getting impatient. "How about you make it worth my efforts, eh?" he said after a few more slurps. Durant stepped forward in response.

"*Dobryj den'*," he said.

"*Ty govoriš' po-russki…?*" Chernomyrdin asked, surprised.

"*Da*," Durant continued. "*I sdelayu vam sdelku...*" And then he leaned forward, resting his hands on the table and let his voice go deep, dark, and cold. "*Yesli vy pomozhete nam, to ya ne budu pasti vas sobstvennyy kishechnik...*" I don't know what he said, but he smiled when he said it—and it wasn't a very nice smile. Chernomyrdin's spoon clinked against the side of the bowl as his hand began trembling. I could see all of the color drain out of his face, and Durant leaned in even closer. "*Vy khotite proverit' menya?*" he asked him again.

"*N-Nyet!*" Chernomyrdin burst out, nearly knocking his bowl over as he shook his hands in front of him. "*Y-Ya schitayu, vy...*" You could literally smell the fear on him.

"*Otlichno...*" Durant replied, nodding, and he went to stand near the entrance. "He shall tell you all that you wish to know, now," he said to me. And sure enough, he did.

Chernomyrdin told us about Bunin's house in Roscoe Village (which, of course, we already knew all about), and about where he liked to work out his favorite vices, including playing pool, drinking hard, random sex, and heavy gambling. In fact, he told us pretty much everything that he'd ever known or even *heard* about Nikodim Bunin, down to how he joined the *Bratva* over a decade ago in Russia, and about his penchant for little girls ever since he'd started up with the *Obshchestvo Drakonisty*. That last bit made my skin crawl. He said that everyone knew that Bunin was running scared now, but not from the police—though he didn't know exactly what he *was* scared of. But he didn't know much about Postyshev, even when Durant took a step toward him when he said it—apparently, he really had told Kingery and Wheaton all that he knew already.

In the end, I figured that we'd gotten about as much as we could out of Chernomyrdin, and I let him get back to his food. But I asked him to keep his eyes and ears open, because Durant wanted information, and this wasn't enough for him. He looked over at Durant, who smiled at him again, and he agreed. Tony and I gave him our cards and told him to call us if he heard anything more. I figured that we had a fifty-fifty chance— Chernomyrdin's fear of getting involved with the *Bratva* vs. his fear of Durant. Knowing Durant and his effect on people in general, I was willing to suggest that we might even have better odds than that, if we let Chernomyrdin stew on it for a while.

"*Prijatnovo appetita...*" Durant said to him as we walked out the door, and Chernomyrdin looked like he was going to be sick.

Durant never did tell me what he'd said to him.

*   *   *

Now, here's where we made a little gamble. It was getting late in the afternoon, but we still had over an hour before it would even start getting dark. Even then, Durant said that an "immature" werewolf probably wouldn't transform until later on in the evening, when the moon was fuller—though he repeated the word "probably" again to make his point about how uncertain all of this was. But given that we only *thought* that Lyn might transform that evening, vs. the fact that we *knew* that Bunin was a dangerous killer, I sent Tony to catch up with Wheaton while Durant and I went in search of Bunin. Like I said, it was a gamble. I didn't want Tony to have to face Lyn alone, but I figured that Bunin was the bigger danger... and I had a score to settle. So Tony took the staff, and I took Durant.

We checked a couple of the haunts that Chernomyrdin had told us about, but it was at the Five Star Bar in West Town, down on Chicago Avenue, that we finally got a break. A few breaks, actually. The Five Star was a neighborhood joint that, like many bars, tended to cater to the locals during the week and pack itself to capacity on the weekends— especially the biker and biker-chick crowd, even though it's right in the middle of Satan Disciples territory. The walls are plastered with photos and posters and stickers of bands, beers, and anything counter-cultural that they could think of, and there was a pool table in the back. Though there was only the one table, from what Chernomyrdin said, it sounded like it was pretty much Bunin's whenever he was in the bar.

We walked to the back, and there were two tough-looking guys playing the table. One had long, greasy blonde hair, and was dressed in a torn, black sweater. His face was gaunt, and he had a scar under his left eye and *Bratva* tattoos on his fingers. The other one was middle-aged, thick and muscular. He wore a tight red tank-top to show off his physique, and the only hair he had on his head was a thick moustache and bushy eyebrows. His neck, torso, arms, and hands were covered in tattoos, including one that ringed his collarbone, a lot like Bunin. His read, "*Я буду достичь небес через ад,*" and a long, black snake curled around and through the letters. When he saw us, he looked surprised and a little concerned. I figured that we didn't look that much like the average clientele, but he also seemed a little too nervous, so I decided that this was our man. But this time, Durant took the lead, saying that this was not the sort of place to show a badge, though he promised to try the polite approach before he went all "bad cop" again. He approached the table and addressed the bald man first.

"*Zdravstvujte...*" Durant said in Russian. The man barely glanced up as he continued playing pool. He was trying just a little too hard to look nonchalant.

"*El este Rus,*" the man grunted in response, nodding to the younger man across the table from him. "*Sunt Român...*" The language he was speaking sounded enough like Spanish to me that I figured out that he was saying that the younger man was Russian, but he himself was Romanian.

"*Pardon*," Durant replied, shifting languages with ease to Romanian. "*Vorbiţi Engleză? Asociatul meu nu vorbesc Româneşte...*"

"*Da*, I speak English," the man answered gruffly. "What you want here?"

"Nikodim Georgiyevich Bunin," Durant said, leaning onto the table. "And I should like to find him very, very soon."

"You are cops?" the younger Russian asked. With a flash, he flipped out a switchblade—one of those curved little kerambit blades that all the hot young turks nowadays think make them look more intimidating. The blade might be small, but that hawk-bill shape is genuinely creepy-looking. I understood why Durant said that this wasn't the sort of place to be flashing a badge around.

Before I could react in any way, I saw a blur of gray, heard a snapping sound and a scream, and the next thing I knew, Durant had the guy pinned to the wall, his arm twisted behind him in a manner that unbroken arms just can't twist. The knife clattered to the floor.

"Do I look even *remotely* like the *poliţie* to you?" Durant growled into his ear. The older man slunk back into the corner while the younger one just whimpered in pain. "*Vy ponyatiya ne imeyete, chto ya nesu...*" he said more quietly. "*You have no idea what I am...*" The Russian looked like he was going to pee in his pants, and I have to admit that I enjoyed it all a great deal. It was exhilarating, seeing one of these guys get what was coming to him.

"We don't know this man you seek," the older Romanian said, stepping forward again. "You go now, you understand?"

"No," Durant replied, letting go of the younger man's arm. When he did, I heard it crack again, and the guy squeaked in pain, slumping to the wooden floor. "I shall go when I am ready, and I shan't be ready until you tell me about Nikodim Georgiyevich Bunin. You are members of the *Bratva*, are you not? The *Obshchestvo Drakonisty*, perhaps?"

"If you help us, I'll call an ambulance for your Russian buddy," I offered.

The older man looked at his friend, then back at Durant, weighing his options. In the end, he nodded and asked us to follow him into a back room of the bar to talk in private. There hadn't been many people in the place, since it was still fairly early in the day, but he wasn't going to take any chances. The room he led us into had screens on two facing walls, with a long, black leather couch wrapping all around the perimeter. In the center, it had its own stripper pole.

"I talk to you," he said to Durant, "and you leave, yes?"

"You talk to me," Durant replied, "and I shall leave, yes."

The man folded his great, hulking arms and resigned himself to talking with us.

"I was in Clămparu clan," he began. "In România, you understand?" The Romanian mafia is broken into various clans, kind of like the Italian mafia here in the United States makes use of various families. One clan focuses on car theft rings, one on bootlegging, etc. Well, the Clămparu clan is the one that controls most of the drugs and prostitution—and virtually all of the prostitution in Spain. In fact, that's where their leader is being held in prison, the last thing I heard. Interpol's "Operation Infra-Red"—the European version of our own Operation Cross Country—netted Ioan Clămparu (AKA, "The Pig's Head"), who's now serving a 30-year term for trafficking more than 100 women into prostitution in Spain. If he ever gets extradited back to Romania, I think he's got a couple of outstanding warrants there as well—including at least one for murder. So when this guy mentioned the Clămparu clan, I started listening real closely.

"But these *Obshchestvo Drakonisty*," he continued, "these *Ruşii*, they begin taking over all business. The *Bratva*, we never have problems, you understand? They do their business, we do ours. But these *Obshchestvo Drakonisty*, they take the girls, they take the money, they take everything. We join them or we die, you understand?"

"Thoroughly," Durant replied. "And this is why you have a Russian tattoo?" he asked, tapping the man's chest.

"*Da*," he answered. "'*Eu voi ajunge în cer prin iad,*' it say."

Durant explained what the tattoo—and the man's Romanian translation—said in English to me: "I'm going through Hell to reach Heaven."

"But what does that even mean?" I asked.

"I was afraid of these *Obshchestvo Drakonisty*," he explained. "They are cruel, and they kill everyone, everyone. But then I realize they are evil only to do good. They bring out the strength, you understand? The beast God create in man. They make it strong, and they kill the evil and the weak. They are *copoi lui Dumnezeu*, you understand?"

"The 'hounds of God'..." Durant translated.

"*Da*, the hounds. They run the *vulpe* to ground, so the hunters can find and kill. They make much noise, they kill much, but they kill to live like God makes them live, you understand?"

I confess that at that point, I really didn't, but I wasn't going to press the issue. There were more important things that we needed to know. Durant realized it, too.

"What about Bunin?" Durant continued. "What about the *vârcolaci*?" The man suddenly looked even more nervous than before.

"You know the *vârcolaci*?" he asked.

"The werewolves, yes," Durant answered. "How are the

Obshchestvo Drakonisty using werewolves here in the United States? Is Bunin one of them?"

"Bunin is *vârcolac*," he said. "He is big *krysha*, you understand?"

"A mafia enforcer…" Durant translated for me again.

"He does much killing, but it is blood for blood, you understand? He is not just *copoi*—he is *lup al lui Dumnezeu*, you understand?"

"A '*wolf* of God'…" Durant translated, though I'd picked that much up myself.

"He hunts the *corbi*, the *vrăjitoare*, as God intended." That part I didn't get.

"He says that Bunin is a werewolf who has been domesticated by the *Obshchestvo Drakonisty* to hunt and kill the witches who are part of the Synod of Crows. He is a witchfinder."

"But Sherri Angelo wasn't a witch," I countered.

"No," he said coldly. "I suspect that she was merely a morsel between meals…" With that, his lip curled into a sneer and he turned back to the man. "Bunin is on the run now. We have found his den in his home. To what other hovel would he crawl to hide? Where can we find Buinin *now*?"

The guy didn't seem to know for certain, but he gave us a bunch of possibilities, including an *Obshchestvo Drakonisty* hangout farther west on Chicago Avenue. It was starting to get late in the afternoon by this time, so we decided to finish up with our friend here.

"If you tell anyone that we've chatted," Durant said as we were leaving, "I will find you."

"*Da*," he replied, nodding. "*Am înțeles*…" But then, just as we were walking out of the back room, he asked Durant a question. "Are you he?" he asked. "Are you *Rătăcitor la Lumina Zilei?*"

"I am," he replied, and the man shuddered. With that, we left.

*   *   *

"Okay, what was that?" I asked.

"That was me attempting the polite approach," he answered.

"No, I mean what was it that he asked you, there at the end? What does '*Rătăcitor la Lumina Zilei*' mean?"

"It means, 'The Wanderer in Daylight,' Detective. I have apparently picked up a bit of a legendary following in Romania as well."

"What's with Romanians?" I asked, as we walked back to the car. "Between Frank Sydor and these guys, is the whole country nuts?"

"Not at all," he replied. "In fact, I am quite taken with both the land and its people. There is a lovely elderly couple just outside of Nagykároly who have distilled my own personal label of *pálinka* for the past fifty years."

"What's *pálinka?*"

"Hmm?" he asked, getting into the car. "Oh, mine is a clear, plum-based brandy, best served from 66-67 degrees Fahrenheit. If its temperature rises above 70 degrees, it is ruined, of course, so one must be very careful when serving it. But I should think that one could use apricots or apples or any other aromatic fruit to make it."

"And *that's* why you like Romania?" I asked. "Because of the brandy?"

"It is an exceptional brandy..." he explained, sinking into the car seat.

I sat down behind the wheel, and a stray thought struck me. These *Obshchestvo Drakonisty* apparently think—at least some of them, on some level—that they're doing God's work. They're out there, slaughtering witches, and they don't seem to view other human beings as anything more than tools or impediments in accomplishing their plans. Maybe more to the point, at least some of them, though they might still look human, have left that essential humanity behind so that they can concentrate on what they see as a holy crusade. So here was my stray, scary thought, and it gave me the willies to think it—*how are they that much different from Durant?* I mean, I just watched him casually snap a guy's arm to get some information. Does he see the rest of us as peers, as means to his ends, or just as fodder for his own, personal war?

Of course, that reminded me that I'd promised to call an ambulance for the Russian guy. In fact, I was surprised that I'd forgotten about it until then. I pulled out my phone and started dialing.

"I have, however," Durant added to his previous thought, "had arguably more than my fair share of uncomfortable dealings with *Russians...*"

Background
From *Краткая История Склады на Протяжении Веков*[1] (Evgeny Konchalovsky, 1830, trans. Andrew Schott)

from *Book 6, Chapter 17*

At this point, it seems appropriate to share an anecdotal episode in which the involvement of the eleventh *Склад*[2] in Moscow played a pivotal role in European politics. It is nearly impossible to overestimate the subtle but crucial influences which the *Склады* and their agents have exerted over history throughout the centuries with their odd affairs, but perhaps this noteworthy incident will provide the reader at least one concrete example which may have, in point of fact, solidified the politics which ultimately led to the Seven Years' War.[3]

It is a little-known fact that, in 1755, there occurred an historically significant convocation between three of Europe's most powerful

---

[1] *Actually, the original report—written at the direct behest of Tsar Nikolai I— is lost to us today, due to the mass purges of the Stalinist regime in the Soviet Union of the 20th century. The only portion of the original Russian document still extant involves a completely different Storehouse during the Holy Roman Empire (which existed in one form or another from 962 to 1806). The section excerpted here is available to us only through a German translation, reprinted in Gerhardt Bremer's* Offizielle Dokumente und Papiere der Russischen Zaren *(1896), which itself was finally translated into English in 1961 by Andrew Schott.*

[2] *That is, "Storehouse." Here—as throughout the document—Schott reflects in his translation the fact that Bremer retains the original Russian word for this storehouse. It is unclear why he did not simply translate it as "Lagerhaus," as one would expect. Perhaps he assumed that Konchalovsky was using "Склад" as a proper name, though this is uncertain, since most of the "Склады" described in Konchalovsky's original work were not, in fact, Russian.*

[3] *Fought between 1756 and 1763 on several battlefronts and engaging the alliances of the major European superpowers of the day—England and Prussia on one side vs. France, Austria, and Russia on the other. In the Americas, this conflict was fought as the "French and Indian War," thus making this arguably the first, true "World War" in European history.*

women at the Schönbrunn Palace[4] in Vienna;—the Tsarina Elisabeth of Russia,[5] the Empress Maria Theresia of Austria,[6] and the Marchioness de Pompadour.[7] The public explanation for this meeting was to celebrate the opening of the orangerie[8] on the grounds of the Schönbrunn Palace, with the Marchioness supposedly bringing her expertise on the subject of orangeries from her experience with *L'Orangerie du Château de Versailles*,[9] and the Tsarina Elisabeth supposedly bringing her appreciation for the same from her experience with her own orangeries at Petrodvorets[10] and Kuskovo.[11] But in truth, the true purpose that brought them together was to address the new political realities which had been created in the wake of the Treaty of Aachen,[12] and to debate their realms' respective places within those realities, without arousing public, international suspicions.

There were, however, two important secondary missions which were being carried out at the same time by the Russian and Austrian delegations, taking advantage of the neutral meeting grounds, both of which were in response to the entourage brought by the Marchioness, which had included such popular luminaries and courtiers of the day as

---

[4]   *A lavish estate built on the Wien River in 1569 by the Holy Roman Emperor Maximilian II as a summer residence and personal retreat. The estate's modern name derives from the* Schöner Brunnen, *or "beautiful fountain," built in 1771.*

[5]   *Elizaveta Petrovna Romanova, Tsaritsa* (царйца—*the term "Tsarina" is an inaccurate transliteration) of Russia.*

[6]   *Maria Theresa, of the House of Hapsburg, who reigned as Holy Roman Empress.*

[7]   *Jeanne Antoinette Poisson (*AKA *"Madame de Pompadour," named for her estate in central France). According to reports, she was so witty and attractive that within three months of meeting King Louis XV at a ball at Versailles in 1745, she was compelled to separate from her beloved husband, Charles-Guillaume Le Normant d'Étiolles, in order to become the king's official mistress (see Antoine's* Louis XV, *1989)—a position of respect and influence within the French court.*

[8]   *The creation of orangeries—conservatories in which the wealthy grew their citrus fruits year-round—had become a popular "fad" amongst the European royal families by the mid-18th century.*

[9]   *That is, "the Orangery of the Château of Versailles" in central France.*

[10]   *In Bremer's original, "Peterhof"—the modern Petrodvortsovy District of St. Petersburg, in Northwestern Russia.*

[11]   *The summer home of Count Petr Borisovich Sheremetev, a few miles East of Moscow.*

[12]   *Schott translates Bremer's "Der Frieden von Aachen" directly. English historians usually refer to the treaty by its French name, "The Treaty of Aix-la-Chapelle" (of 1748), which significantly redistributed the holdings of various European superpowers, shifting alliances dramatically overnight.*

Voltaire[13] and the Comte de Saint-Germain,[14] with his collection of magical stones, intended as entertainments for the imperial peers.

The Tsarina Elisabeth had brought an impressive retinue with her as well, including her beloved Alexei Rozumovsky,[15] who was serving her not only in his capacities as chamberlain and lieutenant-colonel of her life guards, but primarily in his role as the premier agent of her *Склад Одиннадцать*.[16] It appears that Rozumovsky believed that at least one of Saint-Germain's gems, a diamond, did indeed hold special powers to affect change in other substances, and concluded that the visit to Vienna would provide a prime opportunity to retrieve it and return it to Moscow for safekeeping in the *Склад*.

In a similar fashion, the Empress Maria Theresia brought Gerard van Swieten,[17] ostensibly in his role as her private physician, but in reality in the role which she had assigned to him of ridding the Holy Roman Empire of vampires.[18] There is some problem with this account,

---

[13] *François-Marie Arouet, famous author, philosopher, and devout opponent of the Catholic Church. He had been a favorite of Madame de Pompadour's since the creation of her salon at her estate at Étiolles.*

[14] *Acclaimed courtier and popular companion to many heads of state in Europe. His real name is unknown, but he claimed to be the son of Ferenc II Rákóczi of Transylvania, and thus the legitimate heir to the throne of the Holy Roman Empire. But then, he also claimed to have been educated by the Medicis in Italy, to have the power to change the substance of one element into another by use of mystical gemstones, and to be well over 500 years old, so his accounts of his own backgrounds are dubious, to say the least.*

[15] *Oleksiy Grigorievich Rozumovsky, born the son of a poor Cossack in the Ukraine. He originally rose to the attention of the young Elizaveta Petrovna due to his good looks and beautiful singing voice. Through her affection for him, he had quickly risen through the court ranks from a simple* камер-юнкер *("valet," which Bremer translated as "Kammerjunker") to* гофмаршал *(Bremer's "Hofmarschall," or chamberlain, the highest administrator of the imperial court), to* рейхграф *(Bremer's "Reichsgraf," or "imperial count"—naming the new "House Rozumovsky" after his grandfather, Yakov Rozum), to* подполковником *(Bremer's "Oberstleutnant," or lieutenant-colonel) within the Tsaritsa's life guards, or elite cavalry. The next year, in 1756, he was promoted to* генерал-фельдмаршал *(Bremer's "Generalfeldmarschall," or field marshal), the highest-ranking member of the Russian military—though whether that was intended as a reward or as a polite and respectful way to put him "out to pasture" is a matter of some debate.*

[16] *That is, "the eleventh Storehouse."*

[17] *Dutch physician and member of the imperial court of the Holy Roman Empire. He used this position to modernize Austrian medical and educational sciences, establishing (among other things) the Vienna School of Medicine in 1754.*

[18] *There was a common perception that Europe was experiencing an epidemic*

however, as descriptions of van Swieten at this convocation and elsewhere do not match descriptions of him and artistic renderings in other contexts. Commonly, he is described as being a bald, portly, bookish man of short stature, but in this account of the meeting at the Schönbrunn Palace, he is described as *"grand, de bonne forme, avec des cheveux noirs et la barbe coupée, avec la mine austère d'un soldat."*[19] Thus, unless there were in fact *two* Gerard van Swietens working on behalf of the Empress at this point in history, the description given here must be in error; perhaps even conflated with that of Saint-Germain himself.[20] More likely, as anyone with even the smallest amount of investigation might discover, this more clearly matches the description of one Peregrinus Donnacius,[21] with whom the Marchioness had been intimately acquainted in earlier years, having supposedly saved her from assassination by some sort of foreign *automates* at her wedding.[22] This conclusion is supported by an oblique comment by the Tsarina Elisabeth[23] that Donnacius, a former paramour, had been in attendance with the Austrian delegation there at the Schönbrunn Palace, pleasingly unchanged in twenty years.[24]

---

of vampirism at the time (note the specific accounts of alleged vampires such as Petar Blagojević, Arnaut Pavle, Sava Savanović, etc.)—see Barber's Vampires, Burial and Death: Folklore and Reality *(1988), Hamberger's* Mortuus non Mordet *(1972), and van Swieten's own* Abhandlung des Daseyns der Gespenster *(1768).*

[19] *That is, "tall, of good build, with dark hair and clipped beard, carrying the stark bearing of a soldier," a description given by a courtier as also reported in Trintignant's* La Vie Exquise de la Marquise de Pompadour *(1956).*

[20] *See a very similar description of Saint-Germain given in a letter by Horace Walpole, dated 9 December, 1745.*

[21] *Sir Peregrine Donnachie, 18th century British knight and agent of the Crown—holding the "favored agent" status similarly enjoyed by Sir Walter Raleigh in the 17th century and Sir Richard Burton in the 19th century.*

[22] *At L'église Saint-Eustache in Paris in 1741. Among Madame de Pompadour's numerous eccentricities—including a lifelong obsession with time and seeing into the future (for example, see Mitford and Foreman's* Madame de Pompadour, *2001, for an account of her visiting a fortune teller at the age of nine)—was her persistent belief that soulless automata were attempting to kidnap and/or assassinate her, claiming that every few years, they would surprise and attack her (see again Trintignant's* La Vie Exquise de la Marquise de Pompadour, *1956). She maintained that one such attack— at her wedding, no less—was foiled by the visiting Donnachie, whom she said reminded her of her imaginary childhood hero, "l'homme de la cheminée" ("the chimney man").*

[23] *Referenced in* Официальные Отчеты для Императорского Двора Летнего Сезона *(1755).*

[24] *Elizaveta Petrovna was renowned for having a series of lovers, both foreign and domestic. Donnachie had met her during a trip to St. Petersburg in*

As it happens, van Swieten (or Donnacius) became convinced that one of the Marchioness' party was, in fact, a vampire;—specifically, Gilles, the Baron of Retz.[25] In point of fact, it appears that, given the Comte de Saint-Germain's avowed devotion to mysticism and oft-repeated accounts of being immortal, van Swieten had come to believe that Saint-Germain himself was this fiend, masquerading as a human in the court of King Louis XV. Indeed, Saint-Germain was often described as being unusually pale in complexion,[26] but this alone is hardly grounds for such slanderous accusations.[27] Nonetheless, van Swieten found an ally of sorts in Voltaire, who also believed in the existence of vampires[28] and wished to aid him in their ultimate destruction, though he had not been told that van Swieten had suspected his favourite entertainer of being such a creature.[29]

1732. The two enjoyed a romantic flirtation for a brief few weeks, until he left on some unrecorded errand of state—at which point, she became amorously acquainted with Rozumovsky.

[25] *The 15th century Gilles de Montmorency-Laval was a hero of the Hundred Years' War and a compatriot of Joan of Arc. Considered courageous in battle at the time and honored by King Charles VII, it became clear that it was rather his lust for carnage which had made him such an effective warrior when later, in his capacity as the baron of the* pays de Rais—*a barony in the southern part of the region of Brittany—he used his authority to ritualistically and sadistically murder several hundreds of children within his lands. At his trial, he admitted to having sold his soul to Satan for power in 1432 (disconsolate upon the death of his beloved Joan), and he was executed by hanging in Nantes in 1440.*

[26] *See again the letter by Walpole, 1745.*

[27] *It should be noted here, however, that contemporary physical descriptions of Gilles de Montmorency-Laval arguably do match the descriptions of both the Comte de Saint-Germain and Sir Peregrine Donnachie, and that sightings of "Gilles de Retz" were reported for centuries after his execution—the last documented one being an attack upon an elderly widow during the Battle of Leipzig in 1813 (see Stuhlinger's* Völkerschlacht, 2001*). In addition, the libertine Giacomo Casanova mentioned in his memoirs that he noticed that the Comte de Saint-Germain never actually ate any food at the many banquets which he frequented (see his* Mémoires de Jacques Casanova, *1798).*

[28] *See his* Dictionnaire Philosophique (1764), *in which he argued that "vampires were corpses, who went out of their graves at night to suck the blood of the living, either at their throats or stomachs, after which they returned to their cemeteries. The persons so sucked waned, grew pale, and fell into consumption; while the sucking corpses grew fat, got rosy, and enjoyed an excellent appetite."*

[29] *Voltaire was enamoured of the Comte de Saint-Germain, referring to him as "l'homme d'émerveillement" (the "wonder man"), and "un homme qui ne meurt point, et qui sait tout" ("a man who never dies, and who knows everything").*

The weekend was full of intrigues, both political and romantic,[30] but the intrigues of both van Swieten and Rozumovsky came to a head on the final night of the secret conference in Vienna. The Comte de Saint-Germain had entertained the ladies and their companies with his fanciful tales and feats of prestidigitation, never ceasing his talking until late into the evening. Among the sleights of hand with which he amazed them was his famed alchemical trick wherein he took several small sapphires from his purse, dropped them into a glass of champagne (which caused the glass to foam to the point of overflowing), and then poured the contents into a silk handkerchief, from which he then produced one large sapphire of perfect clarity. He also demonstrated the use of a large diamond, with which he was said to have prevented a piece of paper from charring when held over the flame of a candle. Both van Swieten and Rozumovsky were said to have watched this latter bit of chicanery[31] with great interest and intensity.

After the supper and entertainment, the Comte de Saint-Germain retired to the Großes Parterre[32] with two members of the Marchioness' party;—Georges-Louis Arnauld, the Comte de Ponthieu,[33] and his companion, the beautiful Mlle. Rayna du Vilaine, who had just arrived. Apparently, Rozumovsky began following them as they passed the Linden Allee,[34] while van Swieten watched them from the Rusten Allee from the North. After the French trio had gotten far enough away from the Palace, they entered the Irrgarten,[35] where the Comte de Ponthieu began acting most erratically. According to Rozumovsky, the man took on a most threatening aspect and appeared prepared to pounce on Saint-Germain, while Mlle. du Vilaine's voice cooed in an almost alarmingly soothing and attractive manner. At this, the Comte de Saint-Germain

---

[30] *Again, although Maria Theresa was a devoutly religious and conservative woman, both Madame de Pompadour and—particularly—Elizaveta Petrovna were renowned for their amorous adventures.*

[31] *The original word used by Bremer here was* "Machenschaften," *suggesting a level of maliciousness or criminal fraud involved in Saint-Germain's parlour tricks. It is unknown if Konchalovsky's original made use of the Russian cognate,* "махинации," *or if this constituted a gloss on Bremer's part.*

[32] *The large, well-manicured set of ornamental flower beds between the Schönbrunn Palace itself and the grand Sun Fountain, and which forms the hub of the collection of various gardens on the grounds.*

[33] *A recently appointed count of a minor region in France, whose quickly-rising influence in court stemmed largely from his sizeable fortune.*

[34] *One of the main, East-West avenues between the gardens, which include— moving into the gardens from the Palace from South to North—the Lichte Allee, the Finstere Allee, the Linden Allee, and the Rusten Allee.*

[35] *A labyrinth of hedges designed in 1694 by Jean Trehet as part of the French Garden, near the recently expanded Tiergarten (a managerie of exotic animals). It extends over an area of 2,700 square metres.*

produced the large diamond with which he had astounded the company at dinner, and was overheard saying something to the effect that this action should keep the Comte de Ponthieu "at bay," at least temporarily.

It was at that moment that both Rozumovsky and van Swieten burst onto the scene with sabres flashing, entering the Irrgarten simultaneously; Rozumovsky to obtain the diamond for the *Склад*, and van Swieten to slay the man whom he had presumed to be a creature of the night. Mlle. du Vilaine and van Swieten saw one another and each appeared genuinely surprised to see the other;—apparently, they had known each other at some point in the past, though there was obviously no opportunity for either of them at that moment to reminisce. With a loud growl, the Comte de Ponthieu shouted *"Fantôme vivant!"*[36] and leapt forward toward van Swieten, who parried his attack and meant to thrust forward with his own, but was thwarted as Mlle. du Vilaine flung herself upon his back. The Comte de Saint-Germain ran away, deeper into the maze, while the Comte de Ponthieu burst through the hedgerow to escape the labyrinth entirely. Van Swieten growled something as he flung the young woman off of his back and broke through the hedgerow after Ponthieu, while Rozumovsky fled deeper into the Irrgarten in pursuit of the diamond.

Being a stout and hearty military man, Rozumovsky caught up to Saint-Germain with relative ease. He had originally planned a stealthier attempt to obtain the diamond, but under the circumstances felt forced to take it by force, so he came upon Saint-Germain and threatened to end his life with his sword. At this, the courtier simply laughed and said, *"Si un tel résultat était possible, je voudrais offriez bienvenue, monsieur..."*[37] explaining that Porthieu had apparently attacked him to gain through his blood the blessing of immortality, but was enraged when Saint-Germain had told him that his longevity was due to a curse and not a blessing, and that it was thus as non-physical as it was non-transferable. At last, however, the Comte was compelled through less mortal physical violence to turn the gem over to Rozumovsky, asking the agent his birth name as recompense. Rozumovsky formally introduced himself, and then asked Saint-Germain to do him the courtesy of the same. "Isaac Ahasvérus,"[38] the Comte answered him with a wan smile, and then returned to the Palace alone.

---

[36] *That is, "Living ghost!"*

[37] *"If such an outcome were possible, I would bid it welcome, sir..."*

[38] *One final amusement from the Comte de Saint-Germain. "Ahasvérus" (or "Ahasuerus") is thought to have been the name of the so-called "Wandering Jew," who was supposedly cursed to walk the world forever alone as punishment for mocking Jesus Christ on the way to the cross (see Quinet's* Ahasvérus, 1834; Lagerkvist's Ahasverus Död, 1960, etc.*), though Dumas referred to the character as "Isaac" (see his* Isaac Laquedem, 1853*).*

Rozumovsky himself left the Irrgarten through the same gap in the hedgerow left in the wake of Porthieu and van Swieten, though Mlle. du Vilaine was nowhere to be found. He exited the Schönbrunn grounds to the West of the Palace, down the Lichte Allee, and discovered by chance the pitched battle between the Comte de Porthieu and Gerard van Swieten outside of the newly constructed orangerie.[39] He watched in disbelief as van Swieten's sword appeared to slice through the Comte with no effect, whilst Porthieu's blade drew blood at each pass, though both combatants were said to have moved with a practiced speed which Rozumovsky found difficult to follow in the low light of the evening. At one point, van Swieten flung himself at Porthieu so quickly and unexpectedly that both men were sent crashing through one of the great windows on the orangerie's Southern exposure;—they fell into one of the orange tree vaults, and the scent of citrus filled the night air.

Rozumovsky was drawn to witness this fight, and was thus close at hand when van Swieten's blade again appeared to pass through Porthieu, sinking itself deep into one of the ornate pilasters framing the window. The Comte laughed at this, but when van Swieten spied Rozumovsky nearby, with the diamond in his hand, he ripped his sword from the masonry and dashed over to him with such blinding speed that he had wrenched the gemstone from his grasp before Rozumovsky had barely seen him move. Turning to Porthieu, he held the diamond in front of him and lunged once again, this time slicing a great gash in the Comte's side, near to his heart. At this, Porthieu raged once more, though Rozumovsky was shocked that either man was physically able to continue their duel, such was the extent and ferocity of their attacks against one another. But whilst they fought, Rozumovsky took the opportunity to slice at van Swieten's wrist, forcing him to drop the gemstone. He quickly retrieved it from the ground before Rozumovsky could do so, but by then, the Comte de Porthieu had disappeared.

Van Swieten cursed Rozumovsky for allowing a villain to escape, but gave explanation for neither the Comte de Porthieu's actions nor his own. The agent demanded then that the diamond be returned to his custody, as it should not be allowed to fall into the hands of foreigners. Van Swieten growled in reply, "Foreigners? Where were you when 'foreigners' such as Münchhausen and I were fighting for your empire at Özü Kuşatması?"[40] "I was by my Tsarina's side," said Rozumovsky,

---

[39] *At the instigation of Holy Roman Emperor Franz I Stephan, the construction of the orangerie had been begun by Nicola Pacassi in 1754, following plans designed by Nicolas Jadot.*

[40] *His is referring here to the siege of Ochakiv in 1737, while Russia was at war with Turkey. The companion to whom he is referring is Baron Hieronymus Carl Friedrich von Münchhausen, who served as a page to Anton Ulrich, the Duke of Brunswick-Lüneburg, and as a low-ranking*

"not wandering off as you are so wont to do…"[41]

When Rozumovsky again demanded the diamond in the name of the Tsarina, van Swieten simply replied that the agent should return to the Palace and inform Tsarina Elisabeth that he did, in fact, remember her name quite well, and with great affection. He then tucked the diamond into an old leather purse at his side and bowed to Rozumovsky, who bowed in return; but when he looked up afterward, van Swieten had disappeared as surely as Porthieu had done, moments before. Left with nothing, Rozumovsky returned to the Palace to report his failure.

But the resulting effects of this episode were far from over. Tensions rose between the French and Russian delegations, with the French accusing Rozumovsky of open aggression against Saint-Germain, and the Russian and French delegations formally expressing their offense at the Austrians for bringing such a dangerous man as van Swieten to their conference, though both the Marchioness and the Tsarina admitted that they believed him to be, in fact, a British agent.[42] But so immediately had a conflagration of debate arisen that the Marchioness drew their attention to the relative weakness of their diplomatic relations with one another. While England and Prussia were openly developing their own coalition,[43] their own respective realms had been content to bicker privately about borders at a secret meeting in Vienna. If such a tenuous connection existed among them that a diamond might shake their diplomatic relations, then how would they be able to stand together against the English and the Prussians? She

---

member of the Russian cavalry. Münchhausen became famous for exaggerating his adventures when expounding upon them later on in life. It is worthy of note here that there is no record of Gerard van Swieten having served at Ochakiv, though there is evidence to suggest that Donnachie was at the battle for at least some short period of time.

[41] *Bremer included a footnote that the Tsaritsa had similarly referred to Donnachie as* "Странник" *("the Wanderer" or "the Pilgrim"), though he provided no documentation for that claim. The name "Peregrine" does, however, derive from the Latin* peregrinus, *meaning "wanderer" or "alien"—indeed, the German name for the Peregrine Falcon (falco peregrinus) is "Der Wanderfalke" ("the Wandering Falcon"). The key issue in this exchange is that it would appear that Rozumovsky was at least somewhat familiar with this man, with the clear implication that Elizaveta Petrovna had known him as well.*

[42] *Again, another argument that this van Swieten was, in fact, Donnachie, under an assumed name, as the man was known to both of them. The Empress Maria Theresa, however, would almost have to have been complicit in such a deceit—it can hardly be accepted that she would not recognize her own personal physician.*

[43] *An alliance which was expressed formally in 1756 with the Westminster Convention, signed in Whitehall.*

encouraged the Empress and Tsarina to commit themselves and their empires to a formal pact with France, the details of which to be more clearly developed by their diplomatic offices.

Alexei Bestuzhev-Ryumin,[44] whose loathing and distrust for the French[45] had kept Russia and France from allying themselves in the past, was resistant to the suggestion that the two powers could form any form of coalition with Austria, but the repercussions of the "Reversal of Alliances"[46] brought about by the Marchioness which resulted from this episode, in addition to the shifted alliances created by the Treaty of Aachen, generated increased enmity between England and France. At the same time, subsequent to his embarrassingly failed mission to retrieve the diamond, Rozumovsky's influence in the Russian court had quickly waned, and he was soon replaced in the Tsarina's affections by a much younger man.[47] As Rozumovsky's influence decreased, so then did his longtime and crucial support for Bestuzhev. Thus, with his political power crumbling beneath him, and with no voice left in Tsarina Elisabeth's court to bolster him, even Bestuzhev was ultimately forced to admit the need for Russia to ally itself more directly with France and Austria, or else be left on her own to face the coming conflict. When open warfare finally but inevitably erupted between the French and the English,[48] Russia found herself constrained to fight alongside longtime rival France and against longtime ally Prussia. This was but one example of how world politics has been subtly but significantly influenced by the actions of the agents of a given *Склад*.

---

[44] *Grand Chancellor Alexei Petrovich Bestuzhev-Ryumin, arguably the most powerful man in Russia for twenty years, until he lost favor near the end of his tenure.*

[45] *Due, in part to the French alliance with Russia's longtime enemy Turkey, based upon mutual opposition to the power of the Hapsburg dynasty. France's interests in Russia's neighbors Turkey, Poland, and Sweden consistently placed them at cross-purposes to Russian foreign policy.*

[46] *Schott translates Bremer's "Umkehrung der Allianzen" directly. By English historians, this is usually referred to as the "Diplomatic Revolution."*

[47] *Namely, the 27-year-old Ivan Ivanovich Shuvalov—a former page who had caught her fancy. He was at that time Elizaveta's current камер-юнкер, but he quickly rose to the rank of генерал (general) due to her patronage. He used his position in court to further a newfound interest in education and the arts in Russia (see Artemyev and Mikeshin's "Иван Иванович Шувалов (1727–1797), Просвещённая личность в российской истории," 1998). Arguably, this incident with the diamond thus precipitated not only the Seven Years' War—as Bremer is arguing here—but also what scholars have termed "The Russian Enlightenment."*

[48] *The Seven Years' War (1756-1763), informally beginning with fighting over territories in the Americas in 1754.*

Chapter 10
The Royal Disease

So we were driving west on Chicago Avenue. We didn't get very far when I caught a whiff of the food at Habana Libre and started getting hungry. It'd been a long day, and I knew that I wasn't going to be able to function too well on a grumbling stomach. The sun was going down within the next half hour, so I knew that we couldn't take the time to stop at a sit-down restaurant, of course, but by the time that we were crossing Ashland, I felt ravenous, and I couldn't stop thinking about food. So I convinced Durant to let me stop off and grab a quick taco at De Pasada. It's a little place—I mean, seriously, *crazy* little—right next door to Mr. Taco's. It may not seem like much, but they have awesome, one-dollar tacos with a killer salsa verde. I bought a handful of them and the biggest drink that they had and rushed back to the car. I offered one of the tacos to Durant, but he looked at me like I was crazy.

"So you were saying about Russians?" I asked, my mouth full of taco. I wanted to get him talking, because otherwise, it was just the two of us, sitting there on the side of the street, quietly watching me eat.

"Hmm?" he replied, obviously thinking about something else. "Oh, I simply said that I have had several dealing with Russians over the years."

"Anything pertinent to our case?" I asked him to prod him further, crumpling up one wrapper and moving on to the next taco. I don't think that I've ever eaten anything as fast as I wolfed down those tacos. Durant sighed.

"Perhaps," he said at last. "In 1914, I was in Ypres, in Belgium, stalking a werewolf. The month before, I had been at the Battle of the Marne, where I had fought alongside two Americans, actually. The first was an unsettling pilot whom the French called, *'L'Aigle Noir,'* and who, I understand, went down with his plane in 1921 in some remote region or another—which struck me as odd, given Allard's competence behind the stick. The second was a fellow immortal, who turned out to be a distant relative of a fat friar whom I had known in the time of King Richard—solid as an oar, fighting in France because he felt that we who were 'gifted' had an obligation to help the world. In retrospect, he reminds me of another immortal soldier whose acquaintance I had made in 1944—a stout little American Marine named Judson who spoke with an endearing stammer and with a love of history which mirrored my own."

"Ypres?" I asked, trying to get him back on track.

"Oh, yes," he said. "In October, I found and killed a werewolf in Ypres, who turned out to be Prince Maurice of Battenberg, the grandson of Queen Victoria. Somehow—rumor had it, on some hunting trip or what have you in Scotland in 1879—Victoria had acquired at least a tiny trace of the Lycaon virus in her own bloodstream, which she then inadvertantly passed on to her children. It was treated by royal physicians, as it accompanied a strange form of hemophilia—often called the 'royal disease,' since it affected so many of Victoria's later family members—and Maurice's death at my hands was officially whitewashed by declaring that he had been killed in action at the Battle of Ypres. But I ask you, why would the army let a hemophiliac—and a royal personage, at that—serve in a combat situation?" He shook his head as I began shoving my third taco into my mouth. I apologized and promised that it would be my last one.

"Well," he continued, "I should have considered that more of the European royals may have been similarly affected, that it might have been passed on genetically. That was why the lycanthropic Breton king, Conomor, was so terrified to have a child, of course—and why he felt compelled to *behead* both Tréphine and Trémeur. But I had a promise to keep, and I moved on to Africa and to the silent city of vampires near Kôr..."

"I remember you telling me that story the last time," I said.

"Did I?" he asked. He seemed disappointed not to be able to tell it to me again. "Well, did I mention meeting a French Foreign Legion officer named de Saint-Avit in North Africa, who was trying to find Atlantis?"

"In North Africa?" I asked.

"In the sands of the French Sahara, no less!" he laughed. "The fool had fallen hopelessly—and murderously, in fact—in love with a Queen Antinéa, who had claimed that her kingdom was an outpost of lost Atlantis, buried beneath the sands. The man was mad, of course..."

"Anyone who'd believe in Atlantis probably is," I said, washing my tacos down with a gulp.

"Not at all," he corrected me. "But Atlantis certainly never had an outpost in the Sahara."

"You're kidding about that, right?" I asked, laughing so hard that I almost spit out my drink. "You've been to Atlantis?"

"Of course I've not been to Atlantis," he replied with a snort. "The continent was lost thousands of years before my birth in the Great Vril

War against vile R'lyeh, which forever sank them both beneath the sea."

"Of course it did," I repeated, rolling my eyes. "So you're trying to tell me that Atlantis is real?"

"Not the Hollywood version, of course," he clarified. "Mermaids are pure poppycock. But there have been so many grand and horrible cities in the world which have risen and fallen since the dawn of man—and, perhaps, even before then…" He paused for a moment, his mind drifting to something obviously far darker than the flighty story he had originally intended to tell me. But then he came back to himself and continued.

"My friend, João da Silva Guimarães, stumbled across a lost colony of Atlantis, Kuhikugu, well over a century before I myself did with the aid of an archaeologist named Thatch—which was when we first discovered that Daemon there which still haunts my soul. Percy Fawcett and his son were lost, following my trail, half a century after that. Even that globetrotting, illegitimate son of Colonel Richard Henry Savage appears to have crossed the Nohulite Bridge of Light into the city sometime before the Great War, earning for himself the honorary title of 'Itzimin-Chac' from the natives there, before bequeathing the whole thing to his own son later on—as if he'd held the right to do so."

"I'm sorry," I said, wiping my hands and mouth in preparation to get going. "I just can't believe that there's really an Atlantis out there somewhere. That just seems too ridiculous."

"But how can one so easily dismiss the vril-laden, cyan caverns of K'n-yan, or the sunken spires of beautiful Ys, or doomed Sarnath, or the empty ruins of Ib in Mnar, or my own dark experiences in Cornish Lethesow, before it sank beneath the waves itself?" he asked, as if that gibberish meant anything. "There is a reason why syenite and dolomite stones move of their own volition in your Death Valley. Nor can we ignore the terrible truth of the dread corpse-city of R'lyeh—the dreaming monsters of which the more superstitious people of Pohnpei still sing their horrid songs…" He got very quiet and serious again for a minute once he said that. "I myself have heard the chantings of the cultists since that horrible call issued forth from the Antarctic deep in 1997, and I have seen the writings of Mu at Miskatonic, written on brittle palm leaves, describing the great, sleeping Things which yet reside there, slumbering in the deep, waiting to rise again…"

"Palm leaves?"

"Hmm?" he responded, roused from his musings. "Yes. Copeland provided an excellent translation and a critical commentary, though far too many scholars treat his research today—a century later—as the naiveté of a simpler and less critical age. I assume that they should still have copies of his original volumes in the library at the school."

"What school is that?"

"Miskatonic University, as I said," he replied, obviously becoming tired of my questions. "The university in Massachusetts which I founded in 1693. I donated its first books from my own library. We may not have the museum of antiquities of, say, a Barnett College, but over the centuries, I have made certain that the quality of the library has remained of the highest order, including a copy of the *Necronomicon* at Miskatonic University in Massachusetts—though it is, unfortunately, the inferior Latin translation which Wormius created in Spain in the 17th century. He did not even transliterate Abd-al-Hazred's *name* correctly…"

"I've heard of the *Necronomicon*," I said, recalling it from the research that I did for the other book that I wrote. "Nasty stuff."

"Indeed," he said. "When, in 1300, the sorcerer first fell from the sky who—"

"I'm sorry," I interrupted. "What does any of this have to do with the royal families of Europe, Russia, or our case?" He didn't look happy to be interrupted, but the sun had just gone down, I was about to start the car, and I wanted the conversation to come to an end one of these years.

"I had left Europe to go to Africa," he remembered, picking up where he'd left off. "So unbeknownst to me, in Russia, little Tsarevich Alexei was struggling with his own bout of 'hemophilia' in the household of the Tsar. In desperation, after countless physicians had been unable to help the boy from bleeding out from every slight wound, Tsar Nikolay and his wife, Aleksandra Fyodorovna, called upon a mad and debauched self-proclaimed monk and faith healer named Grigori Yefimovich Rasputin to cure him. Between his almost mystical abilities to charm and hypnotize those around him and his simple suggestion of withholding aspirin from the boy—a pain-reliever prescribed for him by the doctors which, being an anticoagulant, had had the unfortunate side-effect of actually worsening his condition—Rasputin was actually able to help Alexei, at least for a time. Of course, the monk was using that time to not only worm his way into the imperial court—and, some say, Aleksandra's bed—but also to perform secret transfusions between himself and the boy. He had recognized the virus for what it was, you see, and he wanted that power for his own diabolical uses."

"You can do that?" I asked. "Change into a werewolf because of a blood transfusion?"

"As I told you before," he reminded me, "one does not become infected with the virus due solely to the festering of an infectious bite. It is a *spiritual* malady of the blood, and thus can be brought about by any one of a number of methods, be it a transfusion, or a witch's curse, or— as Virgil wrote—an herbal potion or salve, or even the merest touch or *gaze* of a werewolf, if it is a mature one. Someone quite close to me was cursed by the chanting of a Pima skinwalker whom we had been hunting in Arizona. You must stop thinking about this from a Hollywood or even a purely scientific perspective. Rasputin wished for power, and he used Alexei to get it."

"Did it work?" I asked.

"Somewhat…" he said. "By 1914, Rasputin had infused enough of Alexei's infected blood into his own, healthy bloodstream that he was beginning to exhibit lycanthropic abilities, albeit without the genetic hemophilia which had thus far prevented Alexei from succumbing to the more wolf-like traits. When Rasputin's noseless former lover, the mad Khioniya Guseva, attacked him, ripping out his intestines with a knife, people at court said that it was a 'miracle' that he had survived. But Rasputin realized that his scheme was working, and that he was changing into something much harder to kill.

"Two years later, Rasputin survived an attempted assassination by conspirators who feared his influence on the Tsar and Tsaritsa, and thus on the Russian court itself. They poisoned him with enough cyanide to kill several men, then shot him three times, then bludgeoned him, then strangled him, and then stabbed him… and yet *still* the fiend survived. In desperation, they finally tied him up into a carpet and threw him several stories down into the icy waters of the Neva River."

"So he drowned?"

"Technically, but only after I shot him again," he said. "Sydney Reilly had helped me enter into Russia, as this was long before he faked his own death in 1925 to defect to the Soviet Union…"

"Reilly was a spy, was he?"

"He was *the* spy," he corrected me. "The blueprint for all spies after him, including my friend, Duško Popov. Born 'Georgi Rosenblum' in the Ukraine, Reilly was recruited in 1894 by Mycroft—well, 'Agent M' to the British intelligence community—and given the codename 'Agent R,' though he used other aliases such as 'Sigmund Rosenblum' and 'Dr. T. W. Andrew' as well. He began working under Melville at Scotland Yard's Special Branch within two years, and by 1919, he had officially joined the ranks of MI1(c), which I'd developed with the War Office in 1909, wearing those ridiculous yellow spectacles and calling himself '*Captain* R'—though he held no rank and Captain Sir George Mansfield Smith-Cumming was his superior. It was a tragedy against humanity when that man sold his soul to Stalin in 1925 to save his own skin. He went on to share every secret that he had, and to recruit Ilya Ivanov and Dr. Nikola to oversee his abominable 'humanzee' project at Sukhumi and Alma Ata."

Humanzees? I didn't even want to go there.

"So… Rasputin?" I asked, changing the subject back.

"Yes," he said. "We found him crawling out of the Neva, his wounds already beginning to heal, and his aspect beginning to change into that of a great beast. I had no idea of his lycanthropy at the time, of course, but I always made it a point to keep blessed, silver cartridges in my Webley in order to remain prepared for as many different sorts of creatures as possible. Thus, when I shot the monster through the forehead, he fell before us, and Reilly kicked his body back into the river."

"What about Alexei?"

"Three years later, he was executed by the Bolsheviks just before his fourteenth birthday, along with the rest of the Tsar's family, save Anastasia, of course."

"They killed the whole family? Even the children?"

"Tsarevichi grow up to be Tsari, Detective," he said. "The Bolsheviks took the entire family down into a cellar and shot them all, including the boy. It is rather telling that, though he was a known hemophilic, Alexei was the hardest to kill. They shot him several times and then bayoneted him, and still the boy would not die. Finally, Yakov Mikhailovich Yurovsky—who was leading the executioners—thought to shoot him in the head, ultimately killing him. They circulated a myth that Alexei's jeweled undershirt somehow deflected the bullets, knives, and bayonets, but the only shirt of such kind that I have ever been acquainted with was worn by the Viking Örvar-Oddr, and I know for a fact that Alexei did not wear this. The sad truth is that he was beginning to change into the same sort of beast that your colleague is in danger of becoming. As decent a human being as the boy had always been, he would surely not have remained so much longer."

"So you're suggesting that murdering a thirteen-year-old boy was a good thing?" I asked, pulling out onto Chicago Avenue again.

"Not really," he replied. "I am suggesting that putting down an infected FBI agent before she kills would ultimately be a kindness to everyone involved…"

I was taken aback by that, and I was about to respond when my phone rang. It was Tony, and he didn't sound like himself at all.

"Tom?"

"What's up, Tony? Any news?"

"Nothin' good, Tom," he replied. His voice was a little shaky. "I got a situation."

"What's going on, Tony?"

"Okay, so Wheaton an' me, we got a lead on Davidge, y'know? By the time I got there, Wheaton'd heard that she's off at Crabby Kim's, down on Western."

"That's the bikini bar, right?"

"Yep."

"I figured you'd like that."

"I did, but we wasn't there long before we hear she's moved on with some guy to *another* bar in Old Irving Park. It's like she's bar-hoppin' her way across Chicago, an' the sun ain't even down yet!"

"What happened to the uniform?"

"I dunno," he replied. "But by the description we was given at Crabby Kim's, the guy she left with wasn't no cop. So we chase after her in Wheaton's car, an' just a couple o' minutes ago, we seen her walkin' down Addison with *another* guy what don't fit the description of either the cop or the guy from Crabby Kim's. They was headin' fer a vacant buildin', so I figured we'd better park an' start followin' 'em. I didn't wanna lose 'em again—especially with the sun goin' down an' all."

"Did you take the stick?" I asked him, and I saw Durant wince out of the corner of my eye.

"O' course I took the stick!" he said. "Wheaton told me I oughta leave it in the car, but I ain't goin' into no vacant buildin' after a suspected potential werewolf without havin' my favorite juju stick with me."

"So what's up?" I asked again.

"What's up is that we walk into this buildin', it gets all dark inside, an' all of a sudden, I hear a crash, an' Wheaton's gone, an' my flashlight is knocked outta my hand, an' I'm all alone here."

"Tony, get out of there!"

"That's what I'm tellin' ya, doofus! I can't! The door we come in by is locked, an' I'm stumblin' around here in the dark, an' I can't *find* no way outta here. I'm swingin' the stupid stick around in the dark like a crazy man!"

"Tony, you're only a couple of miles away from the District 17 Police Station. Call a cop and they'll be there in—"

"They'll be here just in time ta get all ate up, just like me."

"Okay, hold on, Tony," I told him, slamming my foot on the gas. "We're on our way." I figured that I could turn right onto Damen and—

"Tom," Tony said. "Yer like 15 minutes away, at least. I didn't call ya fer that." His voice got quiet and serious. "I called ta tell ya good-bye…"

"Don't talk like that, Tony!" I replied. I was going to say more, but that's when Durant interrupted me.

"Where is this?" he asked, growling. I told him that Tony was off of Addison, about seven miles north on Milwaukee from our present location. As soon as the words were out of my mouth, Durant exploded out of the car, leaping onto Chicago Avenue. He didn't ask me to stop, even though I was doing 45 and accelerating—he just ripped open the door so hard and so fast that I heard the hinges creak as the metal twisted, and with a dark gray blur against the city lights, he was gone.

Funny, I was suddenly reminded of his thousand-dollar shoes…

"Tell Durant he was prob'ly right about Carolyn," Tony continued. "We shoulda just taken her out when we had the chance. I'm gonna be her first doggie dinner."

"I can't tell Durant," I said, yanking Durant's door shut, turning onto Damen, and praying as hard as I knew how to pray. "He's already on his way to save your life."

I tried as hard as I could to sound confident, but I was worried enough that the steering wheel actually bent a bit under the intensity of my grip...

Background
From *Völsungasaga*[1] (13th century, trans. E. Magnusson)

from the *Introduction*

Bor's sons[2] slew Ymir the giant, but when he fell there ran so much blood out of his wounds that all the kin of the Hrimthursar were drowned, save Hvergelmir and his household, who got away in a boat. Then Bor's sons took Ymir and bore him into the midst of Yawning-gap, and made of him the earth; of his blood seas and waters, of his flesh earth was made; they set the earth fast, and laid the sea round about it in a ring without; of his bones were made rocks; stones and pebbles of his teeth and jaws and the bones that were broken; they took his skull and made the lift thereof, and set it up over the earth with four sides, and under each corner they set dwarfs, and they took his brain and cast it aloft, and made clouds. They took the sparks and gledes[3] that went loose, and had been cast out of Muspellheim,[4] and set them in the lift to give light; they gave resting-places to all fires, and set some in the lift; some fared free under it, and they gave them a place and shaped their goings.

A wondrous great smithying, and deftly done. The earth is fashioned round without, and there beyond, round about it lies the deep sea; and on that sea-strand the gods gave land for an abode to the giant kind, but within on the earth made they a burg round the world against restless giants, and for this burg reared they the brows of Ymir, and called the burg Midgard.[5] The gods went along the sea-strand and found two stocks, and shaped out of them men; the first gave soul and life, the

---

[1]   *This saga tells the story of Völsung, king of Hunaland, and his lineage—beginning with his great-grandfather, the god Odin, and continuing forward with his heroic descendants, including Sigmund and his son, Sigurð the dragon-slayer.*

[2]   *The gods Odin, Vili, and Ve*

[3]   *That is, "kites"—birds of prey related to hawks and eagles.*

[4]   *Múspellsheimr ("home of the world-breakers"), a realm of fire and home to the fire jötnar (giants)*

[5]   *Miðgarðr ("the middle enclosure"), or Earth, surrounded by the rest of the Nine Worlds in Norse cosmology; the home of humanity.*

second wit and will to move, the third face, hearing, speech, and eyesight. They gave them clothing and names; the man Ask and the woman Embla;[6] thence was mankind begotten, to whom an abode was given under Midgard. Then next Bor's sons made them a burg in the midst of the world, that is called Asgard;[7] there abode the gods and their kind, and wrought thence many tidings and feats, both on earth and in the Sky. Odin,[8] who is high Allfather, for that he is the father of all men and sat there in his high seat, seeing over the whole world and each man's doings, and knew all things that he saw. His wife was called Frigg, and their offspring is the Asa-stock, who dwell in Asgard and the realms about it, and all that stock are known to be gods.

The daughter and wife of Odin was Earth, and of her he got Thor, him followed strength and sturdiness, thereby quells he all things quick; the strongest of all gods and men, he has also three things of great price, the hammer Miolnir, the best of strength belts, and when he girds that about him waxes his god strength one-half, and his iron gloves that he may not miss for holding his hammer's haft. Balidr is Odin's second son, and of him it is good to say, he is fair and: bright in face, and hair, and body, and him all praise; he is wise and fair-spoken and mild, and that nature is in him none may withstand his doom. Tyr is daring and best of mood; there is a saw that he is *tyrstrong* who is before other men and never yields; he is also so wise that it is said he is *tyrlearned* who is wise. Bragi is famous for wisdom, and best in tongue-wit, and cunning speech, and song-craft. And many other are there, good and great; and one, Loki, fair of face, ill in temper and fickle of mood, is called the backbiter of the Asa, and speaker of evil redes and shame of all gods and men; he has above all that craft called sleight,[9] and cheats all in all things.

---

6   *Literally, "Ash" and "Elm," respectively. Many Germanic peoples found trees to be sacred—note the Donar's Oak of Hesse that was chopped down by Christian missionary Winfrið (aka "S. Boniface") in the 8th century.*

7   *Ásgarðr ("the enclosure of the Æsir," i.e.; the Norse gods)*

8   *Óðinn, the "wild god" of Norse myth who ruled Ásgarðr. He was a consummate shape-shifter who regularly assumed the aspect of wolves, birds, fish, etc., in order to roam Miðgarðr without being recognized. He was skilled at magic, and was renowned for his ability to traverse long distances using his special ship, Skíðblaðnir, or the Asbrú (the "bridge of the gods")—also sometimes called the Bifröst (the "shimmering path")—a "rainbow" portal that opened a corridor between Ásgarðr and the other Nine Worlds. For more information on Óðinn, see Snorri Sturluson's* Ynglinga Sögu *(1225), which also speaks of Óðinn's creation of the bear-shirted berserkir and wolfskin-clad úlfheðnar, both of which were used by King Haraldr Fairhair in the crucial Battle of Hafrsfjord in 872 (see Þórbiörn Hornklofi's* Haraldskvæði, *9th century).*

9   *That is, "magic"*

Among the children of Loki are Fenris-wolf[10] and Midgards-worm;[11] the second lies about all the world in the deep sea, holding his tail in his teeth, though some say Thor has slain him; but Fenris-wolf is bound until the doom of the gods, when gods and men shall come to an end, and earth and heaven be burnt, when he shall slay Odin. After this the earth shoots up from the sea, and it is green and fair, and the fields bear unsown, and gods and men shall be alive again, and sit in fair halls, and talk of old tales and the tidings that happened aforetime.

The head-seat, or holiest-stead, of the gods is at Yggdrasil's ash, which is of all trees best and biggest; its boughs are spread over the whole world and stand above heaven...

In the boughs of the ash sits an eagle, wise in much, and between his eyes sits the hawk Veðrfölnir; the squirrel Ratatoskr runs up and down along the ash, bearing words of hate betwixt the eagle and the worm. Those Norns who abide by the holy spring draw from it everyday water, and take the clay that lies around the well, and sprinkle them up over the ash for that its boughs should not wither or rot. All those men that have fallen in the fight, and borne wounds and toil unto death, from the beginning of the world, are come to Odin in Valhall;[12] a very great throng is there, and many more shall yet come; the flesh of the boar Sæhrímnir is sodden for them every day, and he is whole again at even; and the mead they drink that flows from the teats of the she-goat Heiðrún. The meat Odin has on his board he gives to his two wolves, Geri and Freki,[13] and he needs no meat, wine is to him both meat and drink; ravens twain sit on his shoulders, and say into his ear all tidings that they see and hear; they are called Huginn and Muninn;[14] them sends he at dawn to fly over the whole world, and they come back at breakfast-tide, thereby becomes he wise in many tidings, and for this men call him

---

[10] *Fenrisúlfr*

[11] *Jǫrmungandr ("world serpent"). The wolf and the serpent (or dragon) are often associated with one another in Norse mythology—particularly in connection with Ragnarøkkr, the "twilight of the gods," as world-slayers (see Jens Gundersson's 1999 study,* Odin: Myter og Sagn av Allfader*). The common enemy for this earth-bound wolf / dragon partnership is their uncle, Thor (Þórr), the Norse sky god who controlled thunder and storms.*

[12] *Valhöll ("hall of the dead"), where heroes who had been killed on the battlefield would be taken by the valkyrjur ("choosers of the slain"). It was not an afterlife for just anyone, but reserved only for those who were valr— who had died in combat.*

[13] *That is, "ravenous" and "greedy," respectively*

[14] *That is, "mind" and "memory," respectively. As Gundersson has noted (see* Odin: Myter og Sagn av Allfader, *1999), the ravens and the wolves were in constant competition, both for morsels and for Óðinn's affections. The ravens symbolized his wisdom and his desire for creation and order, while the wolves symbolized his strength and his desire for conquest and valour.*

Raven's-god. Every day, when they have clothed them, the heroes put on their arms and go out into the yard and fight and fell each other; that is their play, and when it looks toward mealtime, then ride they home to Valhall and sit down to drink. For murderers and men forsworn is a great hall, and a bad, and the doors look northward; it is altogether wrought of adder-backs like a wattled house,[15] but the worms' heads turn into the house, and blow venom, so that rivers of venom run along the hall, and in those rivers must such men wade forever...

from *Chapter VII*

Signý[16] brings forth a man-child, who was named Sinfjötli,[17] and when he grew up he was both big and strong, and fair of face, and much like unto the kin of the Völsungs, and he was hardly yet ten winters old when she sent him to Sigmund's earth-house; but this trial she had made of her other sons or ever she had sent them to Sigmund, that she had sewed gloves on to their hands through flesh and skin, and they had borne it ill and cried out thereat;[18] and this she now did to Sinfjötli, and he changed countenance in nowise thereat. Then she flayed off the kirtle[19] so that the skin came off with the sleeves, and said that this would be torment enough for him; but he said—"Full little would Völsung have felt such a smart this."

So the lad came to Sigmund, and Sigmund bade him knead their meal up, while he goes to fetch firing; so he gave him the meal-sack, and then went after the wood, and by then he came back had Sinfjötli made an end of his baking. Then asked Sigmund if he had found nothing in the meal. "I misdoubted me that there was something quick in the meal

---

15   *A house created by wattling, or intertwining twigs and sticks. As such, a "wattled house" might well remind an onlooker of a hibernaculum of intertwined snakes, or adders.*

16   *The daughter of Völsung, and sister to the Icelandic hero, Sigmund. Her evil husband, Siggeir (king of Gautland), murdered Völsung, and attempted to murder Sigmund and his brothers as well by allowing his own mother, a werewolf, to slay them in their sleep.*

17   *To all appearances, Sinfjötli would seem the son of King Siggeir. But in reality, Signý had disguised herself using "skin-changing" (using magic to adopt the appearance of another) and come to Sigmund in the night—thus, Sinfjötli is actually the result of their incest, not the son of Siggeir at all. But Sigmund remained unaware of this fact.*

18   *Signý was a harsh mother. When Sigmund had informed her that her elder two sons (conceived by Siggeir) were unworthy for him to train, she had ordered both of them slain.*

19   *A one-piece garment worn over a smock or under-shirt in the Middle Ages, under the surcoat or outer garment. It was also called a "tunic" or a "cotte," from which we get the modern English word, "coat."*

when I first fell to kneading of it, but I have kneaded it all up together, both the meal and that which was therein, whatsoever it was."

Then Sigmund laughed out, he said —"Naught wilt thou eat of this bread to-night, for the most deadly of worms[20] hast thou kneaded up therewith."

Now Sigmund was so mighty a man that he might eat venom and have no hurt therefrom; but Sinfjötli might abide whatso venom came on the outside of him, but might neither eat nor drink thereof.

The tale tells that Sigmund thought Sinfjötli over-young to help him to his revenge, and will first of all harden him with manly deeds; so in summertide they fare wide through the woods and slay men for their wealth; Sigmund deems him to take much after the kin of the Völsungs, though he thinks that he is Siggeir's son, and deems him to have the evil heart of his father, with the might and daring of the Völsungs; withal he must needs think him in no wise a kinsome man, for full oft would he bring Sigmund's wrongs to his memory, and prick him on to slay King Siggeir.

Now on a time as they fare abroad in the wood for the getting of wealth, they find a certain house, and two men with great gold rings asleep therein: now these twain were spell-bound skin-changers,[21] and wolf-skins were hanging up over them in the house; and every tenth day might they come out of those skins; and they were kings' sons: so

---

[20] *That is, serpents.*

[21] *Again, "skin-changers" were universally believed in once, in Iceland no less than elsewhere, as see Ari Þorgilsson in several places of his history,* Landnámabók, *(12th century), especially the episode of Dufthach (Irish, "Dubhthach") and Storwolf o' Whale. Men possessing the power of becoming wolves at intervals, in the present case compelled so to become werewolves or "loupsgarou," find large place in medieval story, but were equally well-known in classic times. Belief in them still lingers in parts of Europe where wolves are to be found. Herodotus (in his* Ἡροδότου Ἁλικαρνησσέος ἱστορίης, *5th century BC) tells of the Neuri, who assumed once a year the shape of wolves; Pliny (in his* Naturalis Historia, *1st century AD) says that one of the family of Antaeus, chosen by lot annually, became a wolf, and so remained for nine years; Giraldus Cambrensis (in his* Topographia Hibernica, *1188) will have it that Irishmen may become wolves; and Nennius (in his* Historia Brittonum, *830) asserts point-blank that "the descendants of wolves are still in Ossory;" they retransform themselves into wolves when they bite. Apuleius (in his* Metamorphoses, *2nd century), Petronius (in his* Satyricon, *1st century), and Lucian (in his* Ἀληθῆ διηγήματα, *2nd century) have similar stories. The Emperor Sigismund (who reigned over the Holy Roman Empire from 1433 to 1437) convoked a council of theologians in the fifteenth century (the Council of Basel) who decided that werewolves did exist. Dominican prior Johannes Nider wrote his classic treatise on witchcraft (The* Formicarius, *1435-1437) during this Council.*

Sigmund and Sinfjofli don the wolf-skins upon them,[22] and then might they nowise come out of them, though forsooth the same nature went with them as heretofore; they howled as wolves howl but both knew the meaning of that howling; they lay out in the wild-wood, and each went his way; and a word they made betwixt them, that they should risk the onset of seven men, but no more, and that he who was first to be set on should howl in wolfish wise: "Let us not depart from this," says Sigmund, "for thou art young and over-bold, and men will deem the quarry good, when they take thee."

Now each goes his way, and when they were parted, Sigmund meets certain men, and gives forth a wolf's howl; and when Sinfjötli heard it, he went straightway thereto, and slew them all, and once more they parted. But ere Sinfjötli has fared long through the woods, eleven men meet him, and he wrought in such wise that he slew them all, and was awearied therewith, and crawls under an oak, and there takes his rest. Then came Sigmund thither, and said—"Why didst thou not call on me?"

Sinfjötli said, "I was loath to call for thy help for the slaying of eleven men."

Then Sigmund rushed at him so hard that he staggered and fell, and Sigmund bit him in the throat. Now that day they might not come out of their wolf-skins: but Sigmund lays the other on his back, and bears him home to the house, and cursed the wolf-gears and gave them to the trolls. Now on a day he saw where two weasels went and how that one bit the other in the throat, and then ran straightway into the thicket, and took up a leaf and laid in on the wound, and thereon his fellow sprang up quite and clean whole; so Sigmund went out and saw a raven flying with a blade of that same herb to him; so he took it and drew it over Sinfjötli's hurt, and he straightway sprang up as whole as though he had never been hurt. There after they went home to their earth-house, and abode there till the time came for them to put off the wolfshapes; then they burnt them up with fire, and prayed that no more hurt might come to any one from them; but in that uncouth guise they wrought many famous deeds in the kingdom and lordship of King Siggeir.[23]

---

[22] *A common belief of the time was that by wearing the pelts of certain animals, the wearer mystically gained the attributes of that animal. See Verstegen's* classic A Restitution of Decayed Intelligence in Antiquities Concerning the Most Noble and Renowned English Nation *(1605) or Temme's* Die Volkssagen der Altmark *(1839) for later descriptions of the same belief. Temme elsewhere noted that such a skin-changing belt could also be made from the flesh of the back of a hanged man (see* Die Volkssagen von Pommern und Rügen, *1840).*

[23] *Seeing that the youth has the true mettle of the Völsungs, Sigmund allows him to aid in his revenge against Siggeir. Together, they set fire to Siggeir's*

hall, killing the king and Signý as well—who confesses her deception and incest at the end, clarifying Sinfjötli's true parentage.

Chapter 11
Cursed

I raced north on Damen toward Milwaukee, praying that somehow, Durant would get to Tony in time. But I couldn't help but do the math in my head. How fast *was* Durant? Even if he could do, like 60 miles per hour, it would still take him at least seven minutes to get there. Did Tony even *have* seven minutes? I started to put a call in to the District 17 station, but I couldn't get past what Tony said—if any more beat cops came onto the scene, all that they'd end up being is at best a distraction, and at worst, *hors d'oeuvres*.

My adrenaline was raging and my heart was pumping a mile a minute, and I was shocked to hear my stomach growling. I just ate three tacos not two minutes earlier—how could I still be hungry? I slurped down the last bit of my drink and tried to focus on the road. But it was so difficult to do. Anger and fear and worry all rose up in me so hard that I could barely think.

Everything seemed like it was all moving in slow motion. The other cars, the pedestrians on the sidewalks, the traffic lights. The cityscape passed by me leisurely, and bizarrely clearly—like one of those commercials filmed in high resolution, with the action filmed in slow motion. Everything around me was clear, and sharp, and agonizingly slow.

My stomach growled again, and that began to annoy me as well. The whole world became an annoyance, a hurdle to get past. I turned onto Milwaukee, and it seemed like Tony was still a whole world away still. More growling—but this time, I noticed something.

It wasn't my stomach growling—it was *me*. The sound wasn't coming from my belly, but from the back of my throat. Instinctively, in my anger and frustration, I was growling. I'd never done that before, but it'd seemed so natural that I hadn't even realized that I was doing it.

And that's when I had a horrible thought. All this time, I'd been thinking that Lyn was cursed because she'd been *bitten*, but that I was okay because I'd only been *slashed*. But Durant had told me time and again that there are more ways to get infected than just by a bite. The pieces fell together...

The doctors had said that it was a miracle that I hadn't been hurt more than I was, that there was no internal damage. But I remembered what I saw, as I lay there on Bunin's floor—I knew that I was hurt worse there than I was when I woke up in the hospital. I mean, the thing nearly ripped me in half, and I thought that it had broken my right hand, and I *knew* that it had broken some ribs, but I hadn't felt any pain of any kind in days. Thinking about it, I'd been running all over Chicago, and my body didn't even ache. In fact, I felt better than I had in years. I reached down and touched my side, but I couldn't even feel where the scratches had been. I looked in the rearview mirror, but there were no scratches on my forehead. Everything had healed up completely.

I suddenly realized that I hadn't been paying attention to the road at all, and I angrily tried to focus again. The more I thought about it, the more I realized how angry, how aggressive I'd been getting lately, too. This isn't what I wanted to be doing—this isn't *who* I wanted to *become*. I had to try to keep my head together, keep in the game, in the moment.

Again, I looked out at the road. It's hard to explain, but the lights seemed not only brighter, but sharper. All of the colors seemed more saturated, more intense. I rolled down my window, and I smelled a thousand different smells at once—but I realized that I could smell them *all*. It wasn't just a big clump of odors, but rather a collection of clearly distinct scents. It was intoxicating.

But that's when I also picked up that now-familiar scent of almonds.

I pulled the car into the first parking lot I could find, and parked between a Tanning Center and a UPS Store. I jumped out of the car and took in a deep breath through my nose. The smell of almonds was everywhere, with nothing around that should have made that scent. I heard myself growling again, and this time, I gave it free reign. A woman and her little girl were just stepping out of Kriser's next door, but when she heard me, her face went white, and she grabbed her child and ran back into the store.

"What's with the stupid almonds?" I bellowed, but there was no answer in sight. The sights, the sounds, the colors, the smells— everything was suddenly overwhelming. So I got back into my car, rolled up the window, closed my eyes, and tried to get a grip. I prayed again, but this time, I prayed for myself instead of Tony. I prayed that somehow, I could control this, get on top of it.

I started thinking about just focusing on the inside of my car. Let all of the other sounds fall away, and just focus on my own space, my own breathing, the beat of my own heart. I could smell the taco wrappers, the sweet residues in my drink cup, the sweat soaking my shirt, the faintest remnants of Durant's cologne. I hadn't even realized that he'd worn cologne—but knowing him, of *course* he did. It smelled fairly expensive, too, though he'd applied it only lightly. But then, I also smelled echoes of the Five Star Bar, and even Georgiy Chernomyrdin's *ciorbe de burta.*

I was starting to get lost in it all, so I tried a different tactic. I didn't focus on any smells at all. Instead, I breathed through my mouth, kept my eyes closed, and just tried to focus on the sound of my own breaths, and nothing else. I could still taste things in my mouth, but it did help lessen the sensory overload. After a few minutes, I was able to open my eyes and try to process my surroundings in a healthier, more controlled way. Everything still seemed unusually clear to me—and yet strangely flat. That took me a second to figure out, until I realized that I was seeing through the shadows. I could tell that it was dark between the buildings, in the alleys, etc., but I could see so clearly through it that the normal high contrast of a city night just wasn't there—I could see all of the details far too well for that.

And still, that scent of almonds remained. I looked around me—carefully—to see what the source could be. All I saw were moving cars, shopfronts, the cleaners across the street—nothing out of the ordinary. But then, on the corner of Wabansia, across from the library, I saw a strange-looking woman. I normally wouldn't have looked twice at her, but since I was looking for weirdness, she stood out. She was dressed all in black, with a lot of straps and studs and fishnetting for accents. Her hair was obviously dyed black, and she was wearing heavy black eyeliner—basically, a classic Goth. But the woman was probably in her later forties or so, which was a little too old for that look to work. And, more to the point, she was looking straight at me.

We watched each other, and I kept telling myself that this could've been anything. She could've been thinking that *I'm* the one who looked odd, growling like I did. She could've been admiring my car. Who knows? I didn't want to jump to any conclusions, so I just watched her for a while. After about a minute, I decided to check her out. I opened my door and got out to walk over to her. Suddenly, the scent of almonds was so strong that I actually coughed, gagging on it a little. When I looked back at the intersection, the woman was gone.

And so, incidentally, was the smell of almonds.

*   *   *

By the time that I arrived at the intersection of Addison and Milwaukee, about twenty minutes had passed since Tony's phone call. I turned at the Alco building—which looked a lot like Little Bucharest, now that I'd seen them both on the same day—and started scouring the street. Now, there weren't *that* many abandoned buildings to check out along Addison, so it didn't take long to find one with a door smashed open in that characteristic Durant manner. I parked, drew my pistol, and started inside. Yes, I knew that the pistol probably wouldn't help much, but it was a trained reflex.

It was pitch black inside, and yet, I found that I could still see the carnage pretty well. More than anything else, I just lost the *colors* of things. I recalled from high school science class how you have both rods and cones in your retinas that act as photoreceptors, drinking in the images that your corneas and lenses let in. If I remember right, the rods are good with shapes, and can operate in even dimmer light, while the cones are good with color, and can only operate well in brighter light. Judging from how intense all the colors had seemed out on the street, but how well I could still see in this building, I figured that somehow, the Lycaon virus was pumping up the ability of both the rods and the cones in my eyes, but that still didn't make the cones work any better in low light conditions. So physics was still acting like physics, I guess—even in this light, I could see the body parts.

From what I was able to piece together later on, this appears to be what had happened...

*   *   *

Tony was lost in the dark, swinging away at the absolutely nothing that he could see with the Matteh ha Shelomoh, with the vain hopes that if Lyn *did* attack him, he might get in a lucky hit—or at least, hold her at bay until he could find another way out. He called me and I told him to hold on until Durant got there, but both he and I knew that the chances of Durant getting there in time were fairly slim at best. That's when he heard something moving across the room from him, and he dropped the phone to get both of his hands onto the staff.

"Carolyn?" he called out, but no one answered him. He continued to hear something moving across from him—something fairly big.

Knowing that whatever was in there with him was in front of him, he backed up until he bumped up against a wall. Then he started making his way along the wall, feeling for windows or another door that he could use with his left hand. But all he felt was bricks, or the occasional outlet. He did find a light switch and tried it, but there was no power in the building. Whatever was in front of him began to growl, low and quietly.

"Good doggie..." he said, finding the corner of the room. "Nice doggie..."

I don't know if you've ever been in a situation where you were completely—*completely*—in the dark, but it's terrifying. Maybe you've been out on a dark night, or you've been in a basement with the lights off—but usually, there's at least a *little* light to work with, some tiny bit of illumination that helps you at least see some shapes, or to orient yourself in some way. But if it's completely dark—I mean, *pitch* black, like you've got a bag over your head—then after a little while, it can be hard to even tell which way is up and which way is down. That's why it works so well for military interrogators to keep that bag over someone's head when they're questioning them—it's so disorienting that a guy can lose all of his senses, including even a sense of himself.

I say that to emphasize how important it was that Tony kept his head. He didn't panic, and he didn't do anything stupid. He knew that he was totally lost, that he didn't know anything about his surroundings, and that something very, very bad was in the room with him, but he still kept it together enough to keep moving, to keep looking for a way out. For a second, he considered staying in the corner and making his stand there—at least that way, he'd know which direction any attack would have to come from. But then he had the presence of mind to realize that he'd never survive a holding action in the dark against a werewolf. Even if he could miraculously hold out against the first attack or two, all it would take would be for her to get through just once, and it would all be over. So he chose to keep moving along the wall, and keep the growling thing in front of him.

But instead of finding a door, he found that the wall came to another corner—but whether it was a hallway or just an alcove was impossible to tell. He was suddenly awash with conflicting feelings. Yes, this could be a way out; but it also meant turning away from the growl and opening himself up to attack from any one of a bunch of different angles. He had no choice but to follow the wall, but he still didn't like the option.

As he turned the corner, he heard something else—a murmur, almost like a purring, but definitely a human female's voice. It was coming from the same direction as the growls.

"Carolyn?" he asked again, trying to reach her with his words. "Carolyn, this ain't you. Ya gotta try an' fight it, girl!" But the murmur just shifted into a low giggle in response. Something big shifted toward him from the center of the room. With one quick move, the thing was in front of him. It smelled like a wet dog, and he could hear it breathing.

"Tony…?" he heard Lyn's voice whispering.

"Carolyn!" he answered. "Good girl!"

"Tony…" she said again, and he heard her giggle once more. "I don't *want* to fight it…"

He started swinging the Matteh ha Shelomoh in front of him as fast as he could, and he heard her giggle louder. The big thing in front of him stopped moving, and he lost track of exactly where it was. The giggle stopped, and Tony held his breath for what was coming next.

Suddenly, he heard a crashing noise from the room behind him, and the thing in front of him growled—almost barked in reply. He heard the ignition of a flare, and the room was abruptly bathed with light. For a single instant, before he was blinded, he saw in front of him two shapes in the hallway—one was a huge, wolf-like creature that matched the thing that he'd seen at Bunin's house, and the other was a tall, half-human shape that looked decidedly feminine. Out of the corner of his eye, he saw a blur of movement and a flash of silver, and then he couldn't see anything for a few seconds.

But he heard the growling of the great beast and the screeching of Lyn's voice, and he heard the thundering voice of Pieter Durant and the metallic slashing sound of his sword. The werewolf brushed past him, flying toward Durant, but he heard the sword again as it sliced through the air and hit flesh. The wolf howled in pain, whimpered, and then was silent. In front of him, he heard Lyn let out a low growl and then scamper off.

It was all over in a matter of seconds. By the time Tony could see again, Durant was cleaning his blade as he stood over the body of the dead wolf. Its head was lying on the ground nearby.

"Y-Ya made good time..." Tony said, his voice trembling. Durant sighed.

"And ruined my favorite shoes in the process..."

As they watched, the caramel-colored wolf began to change its shape, slowly melting into the form of a human being. Within a minute, the slender shape of a man, covered in tattoos, was clearly visible. The long, greasy blonde hair on the head identified him immediately as the Russian whose arm Durant had so casually broken only an hour earlier.

"That... ain't Bunin..." Tony said, scratching his head.

"Evidently not, Detective de Tullio," Durant replied.

*   *   *

So when I walked into the building, I found the body on the floor, right where they'd left it. I figured that it was a good sign to see the spent flare and a dead Russian instead of pieces of a dead Tony, but then I got to thinking about it a bit harder. Yes, that meant that Durant had gotten there, and yes, he'd obviously killed this guy—I'd recognize the clean slice of that blade of his anywhere. The fact that the guy was naked suggested that he'd probably been in wolf form when Durant had killed him—I didn't figure that the guy would just strip out of his sweater and attack Durant in the nude. But that meant that we were dealing with more werewolves than I'd originally anticipated. We knew about Bunin, and we were concerned about Lyn, but now there was this guy, too. How many others were out there? How many more in this pack?

Tony's cell phone was lying on the floor near the smashed door, so I picked it up and pocketed it to give to him later. Again, I did it as a reflex, but I had to chuckle at myself that seeing a dead, naked *Bratva* thug would suddenly give me such confidence that I'd soon see Tony and Durant alive and well. I called out to them, but didn't get a response, so I kept moving deeper into the building. I found the hallway, and it looked dark and undisturbed to the left, but there was a little light coming from the right—so, of course, I went to the right.

After a couple of twists and turns, I saw light coming from under a door. I called to Tony again, and heard his familiar voice call back, "In here!" from inside the room. I opened the door, but I still wasn't prepared for what I saw there.

The place was an abattoir, strewn with bones and bloody body parts. The stench was—well, it was overpowering. There were Tony and Durant, standing there in the middle of the room, with a lantern on the table, giving some eerie light to the scene. My first thought was that this was the werewolves' den, but Tony quickly disabused me of that idea.

"See this guy?" he said, pointing to a body that looked fresh but horribly torn. "This guy's who we seen her walk in here with. An' this one?" he pointed to another, bloody but more intact. "This guy matches the description we got at Crabby Kim's. This guy over here…" he said, stepping over a severed arm to point to a corpse that had been ripped apart into pieces. "That's our beat cop." Looking more carefully, I could see the shreds of a uniform, as well as his badge, shining in the lantern light.

"And over here…" Durant said, pointing to the corner of the room. I looked, and there wasn't much left of the body, but I could make out a leg and the ribcage, and half of his face. It was Ben Bucher's body.

This wasn't the pack's den—this was just *Lyn's* killing floor.

"B-But…" I started, but I couldn't bring myself to finish the sentence. Luckily, the two of them had had several minutes to let it all sink in.

"She's been killin' 'em all day long, Tom," Tony said. "I'd figure Bucher's been dead since sometime this mornin', an' this beat cop since maybe noon…" I turned to look at Durant.

"But I thought you said that she wouldn't transform until sundown!" I barked at him. "Or later than that, since it'd be her first time." He sighed.

"I wish I knew more about this species of werewolf," he said, mostly to himself. "Perhaps I should consult—"

"You said we'd have time before she changed!" I yelled at him again, and I grabbed him by the scruff of his collar. Yes, I grabbed Pieter Durant in anger, before I even realized what I was doing. His eyes flashed at me for a moment, and then they went cold again.

"I spoke in terms of probabilities, Detective," he said to me quietly, with a cold precision that made my blood freeze. "The only certainty I mentioned was that she would change, and that you should have destroyed her when you'd had the chance. These men are dead because of you and your choices. Live with that..." He took my hands and pulled them off of his coat with ease, brushing his collar down and smoothing out his suit. I looked over at Tony, who just held his arm and looked ashamed.

"Tom," he said at last. "Near as I can figure, she *didn't* change until jus' a few minutes ago. This last guy, he's all torn up with claws an' such. But these first ones?" He looked back at the bodies, lying in bloody piles on the floor. "These was done by hand. An' I'd haveta check with Bill Saunders about this, but them bite marks on Bucher's bones don't look like wolf bites to me. Look at that bite radius, Tom..."

I did, and I had to admit, they looked human-sized. But that just made everything all the more unsettling. That meant that Tony was right—that Lyn had been stalking men, killing them, and then devouring their bodies, all day long—but she'd been doing so as a human being.

"B-But why did she keep killing them?" I asked at last. "I mean, she still had plenty of..." I looked at the flesh on the bones of the bodies. "Why kill more than she was going to eat?"

"Because it was not about the feasting to her, Detective," Durant answered. "It was about the hunt, and about the kill. She murdered these men because she *wished* to do so..." His face contorted into a mask of anger and disgust. "Because she took a great and unholy pleasure in the slaughter..."

We searched the whole building for a while, but the one body that I didn't see was that of Leah Wheaton. I didn't realize it then, but that was going to come up soon enough.

*   *   *

I finally realized that Tony was holding his arm because it had gotten broken when the Russian had passed him in the hallway on his way to attack Durant. The nearest emergency room that I knew of was across Roscoe Village, over in Lake View, so we called the scene in, gave them a description of Lyn, and took Tony over there. We left everything pretty much intact—Lyn met all of the criteria for being a serial killer, and almost nothing in the building would give the cops any other ideas than that. But before we left the building, Durant placed the Russian's head on his body, and pulled a little flask from his *got uechan*—the little leather pouch that he wore at his side, under his jacket. He poured the contents of the flask onto the body, and then carefully placed it back into the pouch. Then he lit a match and tossed it onto the remains. Immediately, the body was consumed with intensely hot, blue flames. Within a few more seconds, there was nothing left there at all. Between Tony's notes from the various bars about who Lyn left with, matching up with the descriptions of these guys in the building, I figured that that part would be pretty simple to explain. A decapitated *Bratva krysha* lying naked in another room? That would've been a little bit more complicated.

So we drove off to get Tony to the hospital, and two things happened that I should probably mention here. First, I commented to Durant about the woman who'd been watching me from the intersection, and he asked if I'd seen any other suspicious people lately. Suddenly, I remembered Miska's.

"There was this old woman this morning at the deli," I said. "A Native American woman. Meskwaki, I think. She kept talking about something called the 'Manetôwa,' if that means anything."

"The dragon…" he muttered.

"Yeah," I replied. "She called it a 'serpent being,' so I guess that a dragon is close enough. And then she told me about Wisaka the Châki-ôtha and his crows and the creation of the world…"

"She called Wisaka the 'Châki-ôtha'?" he interjected. "Are you certain of this?"

"Yeah. What does that mean?"

"It means, 'Allfather,' Detective," he explained. "She was mixing Wisaka with Odin."

"Like, the Viking god Odin?" I asked. "But she's Native American. This old woman was no more Scandinavian than I am."

"She was Synod of Crows," he explained. "Undoubtedly both women were. And, gauging from what you said about the second one, she was perhaps a *wælcyrge*, waiting to see what would happen to you."

"A what?" I asked.

"The *wælcyrie* are Odin's agents, sent to watch warriors and to collect their corpses from the battlefield in order to take them back through the *Asbrú* to *Valhöll*."

"You're losing me again."

"The *Asbrú* is a quantum tunnel," he explained. "A bridge from one place to another in space and time. The ancients used them frequently, and Odin in particular was known to make use of one to move from his realm to our own plane. The Norse called it the '*Bifröst*,' or the Rainbow Bridge—"

"I saw the movie," I said, nodding my head. "Got it. So *Valhöll* is some kind of Viking version of Heaven?"

"According to myth, a place of constant drinking, fighting, and whoring," he explained. "Although I should think that the reality of it is something quite altogether unpleasantly different…" He didn't continue that thought, and I think that I'm glad that he didn't. Instead, he went back to answering my original question. "The Synod have to know about us by now, realizing that we are involved and undoubtedly wondering which way we shall end up falling. But you must understand that whether we speak of Native Americans or the Norse, or the Chinese, or the Zulu, the magicks which they wield are all ultimately stemming from the same source. When one speaks of supernatural power, one must remember that it comes only from God... or *not* from God..."

"Then what's with the whole almonds thing?" I asked, trying to piece it all together.

"When they use their powers, it is not uncommon for the atmosphere to be—" but then, he stopped himself. He turned to look at me with a deep frown crinkling his brow. "You *smelt* the almonds?" he asked quite soberly.

"Yeah," I answered. "Why?"

"Because very few normal human are able to do so..." he answered. He sat and looked at me very, very carefully for a while, and it made me uncomfortable. Part of me wanted to say something, but another part of me was screaming that I should just keep my mouth shut. For good or for ill, Tony broke the awkward silence.

"Guys," he said, "I don't wanna go ta the hospital. I just wanna go home."

"You've got a broken arm," I said, appreciating having something else to talk about. "You're going to the hospital, Tony."

"Maybe it ain't broke," he replied. "Maybe it just got bruised or somethin'."

"It's not bruised," I said. "It's broken, and you're getting it taken care of."

"I don't wanna go ta no hospital, okay?" He was getting pretty adamant back there.

"What, are you afraid they're going to tell you that your arm broke because of your elbow cancer?" I joked, trying to lighten the mood. Tony just sat there in silence. Funny that *that's* what made Durant finally stop looking at me and turn to look at him.

"We should let the man go home, Detective," he said at last.

"No," I said. "He's just being a big baby. We'll be there in a few minutes, and then out of there in an hour, tops. He just doesn't like hospitals, that's all."

"I believe that he has his reasons..." Durant replied. And he turned to face forward, gazing out of the window with a sad, tired look on his face.

"What's going on?" I asked Tony. "What's up?" I glanced at Tony through the rearview mirror, and he just looked uncomfortable. At first, I'd thought it was because his arm hurt, but now I was realizing that it was something else entirely. "Seriously, Tony," I asked again. "What's going on?"

He took a deep breath, and then he let it out slowly.

"It ain't elbow cancer, Tom," he said at last. "It's *lung* cancer…"

Background
From *Daemonolatreiae Libri Tres* (Nicolas Rémy, 1595, trans. M. Summers)

from *Book I, Chapter II*

*How Demons prepare, for those whom they have won by
their Cunning, Drugged Powders,[1] Wands, Ointments and
Various Venoms of the sort: some of which cause Death,
some only Sickness, and some even Healing. And how
these things are not always, or for all Men, poisonous:
since there may be found some who are uninjured by
frequent Applications of them, notably they whose Office
and Business it is to condemn Witches to Death.*

From the very beginning the Devil was a murderer,[2] and never has he ceased to tempt the impious to commit slaughter and parricide. Therefore it is no wonder that, once he has caught men in his toils, his first care is to furnish them with the implements and instruct them in the

---

[1] *It was widely believed that witches spread plague and pestilence by means of these diabolical powders—often made from ground-up human bones (as in the case of the Chinese sorcerors' lónggǔ, Romanian vrãjitorie's oase rău, Navajo shaman's 'áńt'į, etc.). During the visitation of sickness at Milan in 1598, it was popularly held that a band of sorcerers had engaged themselves to disseminate the disease. For the same reason, the plague of Milan in 1629-30 was known as "La Peste degli Untori" ("The Plague of the Plaguebearers"). These wretches daubed walls, doors, and furniture with some purulent matter, and they also scattered magic powders in a circle up and down the streets. To set foot in one of these meant certain destruction. See* Geography of Witchcraft *(1927, Montague Summers), pp. 559-562. See also* An Examen of Witches *(1602, Henri Boguet), chapter xxiii, "Of the Powder Used by Witches."*

[2] *"Ye are of your father the devil, and the lusts of your father ye will do. He was a murderer from the beginning, and abode not in the truth, because there is no truth in him. When he speaketh a lie, he speaketh of his own: for he is a liar, and the father of it" (Jesus Christ speaking to the Jewish leaders in the* Gospel of St. John, *viii, 44).*

practices of witchcraft. And lest the business should be delayed or hindered through lack of poison or difficulty in administering it, he provides them at the very first with a fine powder which must infallibly cause the sickness or death of those against whom it is used: nor does its harmfulness of necessity depend upon its being mingled with a man's food or drink, or applied to his bare flesh; for it is enough if but his clothes be lightly dusted with it. The powder which kills is black; that which only causes sickness is ashen, or sometimes reddish in colour. And since witches are often led by fear or bribery, and sometimes even by pity (of which they claim that they are not entirely destitute), to heal those who have been stricken in this manner, they are not without a remedy to their hand; for they are given a third powder, white in colour, with which they dust the sick, or mix it with their food or drink, and so the sickness is dispersed. And these drugs of varying properties and virtue are distinguishable only by their colour. Claude Fellet (at Mazières, 9th Nov., 1584), Jeanne le Ban (at Masmunster, 3rd Jan., 1585), Colette Fischer (at Gerbeville, 7th May, 1585), and nearly all the women of their fellowship, record that they always found the effects of their powders such as we have said. But this distinction in colours is not so much to ensure the selection of the required poison (for the drugs owe their potency to the Demon, not to any inherent properties of their own), as a visible sign of the pact[3] between the witch and the Demon, and a guarantee of faith. Matteole Guilleraea (at Mazières, 4th Dec., 1584), and Jeanne Alberte (at S. Pierre-Mont, 8th Nov., 1581) add that although the ashen-coloured powder does not as a rule cause a fatal sickness, it has nevertheless the power to kill when it is first received by witches after their enlistment in that army of wickedness; for that initial step has a kind of preference.

But it is a matter of no small wonder that witches not only impregnate with such poisons articles of which the purpose and use is to drive away Demons, but even make use of them during the very time of prayer and the performance of the Sacraments. At Seaulx, 11th Oct., 1587, Jacobeta Weher was envious of the lover of the daughter of her fellow-countryman Pétrone, but could not injure her as she wished; for the girl had emphatically bidden her beware of trying to harm her. But at last, under pretext of doing something else, she infected an asperge[4] with the poison powder and sprinkled the girl with it as she was praying in the church: and at once she was stricken with a mortal sickness and soon

---

3   *"Le Pacte"—the same word is used a century later by the Comte d'Erlette to describe the six-fold* Pacte de le Danse *which governs the vampyre society in his own* Cultes des Goules *(1702, François-Honore Balfour, Comte d'Erlette).*

4   *A device used to sprinkle holy water on a congregation within a church service.*

after died. At Blainville, 16th Jan., 1587, the whole neighbourhood, except Alexée Belheure, had been invited to a feast given by a noble knight named Darnielle on the occasion of his son's baptism.   Ill brooking this slight, she evaded the observation of those who were carrying the newly baptized child and, sprinkling it with a poison powder of this kind, killed it.

And since it is not convenient for them always to keep this powder ready in their hand to throw, they have also wands imbued with it or smeared with some unguent or other venomous matter, which they commonly carry as if for driving cattle. With these they often, as it were in joke, strike the men or the cattle which they wish to injure: and that this is no vain or innocent touch is testified by the confessions of François Fellet (at Mazières, 19th Dec., 1583), Marguereta Warner (at Ronchamp, 1st Dec., 1586), Matteole Guilleret (at Pagny-sur-Moselle, 1584), and Jacobeta Weher whom I have just mentioned.

Yet there are those who, thanks to some singular blessing from Heaven, are immune from such attacks;[5] for witches have not always unlimited power against all men, and Jeanne Gransaint (at Condé-sur-l'Escaut, July, 1582) and Catharina Ruffe (at Ville-sur-Moselle, 28th July, 1587) have recorded that they were more than once informed by their Demons. I remember questioning that woman of Nancy called Lasnier (Asinaria), from her husband the ass-driver, upon the statements of the witnesses, and especially concerning this particular point; and she spoke with great indignation as follows: "It is well for you Judges that we can do nothing against you! For there are none upon whom we would more gladly work our spite than you who are always harrying us folk with every torture and punishment." Jaqueline Xaluētia (at Grand-Bouxières-sous-Amance, 29th April, 1588), freely and without any previous questioning, acknowledged the same. This woman, having long been suspected of witchcraft, was put in chains; but after a little she was liberated by order of the Judge, because she had endured all of the tortured of her questioning in an obstinate silence. After much turning of the matter over in her mind, she could not rest until she had worked some evil upon the Judge who had treated her with such severity; for the filthy rabble of witches is commonly desirous of revenge. Therefore she ceased not to pester her Demon to find some safe and easy way for her to

---

[5]   *King James I in his* Dæmonologie *(1597), Second Book, chapter vi, discusses what power witches may have to harm the Magistrate. "If he be slouthfull towards them, God is verie able to make them instruments to waken and punish his slouth." But if he is diligent in examining and punishing of them: "God will not permit their master to trouble or hinder so good a woorke... For where God beginnes justlie to strike by his lawfull Lieutennentes, it is not in the Devilles power to defraude or bereave him of the office, or effect of his powerfull and revenging Scepter."*

vent her spite: but he, knowing her folly towards herself in this matter, kept pleading different excuses for postponing the affair and inventing reasons why he should not comply with her wish. But at length, since Xaluētia did not cease to importune him, he told her in shame and grief that, in place of that fortune which he had often foretold for her, her own folly and impotence would be exposed and would betray her. "I have always, my Xaluētia," he said, "endured very hardly the unbridled severity of those executioners towards you, and often in the past have I had a mind to be revenged: but I openly admit that all my attempts come to nothing. For they are in His guardianship and protection who alone can oppose my designs. But I can repay those officers for their persecutions by causing them to share in a common disaster, and will strike the crops and fields far and wide with a tempest and lay them waste as much as I am able."

This is not unlike the statement of Nicole Morèle (at Serre, 24th Jan., 1587), that Demons are impregnated and seared with an especial hatred towards those who put into operation the law against witches, but that it is in vain that they attempt to seek to wreak any vengeance against them. See how God defends and protects the authority of those to whom He has given the mandate of His power upon earth, and how He has therefore made them partakers of His prerogative and honour, calling them Gods even as Himself,[6] so that without doubt they are sacrosanct and, by reason of their duty and their office, invulnerable even to the spells of witches. Indeed they are not even bound in the least by the commands of the Demons themselves, even though they may have previously vowed allegiance to them and have been touched with the stain of that oath.

---

[6]   *"I have said, Ye are gods; and all of you are children of the most High," cited from* Psalm lxxxii, 6. *Rémy here takes this verse completely out of context in order to interpret its meaning as saying that those who serve God as His holy clerics tacitly become gods themselves, and thus, are untouchable by evil. This is an inherently dangerous supposition to make, especially for those who would presume to be leaders or spiritual warriors against the Devil—note such verses of warning as* James iii, 1, *or* Galatians i, 1, *which instruct leaders to be on their guard as well, since they, too, are subject to the same temptations and weaknesses as everyone else.*

Chapter 12
You Can't Go Home Again

I suppose it was inevitable. I mean, it's human physics, right? You eat too much fried food, you can have heart problems. You eat too much candy, you can get fat. You smoke too many cigarettes, you can develop lung cancer. Tony was a candy-eating, chain-smoking, fried food junkie, so it really shouldn't have come as a surprise to me that he might have some health problems. And yet, I was still somehow totally floored when I heard about it.

You always think that the people you love are going to more or less go on forever. I mean, you *know* that they won't, but you still live as if you just kind of *assume* that they will. Or maybe, it's just too scary to think about, so you block it out of your mind and pretend that you won't have to deal with it. I dunno. All I know is that somehow, I never expected to lose Tony to cancer. I was more or less prepared for one of us to take a bullet or something one of these days, but I never thought that I might have to stand by and watch him get sick.

I ended up staying with Tony while the doctor checked him out. It turned out that he only had a hairline fracture of the radial bone, but it still needed to be immobilized, so I'm glad that I pressed the issue. I started bringing up the subject of his cancer a couple of times, but he refused to talk about it. As you can imagine, that made for a very long and awkward stint in the emergency room, with long periods of uncomfortable silence, consciously not talking about the elephant in the room.

Durant left after a few minutes to go back to the scene. Part of that was because he had no desire to sit with us at the hospital, but it was mostly because we realized that someone really should be there to walk the investigating officers through what had happened so that they pieced it together the way that we wanted them to. With his Interpol credentials, Durant could jump in and out of potentially complicated questions as he saw fit. To be honest, he also seemed to be uncomfortable being in the same room with me.

I think that he suspected something, but he wasn't ready to say anything yet if I wasn't. I guess that if you've been tracking monsters for that many centuries, you might begin to develop kind of a "sixth sense" about when something is... *off.* I knew that I should tell him what was going on—I really did want to tell him—but again, I have to confess something here: it was all so *amazing.* Like I said before, it was like someone cranked the saturation up on the whole world. Colors kept getting brighter, the contrast kept getting sharper, smells kept getting clearer and more obvious—not in a bad way, but like I could discern all the different smells as well as I could discern different colors. As I walked Tony out to the car, I felt like I was drowning in all of the different sensations, and yet, I've gotta tell ya—I *loved* it.

You know how you're not usually that much aware of smells until something either really good or really bad hits your nostrils? The truth is, you're probably smelling more things than you realize—you're just processing all of those smells on a subconscious level and deciding that most of them are irrelevant to your everyday life. But now, think of when you've tried to smell your favorite food at a restaurant to try to figure out what all was in it. You smelled the oregano, the garlic, the onion, the hint of white wine in the sauce, yadda yadda. You took the time to try to break it all down and separate the various scents in your mind. *Now* picture doing that *all* of the time, with *everything*—without having to concentrate on it.

Instead of just seeing a red car and a blue van, I could smell which one of them was burning more oil. Instead of just seeing a young businessman and a middle-aged woman on the sidewalk, I could smell that he was trying cover up her scent on him with his cologne. I could actually tell that he'd put on cologne, been with her, and then put on more cologne afterwards—I could smell the layers of scents as easily as I could see the layers of his clothing. He'd also snorted cocaine in that suit before, but not today...

But it wasn't just that. When I went to help Tony into the car, he was as light as a feather to me. The guy outweighed me by a hundred pounds, but he felt like he weighed less than Chelsea. I felt strong, and energized, and *healthy.* Don't get me wrong—I knew full well that I was sick, and that I'd have to come up with some way of dealing with all of this before things got out of hand—but I could totally see why Lyn enjoyed this sensation so much. You feel like you're on top of the world, like nothing can stop you, and it feels so good that you never really want it to stop. I'd never been high, but I had to think that it would've felt a lot like this.

Then again, maybe not. When you're on something, your brain tends to get shifted over into the passenger seat, and you're not really in control of yourself or of the situation. But I had total control. In fact, I felt like I had more mental processing power and more physical control over myself than I'd ever had before. While I was driving, I knew exactly how much pressure to put on the gas pedal. I knew exactly how long it would take the car to stop when pressing the brake. I could feel the rhythms of the traffic, and I knew just how and when to dart and weave my way through the other cars to get Tony home as quickly and easily as possible. He left the Matteh ha Shelomoh in my back seat, since he obviously wasn't going to be up to swinging it for a while, and went inside. I honestly couldn't think of anything to say to him, so I just drove myself back home.

When I walked into my own house, the explosion of smells shocked me all over again. I don't mean that in a bad way—it wasn't an unpleasant thing, because all of the smells reminded me of the things that I loved. I could tell where the children had been playing and how long ago by the echoes of odors that they'd left behind them. I could smell last night's dinner—the meals for the last week, if I'm being honest—and the scents triggered my taste buds so that I could actually taste the meals again as I smelled them. But even then, I realized that I could taste not just the chicken burritos, but *every part* of the chicken burritos, every layer of flavor that went into them. I realized that they'd been too salty, with not enough cayenne pepper and the wrong kind of chili powder. And I could taste the medicinal tang of a preservative in the background. I decided that that would be the last time that we would make chicken burritos using seasonings that we'd gotten out of a pouch.

And when I saw Joanna sleeping in our bed, it was a profound moment. She was more beautiful than I'd ever seen her before, and drinking her all in was intoxicating. Things that I'd always found attractive were now riveting my attention—the arch of her eyebrow, the subtle kaleidoscope of colors in her hair, the curve of her neck into her shoulders, etc. Then again, I also noticed every flaw that I'd previously ignored, either consciously or unconsciously. I saw the crow's feet growing at the edge of her eyes, the slightest blotchiness to her skin tone, the pores on the tip of her nose that needed better cleaning, etc.

But the *smell*…! A week before, I would have said that she smelled good if she had just gotten out of the shower, or if she was wearing that really nice perfume that I got for her last Valentine's Day—you know, if she'd smelled clean or fresh. But now, *her* smell, the natural scent that her body gave off was what was drawing me in. I realized that her scent was on everything in the place—on the chairs, the walls, the telephone, my clothes, the children. Smelling her laying there in front of me was like being reminded of the complete personification of everything good in my little encapsulated world of *home*. Even the faint residue of sweat on her clothing was erotic. It was all that I could do not to rush in, grab her, and maul her with kisses the moment that I saw her, but with Flubber there, growling at me, I restrained myself.

I should mention something about Flubber here. He hadn't come to meet me, like he always did. I hadn't noticed it at first, because I was too busy drinking in everything else around me, but he'd only gotten as far as the end of the hallway before he'd stopped short and started whimpering a bit. When I moved toward him, he barked and scampered off toward the bedroom. I'd assumed that he wanted me to follow him, but when I had, there he was, putting himself between me and Joanna, growling, as if he were protecting her. *Protecting* her—against *me*…

I hunched down and called him to come to me, but he just bared his teeth and growled all the more. As he did, I got a whiff of something that I don't think that I'd ever smelled before. I can't even describe it to you, really, because there aren't any words for it. All I know is that I had an immediate, instinctive response to it. As soon as I smelled it, something inside of me registered it as *fear*. I could actually smell Flubber's fear of me.

Of course, that made total sense to me at the time. I was the "alpha dog" in our home, wasn't I? It just made sense that he would have a healthy fear of me. But then I thought back to the last time that I'd been around him, when Durant had stayed for dinner. He'd avoided me and stuck to Durant like glue. At the time, I'd just assumed that it was because he'd taken a liking to the man—but what if it was something more? What if, even then, he'd sensed the changes in me, gotten confused, and was clinging to Durant for security?

I stepped back out of the bedroom to give Flubber some space, and I moved down the hallway toward the kids' rooms. I didn't want to wake them, but I really wanted to see them, to drink their sleeping faces in as deeply as I had Joanna's. The first room that I came to was Chelsea's. I opened her door just a crack so that I could see her, and I was bombarded with scents. I could smell that she'd taken her bath before bed and brushed her teeth, but that she'd obviously snuck a cookie in after that. There was no way that Joanna would've let her get one otherwise. I looked in at her angelic little face, and she seemed so peaceful, laying there. But as I closed her door, something else about her smell caught my attention. It was a subtle thing, and at first I didn't relate it to her scent, but finally, in the end, I couldn't help it.

Smelling her suddenly made me feel *hungry*…

Reflexively, I stepped back in surprise, and almost tripped over a shoe that she'd left in the hallway. I fooled myself into thinking that I could just go to the kitchen and fix myself a snack—that I just had some sort of midnight munchies going on. But as I passed by the open door to the twins' room, I was struck with the same thought again—that I was suddenly ravenous. I felt like I hadn't eaten anything in a week, and everything around me just *smelled so good*. I reached for the door, and I swear to God, I'm almost 90% sure that it was just to close it…

*   *   *

I'll never really know for sure, because I felt someone grab me from behind—and in a flash, I found myself outside in my yard. A new snow was starting to fall, and I could see each snowflake individually, as well as the patterns that they made as they rode the wind down to the ground together. Pieter Durant was standing in front of me now, and I could see that he did not look happy. I could also see that his right hand was resting on that little pouch of his at his side.

"You are *unwell*, Detective…" he said quietly.

"Never felt better…" I replied, quite truthfully.

"My point exactly," he said. "How are your ribs? And your lacerations? Quite fully healed, I suspect?" He absent-mindedly tapped the *got uechan* as he spoke.

"What's your point?" I asked. Oh, I knew that I'd already been made, but like a thousand stupid perps before me—who keep squirming under interrogation, even though they *know* that they aren't going to get away—I still tried to keep up a weak façade. His hand stopped tapping, and I caught my breath.

"Show me your hands," he said, with an intensity that was not to be ignored. I held out my hands, and he flipped them over to see my palms. Hiding was pointless.

"No pentacles…" I whispered, letting the façade crack. "Maybe…" He glared at me from under those bushy brows, and I can barely believe that I got the rest of that sentence out. "Maybe it's only a *slight* infection…?"

"No," he replied, releasing my hands. "There *is* no 'slight' infection. It simply took longer to multiply in your bloodstream. The difference between receiving a bite and receiving a scratch, I should think."

"What does that mean?" I asked.

"I truly do not know," he answered. "There is someone whom we could ask, but…" He sighed and scratched his beard. I knew that part of him was thinking of killing me right then and there—he *had* to have been thinking that. But his heart obviously wasn't in it. He *knew* me. He knew Joanna. He knew the kids. He couldn't just see me as faceless, "collateral damage" any more. And I think that it was at that moment that I finally, really understood why it was that Pieter Durant worked so hard to distance himself from the rest of humanity—how could you do what he had to do, day in and day out, for centuries, and still care for the people that you were inevitably forced to put down? It would have to drive you insane.

So we just stood there, watching the snow fall, for what seemed like forever. Everything that we'd just gone through with Lyn screamed that the smart move would be for him just to whip that sword out of his *got uechan* and kill me right then. The more I thought about how hungry I'd felt back in the house, the more I thought that maybe he should. I really don't know how long we stood there, but the silence was finally broken by my phone, telling me that I had a text message.

"Should I check that?" I asked. It seemed so pointless to read a text, if he was just going to decapitate me in another minute or so. But Durant nodded, and so I looked at my phone. It was from Leah Wheaton, and all it said was "Chicago ave." I assumed that the message referred to the hangout that the guys down at the Five Star Bar had told us about. I showed it to Durant.

"Has anyone heard from Detective Wheaton since the attack on Detective de Tullio?" he asked.

"Nope."

"Then you realize that there is little chance that she still lives," he said.

"Yeah, I know."

"Which would make this almost certainly a trap."

"Yep."

He sighed.

"Just how far gone are you, Detective?" he asked me at last. *"Truthfully."*

"Truthfully?" I replied. "I don't really know. But I think that I've got a handle on it." I really thought that I did... at that moment. He looked into my eyes long and hard, and then sighed again.

"Then let us bait this trap and spring it against them," he said. He grabbed my arm and began dragging me to the car. It dawned on me as we walked that the main reason that I was still alive was that Durant wanted to play "cat and mouse" with monsters again—and that he was once again using me as the cheese for his mousetrap...

*   *   *

"You know," I said, trying to break the silent tension as I drove, "this might even end up being helpful for us."

"What might?" he asked.

"The Lycaon virus," I replied. "I mean, I'm faster and stronger than I've ever been in my life, and all of my senses are heightened. We might be able to make use of that in a fight."

"And that is precisely the reason why werewolves cannot be cured..." he muttered, staring out of the window.

"Excuse me?"

"Do you still not understand the nature of the affliction?" he asked. "The true horror of the werewolf is not in its *bestial* nature, but in its *inhuman* nature."

"I'm not sure I catch the distinction," I replied. Durant scratched his beard again and shifted in his seat to face me.

"Have you ever been to your own Museum of Natural History, here in Chicago?" he asked.

"The Field?" I answered him. "Sure—every school kid in Chicago has. Why?"

"There is an exhibit there of two lions," he said. "The local tribesmen had called them *Kivuli* and *Kiza*—the Ghost and the Darkness—and they believed them to be not lions, but rather the embodied spirits of slain witch doctors."

"Uh huh…" I responded, finding that more than just a little hard to believe.

"Whether they were or were not," he continued, "they were hardly normal lions. In 1898, over the span of only a few months, the pair had slaughtered 135 men who had been working on a railroad near the Tsavo River, in Kenya." He paused for a moment to let the gravitas of that sink in. I confess that, though it certainly sounded like a terrible tragedy, I knew that I wasn't getting the significance of his story.

"That's…" I said, trying to break the pause. "That's really… bad…"

Durant sighed one of his patented sighs.

"You have missed my point."

"I'm sure I have."

"A pair of male lions attacked 135 men in nine months—averaging one man, every other day. But male lions do not hunt in pairs. Ever. They do not even tolerate other males in their territory. These lions were strong and healthy maneaters—both lions were more than nine feet in length. But the only lions who turn maneater are the old or the infirm. These lions dragged their prey back to their lair in the rocks to devour them. But lions do not befoul their dens like that, nor do they even make their lairs in caves such as these two did. These lions licked the skins off of the corpses and then lapped up their blood. But lions do not feed like that. These lions chased their prey up trees. But lions do not climb trees. They defied traps and hunts and multiple gunshot wounds, and still they killed. And, what's more, it appears that they may have only actually eaten 30 to 40 of the men. The rest—nearly 100 men—they killed *merely because they wished to do so*." He paused again to try to let his point sink in.

"Are you saying that they were werewolves?" I asked, still obviously not getting his point.

"Of course not, you idiot," he replied. "What I am saying is that the horror which gripped the men at Tsavo in 1898 was not because so many of their compatriots had been killed by lions, but rather because these lions did not act like lions, and because they appeared to be unstoppable. The horror was not in their ferocity, but rather in their *cruelty*—the sense that it was not their bestial instincts that drove them forward, but rather a cold, hateful, gleeful, unending malevolence that no mere beast should ever possess. In much the same way, the horror of the werewolf is not truly in his claws and fangs, but in his heart. There is a reason why werewolves are drawn first and foremost to hunt the ones whom they love when in human form. Ultimately, the curse draws them not to gain animalistic urges, so much as to lose their humanity. Do you see the difference?"

"I think so," I said, but the immensity of that was hard to wrap my head around.

"Do not ever mistake a werewolf for an animal, Detective," he said. "They are not animals—they are *monsters...*" He stared off into the night again. "And the tragedy of it is that every last one of them ultimately *wishes* to be such a monster..."

We drove on for another couple of blocks in silence as that slowly sunk in. Lyn wasn't becoming more of a beast—she was becoming less of a human being. Whatever it was inside of her that clarified right from wrong, whatever it was that made her *want* to be a good person, that part was rotting away. All that was left was the part that wanted to let loose and do whatever she wanted to do, whenever she wanted to do it—to run, to hunt, to kill, to be in total control in the midst of an uninhibited chaos. It was scary how much that resonated with me.

We were heading south on Kedzie, just about to drive past Palmer Square, when I was hit by a familiar scent again. Durant sat up at the same time.

"Almonds..." I said, and he nodded, his hand instinctively darting to his *got uechan*.

"Witchery..." he replied and spat. "Stop the car." I pulled into West Palmer Court and parked. The last time I parked there was when we investigated a shoot-out between the Insane Orquestra Albany and the Imperial Gangstas about a year before. Somehow, this felt a lot more intense. I shut off my engine, then turned to Durant to ask again for the explanation that I didn't get earlier.

"Okay, so what's the deal with the almonds?" I asked. "Why do witches smell like almonds?"

"They do not," he replied. "But as Wong Li-Shen explained to me, sorcery by definition bends or even breaks the elements of the natural world. When that happens, the very atmosphere around the witch cracks open. The scent from whatever resides on the other side of that crack— which, again, most human beings cannot detect in the slightest—is reminiscent of the smell of bitter almonds."

"Who's Wong Li-Shen?"

"A young man whom I met on my way to help Major Charles Gordon at Kunshan during the Taiping Rebellion in 1864. I could not stomach the audacity of Hong Xiuquan in proclaiming himself our Lord's brother, so I came to China to lend my assistance to Gordon in removing him from power. I came inland to Fóshān, since the city was outside of the 'Taiping Heavenly Kingdom,' and there made the acquaintance of young Wong Li-Shen, who wished to study to become a *wu shen* and join the local *Wūyā Lǐshì Huì*. I spent several days with him and his family, awaiting the open door to move north to Suzhou and Kunshan, and I suggested instead that Li-Shen train as a physician rather than as a sorcerer, pointing him toward the new *Shuāijiāo* academy opened in the city by his 18-year-old cousin, the physician Wong Fei-Hung."

"Did he end up going to study with this Wong Fei-Hung?" I asked.

"I fervently hope so," he replied. "But I was compelled to continue on to Kunshan at the earliest opportunity."

"Okay, but I didn't smell any almonds when I was around Rhiannon," I said.

"You were only human when you were around Rhiannon," he replied with a snort. "These things change, apparently..." The scent of almonds became stronger and more acrid, and Durant opened the door and stepped out of the car.

"So what are we doing now?" I asked, getting out as well. "Why are we stopping here instead of going on to our werewolf trap? I thought we wanted to go spring our werewolf trap..."

Durant walked across Kedzie and into the park. It was surreal watching his dark form silhouetted against the white-covered trees and grass and snow-filled sky—and then seeing him draw that gleaming, silver sword from his side. There was an electricity charging the air, like lightning was about to strike, and I could feel my heart racing in anticipation.

"The witches undoubtedly know much of what we now know," he said, turning slowly in the snow. "They know that you have been infected, and that we are on the hunt. Perhaps they wish to take you down now, whilst they may, or perhaps they wish for some reason to keep us from making this particular rendezvous—but either way, they appear to be making a stand here and now. I should rather meet them out in the open, on my own terms. Wouldn't you?"

I reached for my pistol, but then realized that I had a much better sidearm at my disposal than that, so I opened the back door and grabbed the Matteh ha Shelomoh from my back seat instead. But the moment that I touched it, my hand felt like it was on fire. I dropped it and yelped in pain.

"What's up with the staff?" I asked Durant, but he wasn't listening to me. The wind had suddenly kicked up, making swirls of the snow in the air.

"Prepare yourself, Detective!" Durant yelled back to me. "The Synod of Crows are upon us!"

Background
From *The Cracked Mirror: An Ethnographic Examination of Abnormal Psychology* (Kelly Fontini, 2013)

Similarly, cannibalism echoes the classical theme of *lycanthropy*—not the physical transformation of a human being into a wolf, but rather the psychological aberration wherein people genuinely believe that they have been transformed into an animal, as a means of dealing with the psychic guilt of their consumption of human flesh.[1] In their minds, their cannibalism was not the action of a deranged mind, but rather the result of a curse beyond their control which temporarily removed their humanity from them. They are thus no longer responsible for their actions.

That being said, it is worth noting here that there is a line of thought within many cultures and sub-cultures that the truth is, in fact, the other way around—that it is not lycanthropy which brings about cannibalism, but rather cannibalism which brings about lycanthropy. For those cultures which believe that lycanthropy is genuinely a curse which transforms the individual into a beast, the oldest records suggest that the curse comes as a result of the unlawful consumption of human flesh—a myth to discourage such behavior amongst the people of a given tribal group. Even in the leanest times of famine or hardship, there must be a strong, clear rationale for individuals regarding why they must not, under any circumstances, break that ultimate taboo and resort to devouring one another.

Consider the first lycanthrope, King Lykaon of Arcadia. Ovid's *Metamorphoses,*[2] Pausanías' *Description of Greece,*[3] etc., all tell the

---

[1] *Note that even among the most sensationalistic of the classical and medieval writers, most of them believed that the physical transformations never actually happened—that it was all an illusion of one form or another in the mind of the lycanthrope. See Kramer & Sprenger's 1486 volume,* Malleus Maleficarum, *Pars i, Quaestio 10; Abraham the Jew in* Das Buch der Heiligen Magie der Abramelin der Magier *(1458); or even St. Augustine in his* De Civitate Dei Contra Paganos, *Book xvii, Chapters 17-18.*

[2] Metamorphoseon Libri *(8 AD)*

[3] Ἑλλάδος Περιήγησις *(2nd century)*

story of a king who couldn't believe that Zeus was visiting his household in the form of a man. He attempted to murder Zeus in his sleep, then attempted to fool the god by slaughtering his own youngest son, Nyctimus (or a Molossian hostage—accounts vary), and then serving the meat up to Zeus as an unholy sacrifice, to test his godly omniscience. It's interesting to note that in the *original* version of the story—which Ovid and Pausanías have apparently cleaned up a bit for their audiences—Lykophron[4] tells us that Lykaon not only served Nyctimus up as a sacrifice, but also partook of the child's flesh himself, along with his other sons. Thus, it was not only the family's lack of faith, but more pointedly their *cannibalism* that Zeus cursed them for, changing them outwardly into bestial shapes that mirrored their inner, bestial natures.[5] To the ancient mindset, being turned into a wild, mindless beast—even within the confines of one's own perceptions—was the foulest abasement imaginable, especially for a king.[6]

The underlying assumption in many of these sorts of myths is that cannibalism is addictive—or, perhaps, that it acts like a virus, infecting the cannibal in such a way that once the person ingests human flesh, they are bound to crave it from that point forward. Take for instance the case of escaped convict Alexander Pearce, who escaped from a penal colony in Tasmania with seven other convicts in 1822. Lost and dying of starvation in the wilderness, the group decided to begin killing and devouring one another, one by one, in order to survive. After a few weeks of dyads pairing up against individuals, only two of them were left—Robert Greenhill and Alexander Pearce—and unfortunate Greenhill was the first one to fall asleep. Less than four months after his escape, Pearce had been caught and incarcerated once again, making the cannibalistic deaths all the more tragic because of their pointlessness. But the most terrifying part of the story is that when Pearce escaped again, two years later, with another convict named Thomas Cox, he *again* chose to kill and eat his companion—even though other food sources were plentiful this time. The fact is that he had come to crave human flesh, addicted to it, considering it to be a delicacy better than any other food.[7]

To the mindset of many Native American tribes such as the Cree or Algonquin, someone who engages in cannibalism like this opens

---

[4]   *Lycophron of Chalcis, in his* Αλεξάνδρα *(3rd century BC)*

[5]   *Either the name, Lykaon, or Zeus' choice of changing him and the Arcadians into wolves constituted a pun in classical Greek. Note that* Lykaon (Λυκάων) *is changed into a wolf—a* lykos (Λύκος).

[6]   *Note the humiliation of Babylonian King Nebuchadnezzar II in the Biblical* Book of Daniel, *iv, 30-37.*

[7]   *See the book,* Alexander Pearce of Macquarie Harbour *(by Dan Sprod, 1977).*

themselves up to becoming a *wìdjigò*[8]—a bestial fiend who is compelled to attack, kill, and eat other human beings from that point forward. It becomes a psychological (if not spiritual) compulsion in the person that cannot be denied or overcome. Once one has crossed that threshold, there can be no coming back to rejoin the human race again...

Perhaps the most subtly dangerous aspect of a cultural mythos of cannibalism is that it perpetuates and amplifies itself as the culture fantasy chains[9] about it—it becomes a culture-bound syndrome that magnifies itself geometrically. For example, George A. Romero's classic film, *Night of the Living Dead*, was terrifyingly groundbreaking when it first appeared on the big screen in 1968—the concept of flesh-eating zombies was utterly novel at the time.[10] But the theme has since become so commonplace to the American mindset that even a quick perusal of the horror section of a modern video store shows that a *majority* of contemporary horror movies include cannibalism of some sort or another.[11] We are beginning to assume it as *de rigueur,* and thus it

---

[8] *Or "windigo"—see Brightman's "The Windigo in the Material World" in* Ethnohistory *(1988).*

[9] *An element of Ernest Bormann's Symbolic Convergence Theory (see "Fantasy and Rhetorical Vision: The Rhetorical Criticism of Social Reality," in* Quarterly Journal of Speech, *1972), describing how a group develops cohesion by elaborating on and adding to one another's personal or social narratives.*

[10] *See Roger Ebert's review of the film in the* Chicago Sun-Times, *January 5, 1969.*

[11] *Movies have always mirrored and then influenced the cultures in which they have been created. The argument has been made that to best understand a culture's current zeitgeist, one must look no farther than its horror movies. As Kane notes in his article on "Horror Movies and the American Psyche" in* The Journal of American Film *(June, 2008),*

> *"In the 1930s and 40s—during the rise of the Nazis—the standard English-speaking horror movie made use of monsters with thick, foreign accents who hid in the dark to prey on innocents. In the 1950s—in the wake of the atomic bomb—horror movies tended to feature mutations which had grown from our own radioactive tests and bombs (Japan made a cottage industry of such movies). In the 1960s—during the Cold War—the monsters tended to be those which looked like "one of us," but could in fact be an alien (read: "communist"), etc. A simple analysis of a horror movie such as "Invasion of the Body Snatchers" which has been remade several times will demonstrate the shifts in cultural fears—in the original, 1956 version of the film, the aliens took over your neighbors in the same way that people feared the communists had infiltrated America; in the 1978 remake, the aliens took over authority figures, echoing the overall, anti-authoritarian shift in culture; in the 1993 remake, the aliens took over adults, forcing children to save the world in a culture dominated by kid-centered*

becomes *de rigueur.* The more we think about cannibalism and worry about it, the more it becomes part of our social consciousness—which, ironically, means that it becomes more and more prevalent as a potential social action. "The only thing we have to fear is fear itself" indeed.

This zombie fixation has become so ingrained in the American psyche that last year, when a naked and growling Rudy Eugene assaulted homeless derelict Ronald Poppo on the MacArthur Causeway in Miami by ripping his clothes off and biting off the flesh of his face and his left eye, many people assumed the worst. The Centers for Disease Control and Prevention (CDC) was flooded with phone calls sincerely asking if this might be, in fact, the beginning of an actual "zombie apocalypse"— which is all the more ironic when one realizes that Eugene actually consumed none of the flesh (so it was not, in fact, an act of cannibalism at all).[12] But the CDC nonetheless felt forced to issue a public statement that the "CDC does not know of a virus or condition that would reanimate the dead (or one that would present zombie-like symptoms)." That an official statement was required to be made by the national public health institute of the United States government suggests just how completely our society has feared—and thus, embraced—a cultural mythos of cannibalism, therefore developing and encouraging the very mindsets which bring such acts of cannibalism about.

Of course, Florida is no stranger to this sort of attack. In 2011, Josephine Rebecca Smith attacked and attempted to eat elderly homeless man Milton Ellis, ripping flesh from his face and body with her teeth, claiming that she was a vampire and needed to consume human flesh in order to survive—which didn't alarm the public in the same way that Eugene's attack did a year later, since zombies are cannibals (and thus, terrifying) but vampires are *très chic* (and thus, titillating). For example, since 1992, Tampa's trendy Ybor City neighborhood has been home not only to a strong and growing LGBT community, but also to The Castle nightclub, which caters to Goth sensibilities and styles itself as a

---

imagery; and in last year's most recent, post-AIDS, post-SARS remake, the alien invasion takes the form of an intelligent, infectious disease. Our motion pictures both reflect and create the fears which dominate our cultures, whether we recognize it or not."

One could argue that the modern, American fear of zombies may reflect not only our concerns about diseases and infections, but also the fear that we might become our own monsters—that we might evolve into our own worst enemies.

[12] *The day before the attack, however, saw two notable examples of actual cannibalism—Morgan State University student Alexander Kinyua attacked, killed, and partially devoured his roommate, Kujoe Bonsafo Agyei-Kodie, in Maryland, and Canadian porn actor Eric Newman (aka Luka Magnotta) videotaped himself stabbing, dismembering, and eating Concordia University student Justin Lin in Montreal.*

"vampire" club. There, club-goers can dress in black, wear fangs, and indulge their "sweet tooth" by opening a vein for one another in relatively protected surroundings. In fact, ever since the success of the *Twilight* series of books and movies, more and more young people across the United States have engaged in what is being termed "fantasy biting behavior"—biting one another hard enough to draw blood as both an expression of affection and a means of sexual gratification. Thus, in pushing the socio-cultural envelope in our media to the edges of horror, we create the very society that we depict—which, of course, means that we must continually push the boundaries even further the next time in order to create the desired effect of the scandal of the *avant garde*. In this way, yesterday's shocking horror becomes today's exciting fad becomes tomorrow's bored norm.

So what must tomorrow's *horror* become in order to keep up with our own depravity?

Chapter 13
Manômini

While Durant engaged the witches, I quickly made my way back to the house. Everyone was still asleep, so I crept back into our bedroom and found Joanna, just as I'd left her. I took her sleeping form into my arms and her eyes opened lazily. When she saw me, she smiled and leaned forward to kiss me. But I passed by her lips and sank my teeth deep into the soft flesh of her neck. She tried to scream as I ripped the meat from her bones, but all that did was to make me feel even hungrier. I knew that I had total control of her, that her body belonged to me entirely, and I began to rip her open with my bare hands as she flailed around in vain. Her blood was everywhere, and I gulped it down like a man dying of thirst. Then I heard—

"Detective!" Durant barked at me, slapping me across the face, pulling me off of my wife's dying body. He was in the room with us, and the wind was howling around him. Snow was everywhere, and that's when I realized that we were actually outside. Snow was sticking to the blood on my hands, but I couldn't see Joanna or the bed anywhere. "Chapel!" he yelled again, and slapped me even harder. I wiped the blood from my mouth and realized that it was my own. I was still standing in the park at Palmer Square—I hadn't moved an inch.

"W-What?" I asked.

"I need you *here! Now!*" he yelled. It was hard to hear him over the howl of the wind.

"I-I was back home…" I mumbled, still trying to get my bearings. It looked as though the trees were bending toward us. Everything seemed so unreal.

"What did you see?" he asked me. "Quickly now!"

"I…" I didn't want to remember what I'd thought I'd seen myself do. "Something horrible…" was all that I could get out.

"Is that what you truly want?" he asked me, glaring at me. "In your heart of hearts, is that what you truly wish?"

"No!" I yelled back. "God in Heaven, no…" It was the most horrific thing that I'd ever imagined—made all the more horrifying because, at the moment I had envisioned it, I had *enjoyed* it so much.

"Then push it back and away, Detective," he said as he slashed at something with his sword. He turned back to me. "If a thought comes to your mind and it is not what you truly desire, then you must assume that it comes from one who is trying to tempt you. Do not entertain such thoughts! Pray to God and push them away from your consciousness— let your mind bounce to another thought, any thought! Focus on the snow or the trees or the Brooklyn Dodgers—*anything* but what your mind feels drawn to at that moment!" He slashed again at something behind him, and I saw that it really was a tree that was grabbing at him. He was under attack, but he was dividing his attention to make sure that I was okay. Was that out of compassion? Or was it that he knew that if I succumbed to whatever whammy the witches were trying on me, then he'd have to be fighting on two fronts?

"I'm okay," I told him, but he continued watching me carefully. "I'm fine—don't worry about me!" He slashed again at the grasping branches, but then turned back to me. "The Dodgers moved to Los Angeles sixty years ago, ya fossil! Fight the stupid trees!" It may have been a trick of the light, but I think that he almost smiled at that. Whatever. The important thing is that he turned his attention away from me and toward his attackers. For that matter, so did I. As I looked around, I realized that things were worse than I'd imagined.

The whole landscape was alive and coming at us, and everything— *everything*—smelled like burned almonds. Trees were slashing at us, the snow was sleeting sideways, like tiny ice daggers, slicing a hundred little gashes in our skin. One of the nearby garbage cans suddenly rose up, hung in the air for a moment, and then flung itself at Durant. He was busy fighting off what I believe was a park bench, so I jumped between him and the flying can. It hit me pretty hard, knocking me off of my feet, but I was surprised at how little it hurt. A week ago, that sort of impact would've broken some bones, but now...

Again, I started thinking that this virus might not be as bad as Durant made it out to be. I mean, I was almost as fast, almost as tough as he was. *Maybe that's why he was so scared of me becoming a werewolf,* I thought to myself. *Maybe he's scared that I'll be better than him, stronger.* I began picturing myself once the virus had fully run its course, imagining how powerful I might eventually become—and that's when I remembered his words.

Dear God in Heaven, I prayed, *this isn't coming from me. Please help me think of something else.* I remembered hearing that the worst part of overcoming most addictions usually wasn't the physical withdrawal symptoms, but having to shift your mental gears. Every time you give in to the addictive thoughts or behaviors, you burn deeper and deeper grooves into your neural pathways. It becomes easier and easier to follow the same pathways over and over again, and harder and harder to get your wheels out of the ruts the next time around. Once you let yourself think a certain way, you'll just naturally *keep* thinking that way—and do it more and more as time goes on. The time to stop this line of thinking was right now, before it got any worse—any easier to fall into.

So I looked at the snow in front of me. I just let my mind blank out for a minute, looking at the stark whiteness of the snow. I knew that Durant needed my help, but I also knew that I had to be able to control myself in order to actually be able to help him. So I tuned out all of the commotion and let myself feel the icy slivers against my cheeks, letting all other thoughts drift out of my mind. When I finally felt calm and focused, I looked back up again.

The whole park was one big, white swirl of snow, illuminated by street lamps and flashes of electricity. Garbage was flying past us, and shards of glass were slicing into Durant as he fought off the larger chunks of stone and wood. He had his sword in one hand and a small buckler in the other, trying to defend himself. But even with his speed, there were too many attacks from too many fronts for him to deal with.

This is the wrong strategy, I thought to myself. We were fighting the projectiles, and not the ones throwing them. I tried to focus my thoughts and use the new senses that I'd been given. I couldn't see anything through the snow, the wind and the clatter of combat were too loud to hear anything through, and the scent of almonds was too strong to smell anything else through. But then that gave me an idea. That scent seemed to grow and wane in strength, depending on how much magic a given witch was using at that moment—so maybe I should just try to track that scent.

I closed my eyes and began following my nose. Sure enough, the smell of almonds was coming the strongest from one direction in particular, so I began moving there. I found that if I focused hard enough, I could not only get a sense of the direction, but also the distance. I could almost *see* the figures standing there, wrapped in their scents. I was getting pretty good at this—I could even focus enough so that the witches' magic couldn't stop me. After this, I knew that nothing was going to be able to stop me again, and—

I was doing it again. I was letting them into my skull. If their tempting wasn't appealing to my baser instincts, it was to my pride, and if that didn't work, it was to my pride about *overcoming* my pride. I knew that there was no way that I was going to be able to muscle my way through the temptation to give in to their machinations, so I decided to try a different tactic.

"Dear God," I prayed out loud. "Help me out here. Everything I do that works just comes back to bite me in the end. Please help me do this—there are too many people who need us not to fall..."

I thought of Joanna, and Chelsea, and the twins, and even Flubber. I thought of what would happen to them if I let myself get worn down by these witches, if I let down my guard and actually became what this virus inside of me was trying to make me. I thought of Lyn, and what she was doing right now while we let this fight go on in the park. I thought of all of the people—men, women, children—that monsters like Postyshev and Bunin and the *Obshchestvo Drakonisty* preyed upon. Were there other dens out there like Bunin's? Dark cellars where children were penned up and fattened until the wolves were ready for them?

I started getting angry, and noticed that I was growling again. But that wasn't going to help anyone. This fight couldn't just be about me lashing out in my anger—in fact, that's exactly the sort of thinking that made the wolf inside of me grow stronger. This had to be about something bigger than whatever it is that makes me mad. I had already been losing myself to my aggression too much recently, and I needed to get a handle on it.

That's when I thought of Durant and his centuries of warfare. No one could keep up a mad on for that long—it wasn't a temper tantrum, but a *crusade*. I thought about what God had to feel like, seeing this corruption of his natural creations, this mutilation of the flesh he'd sculpted, and I tried to channel what I was feeling into less of a fury and more of a righteous indignation. I don't know how well I did, but I made it in sight of the two figures who seemed to be the source of the almond smell in the air—a tall man and a short woman. I recognized her right away from our conversation at Miska's deli the morning before—Manômini.

"You have joined the Mahwêwithowa, policeman!" she snarled at me, while her companion focused his attention on Durant. "I trusted you, but you are Manetôwaki now!"

"Why are you doing this?" I yelled over the howling wind. "We're trying to *stop* the bad guys! You're fighting the very people who are trying to stop the monsters you hate!"

She gestured at me, and a bush uprooted itself and flipped toward me. I dodged it fairly easily, given my new reflexes.

"You are not people," she replied. "You and the kîshekwi man," she added, nodding toward Durant. "We thought that you would be different, but you have become one of them, and he will not kill you because he is soft. You both will let the chaos-bringers take you, and with you, everything."

She threw another bush at me, and one of the branches grazed my cheek.

"What on earth are you talking about?"

Manômini closed her eyes, and my mind was suddenly flooded with images—werewolves with blood dripping from their fangs, torn bodies everywhere, a small child in a corner, frozen in fear, too terrified even to scream as she watched her family ripped to shreds in front of her. It took me a moment, but then I recognized the child as Chelsea. I couldn't help it—my reaction was instinctive. I roared so loudly that my teeth ached, and I lunged for the witch with murder in my heart.

"NO!" I heard Durant shout behind me. He was running to me as fast as he could, but I realized that he no longer looked like a blur when he ran. I could actually see his movements fairly clearly now—so was he moving slower, or was I seeing clearer? Durant was so focused on getting to me that he didn't notice the tree behind him, and a huge branch darted at him from behind and burst through his chest. He stopped short and dropped his sword, impaled on the jagged piece of writhing wood.

"Durant!" I yelled back. But he just pointed weakly up at the tall man. I turned and saw that the man's hands were moving the same way that the tree's branches were. He drew his hands together, then slowly apart, and I watched as the branches jutting through Durant began to split and pull apart as well—peeling his torso apart with them.

I drew my pistol and fired three shots into the tall man's chest. I wasn't sure that it would work—I didn't know the rules about how to kill witches like these—but I couldn't stand by and do nothing. The man looked surprised for a moment, then crumpled to the ground. As he did, the winds began to die down a bit, and I could see that we were standing in front of the Old Holy Resurrection Serbian Orthodox Church.

"*Ningozis!*" the old woman cried, and fell to the ground next to the body of the tall man. I turned to Durant, who was slowly pulling himself off of the gnarled and bloody branch.

"Are you okay?" I asked, running over to him. He grunted as he pulled himself off the last bit of the branch.

"Get..." he gurgled, the blood in his throat making it difficult for him to speak. "Get... the woman..."

I turned back to her, but she didn't seem to be going anywhere.

"My son..." she wept, holding the man's body and rocking back and forth. The wind died down to nothing, and the park returned to being a simple, quiet park. "They have murdered you..." she sobbed.

"Woman," Durant said, trying to rise to his feet, but slumping back to the ground. He seemed so unsteady and weak—it was actually kind of scary to see him that way. "Old woman, why did you attack us?"

"The Manetôwaki have murdered you..." she sobbed again, as if she hadn't heard him. Part of me almost felt bad about shooting him. It was a righteous kill, if ever there was one, but no cop ever wants to discharge his firearm.

"You can help us," I said gently, trying to get her attention. "If you know where the... um... the Mahwêwithowa are, where they're keeping their…" I paused because I couldn't bring myself to finish the sentence.

"Their livestock…" Durant suggested.

"If you know where they are," I continued, "we can stop all of this. We're on the same side here…"

"No…" Durant said, trying to rise again.

"You think that you are strong because you are old," Manômini said, sneering at Durant. "But look what my son has done to you. You are not all-powerful, kîshekwi man. But whoever wins the life cup *will* be. The Châki-ôtha has promised us this, and we are faithful."

"You… are a mad, old crone…" Durant rasped, holding his chest together. "Who cannot keep her own family alive…"

At this, the woman dropped her son's body in anger and stood up to face him. The wind picked up again, and I pulled my pistol up to take aim.

"You have over 100,000 miles of blood vessels in your skull, kîshekwi man," she snarled. "And it takes only eight to ten seconds for even one such as you to lose consciousness if I were to shut down the blood flow to your brain. You must hold your organs in with your own hands—do you really expect me to be afraid of you?"

"Try your best," Durant smiled in response, his own blood caking his white teeth. "You've no idea what I can accomplish in eight to ten seconds…"

The woman raised her hands, and I felt the air pressure around us change as the wind began to whip through the night again. It felt like I was sitting on the bottom of a swimming pool, and my ears began to burn.

"Stop what you're doing!" I yelled, but her face was a wild mask of rage. I saw Durant convulse, and I began to put pressure on the trigger. But before I could fire, Durant had bolted from my side, flinging himself toward the old woman. Her eyes were still fixed on where he'd been laying in the snow when he got to her—her brain hadn't even registered that he'd moved. His hands wrapped around her head, and he twisted with a sickening cracking sound, then let go. Her body fell like a rag doll at his feet, right next to the corpse of her son. But as the wind died down again, Durant slumped to the ground as well. I could see that his wound wasn't healing as fast as it normally would have. I ran over to him.

"What's going on?" I asked. "What can I do to help?" He coughed up blood in response.

"Do not become a werewolf…" he said, pulling that little blue vial from his *got uechan*. And then he passed out.

*   *   *

I remembered how to do this, having seen Durant do it on two separate occasions. The stuff in the vial was like lighter fluid on steroids. All I had to do was to pour it over the two bodies, light them on fire, and then within seconds, all proof of the supernatural is gone. Simple. Easy.

But there was only one body in the snow when I turned back to them. Manômini was nowhere to be found. I couldn't help but think of Rhiannon, and that reminded me of how much I really, really hated witches.

At least I could do something about the tall man that I'd shot, I decided. So I sprinkled the liquid from the vial over his corpse, then used a road flare from the trunk of my car to light it on fire. He burst into flame and was utterly gone within a few seconds. All that was left was a large scorch-mark in the grass. I figured that the falling snow would cover that over within the next hour or so.

I dragged Durant and his sword back to my car, and was surprised by how heavy he was. Tony had seemed like nothing to me earlier, but Durant still felt like a load to carry. As I got to the side door, he began to come around again.

"You... handled the bodies...?" he asked, and I assured him that I did. I figured I could explain about Manômini later on. "My amanuensis..." he muttered, and seemed to fall back into unconsciousness. I opened the door and dropped him onto the seat, pushing his legs in behind him.

"Do not..." he mumbled, not quite awake. "Do not write of this, Detective..." So he knew. He hadn't mentioned anything about it up until that point, but apparently, he knew all about that other book. And he hadn't kicked my butt for it or anything.

"I wouldn't worry about it, if I were you," I assured him, setting his sword onto the seat next to him and tucking him into the seatbelt. "As far as I can tell, only about seven or eight people on the planet ever read that book, and most of them were family members."

"Nonetheless," he continued, without opening his eyes. "Do not write another..." and I promised him that I wouldn't.

*   *   *

I had no idea where I was going to drive, at first. I mean, I was afraid to go home, and it's not like I could take him to a hospital. There was no way that I was going to keep our little appointment at the trap on Chicago Avenue, so I just drove around Palmer Square for a few minutes like we were riding on a merry-go-round or something. At last, it dawned on me where I could take him that would be safe, and I headed straight for Tony's place.

I looked over at him, and he still didn't look good. I mean, anyone else on the planet would be dead with a gaping chest wound like that, but I was used to Durant healing immediately. The fact that he was still bleeding was throwing me. With his shirt ripped open, I could see the little silver crucifix that he always wore, covered in blood. I reached over to pull his shirt closed, but as my hand brushed the crucifix, I felt the same burning sensation that I'd felt when I'd tried to pick up the Matteh ha Shelomoh earlier, and I flinched.

With that, Durant roused himself again with a wet-sounding cough. "What—?"

"We're going to get you someplace safe to rest," I told him. "But why isn't the Grail's mojo working for you?"

"There is no 'mojo,' Detective," he sighed. "The Grail is not some sort of magic talisman. But this wound is magic at its core, and I have not been in contact with the Grail for some time…"

"I just assumed it was in that bag of yours, with everything else in the world."

"The Cup of the Christ, stuffed into a leather pouch?" he growled. "I should never allow such a sacrilege…!" He drowned out his own grouching with another round of coughing.

"So where *is* it?" I asked. He coughed a bit more, then let his gaze pass out of the car and into the night.

"It is safe…" was all he'd say. We continued to drive in silence for a while after that. As we came to a stoplight, I looked over, and I was happy to see that his chest wound looked a little smaller. So he was healing—just not very fast.

"Incidentally," he said, turning back to look at me. "We may fight a common enemy, Detective, but never deceive yourself into believing for one moment that we fight on the same side as the damnable Synod of Crows."

"But why not?" I asked, a little shocked that he'd bring that back up with such vehemence. "They could be pretty potent allies, if you ask me."

"Do you know how a witch develops a power such as telekinesis of this magnitude?" he asked me, holding the wound in his chest closed as it continued to heal. The scratches on his face and hands appeared to have healed completely already. "The power to bend the trees to their will, or to fling a park bench through the air like these witches did tonight?"

"No, but…"

"There are many ways, of course, but most commonly, they must pledge themselves to Satanic beings—though they may refer to them as the Châki-ôtha or Manidoo or the Tchaga or Odin or what have you— through the sacrifice of a loved one, usually a child. They must make the child's death as long and as excruciating as possible—and believe me, the Meshkwahkihaki knew the art of keeping a person alive and conscious almost as well as the Apache did. Then they usually either drink the child's blood or feast on their still-beating heart. This is the *least* offensive ritual with which I am all too personally familiar..."

I thought of the little old woman who'd patted my hand at the deli the other day. It was hard to picture her doing what he was talking about. Then again, I've seen a lot of horrible things on the job over the years, perpetrated by a lot of decent-seeming people who looked far more innocent than she did. You can't assume that someone's okay because they smiled at you, or assume that they're guilty because they didn't.

"This woman may or may not have loved her son," he continued, "but how many other children had she given over to Satan to bring her the power which she wielded against us this night? When the witches bemoan that the wolves are taking their children, they are not acting as protective parents—they are acting as competitors, fighting over table scraps..."

*   *   *

I'd called ahead, so Tony was waiting for us. He was as shocked as I had been, watching me put Durant's arm over my shoulder and walking him inside.

"Youse guys fight King Kong or somethin'?" he asked, holding the door open for us.

"Or something..." I answered and brushed past him. Funny, but as I did so, I could actually *smell* the cancer on him. I can't really describe to you what it was like—the closest that I can come is to say that it reminded me of a musty smell, like a rotting piece of wood in an old basement somewhere, but that's not quite right. It was faint, in the background behind the scent of cigarettes and dinner and coffee, but it was there nonetheless.

"D'ya use my stick on 'em?" he asked, closing the door behind us.

"It is not your 'stick,' you..." Durant began to respond, but his own coughing interrupted him.

"Nope," I said, laying Durant down onto Tony's ancient couch. You have to understand, between the divorce settlements and Tony's bizarre personal tastes, his apartment looked like a rummage sale had vomited into the room. "There's something wrong with it."

"There is nothing wrong with the Matteh ha Shelomoh..." Durant replied.

"Yes, there is," I corrected him. "Maybe the witches messed with its magic, but it burned me when I tried to pick it up."

"Witches?" Tony asked.

"The Matteh ha Shelomoh is not 'magical,' Detective," he growled, "any more than the Grail is. One does not make use of magicks to confront magicks—that merely compounds the problematic issues at hand."

"What about fighting fire with fire?"

"A tactic which only works if one is very competent and very careful," he replied, shifting himself uncomfortably. "And even so, one may often still be burned just as badly by the very 'tool' which one thinks one controls."

"Can we go back to th' *'witches'* part?" Tony asked.

"Okay, then what is it?" I asked, staying on the subject at hand. "Why does this stick work when nothing else does?"

"It is the Staff of Solomon, and its effectiveness is due to the slender thread of vril embedded within it," he replied, as if that should be a good enough answer to my question.

"What's 'vril'? You've mentioned it a couple of times now."

"Vril is…" He crinkled his brows in mid-sentence, as if trying to figure out how to explain it to us. Finally, he just said, "Vril is complicated. For the nonce, let me simply say that just as gold is an excellent conductor of electricity, and cavorite is an excellent conductor of gravity, and iron is an excellent conductor of magnetism, vril is an excellent conductor of more… *exotic* energies. Vril—or orichalcum, as the ancients named it—is a rare and powerful element, and one which should not be left in the hands of Neanderthals such as Detective de Tullio…"

Okay, I have no idea what cavorite is, and "for the nonce?" Really? Sometimes Durant slips, and I'm reminded of how really, really, horribly old he is. But since he seemed like he needed to rest, I decided not to keep pressing him for answers. Tony and I retreated into the kitchen, where I poured myself a glass of water and asked him how he was doing. He answered that painkillers were awesome, and that his arm didn't hurt at all. I clarified that I wasn't just asking about his arm, and he quickly changed the subject.

"Oh, while ya was out, we got a call from that Chernomyrdin guy," Tony said, diverting the conversation. "He said he got a name fer th' top whatyacallits, *Avtoritet* or whatever, over all o' them *kryshas*."

"Bunin…" I said, nodding.

"Nope," he replied with a big grin. "Yer gonna love it."

"Okay…" I said, swigging the last of the glass, swallowing with a loud gulp, and then sighing. "Go ahead and shock me, Tony."

"It's *Sydor*…"

Background
From *Malleus Maleficarum*[1] (Heinrich Kramer & Jakob Sprenger, 1486, trans. G.L. Burr)

From *Pars ii, Quaestio 2*

Is it lawful to remove witchcraft by means of further witchcraft, or by any other forbidden means?

It is argued that it is not; for it has already been shown that in the *Second Book of Sentences*,[2] and the 8th Distinction,[3] all the Doctors agree that it is unlawful to use the help of devils, since to do so involves apostasy from the Faith. And, it is argued, no witchcraft can be removed without the help of devils. For it is submitted that it must be cured either by human power, or by diabolic, or by Divine power. It cannot be by the first; for the lower power cannot counteract the higher, having no control over that which is outside its own natural capacity. Neither can it be by Divine power; for this would be a miracle, which God performs only at His own will, and not at the instance of men. For when His Mother besought Christ to perform a miracle to supply the need for wine, He answered: Woman, what have I to do with thee?[4] And the Doctors explain this as meaning, "What association is there between you and me in the working of a miracle?"[5] Also it appears that it is very rarely that

---

[1] *This work—" Der Hexenhammer," or* "The Hammer of Witches"*—became the textbook of its day for clergy and scholars in the proper understanding of and reaction to perception of the prevalence of witches in the pre-Reformation world, quickly eclipsing Johannes Nider's earlier text,* The Formicarius *(1435-1437).*

[2] *The second book in Bishop Peter Lombard's seminal* Libri Quattuor Sententiarum *(1150), a four-volume textbook on systematic theology and Biblical commentary.*

[3] *The books of the* Libri Quattuor Sententiarum *were broken down a century later into "Distinctions" (or chapters) by Alexander of Hales, a British Franciscan who taught at the University of Paris..*

[4] *See the account of the wedding at Cana in* The *Gospel of St. John, ii, 1-11.*

[5] *That is, "Should I do a miracle of God simply because a human asked for it?" Other Catholic theologians, however, have taken this section of Scripture in a different way, leading to the popular dictum, "Quod Deus*

men are delivered from a bewitchment by calling on God's help or the prayers of the Saints. Therefore it follows that they can only be delivered by the help of devils; and it is unlawful to seek such help.

Again it is pointed out that the common method in practice of taking off a bewitchment, although it is quite unlawful, is for the bewitched persons to resort to wise women, by whom they are very frequently cured, and not by priests or exorcists. So experience shows that such curses are effected by the help of devils, which it is unlawful to seek; therefore it cannot be lawful thus to cure a bewitchment, but it must patiently be borne.

It is further argued that S. Thomas[6] and S. Bonaventura,[7] in Book IV, dist. 34,[8] have said that a bewitchment must be permanent because it can have no human remedy; for if there is a remedy, it is either unknown to men or unlawful. And these words are taken to mean that this infirmity is incurable and must be regarded as permanent; and they add that, even if God should provide a remedy by coercing the devil, and the devil should remove his plague from a man, and the man should be cured, that cure would not be a human one. Therefore, unless God should cure it, it is not lawful for a man himself to try in any way to look for a cure.

In the same place these two Doctors add that it is unlawful even to seek a remedy by the superadding of another bewitchment. For they say that, granting this to be possible, and that the original spell be removed, yet the witchcraft is none the less to be considered permanent; for it is in no way lawful to invoke the devil's help through witchcraft.

Further, it is submitted that the exorcisms of the Church are not always effective in the repression of devils in the matter of bodily afflictions, since such are cured only at the discretion of God; but they are effective always against those molestations of devils against which they are chiefly instituted, as, for example, against men who are possessed, or in the matter of exorcising children.

Again, it does not follow that, because the devil has been given power over someone on account of his sins, that power must come to an

---

imperio tu prece, Virgo, potes"—*"That which God can do by power, you, O sacred Virgin, can do by prayer" (from Alphonsus Maria de Liguori's 18th century work,* Le Glorie di Maria)—*arguing that all miracles are ultimately wrought through Mary's express will. As Bernardus Claraevallensis (Bernard of Clairvaux) taught in the 12th century,* "Totum now uoluit habere per Mariam"—*"Such is God's will, that we should have all through Mary" (see his* "Sermo de Aquaeductu," *collected in the* Sancti Bernardi Opera Genuina, *1854).*

6   *Thomas Aquinas, Italian Dominican and theologian.*

7   *Bonaventure, Italian Franciscan and theologian.*

8   *Again, from Peter Lombard's* Fourth Book of Sentences, *Distinction 34.*

end on the cessation of the sin. For very often a man may cease from sinning, but his sins still remain.[9] So it seems from these sayings that the two Doctors we have cited were of the opinion that it is unlawful to remove a bewitchment, but that it must be suffered, just as it is permitted by the Lord God, Who can remove it when it seems good to Him.

Against this opinion it is argued that just as God and Nature do not abound in superfluities, so also they are not deficient in necessities; and it is a necessity that there should be given to the faithful against such devils' work not only a means of protection (of which we treat in the beginning of this Second Part), but also curative remedies. For otherwise the faithful would not be sufficiently provided for by God, and the works of the devil would seem to be stronger than God's work.

Also there is the gloss on that text in *Job*. There is no power on earth, etc.[10] The gloss says that, although the devil has power over all things human, he is nevertheless subject to the merits of the Saints, and even to the merits of saintly men in this life.

Again, S. Augustine[11] says: No Angel is more powerful than our mind, when we hold fast to God. For if power is a virtue in this world, then the mind that keeps close to God is more sublime than the whole world. Therefore such minds can undo the works of the devil.

Answer. Here are two weighty opinions which, it seems, are at complete variance with each other.

For there are certain Theologians and Canonists who agree that it is lawful to remove witchcraft even by superstitious and vain means. And of this opinion are Duns Scotus,[12] Henry of Segusio,[13] and Godfrey,[14] and all the Canonists.[15] But it is the opinion of the other Theologians, especially the ancient ones, and of some of the modern ones, such as S. Thomas, S. Bonaventura, Blessed Albert,[16] Peter à Palude,[17] and many

---

[9] *Here, the authors are arguing for the need for priestly confession to remove the sin from one's soul.*

[10] *Kramer and Sprenger here allude to the Biblical* Book of Job, *xli, 33-34, which speaks of God's authority by saying, "There is no power upon earth that can be compared with him who was made to fear no one. He beholdeth every high thing, he is king over all the children of pride."*

[11] *In his* De Moribus Ecclesiae Catholicae et de Moribus Manichaeorum *(388). Note that Augustine was uniquely qualified to write apologetics against the Manicheans, since he himself had spent several years as one in his youth.*

[12] *John Duns Scotus, British Franciscan and theologian.*

[13] *Enrico da Susa (aka, "Hostiensis"), Italian canonist.*

[14] *Godfrey of Fontaines, Belgian theologian who taught at the University of Paris.*

[15] *The contemporary experts in canon law (i.e.; the organization and authority structures of the Church).*

[16] *Albert of Cologne, German Dominican and theologian.*

[17] *Peter Paludanus, French theologian and archbishop.*

others, that in no case must evil be done that good may result, and that a man ought rather to die than consent to be cured by superstitious and vain means.

Let us now examine their opinions, with a view to bringing them as far as possible into agreement. Scotus, in his Fourth Book, dist. 34,[18] on obstructions and impotence caused by witchcraft, says that it is foolish to maintain that it is unlawful to remove a bewitchment even by superstitious and vain means, and that to do so is in no way contrary to the Faith; for he who destroys the work of the devil is not an accessory to such works, but believes that the devil has the power and inclination to help in the infliction of an injury only so long as the outward token or sign of that injury endures. Therefore when that token is destroyed he puts an end to the injury. And he adds that it is meritorious to destroy the works of the devil. But, as he speaks of tokens, we will give an example.

There are women who discover a witch by the following token. When a cow's supply of milk has been diminished by witchcraft, they hang a pail of milk over the fire, and uttering certain superstitious words, beat the pail with a stick. And though it is the pail that the women beat, yet the devil carries all those blows to the back of the witch; and in this way both the witch and the devil are made weary. But the devil does this in order that he may lead on the woman who beats the pail to worse practices. And so, if it were not for the risk which it entails, there would be no difficulty in accepting the opinion of this learned Doctor. Many other examples could be given.

Henry of Segusio, in his eloquent *Summa*[19] on genital impotence caused by witchcraft, says that in such cases recourse must be had to the remedies of physicians; and although some of these remedies seem to be vain and superstitious cantrips[20] and charms, yet everyone must be trusted in his own profession, and the Church may well tolerate the suppression of vanities by means of others vanities.

Ubertinus[21] also, in his Fourth Book,[22] uses these words: A bewitchment can be removed either by prayer or by the same art by which it was inflicted.

Godfrey says in his *Summa:*[23] A bewitchment cannot always be removed by him who caused it, either because he is dead, or because he does not know how to cure it, or because the necessary charm is lost. But if he knows how to effect relief, it is lawful for him to cure it. Our author

---

[18]   *Of his* Quaestiones super Libros Metaphysicorum Aristotelis *(1297).*
[19]   Summa super Titulis Decretalium *(13th century).*
[20]   *That is, "spells."*
[21]   *Ubertino da Casale, militantly strict Franciscan theolgian.*
[22]   *Of his* Arbor Vitae Crucifixae Christi *(1305).*
[23]   *That is, in his extended commentary on S. Thomas Aquinas'* Summa Theologiæ *(13th century).*

is speaking against those who said that an obstruction of the carnal act could not be caused by witchcraft, and that it could never be permanent, and therefore did not annul a marriage already contracted.

Besides, those who maintained that no spell is permanent were moved by the following reasons: they thought that every bewitchment could be removed either by another magic spell, or by the exorcisms of the Church which are ordained for the suppression of the devil's power, or by true penitence, since the devil has power only over sinners. So in the first respect they agree with the opinion of the others, namely, that a spell can be removed by superstitious means.

But S. Thomas is of the contrary opinion when he says: If a spell cannot be revoked except by some unlawful means, such as the devil's help or anything of that sort, even if it is known that it can be revoked in that way, it is nevertheless to be considered permanent; for the remedy is not lawful.

Of the same opinion are S. Bonaventura, Peter à Palude, Blessed Albert, and all the Theologians. For, touching briefly on the question of invoking the help of the devil either tacitly or expressedly, they seem to hold that such spells may only be removed by lawful exorcism or true penitence (as is set down in the Canon Law concerning sortilege), being moved, as it seems, by the considerations mentioned in the beginning of this Question.

But it is expedient to bring these various opinions of the learned Doctors as far as possible into agreement, and this can be done in one respect. For this purpose it is to be noted that the methods by which a spell of witchcraft can be removed are as follows: - either by the agency of another witch and another spell; or without the agency of a witch, but by means of magic and unlawful ceremonies. And this last method may be divided into two; namely, the use of ceremonies which are both unlawful and vain, or the use of ceremonies which are vain but not unlawful.

The first remedy is altogether unlawful, in respect both of the agent and of the remedy itself. But it may be accomplished in two ways; either with some injury to him who worked the spell, or without an injury, but with magic and unlawful ceremonies. In the latter case it can be included with the second method, namely, that by which the spell is removed not by the agency of a witch, but by magic and unlawful ceremonies; and in this case it is still to be judged unlawful, though not to the same extent as the first method.

We may summarize the position as follows. There are three conditions by which a remedy is rendered unlawful. First, when a spell is removed through the agency of another witch, and by further witchcraft, that is, by the power of some devil. Secondly, when it is not removed by a witch, but by some honest person, in such a way, however, that the spell is by some magical remedy transferred from one person to another; and this again is unlawful. Thirdly, when the spell is removed without imposing it on another person, but some open or tacit invocation of devils is used; and then again it is unlawful.

And it is with reference to these methods that the Theologians say that it is better to die than to consent to them...

Chapter 14
Ad Vitam Æternam

Frank Sydor was dead. I knew that he was dead. He'd worked for a vampire named Ruthven as his *vrăjitorul*—a necromantic witch who murdered people using a powder called *oase rău* or *'áń't' į* or whatever. I *knew* that he was dead because I'd seen his dead body hanging outside the Richardson Library on the DePaul University campus a couple of years ago after Ruthven had no more use for him. How on earth could this werewolf *Avtoritet* who was leading the rest of the *Obshchestvo Drakonisty* in Chicago—be Sydor?

"Was Chernomyrdin sure about that?" I asked Tony.

"Oh, he was positive," he answered, chuckling. "The guy's name is *Teodor Pompiliu Sydor*. Ain't that a trip?"

Another Sydor? How many of them were there?

"A relative, do you think?" I asked him.

"His father..." we heard Durant mutter quietly from the couch. I walked back into the room and he was trying to sit up, dripping blood all over Tony's couch—but then again, with that couch, it was probably an improvement. The whole place was beginning to smell like blood.

"What?" I asked.

"I believe that I may have heard of this Teodor Pompiliu Sydor," he said, clutching his chest. "If so, then I believe that he is the *father* of František Yevhen Sydor."

"Ya knew about 'im an' ya never thought ta mention 'im?" Tony snorted.

"No, when we interacted with Sydor the Younger a few years ago here in Chicago, it never dawned on me to make the offhand observation that his father was still alive and lived in Romania," he said, wilting back onto the couch. "How foolish of me..."

"Did you know that he was a werewolf?" I asked.

"Of course not," he answered with a cough. "I've never met the man. I knew only that Sydor's father, Teodor, was some sort of criminal, and that the son had broken from the family to follow the witchery way, serving the vampyri. Perhaps the father now masquerades as your Nikodim Bunin..."

"Yeah, that—can we get back to that 'witches' thing now?" Tony repeated. "An' ain't he s'posed ta be healin' better'n this?" he asked me, pointing to Durant.

"That can't be," I told Durant, ignoring Tony for the moment. "Bunin's way too young to have been Frank Sydor's father."

"A werewolf's constitution can allow him to be quite long-lived," Durant said, closing his eyes. "I've known of some who had reached hundreds of years in age, though the vast majority of them do not, of course…"

"So why is that an 'of course' kind of statement?" I asked. Obviously, I had a vested interest in finding out more about a werewolf's life expectancy. Durant opened his eyes again for a moment to look at me.

"Because, unlike the vampyri, werewolves do not often hide themselves or their rampages," he said sternly. "They cannot control the beast within them, nor do they *wish* to. Thus, they tend to lose control and over-predate their hunting grounds until they are finally found and put down…" He kept his eyes on me for several more seconds before he added, "Usually, by me…"

*   *   *

While Durant slept, I explained to Tony about the Synod of Crows and the attack at Palmer Square, and that something about that magical wound was keeping Durant from healing like he normally would. Of course, having said that, I could see that the hole in his chest had closed, and he'd stopped bleeding, now that he'd been given a chance to rest for a bit. I suggested that Tony do the same, since it had been a hard night on him as well. Given everything that we'd gone through over the past couple of years, Tony was able to roll with all of that weirdness pretty well, and he took me up on my offer to get some shut-eye.

Me, there was no way that I was going to sleep. In fact, I actually felt wired. While both of them rested, I paced around Tony's apartment like a caged animal. I raided his refrigerator and ate the last few pieces of cold fried chicken, washing them down with a couple of cans of Tony's Coke. But I was still thirsty, and I was still hungry. What sounded good was to go out and get a thick, rare steak, but I reminded myself that I'd promised Tony not leave them alone.

So I tried not to think about it, and instead thought of Lyn. Where would she have gone? Was she the one who'd sent the text from Leah Wheaton's phone? Had Bunin? Or had Wheaton somehow survived and sent it herself?

Tony's neighbor came home early in the morning, around three o'clock—not only could I hear her in the hallway, but I could smell her perfume. Tony had said that she was some kind of a dancer, and I could smell the mingled scents of dried sweat and stale beer still clinging to her. I felt myself getting hungry again.

That's when I remembered my dad talking about that time as the "hour of the wolf"—smack dab in the middle of the night, when you've either fallen into your deepest sleep, dreaming your most intense dreams, or when you're just tossing and turning, lost in your deepest fears. It's the hour when peasants always thought that the wolf would prowl around outside of your door, when the ghosts and goblins were out haunting the darkened streets. It's the time of night when you're most tempted to lose yourself to whatever terrors lurk in the deepest parts of your heart. People always tend to think that that sort of thing is supposed to happen at midnight, but my dad argued that the scariest time of night was closer to three, because by then, you were so far into the night that you knew that you really should be sleeping, and yet, you were still hours away from the dawn. It's a time for hopelessness—and that always breeds the worst kinds of terrors.

So I pulled myself back and tried to think about something else other than the gnawing hunger in my belly. I tried to focus on Joanna and the kids, but that didn't help. I tried to pray and ask God to make the hunger go away, but it didn't. I picked up a book and started to read it, but when I turned the page, I realized that I had no idea what it was that I'd just read. I could smell Durant's blood everywhere, and it distracted me horribly. I walked over to look at his wound, and from the outside, it looked completely healed. I leaned over a bit to look at it more carefully, but as I did, I could… I don't know how to describe it. I could *feel* Durant's crucifix as I got nearer to it, and it… *hurt*… I can't tell you if it was the cross itself or the fact that it was made of silver, but whatever it was, it made me pull back instinctively with a low growl.

Durant woke up with a start, and before I realized that he had even moved, his hand was gripping my wrist.

"What are you doing, Detective?" he asked quietly.

"I—I was checking your wound," I stammered. "It looks like you've healed up pretty well now." He watched me for a moment, scrutinizing me with a cold intensity. Finally, he let go of my wrist and lay back down. It was only then that I realized that his other hand had been resting on that little *got uechan* of his.

"I shall not be quite myself until I have the opportunity to partake of the Grail once more," he said, "but I should think that I shall soon be up to the task of picking up where we left off earlier this evening." He picked at the tattered, bloodied shreds of his shirt. "But I shall need a change of clothes and a wash before I should do so."

I plopped down into the chair opposite of him and thought about what he just said. He was the guardian of the Holy Grail, right? The

Cup of Christ, or whatever you want to call it. If you believe the legends, the Grail is this miracle-working medical wonder, and Durant had possessed the thing for over 1,500 years. And yet, as near as I could figure, the only thing that he'd ever used it for was to keep himself alive and kicking.

"Okay, I've got a question," I said, leaning forward. "So the Grail can heal anything, right?"

"Anything that one *wishes* to be healed of, yes," he replied, sitting up.

"Even cancer?"

"What is your point, Detective?" he asked, frowning.

"My point is, why don't you *use* it to cure cancer? Or AIDS? Or any of the things that people die from every day? Couldn't you share the wealth a little bit and work to *save* lives instead of just *taking* them all the time? What about all of the people you could heal with the thing?" And then, because I couldn't help myself, I added, "What about people like Tony?"

"What about them?" he asked.

"Why not let him take a sip?" I replied. "Why not use that thing for somebody *else's* benefit for a change?" He frowned harder, and then let out one of his trademark sighs.

"Do you truly believe that what the Grail has provided me all these years has been for my benefit?" He shook his head. "You understand nothing about the millstone of immortality…"

"But think of all of the people you could help!" I pressed.

"*Which* people, Detective?" he asked, leaning forward toward me. "*Whom* would you have me help? Those with cancer? Or AIDS? Or heart disease? Or pneumonia? Or the common cold? Where is the bold black line to be drawn where you would agree, 'We shan't help *that* person…' when we could certainly do so? Just how would you suggest that we regulate the use of the Grail—if, indeed, you would regulate it at all? If you would not, then the world would surely descend into anarchy—and if you would, then why judge me so harshly for drawing the same such line at a different point to where you would do so?"

I confess that I hadn't thought about it like that. I mean, would I really suggest that Durant should just set up a shop front where people could come in and take a sip? Even if he kept the doors open 24 hours a day, 365 days a year, the line out front would never end. No, scratch that—there wouldn't be a line, because somebody powerful enough or rich enough or high enough up in the government would just come in and take it over before the first day was through.

"The Grail is not a magical healing machine, Detective," he continued, lying back again into the couch. "That is not—nor has it ever been—its purpose."

"Then what's the point?" I asked. "Isn't that what Jesus would have wanted you to use it for? To help people?"

"Indeed," he said, crossing his arms. "And yet, Lazarus died twice…"

"What?" I asked.

"Lazarus," he said. "A friend of the Lord's who lived with his sisters in the town of Bethany."

"Yes, I know the story," I said. "But what are you getting at?"

"Our Lord brought Lazarus back from the dead. Why do you believe that he did such a thing?"

"I guess because Jesus didn't want his friend to be dead," I suggested.

"But Lazarus *is* dead now, as we speak. Though he was brought back from his grave, he eventually made his way back to it, as all men—" He stopped in mid-sentence, struck by the irony of what he, of all people, was arguing. "Lazarus died, as all men must ultimately do some day. If the Lord brought him back because, as you say, he did not wish his friend to be dead, then does that not mean that his plans for resurrecting Lazarus were ultimately thwarted?"

"No…" I answered. "I guess, maybe a little? I don't know…"

"The miracles which our Lord performed were not merely out of a desire to alleviate the temporary dispositions of uncomfortable people, Detective," he continued. "He did not spend his limited time amongst us simply to heal this person or that one for a moment here or a day there— he had an entire world to heal, by a much greater and more profound action, which would affect people on a much deeper and more eternal level than any mere physical healing."

"Then what was the point of healing anyone?" I asked, getting frustrated.

"Oh, in part, it was borne from the fruit of his compassion, surely," he answered. "He could not stand by and watch the suffering of his children and do nothing. But ultimately, the reason why Jesus Christ brought Lazarus back from the dead—the reason why he waited three days until everyone would *know,* beyond a shadow of a doubt, that Lazarus was utterly and truly dead—was to glorify God in the process, not in the end to keep Lazarus from dying. For Lazarus has now been in his grave for nearly two millennia since, and our Lord had to know that this would happen. Neither Christ nor Lazarus was afraid of death, as so many appear to be today, because they both knew what lay beyond it."

I had to admit that he had a point. I didn't *like* it, but it made a certain degree of unpleasant sense to me when I heard it. Otherwise, what *was* the point of bringing Lazarus back, knowing that he'd just have to die all over again?

"The purpose of the Grail," he continued, "the purpose of *any* of the miracles which our Lord's life and death have brought about, really, is to glorify God. The healings which have thus been wrought by his hands— or, by extension, by the Grail—are only the particular means to that end. When we emphasize the results of the miracles instead of their purposes, then we distort them in our minds, making them about *us* instead of about *God*, and that is a travesty of the most profound measure. The work of God is not to exalt and serve the will of Man, Detective—it is the work of Man to exalt and serve the will of God."

That last bit... At first, it struck me as being more than a little trite-sounding—*We just need to serve God...* But the more I thought about it, the more uncomfortable I felt about how many times I'd just tossed a prayer up to God, asking him to do this or that for me, like he's some kind of cosmic concierge whose whole job it is to do whatever I suddenly decide needs to happen here or there. If there really is a God, then I think maybe we too often treat him like the hired help instead of the guy in charge—and if there is no God, then all of those prayers are ridiculous in the first place, like Tony had argued about the Ouija boards. Either way, I figure that we probably ought to re-think how we pray.

"I just don't want Tony to die..." I said at last. He frowned again—but this time, it seemed more pained than frustrated.

"This life is infinitely more complicated than to be founded and turned upon what you or I want to happen within it, Detective," he said, with a gentleness that seemed very alien to what I thought that I knew about Pieter Durant. "And that simple truth is far more often a blessing than it is a curse..."

*   *   *

In the morning, after Tony chewed me out for eating all of his food, we had a planning session. I tried calling Leah Wheaton's phone, but it just went to voicemail, so we had to make decisions based on the little bits of information that we had at hand. We knew that Lyn was out there, and definitely dangerous. We knew that *someone* had texted me from Wheaton's phone, trying to get us to go to somewhere on Chicago Avenue, but on the way there, we'd gotten waylaid by the Synod of Crows—so was it really from Wheaton, had it really been sent by the witches, or had it been intended to draw us into a completely unrelated trap from the *Obshchestvo Drakonisty*? We knew that Bunin was one of them, but what was his relationship to this Teodor Sydor? So many questions, so many intertwining tracks to follow, but no clear path.

That's when Durant reached into his leather bag and pulled out a little box. It looked very old, with a domed cover that looked like it was made out of lapis lazuli. He opened it up, and I could see that it was an old-fashioned compass. As he looked at it, the needle spun a bit and then pointed due east, toward the North Center neighborhood.

"That thing is broken. North is that way," I said, pointing out the window.

"But that is hardly what we are looking for," he replied, snapping it shut and putting it into his coat pocket. "It suddenly dawned upon me that your investigative skills have ultimately provided us more altercations and clues than any consequent conclusions. Instead, I thought that perhaps we should simply go to the source and find the wolves' den."

"They got a den?" Tony asked.

"Wolf packs *always* have dens," Durant responded.

"Then why wasn't we lookin' fer that in the first place?"

"Because Bunin and Agent Davidge appeared to be the more immediate problems with which to contend, and because I wished to see how you were going to deal with them. But now, it is time to cut through the cloth and take the fight to the fiends' own doorstep, whether that trail leads us to your particular culprits or not."

"So you're saying that that thing points toward what you're looking for?" I asked, pointing to the compass in his pocket. "*Anything* that you're looking for, no matter where it is?"

"Not precisely, no," he answered, gathering his coat and pulling his shirt together as best he could. "The compass points one to that which one desires the most intensely at a given moment. At this moment, what I desire is to find the den."

"Then why didn't you just '*desire*' to find Bunin or Lyn yesterday?" I yelled. "Why have we been running all over creation, getting all but killed, when you could've just pointed us to them all the time?" Before he could answer, I added, "For that matter, why did you waste that stupid bottle of wine the last time instead of using this compass thing to find us?"

Durant sighed. "Because the compass points to *what* one desires, not to *whom* one desires." He stood up and buttoned his jacket over his ragged shirt with as much dignity as he could muster. "I was forced to make use of one of my bottles of Château Climens, 1811, to track you and your family during our last adventure because you are not, in fact, inanimate objects or places."

"Then why didn't you just have it look for my shoes or something?" I asked. "Or Joanna's car?"

"There is no 'tricking' the compass, Detective," he said, with that patented exasperation creeping into his tone. "It knows what it is that you *truly* wish to find, even if you yourself do not. Are you coming with me, or shall I continue on alone?"

*   *   *

While Tony and I got ourselves ready, Durant disappeared for about fifteen minutes. He came back cleaned up, with his beard trimmed, wearing a perfectly pressed, tailored, Navy blue suit that I later found out had been made for him by Anderson & Sheppard when they were still at London's Savile Row. He was still wearing that same black Burberry overcoat (or one just like it), but I saw that he had changed his shoes—again, probably a pair that was worth more than a month's pay as a cop. It never ceased to amaze me that a man so focused on action would take the time to dress like such a fashion plate. It also dawned on me that I had no idea where he disappeared *to* when he'd leave.

"Are we ready?" he asked impatiently in the doorway.

"Just waiting on you," I replied. "Do you have a hotel in town or something?"

"No," he replied, and walked out the door. I shook my head and followed him out, but then I noticed that Tony was coming along, too.

"You'd better sit this one out, Tony," I said, stopping him. "With that broken wing, you need to rest more than we need you along. Or maybe you could do some legwork to find out more about this Sydor guy…?"

"That's a load o' crap an' you know it, Tom," he replied.

"What are you talking about?"

"Okay, let's get inta this," he growled. "Coupla days ago, you was in the hospital after Ben Bucher an' me scooped up yer guts an' stuffed 'em back into yer belly!"

"It wasn't really as bad as all that…" I started, but Tony just held up his hand.

"I'm a detective, too, Tom" he snapped. "I ain't stupid. Carolyn gets attacked by a werewolf an' then she gets all better real fast, an' she tries to eat me last night. *You* get attacked by a werewolf an' then get all better real fast, an' I'm just s'posed to be all happy an' joyful that yer up an' at 'em an' eatin' all my chicken? I can't say as I know *exactly* what's goin' on with ya, but I can do the math, an' I figure that everyone'll be a lot safer with me watchin' yer back intead o' lettin' ya go through it all by yer lonesome."

"Durant is with me," I said.

"Yer all by yer lonesome," he replied, pulling out his pistol and checking the magazine to make sure that it was loaded. "He ain't watchin' yer back, Tom—he's just waitin' fer ya ta do somethin' worth killin' ya for…"

I'd known Tony for almost a decade, but every once in a while, he reminded me that I too often took him for granted, sometimes confusing bad grammar and a sloppy appearance with ignorance on his part. We all have our little prejudices, and the most dangerous ones are the ones that we don't realize that we have. But Tony was right—he wasn't stupid by a long shot, and I shouldn't have assumed that he was going to be. On top of that, he just told me that he'd known that I'd been infected with the same thing that had turned Lyn against him the night before, but rather than run away from me in fear, he'd committed himself to sticking by me. Not many people in this world have the loyalty or the kind of even keel in the midst of a sea of chaos that Tony did, and I realized just how lucky I was to have been his partner for all these years.

"Just stay back when things get hairy," I said as we walked out into the hallway.

"Bad choice o' words..." he chuckled, closing and locking his door behind us.

*   *   *

We drove east, with Durant checking his compass every once in a while to suggest a turn here or there. But no one was really chatty, and that gave me time to think. I knew that Durant had said that the Lycaon virus couldn't be used or channeled to help us, but I just wasn't sure that I believed him. There just had to be a way that we could use all of this to our advantage.

"What about that diamond?" I asked at last, breaking the silence.

"What?" he asked.

"That diamond," I repeated. "The one you used on Billy th—I mean, on Ruthven..."

"The diamond of the Comte de Saint-Germain?" he replied. "What of it?"

"You said that it could control changes, that it could *prevent* changes," I continued. "It kept him from shapeshifting when you were fighting him, right? Couldn't I use that to keep myself from, y'know, wolfing out?" Durant closed his compass and looked out of the window.

"Who's got a what now?" Tony asked.

"The diamond could indeed prevent you from, as you say, 'wolfing' in form," Durant said at last, turning back to face me. "At least, for a time..." He let that last bit sink in for a second "But for the diamond to be effective, you must *consciously will* yourself not to change."

"No problem," I said. "There's no way I'm going to let myself turn into..." I thought of that huge, gray wolf, tearing at me at Bunin's house, ripping into Lyn's bleeding flesh. "I'm not going to let myself change into something else..."

"Again, you misapprehend the nature of the infection," Durant replied with a sigh. "To be a werewolf changes not only your form, but your heart. You become the wolf, not from the *outside-in*, but from the *inside-out*. You will remember that Agent Davidge made her first kills yesterday long before she ever changed her outer appearance." Yes, I knew that. I remembered that. I just didn't want to think about that. Besides, hadn't Lyn been emotionally damaged goods long before that creature ever sank its teeth into her? When she realized the new power surging through her, it had just flipped switches in her that had already been there—switches that weren't in me.

"You shall progressively change inside before your body finally metamorphosizes into its lupine shape," Durant continued. "At some point—even with the diamond on your person, perhaps allowing you to prevent the physical transformation—eventually, you shall *want* to change." His eyes burned so intensely under those brows that I couldn't look at him, so I just focused on the road. "In the end, you shall *want* to be the wolf, Detective," he said. "You shall *want* to revel in its power and in its unbridled lusts. Nearly everyone who has ever been infected has ultimately fallen."

"But that won't happen ta Tom," Tony interjected from the back seat. "He wouldn't ever do that, no matter what kinda juju was messin' with 'im, would ya, Tom?" I wished that I'd had the confidence to agree with him, but I was beginning to wonder myself.

"Let me tell you about a man named Waldo," Durant said, crossing his arms as he wound up into one of his stories. "An opponent and sometimes ally of a detective acquaintence of mine who kept offices at Berkeley Square, he had been bitten by a French werewolf outside of Toulouse, but he used a combination of various salves and elixirs—and sheer force of will—to keep the beast within him at bay for years. Instead, he used the same physical abilities with which you yourself are obviously becoming enamored to commit daring crimes and to cement his name as a 'wonder' in Europe, claiming that they stemmed from a rare strain of syringomyelia. He was strong and fast and durable beyond all normal human limitations, and he reveled in his body's changes, even as he resisted the final transformation into full-blown lycanthropy."

"So it can be done," I said.

"For a time, Detective," he replied. "A man with an iron will like Waldo's could resist for a time, but only for a time. He even attempted to live as an honest man at one point, hiring himself out for exorbitant fees to perform perilous tasks which 'lesser' men could never accomplish. He thought that he could control it—and, in his ignorance, he allowed the virus to be passed on to the next generation by producing a son. But in the end, the beast took over and Waldo became a prowling monster, ironically ultimately locked into his lycanthropic form by an evil genius named Nikola in order to be directed to commit the most heinous acts."

"An' that's when ya killed 'im, right?" Tony said.

"In point of fact, I did not," he answered. "I fought with him, yes, but he died in the flames of a dirigible crash indirectly caused by that conflict. An accomplice of his named Späh had smuggled the fully transformed Waldo on board in Frankfurt in a crate, convincing the crew that Waldo was, in fact, a large Alsatian named Ulla. When I caught up to the craft just outside of Lakehurst and found that Späh had made repeated trips to the cargo hold to feed his 'dog,' I pieced together what had happened and grappled with both of them on the catwalk between the gas cells. It was in fact the discharge of Späh's Luger—smuggled onto the Hindenburg inside of an expensive doll—which sparked the conflagration that ultimately destroyed the craft and most of its passengers."

"Wait," I stopped him. "You're telling us that *you* caused the Hindenburg crash?"

"No," he replied, obviously a little frustrated. "I am telling you that *Späh* caused the crash when he shot me. I must say, for a detective, you often lose your attention to the wrong details..." He pulled out the compass and opened it again, even though we hadn't made any turns since the last time he'd looked at it.

"Where do you even find this sort of stuff?" I asked, trying to change the subject. "More junk from that warehouse in Russia, where you got the wine?"

"Off the shores of Hispaniola, in 1769, actually," he replied, snapping it shut again. "I retrieved the compass from a decidedly eccentric fellow who was quite clever and quick with his sword. He was terribly helpful to me as I foiled the efforts of Baron Saturday to use black magicks to oust the French and Spanish and establish a new, independent vodoun state upon the island. Having said that, I am almost certain that the pirate was more interested in taking the Baron's ship for his own than in actually attempting to thwart the vile fiend's plans."

"That good a ship, huh?" Tony asked.

"It was in tatters, in point of fact," he said, his voice sounding almost light for a change. "But it was nonetheless quite a nimble little vessel. I myself had fought against the same ship some fifty years earlier, off the coast of the Carolinas, when it had been captained by Raphael Adolini and called *La Muerta Negra*. In the interim, it had been found by British pirates adrift in the Bermuda Triangle and rechristened."

"So the compass originally belonged to this pirate guy?" I asked.

"Not at all," he replied. "As I was saying, the compass had originally belonged to Baron Saturday himself—a spiritualist from Saint-Domingue who, I believe, is still worshipped by vodouist *sèvitès* as one of their loas. He painted his face white and black to resemble a skull, and he was quite imposing in his own right. The slaves of the region considered him a god, though they were nonetheless terrified of him, and rightly so. If it had not been for the pirate's insatiable greed happening to coincide with my own purposes, the Baron might well have taken over the whole island—perhaps even the entirety of the Caribbean before he was finished. The pirate was merely a deluded madman who claimed to have been using the device for decades, though he hardly seemed old enough for that to be true."

"And how old are you again?" I asked.

"A millennium and a half," he answered. "Why?"

"Because you hardly look a day over a hundred," I replied. He sighed again, but I think I made my point. "Seriously, think about what you just told me earlier about Bunin and how old a werewolf can get. How do you know that guy didn't find a Fountain of Youth somewhere or something?"

"Because there *is* no Fountain of Youth," he answered me. "At least, not properly so."

"Waitaminute!" Tony said, grabbing Durant by the shoulder. "Whaddya mean? There's a *sorta* Fountain o' Youth out there?" The look that he flashed at Tony quickly convinced him to remove his hand.

"There are at least half a dozen different ways to approximate Ludwig Prinn's formula for the *elixir vitae*—and all of them end in horror and tragedy," he growled at us, suddenly serious again. "I myself found that two-century-old heretic, Prinn, hiding in the ruins of a pre-Roman tomb and burned him at the stake five hundred years ago, but his damnable book still rots souls to this day. Men were not meant to live forever on this earth…"

"No men except for *you*, right?" I replied.

"I stand by my statement," he said quietly. "Men were not meant to live forever on this earth. *None* of us…"

Background
**From *La Tragèdia de Perseval, lo Cavalièr Que Pòt Pas Morir*
(Bertran de Born,[1] 1184, trans. J. Argento)**

Though I may be born a thousand times,
every day given a new name, a new life,
a new face with which to greet eternity,
ever young in the light of an aging sunlight,
still I would rather spend a single lifetime with you,
my beloved, my lady, my pale blossom,[2]
than to live the lifetime of the spheres without you.
    But we were fated to part
    at a generation's end,
    and I am preserved forever alone.

I bear the precious cross[3] laid upon me

---

[1] *The lord of Autafòrt, protégé and favorite troubadour of Eleanor of Aquitaine, wife to King Henry II of England. Bertran wrote his verses in Occitan, an early Romance language descended from Latin and similar to Catalan. This genre of verse—known as a "planh"—is a tragic form, usually used to mourn the passing of a great person who has recently died (such as Bertran's 1183 verse,* Mon chan fenisc ab dol et ab maltraire, *written on the death of Henry and Eleanor's eldest son, Henry). Ironically, Bertran here is using a planh to mourn the fact that the Grail knight, Sir Perseval,* cannot *die as mortal men do.*

[2] *Bertran's "ma florblanca" here may indeed be a poetical description of the woman's complexion, as Argento appears to believe, but since Chrétien de Troyes'* Perceval, le Conte du Graal *(1181) names the knight's beloved "Blanchefleur," there is good reason to believe that both names may actually point back to the original name of the Welsh princess—perhaps "Gwynblodau" or the like. Then again, Bertran's "ma domna amar" ("my beloved lady") in the same line may similarly point back to the character's name in* The Mabinogion *(an 11th-13th century collection of Welsh folktales)—"Angharad" ("my beloved one").*

[3] *Again, a questionable translation of the original Occitan. Bertran's "crucific d'argent" almost certainly refers to a "silver crucifix"—a more literal translation should read, "I wear the silver crucifix which you gave to*

on the night when we were wed,
the weighty burden of two loves,
each the cry of my heart,
each the author of my fate,
each the director of my path,
but neither the consort of the other.
>   Would that I could bear the one
>   and the other at the same time,
>   and serve both of my loves.

But the Cup of Christ holds not the marriage wine,
nor the family home His tomb and blood,
so I find myself set upon a solitary path,
with no one destined to walk beside me.
I see kings and princes wither,
I see kingdoms and empires fall,
but only God sees my footsteps alongside them.
>   I walk in daylight,
>   but always the darkest nights
>   ever haunt my thoughts.

Long life is a blessing for which monarchs strive
and they are called wise to do so,
but when one is older than the mountains,
then how can one's heart be warmer
than the stones which one outlives?
How can one express more kindness
than the hills under which one's beloved lies?
>   To know this length of days
>   is to outlive the very stars
>   and to outlive the light which they bear.

The sterling and the tournois[4] may purchase
all of the things for which a man may wish,
but they can never buy the joy which he seeks
and which may only be found
within the sharing of another loving heart.
Though he may rest his head on silken pillows
and eat the finest meats, he can yet live alone.
>   Thus is the lowliest beloved beggar
>   a master of greater wealth

---

me."

[4] *Units of currency—the sterling (i.e.; the Paris livre) was worth 25 sous, and the tournois was worth 20 sous.*

than the highest lonely king.

I stand alone atop a stonework wall
whose battlements face the north,
and I see the setting sun at my side.
My children's children's children died long ago,
when these walls were still young,
and many times has this same sun set
since their children's children stood where I now stand.
      Would their children even know
      the name of their forebear
      who stands watch over them today?

May Artús[5] sleep with his Guilalmer[6] until he reawakens,
and may all lovers rest alongside one another in Paradise,
all save the one who never rests, who walks unloved,
who faces demons and knaves and kings alike
to bear the sword and shield of righteous honor,
who shall never know the warm embrace of the sleep
which calls all men home to see their God at the last.
      All men save one,
      that Perseval of Evrawc,
      the knight who cannot die.

---

[5] *King Arthur—who, according to legend, rests with his queen in Avalon until he is most needed, when he will rise again.*

[6] *Queen Guinevere.*

Chapter 15
Bondage

The world is a complicated place, and that makes it hard for people looking for broad categories and simple answers. Rains come, babies die, and all sorts of horrible things go on every day. But there are also rainbows, and babies being born, and all sorts of wonderful things going on every day. So is the world a terrible place with just enough bright spots to make it bearable, or is it a beautiful place with just enough rotten bits to remind us that it's not perfect? It kind of depends on the attitude you walk into the discussion with, I suppose.

But the more complicated something appears, the more people naturally try to simplify it—and the more emotionally complicated a truth is, the more irrational people will tend to become about the need for simplifying it away. For instance, by the end of World War II, Adolf Hitler had murdered six million Jews. That's not only horrible—it's conceptually "icky," and it's hard to wrap your emotions around a truth that unpleasant. So there will always be people who try not to think about it or who live like it never happened—in fact, there are even some who deny that it *ever did* happen, since it's too vile a truth for them to accept. On the other hand, there are those who will tell you that Hitler killed ten million Jews, maybe twelve—and if you remind them that it was only *six* million ("*only* six million..."), they'll accuse you of trying to whitewash history and dismissing the suffering of all those who died. Their moral hysteria perceives your rationality as a lack of moral outrage.

As a cop, I recognize the crucial importance of a controlled moral outrage—we have to let our conscience be sensitive enough to the horrors of the world around us to motivate us into action, but we also have to train our intellect to keep us sharp enough, clear enough, that we can keep our focus on the actual evidence in front of us, and thus effectively bring an end to the things causing the outrage. I can't catch a murderer if I don't care, but I also can't catch him if I feel *so* much, or *so* strongly, that I get lost and let myself inflate or even invent evidence, missing the *real* clues.

So when I describe to you the place that Durant's compass directed us—when I describe why the *Obshchestvo Drakonisty* became involved in human trafficking in the first place—well... any time that you talk about human trafficking, things get "icky," and people get weird about hearing that.

Some people are so horrified by the concept that they pretend "it can't happen here," and they stick their heads in the sand while other people suffer because of their willful ignorance. Part of them realizes that, and their feelings of guilt force them to stick their heads deeper in the sand to avoid the shame of doing nothing. But the truth is, as bad as things are in distant Bangkok or Moscow, there's also human trafficking in Naperville, too, whether we want to admit it or not.

But then there's always going to be the well-meaning bleeding hearts who allow themselves to accept the truth—and in reaction to their earlier ignorant indifference, they'll inflate numbers, invent statistics, and treat anecdotal evidence as if it's the same as investigated evidence—and that's *deadly* to an investigation that might actually be able to help change things. For instance, one agency trying to combat the human trafficking industry estimated and documented that there are over 300,000 underage sex slaves in the world, being abused against their will—but they arrived at that statistic by doing their own informal search of the internet for pornography, estimating the number of girls who looked under-aged to them, and then assuming that, since they *seemed* young, they must be engaging in these acts under duress. Are there over 300,000 underage sex slaves in the world? Maybe there are, but we can't use that statistic as a starting point for investigation, because it's bogus evidence. Maybe there are ten times that many, but who knows? In 2003, *Newsweek* ran a story talking about the Mall of America in Minnesota as a major hub for human trafficking in the United States—a crucial bit of evidence that made every cop in the Midwest sit up and take notice. However, they had to issue a retraction later, admitting that they had no evidence to back that accusation up, that they'd included the information based totally on unreliable hearsay. No arrests, much less convictions, have ever been made related to human trafficking in the Mall of America, and no law enforcement records document any such activity going on there. And yet, in our hyper-Googled world, people keep quoting that same non-truth, then cross-quoting each other, citing and re-citing something that just isn't true. It's crap like that that makes investigative operations like Cross Country difficult, because we're always having to sift through the false evidence to find the real stuff that's going down. Even the Minnesota legislature brought the Mall of America thing up and tried to make decisions based on retracted facts that never had any evidentiary basis in the first place. Is there human trafficking going on at the Mall of America? Or at the Super Bowl? Or at the Olympics? Maybe there is, but there's absolutely no *evidentiary* reason for us to assume that there is, though people just keep insisting—emotively—that it's true. But if you try to explain that to some activists, they'll become morally indignant and accuse you of not caring enough—of not having enough moral outrage. But all of that is complicated, and we really prefer emotional simplifications that paint with wide, moral brushstrokes and make it easier for us to sleep at night.

So every year, missionaries raise money to go to Africa and buy slaves at slave markets so that they can set them free… and end up economically supporting the very slave trade that they were intending to undermine, because the slavers don't care what happens to their product after it's sold—they simply want the money that comes from the sale. In fact, those young people that the missionaries free usually go back to their villages to be reunited with their families… and are then often recaptured the same way by the same slavers who captured them in the first place. The truth is, slavers often actually *appreciate* the effort of the missionaries, since it lets them sell the same slaves over and over again. It doesn't help the victims to pretend that none of this is happening—but it also doesn't help them to ignore the facts and throw a lot of well-intentioned idiocy at the problem.

All this is to say that when I tell you that we were directed to an innocuous-looking storefront between Hamlin Park and Roscoe Village, it doesn't help to try to deny it. The fact is, criminals tend to be drawn to two kinds of areas—the kinds of places where you'd expect gangs to hang out, and the kinds of places where you'd *never* expect gangs to hang out. Would I expect gang activity in Englewood? Absolutely. Would I expect it in a nice little place like Hamlin Park? Not so much, no—they've worked so hard to clean up their neighborhood. Then again, we're not talking about street gangs like the Insane Deuces or the Latin Kings, who like being seen because they want to control a neighborhood as their "turf," and we're not even talking about the *Bratva*, who are trying to muscle in on the organized crime in Chicago through fear and blitzkrieg tactics—we're talking about the *Obshchestvo Drakonisty,* who are hunting humans for their own depraved reasons. Criminals are drawn to Englewood because it feels like home to them. Criminals are drawn to Hamlin Park or Roscoe Village because it feels like *your* home to them… and they want either the anonymity or the unprepared hunting ground that they think your home will provide them.

But even after I say all of that, I have to confess that when we walked inside the store and saw that portly, middle-aged man sitting calmly behind the counter in the bright morning sunlight, my first instinct was that Durant had led us on a wild goose chase. In fact, I almost said exactly that—I almost ignored the clues and made assumptions because this wasn't what I expected to find, but then I smelled something. *Two* somethings, actually. I smelled what reminded me of how Flubber smells when he comes inside from the rain, and I smelled the slightest hint of old blood.

"Can I help you gentlemen?" the man asked us with a pleasant smile.

"Where?" Durant asked with a sharp edge to his voice. The man looked confused for a second.

"Excuse me?"

"Where?" he growled again, vaulting over the counter and grasping the man by the throat. Tony and I both lurched forward to stop him, but that's when I saw the man's face change. It contorted into a hideous scowl of hatred and fury, and I saw his teeth sharpen.

"Back, Tony," I shouted, whipping my arm around to stop him. In fact, I think that I hit him hard enough that I might've knocked the wind out of him.

"*Where?!?*" Durant shouted as he gripped the man tighter, but he continued to transform. Somehow, I thought it would have taken longer, but he was already sprouting reddish-brown fur and ripping through his clothes. His fingers turned to claws, and he began to slash at Durant furiously. With a disgusted growl of anguish, Durant twisted him quickly with a sick, snapping sound, and the man's now-limp body slumped to the floor. Durant looked down at his torn sleeves.

"I despise werewolves..." he said with a sigh. The man's body again morphed in front of us back into a normal human form, like watching a stretched rubber toy shrinking back into shape. Durant drew his sword and sliced the man's head off cleanly, wiped the sword spotless on the man's pants, then performed his regular clean-up ritual with the little blue vial. "We shall have to search this place," Durant said, putting his sword away as he opened the door to a back storeroom. "The den will be well-hidden, to be sure." Tony went through another door to look through the office. I stood in the center of the store, cleared my head, and let my senses loose.

I could smell the man behind the counter—his aftershave, the soap he'd used earlier that morning, the coffee he'd had with his breakfast of eggs and sausages. I could smell the sweat and musk from his change. I could even smell the faintest scent of death already beginning. But I had to pull back, because I was finding myself getting lost in it. I listened, and I could hear the heat kicking on from a furnace—probably downstairs. So I followed the sound and walked into the storeroom, where the door to the basement of the building stood open. Durant had already gone down and was standing in the middle of the room, looking frustrated. The place was fairly sparse, but sure enough, there was the furnace that I'd heard.

"There's nothing here!" he shouted, taking a can and flinging it against the brick wall. It burst open, and I watched the contents splatter and form patterns, seemingly in slow-motion. Again, I had to pull myself back and re-focus. I could smell that musky, "wet dog" scent down here even stronger than upstairs. So I stopped and focused only on that smell. It almost seemed like something that I could see, like it was a trail of footprints left in mud, but it was a trail of scents left in the air. I followed that trail until it took me behind the furnace, to a stack of boxes piled up in the corner.

"There…" I said quietly, pointing in that direction. It was like I was walking through some sort of a dream, like it was all somewhat unreal. Durant pulled the Matteh ha Shelomoh out of his *got uechan* and handed it to me—I hadn't even noticed that he'd gotten it out of the car in the first place.

"You shall need this," he said. I began to reach for it without thinking, but the moment my hand reached it, I felt that burning sensation again, and I jerked back in pain.

"I can't…" I said, the pain rousing me. "I can't touch it." His eyes narrowed as he watched me. He was so hard-looking that, for a moment, I actually thought that he might draw that sword out and kill me. So when he reached into his bag, I found myself stiffening and preparing for attack.

Instead, he pulled out a pair of gloves—really, really old-looking gloves. In fact, they looked hand-made.

"Put these on…" he said.

"What are they?" I asked.

"Gloves."

"Yes, I know that, but how are they going to help me?" He sighed, obviously frustrated at having to explain himself.

"They are lined with special wolf fur, and they should give you a measure of protection against the vril in the staff," he answered. I put them on, and they felt amazing. Not only were they well-crafted and incredibly soft, but something about the wolf fur made me feel… comfortable…

"These are great," I said. "Thank you. Did you make them yourself?" His face darkened just a bit—almost imperceptibly, but I was noticing even the smallest detail better and better.

"No," he said quietly. "My daughter made them…" I could tell that this was something important, and that made me appreciate them all the more. Durant always did have a soft spot when it came to thinking about family.

"Then it's an honor to wear them," I said, trying to show that I understood what it meant to him. But the expression on his face turned to pain, and I realized that I'd said the wrong thing. When I thought about it a bit more, it dawned on me that he'd just given me maybe the only thing that he still had from his daughter—a beloved keepsake, irreplaceable—so that I could wield the weapon that his dying friend had given him, even though I was turning into exactly the sort of monster that he'd hunted for centuries. Wearing the gloves wasn't about honor at all—it was a tragedy...

*   *   *

We moved the boxes, and sure enough, there was a panel behind them. I'm certain that there was some sort of secret, special mechanism that would've opened the thing up, and that we'd have found it if we'd looked for it, but Durant just ripped the thing open with his bare hands and burst through the opening. We walked down a sloped corridor until we reached another, heavy door. Durant again ripped this one open with ease. Inside, what we saw curdled my blood.

I'd thought that what I'd heard about Bunin's basement meant that he'd been some sort of serial killer, but now I realized that his house was nothing more than a little way-station of a much larger operation. We walked into a large, central room that had *dozens* of small cells around its perimeter, with half a dozen padded red doors clumped in the back wall, and a couple of leather belts hanging on the wall next to them. In each cell were at least two young people, ranging in age from ten up to their early twenties. In Bunin's house, the cells had been soundproofed, but here, we were deep enough underground that nobody could hear their occupants, so these cells were little more than cages with barred doors. Throughout the room were the chunks and shreds of the carcasses of fresh kills.

"Dear God in Heaven..." I whispered.

"Indeed..." Durant growled in response. "This... is not the first time that I have seen one of these abominable places..." I turned to him in shock. This was the worst place I'd ever been in my whole life, and it's nothing new to him? I mean, I knew that he'd seen everything, but I guess that I never really realized what that meant until that moment. Looking around that horrible room, I saw the motivation for every century of his long fight against evil.

The children shrunk back in their cages, obviously terrified. Strangely, that surprised me. I guess I kind of assumed that they should've been excited to be rescued, but then I thought about how traumatic their ordeal must have been. Not only had they been captured and taken from their families, not only had they been locked behind bars and treated horribly, but because of the set-up of this room, they'd been forced to watch and see what the werewolves were doing to their fellow captives. They knew exactly what awaited them whenever somebody walked through that door—it was just a matter of seeing which cell the abuser went to first.

"Satan has ever sought the torment of children..." Durant said darkly.

"Because they're defenseless?" I asked.

"Because they are innocent," he answered, his voice low. "This makes them corruptible, but it also makes them more purely and completely terrified than most adults—and, at his core, the Devil is a sadist. He revels in the suffering of others because he knows that his own end will be terrible indeed."

"Like a wounded animal," I suggested, "just trying to lash out and hurt as many other people as he can before he finally goes down."

"Just so," he said. "He knows that he lacks the power and ability to hurt outright the God who created him, but he nonetheless desires to wound his Maker, even if only obliquely. And what better way to hurt a Father than to hurt his children...?"

I looked around the room, at the huddled, terrified children, and thought of Chelsea and the twins.

"We have to get these children out of here," I said, suddenly angry. I grabbed my cell phone to call Tony upstairs, but we were too deep underground for me to get a signal. "Can you go get Tony while I open these cages?" I asked. He sighed, then disappeared in a blur. There were keys hanging on a hook near the door, so I grabbed them and took them to the first cell. The children inside started crying as I approached.

"It's okay," I said, reassuring them. "I'm a police officer. I'm here to take all of you home." I repeated it loudly enough for the other children to hear, but only some of them seemed to really hear me. Most of them were so traumatized that they just shrank to the backs of their cages and cried. My heart broke as I opened up the cages as quickly as I could. How could anyone do this to a child? To *any* other human being?

But then I figured that the *Obshchestvo Drakonisty* didn't think about their captives as fellow human beings, really. They obviously thought of them as human cattle—a means of keeping their werewolf *kryshas* fed and happy. I saw that several of the older girls were just wearing their underwear, and I felt my moral outrage rising into a low growl in the back of my throat.

I began to wonder if the werewolves even saw *themselves* as human any more. Maybe they considered themselves an entirely separate species now—as wolves who occasionally turned into humans, instead of the other way around. Maybe it wasn't really cannibalism so much as inter-species predation. That thought made it only slightly more endurable as I stepped over body parts to open more cells. By the time any of the children had risked coming out of their cages, Tony and Durant were back in the room. Durant started on the other side of the room, ripping the cage doors off at the hinges, while Tony just stood in the door in horror—and then turned aside and threw up. In all of the crime scenes we'd been to over all of these years, I'd never seen him lose it like that. My first thought was that it must have been because of the cancer, but then I stepped in a pile of entrails and it struck me—we were in an enclosed room filled with piles of rotting flesh everywhere. The stench had to be horrible, nearly unbearable. With my new, enhanced senses, it should have hit me even harder than it had Tony, but I suddenly realized why it hadn't: to me, the place smelled really, really good. In fact, I was finding myself getting hungrier and hungrier with every step. But I remembered what Durant had told me at Palmer Square, and I tried to make my thoughts bounce to something else.

So I prayed to God that I could think about the Brooklyn Dodgers.

First baseman Jackie Robinson was a personal hero of mine. Roy Campanella came up as catcher the next season. *My stomach growled...* Who was the pitcher that came up the next year? Don Newcombe! He was a Cy Young Award winner, for crying out loud—how could I forget him? Sandy Koufax started in as a pitcher in what... 1955? But he stunk until 1961. *I was so hungry...* Why did he stink? He was injured half the time, he was out of shape, he was young and raw. *These kids were so young...* By 1961, they were in Los Angeles, right? Who was that fast shortstop that they'd had...?

"Tom...?" I heard Tony call out. He was standing in the middle of the room, and he looked like he was in shock. "What *is* this place, Tom?"

"A larder for *La Société des Dragonistes*," Durant answered, opening up the final cell. The children were still crying, and they were having trouble coming out. We'd gotten them to the scariest point that they'd been at for weeks—we'd given them the horror of hope, but they were still surrounded by the evidence of the inevitability of their own deaths.

"Get..." I started, but I found that I was struggling to express a coherent thought. "Get... them out... out of..." It was all coming out as low growls. Durant was watching me carefully.

"Hey, kids," Tony shouted out, snapping back to his senses. "Anyone wanna get outta here with me an' go home to yer famlies? Let's all go upstairs. C'mon, let's go..." The older ones helped the younger ones, and they all started moving toward the door. All of a sudden, one of the littlest kids made a break for it and started running— and after that, it was a mad free-for-all as kids were falling over themselves trying to get out. Tony and the older ones tried to keep order, but it was like herding a rioting bunch of terrified cats. I knew that I couldn't help—I was doing everything I could just to keep it together. Durant was standing there, watching me.

"Yes, a child is uniquely capable of being thoroughly and utterly terrified," he said at last, and there was something about the clarity of his voice that reeled me in. I used it to try to focus myself back and shut out the smells and thoughts that were filling my mind. Such horrible thoughts… "The intensity of their terror stems primarily not from their innocence being ripped from them, nor from their uncanny ability to feel every emotion completely and uninhibitedly, but ultimately from their ignorance. They cannot comprehend what is happening to them, nor why anyone would torment them in this way, nor why their loving parents are not there to protect them from their torture. Their entire cosmology is torn out from under them, and they are left physically and emotionally alone, without a shred of hope. And this is Satan's delight. This is what you and I must take our stand against. Throughout history, the Devil has made use of the Ježibaba and the Baba Jaga, Yeitso and the yeibichai, the luchorpán and the bogeymen to hunt, terrorize, torture, and devour children, because it is the simplest way to cause the greatest amount of horror to the people whom God loves."

"Boogie-man… is real?" I asked, trying to hold onto what he was saying.

"There are no supernatural creatures hiding under one's bed at night…" he replied, stepping toward me, his hand on his *got uechan*. His voice was calm and measured. "But the bogeymen were quite real, I assure you. Were you aware that the words, 'bug,' 'bag,' and 'boogie-man,' are all derived from the same root word? There is good reason why the children of the world should fear a man who comes in the night with a sack…" He stood in front of me and his eyes latched onto mine. Mine latched right back onto his and I tried to focus on him and him alone. It was hard to look into those eyes for very long—they burned like some sort of cold fire.

"The Comprachicos of the 16th and 17th centuries would abduct small children from their homes while they slept," he continued in that same quiet tone of voice, providing me a center. "They would tuck them into bags and steal them far away. You must understand that the call for dwarves and fools and circus freaks was great in those days, and so the Comprachicos would mutilate the children in order to stunt their growth, artificially deform their bodies or faces, and otherwise convert them into man-made monsters which could then be sold to a court or circus for profit." I could finally find myself able to breathe normally again. My mind was clearing—but I realized that what he was saying was something terrible, and part of me wanted to climb back into those horrible, wonderful smells.

"But the Comprachicos were pikers compared to the Torbalan. Where the former were simply bands of cruel men who sought personal profit through the suffering of the defenseless, the Torbalana are dark and foul creatures which stuffed children into bags and stole them away in order to feed upon them. And I have found them in nearly every culture on the planet. The Spanish call them *el hombres del saco;* in Turkey, they are the *Öcü;* in India, the *Bori Baba;* in Africa, the *Antjie Somers;* and the list goes on. The Dutch refer to *Zwarte Piet*—"

"Wait!" I stopped him. There was something that I remembered there. *Zwarte Piet—Black Pete.* "I've... heard of that one. Works with... with Santa Claus? In... in blackface...?"

"Sinterklaas," he corrected me. "To the Dutch, Sinterklaas may bring presents to good children in his bags, but his dark minion, Zwarte Piet, then uses those now-empty bags to stuff the naughty children into, torturing them and mutilating them into new Zwarte Pieten who will then later abduct still more children. One can easily see how the Dutch have conflated the historical Comprachicos, the Torbalana, and the good Turkish bishop, Nicholas, with the Odinist tales of the white-haired god flying through the sky in his sleigh, off on his Wild Hunt. Nonetheless, there are often slivers of truth hidden amongst the trees of myth, and the Torbalana are a perfect example of this. Even in Vietnam, they speak of the *ông ba bị,* which uses its *bột xương*—in truth, a form of *oase rău*, not at all dissimilar to the *'áńt'į* which František Sydor used against your friend...?" He stopped for a moment, and I realized that he was asking for her name. He'd forgotten her name.

"Karen..." I answered quietly. He remembered all of these horrors, for all of these centuries, but couldn't be bothered to remember her name... *Karen Gage...*

"Yes, Karen. The *ông ba bị*—like to many such witch-monsters— uses these powders to lull the children into a deeper sleep, from which they never truly awaken. The Torbalana delight in the taste of child-flesh, and in the horror which this brings to the children's families."

"Hansel and Gretel..." I muttered, clearing my mind.

"Excuse me?"

"The old story of Hansel and Gretel," I said again, finally myself again. "There was this witch that wanted to eat them. That's the whole point of the story—they were lost in the woods and the witch captured them to cook them and eat them."

"Just so," he replied. "One of the Torbalana known as Frau Perchta. But tell me the truth, Detective," he said, leaning in close. "Can you imagine a horror worse than a monster who would wish to devour an innocent child?"

For a moment, his gaze was so intense that I couldn't breathe— because I knew that he was testing me, and because a minute earlier, I honestly don't know what I could've said in response.

"That's about the worst thing that I can imagine," I answered at last. "I'd rather die than become something like that." I looked him straight in the eye and kept looking at him until both of us knew that I meant what I'd said.

"Excellent," he said with a nod of his head.

Maury Wills, I thought to myself. *The shortstop who stole all those bases was Maury Wills...*

*   *   *

At that moment, we heard one of the red doors opening behind us, and out came Bunin, with his arm around the neck of a crying girl who was maybe 18. With all of that padding on the door, he must not have heard anything that had been going on out in the main room. We both spun around, and when he saw Durant, his face went white.

"*Bozhe moi!*" he cried hoarsely. "*Vy Strannik...*"

"*Da*," Durant replied with a snarl. "*I vy Nikodim Georgiyevich Bunin. Dobroe utro...*" Bunin let the girl go and jumped for one of the belts on the wall. As soon as he touched it, I saw his body begin to contort, and dark brown fur began to bristle all over his body.

Dark brown, not gray.

"Kill it, Detective!" Durant shouted, dashing over to Bunin and grabbing him. "Kill it! *Now!*" Bunin struggled in his grasp as he continued to change. I ran over and raised the staff above my head to strike, but I couldn't get past the fur color. Bunin wasn't the monster that had attacked us that night in his house. The big bad wolf was still out there somewhere.

"Change back!" I growled at him, bringing the staff closer to his twisting face so that the vril could burn him. "Change back to human, or I'll take you out right now!" The metamorphosis stopped, and he stopped struggling. For a moment, I couldn't tell if that was because he understood me, or because the vril had messed with him somehow. But then, he gritted his teeth and I watched him slowly shift back into his human form.

"What are you doing, Detective?" Durant yelled. "Destroy the fiend!"

"He's not the one," I said, and I yanked the belt out of his hand. "He's not the one that I'm looking for." As I waited for him to change, I realized that the leather in the belt wasn't what I was expecting—it was softer and thinner than cowhide. I dropped it and recoiled in horror when I realized that it had been made from tanned, human skin. That's when I noticed that the girl was still there, shaking, with her back up against the wall.

"Go upstairs!" I shouted, pointing to the door. "We're police officers, and the rest of your friends are upstairs!" Slowly, trembling, she began to back away and move to the door. "Go on, hon—it's okay..." I said with a little more gentleness. She'd been through enough, and I didn't need to be adding to it. "You're going to be okay now. I promise."

Let's be honest—very few of these kids were ever going to be "okay" again. They were going to need a lot of counseling and a lot of TLC, and they were still going to be wounded people for a long, long time to come. I suspected that there were going to be a lot of vegetarian non-dog owners in that group, and that very few of them would ever be comfortable going down into a basement again. But the girl understood me and broke into a run out of the room and up the corridor to Tony.

I checked, but there wasn't anyone in any of the rooms behind any of the other doors. With that, I turned back to Bunin. Durant was whispering something into his ear, and the guy began shaking uncontrollably. He was ready for me to question him.

"Where's the rest of the pack, Bunin?" I asked.

"N-Not here," he stammered. "Is morning, is not here!" Durant pulled one of his arms up behind him with a cracking sound, and he yelped in pain.

"Where?" he growled.

"Different places," Bunin replied. "All different places..."

"Any more places like this?" I asked him. "Any more cages with any more children?"

"No..." he answered. Durant whispered something else to him, and he lost control of his bladder. "No, not yet, I swear!" he screamed. "*Klyanus' Bogom!* I swear to God this is only one!" And if you'd have been standing there, watching his dark eyes rolling around in utter terror like I was, smelling the fear rolling off of him in waves like I did, you'd have believed him, too.

"Not even at your place on Chicago Avenue?" I asked. He started crying.

"That was trap," he said, his words coming out in tearful bursts. "Ten *oborotni* wait to pounce, but you do not come. No one want to meet the *Strannik* alone, not out in open," he added, glancing back at Durant. "He kill us for sport. Like the *volkodav*—the wolfhound—he hunt us."

"No hearts here bleed for you, Nikodim Georgiyevich..." Durant growled.

I felt my aggression rising again. Remember what I said earlier about controlled moral outrage? It was like I could hardly contain it, like it was in control of me. All I wanted to do was to rip Bunin's throat out and... and the thoughts that went through my mind were exactly the sorts of thoughts that must go through a werewolf's mind all of the time, and I prayed to make them go away.

"What did you do to Leah Wilson? What kind of a monster does *any* of this to people?" I asked him, looking around the room. "You're not even a true werewolf, are you? You're a *wannabe*." I pointed to the belt on the ground. "You need something like that belt to make you change. Did you take that off of one of your kills?"

"No…" I heard a voice behind me, back at the doorway at the base of the corridor. I turned around to see the muscular, tattooed Romanian from the Five Star Bar standing there, with four werewolves panting next to him in the doorway. "No, I stripped flesh from back of my dead son and made belt myself, you understand?"

"Crap…" I said, kicking myself for not putting it together earlier. "That guy's Papa Sydor, isn't he…?" And how did the werewolves get past Tony? What was going on upstairs?

"*Da*," the Romanian said to me, nodding. "*Şi salut din nou, Rătăcitor…*" he said to Durant, with a smile that spread his thick, gray moustache across his face. He was shirtless, and I could clearly see the serpent tattoo around his neckline—but now I could also see the large crucifix under it, filling his chest. There were huge wolves wrapped in serpents on either side of the base, their faces turned upward toward the crucified Christ. He was the *Avtoritet,* their leader.

Bunin started laughing, and mumbled something under his breath that I didn't catch.

"That's it—I've had my fill," Durant said, reaching up and snapping Bunin's neck. Somehow, that just didn't seem like enough justice for all that he'd done. It just seemed… anti-climactic… Then again, it really didn't bother me that slime like Bunin was done sucking air. I felt that growling outrage rising in me again.

"So you're the 'Alpha dog' around here?" I asked Sydor as Durant dropped Bunin's body to the ground.

"The what?" Sydor replied, frowning.

"The leader of this pack," I said. "The strongest one here."

"*Da*," he answered me, flashing that same, big smile. "Strongest one here."

"Then he is the one whom you must kill, Detective," Durant said. "Leave the others to me." *Sure—just give me the strongest one, why don't you?* I thought. With that, the four werewolves split up and started to circle around. Durant drew his sword with a flash and stepped away from me. Sydor just stood there and faced me from across the room.

"You want kill me, yes?" he asked. I watched as the werewolves padded past the empty cages, and the overpowering smell of their musk and the blood around me made me almost dizzy. "You want kill old Sydor?"

"I'm really beginning to…" I growled back. I found myself gritting my teeth, and the palm of my hand began itching. I heard the other wolves panting and snarling, and it excited me.

"But you are one of *us*," he said, chuckling. "I smell serpent on you. Why did *Rătăcitor* not bring his cup to save you, eh?" He nodded to Durant. "Because he know you too far gone, or not far enough? Because he know you no really want to be saved, maybe?" I glanced over to Durant, too, reflexively. Why *hadn't* he offered to let me drink from the Grail? *Could* it save me? And—maybe more importantly— why hadn't I ever thought to ask for it?

"I know what you want," he continued. "You want killing, yes—but not me, no..." He smiled and pointed at Durant. "You want man-flesh..."

I followed his pointing and looked fully at Durant, and he turned to look at me. His eyes narrowed, and he backed up, away from me, his sword arcing between me and the approaching werewolves. I was beginning to breathe heavy, and my mind was swirling around.

"Detective," I heard him say to me, as if through a fog. "Bounce your thoughts..."

"Detective," Sydor said, and his voice sounded like a warm blanket. "Embrace chaos—follow your heart..."

Background
From *Ophiolatreia: An Account of the Rites and Mysteries Connected with the Origin, Rise, and Development of Serpent Worship in Parts of the World* (anonymous, 1889)

Mr. James, in his MSS. in the possession of the New York Historical Society,[1] states, "that the Menominees translate the *manitou*[2] of the Chippeways by *ahwahtoke*," which means emphatically a snake. "Whether," he continues, "the word was first formed as a name for a surprising or disgusting object, and thence transferred to spiritual beings, or whether the extension of its signification has been in an opposite direction, it is difficult to determine." Bossu[3] also affirms that the Arkansas believed in the existence of a great spirit, which they adore under form of a serpent. In the North-west it was a symbol of evil power.

Here we may suitably introduce the tradition of a great serpent, which is to this day, current amongst a large portion of the Indians of the Algonquin stock. It affords some curious parallelisms with the allegorical relations of the old world. The Great Teacher of the Algonquins, Manabozho,[4] is always placed in antagonism to a great

---

[1] *Edwin James'* Outline of the Paradigma of a Chippeway Vocabulary *(1830), and his* Essay on the Chippeway Language *(1833), both folios placed on reserve at the Society's Albany branch. A trained physician, James had served as botanist and geologist for Maj. Stephen Harriman Long's 1820 expedition, which explored the Rocky Mountains.*

[2] *A word meaning both "snake" and "spirit" in many Native American languages—which was why the Menominee (or Mamaceqtaw) used a completely different word to translate it when referring to the Great Serpent—a horned monster that lives underwater. The Potawatomi (or Bodéwadmi, or Neshnabé) among the Ojibwe differentiated the meanings of "mnito" in their language by consistently using "Gchi-Mnito" ["Great Manitou"] to refer to their almighty sky god and "Mji-Mnito" ["Evil Manitou"] to refer to the Great Serpent.*

[3] *Jean-Bernard Bossu, a French captain and adventurer who traveled extensively in America—particularly amongst the Arkansas [aka Akanças] tribe, as chronicled in his* Nouveaux Voyages dans l'Amerique Septentrionale *(1777).*

[4] *The Menominee name for the Trickster, also called "Nanabozho" by the*

serpent, a spirit of evil, who corresponds very nearly with the Egyptian Typhon,[5] the Indian Kaliya,[6] and the Scandinavian Midgard.[7] He is also connected with the Algonquin notions of a deluge; and as Typhon is placed in opposition to Osiris or Apollo, Kaliya to Surya or the Sun, and Midgard to Wodin or Odin, so does he bear a corresponding relation to Manabozho. The conflicts between the two are frequent; and although the struggles are sometimes long and doubtful, Manabozho is usually successful against his adversary. One of these contests involved the destruction of the earth by water, and its reproduction by the powerful and beneficent Manabozho. The tradition in which this grand event is embodied was thus related by Kah-ge-ga-gah-boowh,[8] a chief of the Ojibway.[9] In all of its essentials, it is recorded by means of the rude pictured signs of the Indians, and scattered all over the Algonquin territories:

Potawatomi—though his name should properly be expressed as "Wenabozho," since the particle "N-" expresses the concept of a personal connection with the speaker [i.e.; "my Wenabozho"]. He is often portrayed as a rabbit, and is thus also called "Chi-Waaboozo" ("Great Hare").

[5] *Actually, Typhon (Τυφῶν) the chaos-bringer—who, with his wife, Echidna ('Εχιδνα), acted as the "father and mother of all monsters"—was a Greek monster, not an Egyptian one. Though Herodotus (in his 5th century BC text, Ἡροδότου Ἁλικαρνησσέος ἱστορίης) does connect the Greek Typhon myths to Egyptian myths about Set, Typhon's mortal enemy is Zeus, Greek sky god of the thunderbolt.*

[6] *An evil god (one of the nāgás—the serpentine gods of Vedic mythology) who lived under the waters of the Yamuna River. Interestingly, Kāliya's mortal enemy was Garuḍa, the eagle—much as the Potawatomi tribe's water monster's mortal enemy was Cigwe', the thunderbird creature of the sky.*

[7] *In Norse mythology, "Midgarðsormr" (also called the "Jörmungandr") is the offspring of jötnar Loki and Angrboða. In the final battle of Ragnarök, the Midgarðsormr and his mortal enemy, Thor (god of thunder) are fated to kill one another. Note that in all three cited cases—Typhon, Kāliya, and the Midgarðsormr—the archenemy of the serpent is a sky god (particularly, a god of thunder), much like the serpentine Tiamat's mortal enemy was the storm god, Marduk, in ancient Sumeria, or sky god Zhù Róng fought water dragon Gònggōng in ancient China. In all of these myths, the underwater serpent god (and, by association, the water itself) represented the forces of chaos and destruction, and the sky god represented the forces of order and light.*

[8] *George Copway (1818-1869), who served as chief to the Ojibwe, medicine man to the Algonquin and Iroquois, and Christian missionary to the Saugeen. He also helped to translate the* Gospel of St Luke *and* The Acts of the Apostles *into Ojibwa, published his memoirs as* The Life, History and Travels of Kah-ge-ga-gah-Bowh *(1847), and printed his weekly* Copway's American Indian *newspaper in New York City in 1851.*

[9] *The Ojibwe, aka "Chippewa" tribe.*

One day, returning to his lodge from a long journey, Manabozho missed from it his young cousin, who resided with him, he called his name aloud, but received no answer. He looked around on the sand for the tracks of his feet, and he there, for the first time, discovered the trail of Meshekenabek, the serpent.[10] He then knew that his cousin had been seized by his great enemy. He armed himself, and followed on his track, he passed the great river, and crossed mountains and valleys to the shores of the deep and gloomy lake now called Manitou Lake, Spirit Lake, or the Lake of Devils. The trail of Meshekenabek led to the edge of the water.

At the bottom of this lake was the dwelling of the serpent, and it was filled with evil spirits—his attendants and companions. Their forms were monstrous and terrible, but most, like their master, bore the semblance of serpents. In the centre of this horrible assemblage was Meshekenabek himself, coiling his volumes around the hapless cousin of Manabozho. His head was red as with blood, and his eyes were fierce and glowed like fire. His body was all over armed with hard and glistening scales of every shade and colour.

Manabozho looked down upon the writhing spirits of evil, and he vowed deep revenge. He directed the clouds to disappear from the heavens, the winds to be still, and the air to become stagnant over the lake of the manitous, and bade the sun shine upon it with all its fierceness; for thus he sought to drive his enemy forth to seek the cool shadows of the trees, that grew upon its banks, so that he might be able to take vengeance upon him.

Meanwhile, Manabozho, seized his bow and arrows and placed himself near the spot where he deemed the serpents would come to enjoy the shade. He then transferred himself into the broken stump of a withered tree, so that his enemies might not discover his presence.

The winds became still, and the sun shone hot on the lake of the evil manitous. By and by the waters became troubled, and bubbles rose to the surface, for the rays of the sun penetrated to the horrible brood within its depths. The commotion increased, and a serpent lifted its head high above the centre of the lake and gazed around the shores. Directly another came to the surface, and they listened for the footsteps of Manabozho but they heard him nowhere on the face of the earth, and they said one to the other, "Manabozho sleeps." And then they plunged again beneath the waters, which seemed to hiss as they closed over them.

It was not long before the lake of manitous became more

---

[10]   *The "Mji-Mnito" or "Great Serpent," the father of all water monsters and the personification of evil. Also called a "mishibijiw" or "michipeshu" by mid-western tribes, or an "apotamkin" by north-eastern ones.*

troubled than before, it boiled from its very depths, and the hot waves dashed wildly against the rocks on its shores. The commotion increased, and soon Meshekenabek, the Great Serpent, emerged slowly to the surface, and moved towards the shore. His blood-red crest glowed with a deeper hue, and the reflection from his glancing scales was like the blinding glitter of a sleet covered forest beneath the morning sun of winter. He was followed by the evil spirits, so great a number that they covered the shores of the lake with their foul trailing carcasses.

They saw the broken, blasted stump into which Manabozho had transformed himself, and suspecting it might be one of his disguises, for they knew his cunning, one of them approached, and wound his tail around it, and sought to drag it down. But Manabozho stood firm, though he could hardly refrain from crying aloud, for the tail of the monster tickled his sides.

The Great Serpent wound his vast folds among the trees of the forest, and the rest also sought the shade, while one was left to listen for the steps of Manabozho.

When they all slept, Manabozho silently drew an arrow from his quiver, he placed it in his bow, and aimed it where he saw the heart beat against the sides of the Great Serpent. He launched it, and with a howl that shook the mountains and startled the wild beasts in their caves, the monstre awoke, and, followed by its frightful companions, uttering mingled sounds of rage and terror, plunged again into the lake. Here they vented their fury on the helpless cousin of Manabozho, whose body they tore into a thousand fragments, his mangled lungs rose to the surface, and covered it with whiteness. And this is the origin of the foam on the water.

When the Great Serpent knew that he was mortally wounded, both he and the evil spirits around him were rendered tenfold more terrible by their great wrath and they rose to overwhelm Manabozho. The water of the lake swelled upwards from its dark depths, and with a sound like many thunders, it rolled madly on its track, bearing the rocks and trees before it with resistless fury. High on the crest of the foremost wave, black as the midnight, rode the writhing form of the wounded Meshekenabek, and red eyes glazed around him, and the hot breaths of the monstrous brood hissed fiercely above the retreating Manabozho. Then thought Manabozho of his Indian children, and he ran by their villages, and in a voice of alarm bade them flee to the mountains, for the Great Serpent was deluging the earth in his expiring wrath, sparing no living thing. The Indians caught up their children, and wildly sought safety where he bade them. But Manabozho continued his flight along the base of the western hills, and finally took refuge on a high mountain beyond

Lake Superior, far towards the north. There he found many men and animals who had fled from the flood that already covered the valleys and plains, and even the highest hills. Still the waters continued to rise, and soon all the mountains were overwhelmed save that on which stood Manabozho. Then he gathered together timber, and made a raft, upon which the men and women, and the animals that were with him, all placed themselves. No sooner had they done so, than the rising floods closed over the mountain and they floated alone on the surface of the waters; and thus they floated for many days, and some died, and the rest became sorrowful, and reproached Manabozho that he did not disperse the waters and renew the earth that they might live. But though he knew that his great enemy was by this time dead, yet could not Manabozho renew the world unless he had some earth in his hands wherewith to begin the work. And this he explained to those that were with him, and he said that were it ever so little, even a few grains of earth, then could he disperse the waters and renew the world. Then the beaver volunteered to go to the bottom of the deep, and get some earth, and they all applauded her design. She plunged in, they waited long, and when she returned she was dead; they opened her hands but there was no earth in them.

"Then," said the otter, "will I seek the earth:" and the bold swimmer dived from the raft. The otter was gone still longer than the beaver, but when he returned to the surface he too was dead, and there was no earth in his claws.

"Who shall find the earth?" exclaimed all those left on the raft, "now that the beaver and the otter are dead?" and they desponded more than before, repeating, "Who shall find the earth?"

"That will I," said the muskrat, and he quickly disappeared between the logs of the raft. The muskrat was gone very long, much longer than the otter, and it was thought he would never return, when he suddenly rose near by, but he was too weak to speak, and he swam slowly towards the raft. He had hardly got upon it when he too died from his great exertion. They opened his little hands and there, clasped closely between the fingers, they found a few grains of fresh earth.[11] These Manabozho carefully collected and dried

---

[11] *As Spence noted in his* Myths of the North American Indians *(1914), the Algonquin version of this myth has Manabozho (known to the Algonquin as "Michabo") actually causing the flood by wading into the water after his hunting dogs. Afterwards, "Michabo dispatched a raven with directions to find a piece of earth which might serve as a nucleus for a new world, but the bird returned from its quest unsuccessful. Then the god sent an otter on a like errand, but it too failed to bring back the needful terrestrial germ. At last, a musk-rat was sent on the same mission, and it returned with sufficient*

them in the sun, and then he rubbed them into a fine powder in his palms, and, rising up, he blew them abroad upon the waters. No sooner was this done than the flood began to subside, and soon the trees on the mountains and hills emerged from the deep, and the plains and the valleys came in view and the waters disappeared from the land leaving no trace but a thick sediment, which was the dust that Manabozho had blown abroad from the raft.

Then it was found that Meshekenabek, the Great Serpent, was dead, and that the evil manitous, his companions, had returned to the depths of the lake of spirits, from which, for the fear of Manabozho, they never more dared to come forth. And in gratitude to the beaver, the otter, and the muskrat, those animals were ever after held sacred by the Indians, and they became their brethren, and they never killed nor molested them until the medicine of the stranger made them forget their relations and turned their hearts to ingratitude.

---

earth to enable Michabo to recreate the solid land." Note the similarities to the Biblical story of Noah also sending out a raven and then three sorties by a dove in The Book of Genesis *viii, 6-12, to discover much the same thing (the Mesopotamian Utnapishtim does something very similar as well in the ancient* Epic of Gilgamesh*). It is significant that remarkably parallel deluge stories may be found in the otherwise disparate histories of Chinese, Greek, Navajo, and pre-Inca peoples (see Rosenberg's* World Mythology, 1989*), as well as the Manu myth of ancient India, the Tiddalik myth of the Australian aboriginal peoples, the Pūluga myths of the Andaman Islands, and even the Finnish legends of Väinämöinen's blood. That these various myths may in fact all point back to an original, corrupted narrative of a single, worldwide flood has been argued by various scholars to various degrees, including Sir Charles Leonard Woolley from his work at Ur (see Young, 1977), Eric Schmidt from his work at Shurrupak (see Bailey, 1968), Claude Albritton in his* Catastrophic Episodes in Earth History *(1989), etc.*

Chapter 16
Cavete Lupus

A recovering alcoholic gets handed a beer at a ball game. A porn addict's finger hovers over his mouse button. A gambler who wants to quit is sent by his boss to a convention next to a casino. A girl with low self-esteem is complimented by a guy who's making moves on her at a party. There are times in your life when you're thrust into the moment and forced to make a decision about who you want to be—not just about what you're going to do next, but about what kind of person you're going to become in the next few seconds, for good or for bad, from that point forward. Are you going to fall off the wagon? Are you going to decide that your body and your self-image are precious to you? Which way are you going to go with your next step, your next breath?

Everything physical in me wanted to let go and run free. I felt tied down, constrained, trapped. But if I could rip through all of that and just *do*—not think, not plan, just *act* and do whatever felt good at that moment, then I'd be free. My whole world had turned red, and all I smelled was blood. I swear that I could hear the blood rushing through Durant's veins, even though I couldn't hear his words any more. My teeth hurt, and I wanted to run on all fours like my brothers. I wanted to feel strong and powerful and free and happy.

That's what my body wanted, what it craved. But then Durant's words from the night before echoed in my mind: *This life is infinitely more complicated than to be founded and turned upon what you or I want to happen within it...*

Surely we're more than just the sum total of our cravings, aren't we? Tony's more than just a chain smoker. Nate Kingery is more than just a guy who's going to Alcoholics Anonymous. I'm more than just what this sickness was trying to make me become. What I desperately *want* to do isn't what I absolutely *have* to do.

I suddenly remembered my pastor sharing an old Cherokee parable about a grandfather telling his grandson that in every man, there are always two wolves fighting for control. You can break it down that one is evil and one is good, or one wants you to turn left and one wants you to turn right, or one wants you to take a drink and the other tells you to stand tough, whatever. The point is, the wolves are always fighting, and the strongest one will always win.

"But which one is the strongest one?" the little boy asks him.

"The one that you *feed*..." the grandfather answers.

My body wanted to take that drink, click that button, go to that casino, give in to what would make me feel good. That's what I craved. But I knew that if I did, then that's the wolf I'd be feeding, and the other wolf, the man that I really am inside, would starve to death. It would feel like freedom at the moment that I gave in, but even saying it that way proves the point—I'd be *giving in*. It would feel like freedom, but it would make me a slave to my lusts instead of the master of my own mind.

You have to understand that all of this went through my mind in a split second, in the space between heartbeats. I'm spelling it all out for you now, but it really was more of a clash of gut feeling vs. intuitive discernment—a flash of insight more than a thought-through argument. But then I took a moment to think about Joanna and how hard I'd been trying to be the kind of husband she deserved. I thought of my children, and how much I loved being the kind of father that they could respect and love. Would giving in now make me more or less the man that I truly wanted to be?

"Dear God..." I said to myself—though, to be honest, I might've said it out loud, too. "This isn't who I want to be, and it's not who you want me to be. Give me strength..."

I'm not really much of a long-winded prayer type of guy. That was pretty much it. I don't know if you could say that God gave me the strength I prayed for, or if I just needed to take that moment to make my own decision about whether to turn left or to turn right, but I realized that I'd just passed through that moment of personal epiphany that I was talking about before—that moment when you decide the person that you're going to be from that point forward.

I decided to be Tom Chapel at his best, not some animal that only looked like him sometimes.

Now, I know that Durant had told me to go after Sydor and to leave the other wolves to him, but when I saw them begin to lunge at him from four different sides, I couldn't stand back and do nothing. I don't think that I would've called Pieter Durant my friend, but he was my partner, and he was one of the good guys, and there was no way that I was going to let these monsters sink their teeth into him.

So I jumped for the one closest to me, swinging the Staff of Solomon at it as hard as I could. I guess that I expected that it would act like it did with revenants and stuff like that, smashing through the wolf like swinging a baseball bat through a jello sculpture. Instead, it more just acted like a baseball bat, period. I hit the wolf across its side, and it felt like smacking a side of beef. But the werewolf yelped and swung to the side—it obviously hurt. But then the thing spun around and faced me, growling and frothing at the muzzle. A week earlier, I would've been scared out of my mind, but at that moment, I just really, really wanted to kill one of these things.

"Come on!" I snarled back at it.

The thing leapt at me with blinding speed, raking me with its claws. But I'd become pretty fast, too, and I was able to dodge to the side enough that the claws only slashed my left arm as the wolf passed by me. It hurt, of course, but it felt different than it had at Bunin's house. Somehow, I found the pain invigorating, like it actually helped me focus on the fight. I roared back at the thing and swung the staff, smashing it on its spine. Again, it whined in pain.

Out of the corner of my eye, I could see Durant grappling with the other three. He was having trouble slashing with his sword, since they were in so close and all over him, and I could see that he was covered in blood—but how much of it was his and how much of it was theirs, I couldn't tell. Sydor was just standing there, watching us all.

My own opponent had spun around again and was preparing for another pounce. Its bright eyes were like two green fires, and they flashed when the thing jumped at me again. But this time, I was ready, and I swung the staff just as it got on top of me, sweeping at one of its legs. I heard a loud cracking sound, and the wolf crumpled to the killing floor, howling in pain, its leg shattered in a compound fracture that shoved the bone through the skin. I seized the opportunity and made the first move this time, smashing my staff down onto its head. Again, I heard a crack, and the beast stopped moving altogether.

Turning around, I saw that Durant was still furiously fighting two of the creatures—and the fresh body of a naked, heavily tattooed man lay in two halves on the ground nearby.

"Why you fight us, brother?" Sydor called out to me. I turned to face him.

"Because I'm not your brother," I answered. "I'm a human being."

"*Da*," he replied, nodding. "But man is made in wilderness first, yes? Dumnezeu make man before he make *Grădina Edenului*, you understand? Man is not made for garden, but for hunting. To be a man is to hunt, to kill, to feed, to mate—that is a man, yes?"

"That sounds more like a vampire to me," I said. Sydor spat on the ground in disgust.

"*Nu!*" he growled. "They hide in dark like *viermilor* and live off man like *lipitori*, like blood-suckers. They are *paraziți*, you understand?"

"Parasites…"

"*Da*, parasites. They suck at us like *tenii* in a sheep's guts. Are you sheep, or *teniei*, or wolf, brother? Are you prey or parasite or predator?"

"None of the above," I replied. When had he gotten closer to me? I hadn't noticed him getting closer. "Life is bigger than that, bigger than just 'kill or be killed' to get by."

"*Nu!*" he growled again. "That is *all* life!"

"That's only *part* of life," I growled back, "but not all. It's family and love and doing the right thing *because* it's the right thing to do. I became a cop to save people. Durant saves people." I had forgotten about Durant. I turned back to see him, and he was down to one assailant. But I could now see that his left arm was shredded, hanging from his shoulder by only a few tendons, and that his side had been bitten open. Could Durant even *get* infected?

"Why you think we *made* you, Detective?" Sydor asked me, standing right in front of me now. I confess that I hadn't really thought about it in those terms. I'd just assumed that Lyn and I had stepped into the wrong place at the wrong time. But he was suggesting that there was a *purpose* to it? Somehow, that was a scarier possibility.

"Because you blame me for the death of your son?" I suggested. Sydor just threw his head back and laughed in reply.

"My son? *Fii serios…* You really think I care about that *javră* after he leave us for vampyri?" He laughed again, but I could hear an anger in the back of the sound.

"Didn't you?"

"*Nu,*" he growled in reply. "I am of great *Skorzeny* pack, but František? He was lapdog for spellcasters and bloodsuckers—decadent masters who use him, and he love them for it." He spat on the ground in disgust. "I myself hang him when I find him, and I myself come back and tear flesh from his rotten back in morgue to make belts for my pack. The *mârţoagă* deserve his fate, you understand?"

Sydor's *father* killed him? We'd just always assumed that it had been Ruthven who'd done it, to cover his tracks after the younger Sydor had outlived his usefulness. But it was this Teodor?

"Then why?" I asked him. "Why did you turn Lyn and me?"

"Who say *I* turn you?"

Out of the corner of my eye, I saw the werewolf that I'd beaten limping out of the door. I thought I'd killed it, but I guess that these monsters really were as tough as Durant had warned me about. It turned for a moment on its way out to look at me in pain, and I felt a sudden shock of recognition—I knew those eyes. The creature was Lyn Davidge.

I started to run after her, but Sydor's thick-muscled arm darted out to me and held me tight. I turned to him, and saw his teeth begin to grow, and his eyes burned with an unholy fire. His face twisted and split, but unlike the other transformations I'd seen, he didn't seem to be in pain as he changed. Instead, he seemed to relish it. I tried to wriggle out of his grasp, but even with my growing strength, his hand was holding me like a vise. I turned to look back at Durant just in time to see him slice his final opponent in half with his sword. His own face was ripped badly, but I could see that his left arm and the hole in his side had already started to heal. Still, he stopped and leaned on his sword to take a breath for a second. I don't think that I'd ever seen Pieter Durant exhausted like that before. Maybe no one ever has…

Behind him, I saw Nikodim Bunin begin to move a little…

But before I could get a good look, Sydor spun me around to look back at him. He was growing to an enormous size, with gray fur bristling all over his tattooed muscles. His thick moustache spread out across his growing muzzle, and he smiled. Seeing a werewolf smile at you is not a pleasant thing, let me tell you. His shoulders broadened and thickened, and by now, his legs had grown and contorted enough that they had ripped out of his jeans. In front of me now stood the biggest, nastiest thing I'd ever seen in my life.

"You're under arrest…" I said, and the wolf growled back in response. I tried to swing the staff at him, but I was too close to get much of an arc. Instead, when I hit him, he just winced a bit from the touch of the vril and howled back at me in anger. With one wave of his arm, he smacked me to the side with ease, knocking the staff from my hand. As I lay there on the charnel house floor, I realized that the werewolf that I'd just beaten—Lyn—was *nothing* compared to the power of this monster. I kicked at his leg with both feet, hoping to at least knock him off-balance for a moment, but it was like kicking a fire hydrant. He slashed at my leg with his other hand, ripping four large gashes into it. This time, I can honestly say that it just hurt a lot. Then he leaned down to me and opened his huge jaws over my face.

That's when Durant hit him full force from the side, slashing him open with his sword. Now, my experience up to that point with Durant was that when he came at something with that sword, that was pretty much the end of the fight. But not this time. Sydor howled in pain, and his blood started splattering everywhere, but he spun back so fast that even Durant couldn't dodge his attack. He brought his claws around and sliced the Grail Knight open across the belly, almost cutting him in half and knocking his sword out of his hand. Durant flew back about ten feet and landed in a pile of bones near the wall of doors. About six feet behind him, I could see Bunin beginning to sit up.

Sydor picked me up like I was a ragdoll and threw me across the room, slamming me into the open door of one of the cages we'd freed the kids from. I could feel several ribs give, and my right arm popped out of its socket. Seeing that I was down, Sydor turned back to Durant, who was—incredibly—holding himself together and beginning to stand to face him again.

I wished that I could help, but that's when I noticed that my left arm—where Lyn had slashed me—was now healed. As I lay there, I could actually feel my ribs beginning to knit themselves back together. Was that the way that it was with Durant? I dunno, but it was freaky. So I pulled myself up and stumbled over to the wall. I took a deep breath to prepare myself, then slammed my right shoulder against the wall, popping my arm back into place. The only way that I can describe the pain of that is to say that it felt like someone hit me in my shoulder with a sledge hammer. I leaned against the bars of the door for a minute, until I could feel the muscles of my shoulder pulling themselves together as well. Then I turned back around to see what was going on with Durant.

His sword was laying about three feet from him, and Sydor was on top of him, ripping at him savagely with his claws. But Durant had some little silver dagger that he was using to slice and stab at Sydor so fast that it was nothing but a silver blur, even to my eyes. It was a horrifying, gory race to see which one would shred the other one first.

Continuing to stumble, I made my way over there as fast as I could, slipping and sliding on the pieces of victims on the ground. As I finally reached the sword, I watched as Sydor bit deeply into Durant's shoulder, then ripped the flesh out and gulped it down. As he leaned back, I saw that Durant had all but disemboweled the monster, and that both of its legs appeared to be broken at several places.

I picked up the sword, and I felt it burning my hands, even through the gloves. I shifted it to my right hand, but my left palm still burned like it was on fire. I lifted the blade above my head and brought it down with all of my strength onto Sydor's head, chopping off the back half of it. He turned around and growled at me in pain, his eyes beginning to glaze over. Holding the sword was excruciating, but I swung it again at Sydor's neck, and his head tumbled to the side. The entire bulk of his body landed full on Durant, and I dropped the sword, instinctively ripping off my gloves in pain. Both hands were all red and puffy, like a first degree burn.

On my left palm was the clear, blistered outline of a pentacle…

*   *   *

I heard a growl to my right, and I turned to see Bunin standing there, his head unnaturally cocked to one side and his neck still bulging from where Durant had broken his neck. He had reached the leather belt and was beginning his transformation again. I knew that I didn't have the strength in me to do much to stop him, and Durant wasn't moving underneath Sydor's now-shrinking corpse. Bunin coughed as he began to laugh, his features already beginning to contort into those of a wolf.

"You die now, *polismen*…" he growled, walking toward me.

"Aw, shut up!" I heard Tony shout as he smacked Bunin across the face, using the Matteh ha Shelomoh with his one, good arm. Bunin went down like a sack of wet cement.

"Tony!" I yelled.

"Yep," he said, dropping the staff and running over to me. "What happened here?"

"What happened to you?" I asked, quickly pulling the glove on to cover my left hand.

"I took th' kids straight across Belmont to that Twinkling Stars Daycare place an' called it in, 'cuz I sure wasn't gonna leave 'em standin' upstairs in this place, an' I figgered I could use th' help o' people what know what they're doin' with kids." I looked at him in shock at how smart that was. "What?" he asked, looking confused. "Ya think I was gonna leave 'em with a mailman or somethin'?"

"No," I replied, chuckling. "I just… never mind…" I reached over and hugged him. "I'm just happy to see you, partner…" He gave me a quick and somewhat uncomfortable hug in return, then pulled away.

"Where's Durant?" he asked.

I ran over to him and pulled Sydor's body off of him. We could see that he was still breathing, but God only knows how. He was ripped up so horribly that he looked almost as bad as the rest of the bodies in the room. But again, I could see that his face was already healing, that his shoulder was beginning to fill in, etc. I reached over and tried to put his organs back inside of his body so that he could heal correctly, and he moaned in pain.

"That… had ta suck…" Tony said, watching me.

"For me or for him?"

"Yep."

Bunin began to move again, and I realized that he was still alive. He was lying next to the dead body of one of the werewolves Durant had killed earlier, and I saw that the corpse wasn't exactly naked—it had on one of those leather belts that Bunin had tried to use to transform himself before. I looked over, and so did the other two corpses. Apparently, only a werewolf as powerful as Sydor could change at will—at least, during the daytime. Maybe it took something like one of those belts to help them transform otherwise. That would explain why Bunin was still alive. He wasn't a werewolf wannabe—he was a full-fledged werewolf.

He was starting to sit up, so I grabbed him by his collar and yanked him to his feet.

"What's going on here?" I shouted.

"Wh-What?" he replied.

"What's going on?" I repeated. "Sydor said that he turned me for a reason! Why? What's the plan, Bunin?"

He looked confused for a second, then started to laugh. Blood from the head wound that Tony had just given him flowed into his mouth and he began to cough.

"What?!?" I shouted louder.

Bunin stopped laughing and looked at me, and his brow furrowed in surprise. "You really don't know, do you, *polismen*?"

"Know *what*?"

"You part in this," he replied, coughing. "You really don't know what is coming, do you? Why Ruthven was even here at all?" I picked him up and slammed him back down onto the ground in frustration, and I was surprised when a snarl erupted from my throat.

"Tell me!"

Suddenly, a silver streak whipped through the air, and I could feel that burning heat coming off of it as it passed by me. Bunin's head flipped away from his body, and Durant stood beside me, bleeding and breathing heavily.

"He was going to tell me what's going on!" I growled at him.

"He was toying with you," Durant replied, slumping down onto the ground in exhaustion. "Playing for time…"

"You could've waited for another minute or two!"

"Why?" he asked, leaning over and wiping his sword against Bunin's leg to clean it. "So that whatever he was waiting for would come about? A great deal can occur in the span of a minute or two, Detective."

"But why did they do this to me?" I barked at him. "Sydor did this for a reason, and I want to know why!"

"I have no idea why," Durant replied, sliding his sword carefully into his *got uechan* again.

"Don't you even care?"

"In point of fact, I do not," he said, finally looking me in the eyes. He looked so incredibly tired. "There are far larger stakes at play here than *why* I shall have to kill you soon—including the fact *that* I shall have to kill you. The why and wherefore questions of life interest me very little."

"The why is everything!" I growled back at him, pacing back and forth like an animal in a cage. "Why does a killer stalk this prey rather than that one? Why only on Saturdays or Tuesday mornings? Why only in this neighborhood, and never that one? It's the why *behind* the what that makes all of the difference in life!"

"I tend not to think in those ways," he said, matter-of-fact.

"Which is why you need a detective!" I snapped.

"Which is why I need a detective," he answered me back. Tony had just been standing there quietly, but at that point, he chimed in, addressing Durant.

"Did you just say that yer plannin' ta kill Tom?"

Yeah, I'd heard him, too. I just hadn't wanted to think about it. But obviously, a part of me knew that he'd been planning it for a while now. And, to be honest, a part of me knew that it was almost going to have to come to that.

"You have killed Sydor by your own hand," Durant said to me. "Do you feel any different?"

"No," I replied. "Why? Am I supposed to?" He just sighed and let his chin drop to his chest.

"I had hoped so…" he said quietly.

"What's goin' on here?" Tony asked again. Durant just sat there for a few moments, breathing and quietly healing.

"Detectives," Durant said at last, his voice softening just a bit. "As much as you want answers to your situation, it is inherently dangerous to seek them from monsters such as Bunin or Sydor. When one plays with a flame, one tends to get burned—when one plays with a manipulator, one tends to get manipulated. Never allow yourself to be drawn in by a fiend who obviously feels that he has the upper hand in an engagement."

"But I had the jerk, and Tony had the staff," I replied. "And you were right there with your sword. There wasn't anything that he could've done to us."

"It is never really about firepower, Detective," he said, sighing again, "but merely about *power*. The ability to control the outcome of a situation—the ability to control the other individuals *within* the situation. Sometimes that power comes from a weapon, sometimes it comes from a position of authority, and sometimes it comes from simply knowing that you possess information that your enemy desperately desires. In that final situation, no matter how much firepower your enemy has arrayed against you, the truth is that *you* then hold all of the power because you control the situation."

I knew that he was right. I remember this one time when a guy robbed a convenience store downtown and held us off for, like, two hours. In the end, we found out that he didn't even have a real gun. But for two hours, he was the petty little god of that convenience store.

"Do you think that Bunin even knew anything?" I asked quietly.

"We shall never know," he replied. "But whether he did or not is irrelevant. He recognized that the mere appearance that he knew something gave him power over you, and that is something which you must never allow to happen in this battle. Even if he would have told you something—and even if he would have told you the *truth*—he would have done so in a manner which would have aided him and compromised you."

"Let's get back ta somethin'," Tony chimed in. "Yer plannin' ta kill Tom?" Durant just sat there on the ground with a pained expression on his face. Maybe it's just me, but I could've sworn that the expression got even more pained when he heard Tony's question.

"Why did you ask if I felt any different?" I asked him.

"Because," Durant replied, rising to his feet with a loud groan, "there was always that… possibility…"

"What possibility?"

"In some rare cases, a werewolf may cure himself by severing the bloodline and killing the werewolf who infected him by his own hand—so long as the victim has not allowed himself to transform as of yet." He turned and looked at me, and his face seemed to ache with sadness. "This is why I tried to give you the chance to kill Sydor…"

And that's when it dawned on me. That's why he'd been putting up with us running all over town like idiots. That's why he'd been so focused on finding the den once we figured out who the *Avtorityet* was. That's why he'd taken on four werewolves by himself and left Sydor to me. In fact, the more I thought about it, I wondered if that's why Sydor was even still alive for me to kill there at the end. All of that punishment, enduring all of that pain—Durant had gone through all of that and almost died *for me*, rather than just killing Sydor himself, in the vain hopes that I might be able to end my own curse right then and there.

"An' now, yer just gonna kill 'im?" Tony asked. "Yer just as bad as them werewolves, Durant! Yer a monster too!" Durant's eyes never left mine, and I could see the pain in them.

"Tony…" I said quietly. "Just… stop…"

This man, this centuries-old monster-hunter, had just put his life and his whole Divine mission on the line to save me—a monster. How could I explain to Tony that at that moment, I saw Durant as the greatest hero that I'd ever known?

"Why didn't you tell me?" I asked him.

"Why raise hope needlessly for us both?" Durant replied. "I would not add that pain to the rest of what would need to be endured."

"I understand," I said, nodding. I took a deep breath and realized what needed to be done next. "Tony," I said, getting his attention off of Durant. "This is almost over. But something has to happen now that… that *has* to happen." I felt the pentacle itching on my left palm, and I knew that if Durant didn't end this some time *today*, I'd end up becoming like Lyn. I'd rather die than to let that happen.

"Ain't gonna happen," Tony said, realizing what we were talking about.

"It *has* to happen," I replied. "And I need you to… You have to explain all of this to Joanna, Tony." He started shaking his head, but I kept talking. "She has to know how and why I died, Tony. But you have to explain to her that Durant was *saving* me, that I *wanted* this, you understand?"

"I ain't doin' it, Tom," he said. "There's gotta be another way."

"Is there?" I asked Durant. He sighed, then dropped his gaze to look at Sydor's severed head.

"There's gotta be…" Tony said again.

"I don't think so, Tony," I replied. "So help Joanna and the kids understand why it had to be like this. I don't want them angry with me or you or Durant or God. This was Sydor's doing, and he's paid for it."

"The truth of it is, Tom, *everybody* dies," Tony said… but then he looked over at Durant. "Okay, almost everybody. But if ya get all mad at God 'cuz he let somebody die, then I'd've gotten mad at 'im a long time before this, 'cuz if I thought his job was keepin' people alive, then he's been suckin' at his job fer, like, *ever*, ya know?" Funny, I never thought of Tony as a theologian. "But I can't promise that they won't hate Durant over there fer killin' ya…" Durant frowned and squatted down on his haunches to look at Sydor's head more closely.

"You've got to help them try," I said to Tony. "They're the only family he's got left, and I don't want him to lose that. Don't let Sydor steal them away from both of us…"

"Maybe I'll tell 'em that I had ta finish ya off instead…" Tony said, tears welling up in his eyes. "They… They'll fergive me a lot better'n him, I think."

I have to admit that I got a little misty at that point, too. What these two men were willing to sacrifice for my sake—it was humbling, and I wondered what a guy like me had ever done to deserve men like these as partners and friends.

"Okay, Durant," I said at last. "Let's do this." He didn't seem to hear me.

"Hey, Durant," Tony shouted. "Get in th' game…"

"Detective," he said, standing up with a start. "What color were the eyes of the creature that attacked you at Bunin's home?"

"Bright blue," I answered. He smiled—I wasn't expecting him to smile—and turned Sydor's head toward me with the toe of his shoe. His eyes were open, and I could see that they were green.

"That…" I gasped. "Are you saying that Sydor's not the guy who attacked us…?"

"Sydor is not the guy who attacked you," he replied, smiling broader. "This is not over yet."

"But he said that he was the Alpha of the pack…" I said, not wanting to let hope creep back in, now that I'd resigned myself to death.

"No, he said that he was the strongest one in the room," Durant corrected me. "The two statements appear not to have been synonymous…"

"Or he lied," Tony offered.

"But we've got no leads, and no place to point your compass," I said. "How would we find the real head of the bloodline by nightfall tonight?" Durant began to smile again.

"Come," he said, trotting painfully toward the open door leading upstairs. "I shall need a telephone…"

"What?" I asked, trying to follow him. "What are you thinking?"

"There's a thread of hope upon which to clutch, Detective," he answered, pulling that little blue vial out of his *got uechan*. "A very slender thread indeed. Someone with whom I have not spoken in some time…"

"Are you actually going to need that?" I asked him, pointing to the rotting piles of body parts all over the room already. "I don't think that four more hacked-up corpses are going to make that much more of a difference, do you? And we'll need the evidence for these kids…"

Durant reluctantly agreed, putting the vial back into his bag. Tony almost looked disappointed to miss whatever big show Durant had planned for that room.

"Tell me, Detective," he said, beginning to walk up the corridor. "Have you ever been to Cincinnati…?"

Background
From *Witch-Songs of the Navajo Medicine Chiefs* (John Gregory Bourke,[1] 1887)

There are many and sundry examples of the American Indian's belief in the transformation of the human body into the form of a wild beast. The Navaho's *yenalyosi*[2] is but a single expression of this. To the Indian mind, it is simply a common truth that the medicine chief is able to not only commune with the spirits of Nature, but also to affect changes within his own body that make him one with that Nature physically.

Such men bless the urine of cows and humans, draughts of which the men of the tribe drink in great measure, as they believe that the *nirang*[3] gives them strength and potency. As with the Apache, the first thing which a brave might do upon rising in the morning is to smear the *nirang* of a cow or bull liberally upon his hands and face. But the urine of a wolf is never used in such a ceremonial manner, since the Navajo view a natural connexion between the wolf and the witch. Indeed, though they name the wolf in their language is *"ma'ii tsoh,"* they nonetheless often call the beast by the name *"mai-coh,"* or witch.

Thus, when a medicine chief assumes the shape of an animal such

---

[1] *A cavalryman and hero who fought in the Apache Wars from 1870 to 1886, Bourke was a self-trained ethnologist, particularly interested in the religious beliefs of Native American tribes such as the Navajo, Apache, and Zuni tribes. He is most well-known for his scholarly work,* Scatalogic Rites of All Nations. A Dissertation Upon the Employment of Excrementicious Remedial Agents in Religion, Therapeutics, Divination, Witch-Craft, Love-Philters, etc. in All Parts of the Globe *(1891).*

[2] *Here, Bourke appears to be referring to the Navajo "yee naaldlooshii" (which, literally translated from the Diné bizaad, means "with it, he goes on all fours"). The medicine-man (or "'ánt'įįhnii") was believed to be able to take on the form and powers of an animal by placing that animal's skin on his person and running on all fours like the creature—such as a wolf, a bear, or a coyote. Whether the 'ánt'įįhnii could truly do this, or if the sensation of transformation was simply the result of a peyote-induced hallucinatory ecstasy, is a matter of debate.*

[3] *That is, consecrated urine.*

as a hare, he is usually perceived by his tribe as being a force for *hózhó*,[4] or good. But when he assumes the shape of a wolf, he is seen as a *mai-coh*, and is feared by his tribe. The witches are associated with the night, darkness, chaos, and death. They are known to devour the flesh of corpses and infants, whether while in their wolf forms or in their human forms, which is the main reason why the Navajo build a *hooghan* or small house over their corpses.[5] After mourning for their loved ones, the Navajo then forget the deceased and never again speak their names, so as not to offend *Chinde*, their Devil.[6]

The Indians also fear that continued contact with the corpse, or even indeed the very memory of the deceased, would bring them into *hóchó*, or ritual ugliness.[7] Since witches and wolves were known to feast upon these *hóchó* corpses, then witches and wolves must similarly be associated with *hóchó*, and are both thus to be equally feared.

The truth is that the *yenalyosi*, known also as a "skin-walker," is a necessarily evil creature, and the white man should not presume to associate him with a "white magic" as opposed to a "black magic" in his dealings with the red savage. To devour the flesh of another human is

---

[4]   *An idealized condition of positive balance of the best parts of life, summarized in this manner by Witherspoon: "The goal of Navajo life in this world is to live to maturity in the condition described as* hozho, *and to die of old age, the end result of which incorporates one into the universal beauty, harmony, and happiness" (see his* Language and Art in the Navajo Universe, 1974).*

[5]   *They were known to leave the body where it lay and build the makeshift hogun around it. When this was not possible, they usually attempted to bury the body in shallow graves near where their families live. The hoguns gave little protection for the remains, and it was thus not uncommon for wild animals to ravage them and devour their bodies in full view of the Navajo encampments (see the testimonies of Dr. John Menard and Lt. George E. Ford in Yarrow's* A Further Contribution to the Study of the Mortuary Customs of the North American Indians, 1881).*

[6]   *Actually, a ch'įįdii should not properly be associated with the Devil, as such, but rather is a malicious ghost, or the spiritual part of a deceased person which did not enter with them into eternal happiness. To avoid contact with these ghosts—known to be used by witches to harm the living—family members often burned the personal effects of the deceased and refused to speak their names.*

[7]   *The Navajo saw all things that were ugly or deformed as being necessarily out of harmony with Nature or evil—and thus, the logical opposite of hózhó—and avoided ugliness at all costs, fearing that contact with deformity would bring them similar disharmony. They were therefore known not only to abandon the dead bodies of their loved ones, but also the living bodies of any deformed or ugly infants, leaving them outside of their camps to be killed by the elements or scavengers (see the Leightons' excellent study,* The Navajo Door, 1945).*

considered the highest sin in their culture, under any circumstances. Once the *yenalyosi* has done so, he has crossed inexorably onto the path of *hóchó,* and is lost to the human race. Any contact with him is dangerous, and he must live in the wilderness alone.

Background
From *The Medicine-Men of the Apache* (John Gregory Bourke, 1892)

The chiefs of the tribes of the Southwest, at least, are not *ipso facto* medicine-men; but among the Tonto Apache[1] the brother of the head chief, Cha-ut-lip-un, was the great medicine-man, and generally the medicine-men are related closely to the prominent chiefs, which would seem to imply either a formal deputation of priestly functions from the chiefs to relatives, or what may be practically the same thing, the exercise of family influence to bring about a recognition of the necromantic powers of some aspirant; but among the Apache there is no priest caste; the same man may be priest, warrior, etc...[2]

The medicine-men of the Walapai,[3] according to Charlie Spencer,[4] who married one of their women and lived among them for years, were in the habit of casting bullets in molds which contained a small piece of paper. They would allow these bullets to be fired at them, and of course the missile would split in two parts and do no injury. Again, they would roll a ball of sinew and attach one end to a small twig, which was inserted between the teeth. They would then swallow the ball of sinew, excepting the end thus attached to the teeth, and after the heat and moisture of the stomach had softened and expanded the sinew they would begin to draw it out yard after yard, saying to the frightened squaws that they had no need of intestines and were going to pull them all out. Others among the Apache have claimed the power to shoot off guns without touching the triggers or going near the weapons; to be able to kill or otherwise harm their enemies at a distance of 100 miles. In nearly every boast made, there is some sort of a saving clause, to the

---

[1] *The Dilzhę'é, a group within the Western Apache nation.   Other Apache tribes referred to them as the "Koun'nde" ("crazy people"), and thus, the Spanish called them "Tonto" ("foolish") Apache.*

[2] *See Herbert Spencer's* Ecclesiastical Institutions: Being Part VI of the Principles of Sociology *(1886).*

[3] *That is, the Hualapai—a Native American community living in Arizona along the Colorado River.*

[4] *A white Indian trader from Missouri who went to live with the Hualapai in 1869.*

effect that no witchcraft must be made or the spell will not work, no women should be near in a delicate state from any cause, etc.

Mickey Free[5] has assured me that he has seen an Apache medicine-man light a pipe without doing anything but hold his hands up toward the sun. This story is credible enough if we could aver that the medicine-man was supplied, as I suspect he was, with a burning glass.

That the medicine-man has the faculty of transforming himself into a coyote and other animals at pleasure and then resuming the human form is as implicitly believed in by the American Indians as it was by our own forefathers in Europe. This former prevalence of lycanthropy all over Europe can be indicated in no more forcible manner than by stating that until the reign of Louis XIV, in France, the fact of being a were-wolf was a crime upon which one could be arraigned before a court; but with the discontinuance of the crime the were-wolves themselves seem to have retired from business. In Abyssinia, at the present day, blacksmiths are considered to be were-wolves, according to Winstanley.[6] The Apache look upon blacksmiths as being allied to the spirits and call them "*pesh-chidin*"—the witch, spirit, or ghost—of the iron.

---

[5]   *A half-breed Apache scout who had served with Bourke during the Apache Wars from 1870 to 1886.*

[6]   *William Winstanley, in his 1881 book,* A Visit to Abyssinia: An Account of Travel in Modern Ethiopia.

Chapter 17
Mkogisos

Tony stayed with the kids to be there when the cops arrived, while Durant and I drove just outside city limits to a private airport that I never even knew existed. It took us about 45 minutes to get there, but by the time we did, a plane was all prepped and ready for him. In fact, as near as I could tell, it was the only plane that flew out of that airport. Ever.

And what a plane it was. Long, black, and sleek, it was to jets what a black stretch limo is to Buicks. The front looked a little bit like a Concorde, since the nose had that strange dip downward, but the rest of the thing almost looked more like a missile than a plane. The front two wings were short—only about six or seven feet long—extending from just behind the cockpit. And the back two wings were much longer, though still nowhere near as long as a normal plane's wings, sweeping upward in a gently curved "V" shape. Basically, it was the opposite of any plane I'd ever seen.

"What kind of plane is this?" I asked, feeling like I was stepping into a sci-fi movie.

"The Raven is a prototype which your Lockheed Martin was kind enough to build for me," he answered, all but dragging me along to the plane with him. "And an exceptionally fast one at that…"

We were met at the hatch by a stunningly beautiful attendant and a dark-haired man who was obviously the pilot.

"All ready to go, Mr. Durant," the pilot said.

"Excellent as always, Cliff. Thank you," Durant replied. "And you, Victoria?" he asked the attendant as we began to climb aboard. "Do you have everything prepared as well?"

"Of course, sir," she said with a decidedly British accent. From her smile and the way that her face beamed when she caught sight of him, I could tell that she obviously had some sort of feelings for Durant, though he barely seemed to notice her. For that matter, neither of them seemed to notice the fact that the two of us were covered in blood, and Durant's clothes were a shredded mess. We'd both long since healed, for the most part, but we still had to look like we'd just stepped out of a meat grinder. Both Cliff and Victoria were acting like it was a normal day at the office.

Then again, if they worked for Durant, maybe it was.

The inside of the plane was even nicer than the outside. It was paneled in mahogany, and the four leather, quilted chairs were huge and plush. The walls of the cabin—including almost the entire back wall—were covered in book shelves filled with what had to have been first editions of books from centuries of collecting and little wooden carvings that I recognized as the work of Durant himself. In front of the door in the back wall was an ornate, hand-made, mahogany desk. My grandfather was a carpenter, so I couldn't help but be drawn to it immediately. Durant noticed me admiring it.

"Gillow's made this for me in the late 18th century," he said, walking over to it. I made note of the sheer size of the thing, then glanced back at the hatch to the plane, then back at the desk again.

"How did you get it in here?" I asked.

"Hmm?" he asked, picking up some papers from a carved ebony tray on the corner of the desk. "Oh, we had the Raven built around it, of course…"

"Please take your seats," we heard the pilot say over the speakers. "We'll be taking off momentarily." Each of us sat down in one of the plush, leather chairs, and I have to tell you, it was the most comfortable chair I'd ever sat in in my whole life.

"So, is Victoria going to come out and tell us where the exits are?" I asked, joking.

"No. Why do you ask?" Durant replied, totally seriously. I looked back at him to respond, but then it struck me that I couldn't actually picture Durant ever flying in a common passenger plane. Maybe he'd never even heard the classic stewardess speech before.

"Never mind," I said, and let it drop.

When the plane took off, it felt like we were being shot out of a high-powered rifle, but it was still the quietest takeoff that I'd ever experienced. I looked over at Durant, and he was just reading his papers like nothing was going on. Soon, my body began to adjust to the acceleration, and Cliff came on again to let us know that it would soon be safe to get up and move around the cabin.

"So, is this Cliff guy your personal pilot?" I asked.

"One of them, yes," he answered, setting the pages down to face me. "He was named after his grandfather, a pilot whose acquaintance I made here in America between the wars who worked for me in a similar capacity."

"Did he fly a plane like this?" I joked again. *No* one *ever* flew a plane like *this…*

"No," he said. "But he did have a remarkable engine of his own with which he—"

"Excuse me, sir," Victoria interrupted us, stepping into the main cabin from a forward one, "but would you care to change now?"

"Absolutely…" Durant sighed with relief. "Which suit did you lay out for me?"

"The charcoal Kilgour, sir," she answered warmly, "with the royal blue Charvet tie. You always look so smart in that one." I couldn't help but turn and smile at her when she said that last bit, and she couldn't help but blush when I did. Again, Durant didn't seem to notice.

"You've impeccable taste, Victoria," he said, beginning to strip as he walked to the polished door at the rear of the cabin. "I shall wash and dress, and then we can chat a bit, Detective." He took off his shirt, and for the first time, I realized just how big Durant really was. Muscles rippled over muscles, and all of them were covered in scars. Were those scars from before he found the Grail, or was there a limit to how much even the Cup of Christ could heal? I turned back to see Victoria trying very hard not to look at him. Somehow, it made me feel good to know that there was someone out there who cared for him like that, even if he might never realize it himself.

"Oh," he added, turning back to her. "And please find something for our guest as well."

"Of course, sir," she said, and he disappeared into his private quarters and shut the door.

Victoria didn't give me one of Durant's suits, which is okay, since it probably would've fit me like a tent. Instead, she brought me a clean shirt and a moist towel to clean myself up with.

"Have you worked for Durant for long?" I asked her. She just smiled sweetly and demurely removed herself back to the forward cabin so that I could have some privacy. In the five minutes or so that it took me to clean up and change my shirt, Durant had emerged from the rear, completely clean and dressed in the suit and tie that she'd picked out for him. And yes, it was a perfect combination.

"So why are we going to Cincinnati?" I asked him, buttoning my last button.

"To visit the tunnels of the Lost Children, of course," he answered cryptically.

*   *   *

I've never been a big fan of Cincinnati. For one thing, they're on Eastern Standard Time, and that drives me crazy—no one who has to get up before six in the morning should ever have to stay up until 11:30 just to watch the nightly news. For another, they have the world's weirdest chili. Oh, there are some people who love it, but a runny, red, sweet meat sauce that they make with chocolate and cinnamon, and then pour over macaroni? That's just not chili to me. My dad always said that chili should be thick enough that you can eat it with a fork.

Anyway, as Durant explained it to me, the city of Cincinnati tried to build a subway system there in the early part of the last century. They'd been told that it would cost $12 million, they budgeted $6 million for it, and—go figure—they ran out of money before they could finish the project. So they have a couple of miles of unused tunnels under the city that they've locked up and spend over $2 million a year nominally maintaining, since it would cost almost $20 million to demolish it. They swear that the tunnels are completely empty, but there's a population of homeless people that live there anyway, as well as a very special population *within* that population.

As you might imagine, now that you have more of a sense of how the world really works, there's a small but significant number of people out there who have had some sort of brush with the dark, twisty, supernatural underbelly of life, and have come out the other side... scarred... one way or another. They aren't evil or anything, but they are cursed, or malformed, or just plain wounded in ways that the normal world simply couldn't understand. Somewhere along the line, those on the West Coast began to congregate in Seattle, those on the East Coast in New York, and those in the Midwest found a place for themselves in the abandoned subway tunnels under Cincinnati. They are called the "Lost Children," and they've carved out a little community for themselves there. I asked Durant if that would be dangerous—if the vampires' Covenant or the witches' Synod of Crows or the werewolves' *Société des Dragonistes* ever found out about these people, and all of them were congregated in the same place at the same time, then couldn't they be a danger to one another, living like one big target like that?

That's when he told me about Mkogisos.

"He was born in February of 1839," Durant told me, "so his mother called him *Mkogisos*—'Little Bear'—because to the Bodéwadmi, February was the month of the little bear. But that particular February was a hard month to be born in, as the tribe had marched from September to November to their new 'home' in Kansas, pressed as they were by Jackson's Indian Removal Act. Chief Menominee had held out as long as he could, but in the end, the whole tribe was forced to move so that the state of Indiana could be given completely to its white settlers. Dozens of members of the tribe died under those harsh conditions. When Jackson heard of this, his only response was the single word, 'Good,' may he rot..." Durant stopped for a moment and sighed, remembering.

"They were exposed to typhoid, forced to eat rations which the soldiers guarding them refused, and prodded along by the taunting and abuse of the United States military. I myself was in London at the time, hunting a demon which called itself 'Spring-Heeled Jack,' and knew nothing of this until the forced march was already completed. Little Mkogisos was one of the first infants born to the Mshkodésik band of the Bodéwadmi tribe in Kansas—though hardly a replacement for the dozens lost along the way.

"In 1852, a group of Mshkodésik broke away from the tribe and settled in what is now Texas, along the Sabine River. They were considered renegades by the United States, but they were not warlike or aggressive—they simply wanted their own land and autonomy. Teenaged Mkogisos and his family were among them. But after a few years of relative freedom, the constant harassment by the whites had hardened the band, and they began fighting back in ways that Mkogisos and his family could not condone. Taking a stand for honor in 1869, Mkogisos was ultimately forced to fight a young brave named Zibiwes, the son of the chief of the band. When he killed the brave, Mkogisos was forced into exile. Disheartened, he took the name, 'Foolish,' for himself, and rode away from everyone and everything that he knew. A lesser man might have become an outlaw, a bitter and resentful man who despised those around him—particularly the white men. But Mkogisos was not such a man.

"As God's grace would have it, he soon ran across a Texas Ranger whom he had known as a child, and the two rode together for several years. He suggested to the Ranger that they roam Texas, New Mexico, and Arizona, ever staying on the move in order to fight evil wherever they may find it, defending those who could not defend themselves. I am told that he did so in remembrance of what his mother and the Bodéwadmi had told him in his childhood about me in years past, though he had never met me himself. If this is true, then I take that as the greatest honor." Durant's eyes misted just the slightest bit, and then he continued.

"We did finally meet in 1881, when I was passing through Tombstone, following the spoor of an Apache vampire whose path I never did cross. There, I met Wyatt Earp and Bat Masterson, though the latter was suddenly called away back to his Dodge City by an urgent telegram."

"Did you see the gunfight at the O.K. Corral?" I had to ask.

"No," he replied with a gentle chuckle. "I was gone from town long before that overblown altercation took place. But that summer, I met Mkogisos and his companion while they were on the trail of a Pima skinwalker. We worked together, but during that time, Mkogisos was cursed by the skinwalker's damnable chanting. He was the only man I'd ever seen with the strength of character to fight the transformation into a beast—and ultimately, we were able to halt the advancement of the curse. But he was nonetheless... *changed*... by the encounter. His friend married and moved to Boston to be near his brother's family, while Mkogisos and I continued to travel together for a time.

"In fact, he was with me when I visited Abel Guevez de Argensola in Georgetown, Guyana to discuss the Indians of Parahuari, in the jungles of Venezuela. He told us of a strange 'bird girl' whom he named Rima or Riolama or somesuch who talked with animals, but we considered him a bit of a babbler. We were, however, able to follow the information which we received from him and rediscover the city of Kuhikugu, with the aid of an eccentric archaeologist friend.

"We ultimately parted ways in 1888, after investigating a particularly gruesome murder spree of prostitutes in London committed by an apelike brute called Edward Hyde. In the wake of that horror, Mkgosis missed his prairies, and I had work yet to do on the continent. I did not see him again until I was in Cincinnati in 1966, investigating the murder of the Bricca family. A fear-monger was involved—the same species of monster as the one which surfaced in Willow Park, California, in 2000—and I tracked the thing to the abandoned tunnels beneath the city. There, I ran across Mkogisos, who had been living for decades as the protector of the Lost Children. Believe me, Detective, when I say that these people are in no danger, so long as Mkogisos is there to safeguard their lives."

"And he's been there ever since?" I asked.

"So far as I know," he said. "The only thing which would drive Mkogisos out of those tunnels would be his death, and I cannot imagine the threat which could easily bring that about. I gave him my Komondor for company, a loyal and intelligent dog whom I called Élénk."

"But you didn't stick around?"

"No. I was called away to work alongside an American agent with a complicated mechanical device disguised as a common pen to thwart the efforts of Dr. Nikola to make use of an American B43 nuclear bomb which he had salvaged off of the coast of Okinawa in 1965. Thus, we left Cincinnati to fight the fiend at his base of operations in the dormant volcano which formed Southern Thule in the South Sandwich Islands. Such villains were so enamored with the use of chrome as a decorating theme in those days..."

"The Raven will be landing in Cincinnati in five minutes," Cliff's voice informed us over the speakers.

"That's a great name for this plane," I said.

"It was named in honor of an old friend," he explained, "who was himself scarred deeply by horror in his lifetime."

"Waitaminute," I said, looking down at my watch. "We've been in the air for a little over fifteen minutes. Are you telling me that it took more time for us to drive to the airport than it did for us to fly from Chicago to Cincinnati?"

"Indeed," he replied. "The Raven has a top speed of 2,400

kilometers per hour, Detective. We could be in New York in less than an hour's time…"

*   *   *

We set down at a private airport outside of town. The place looked nearly identical to the one outside of Chicago. As we prepared to leave, Durant told his staff to have the plane refueled and ready for a return trip as soon as was physically possible. Cliff jotted down some notes, and Victoria brushed off absolutely nothing from Durant's shoulder, plucking invisible lint from his lapel in a decidedly caring and protective fashion.

"Take care, sir," she said with genuine concern.

"Be ready," he said in reply, and dashed off to the Jaguar F-type that was waiting just off of the tarmac for him. I shook Victoria's hand and promised to try to keep him safe and bring him back in one piece. That brought a quick frown from her, followed by a sincere smile.

"Thank you," she responded, and she stepped back into the plane, wiping her eyes as she did so.

When I got to the car, Durant was in the passenger seat.

"I despise automobiles," he said when I asked him if I was driving. "They are a necessary means to an end, but I refuse to ever attempt to drive one."

So I got behind the wheel of a high-performance driving machine, and it was a thing of beauty. He directed me up Interstate 75 until we came to an exit for the Western Hills Viaduct. We went west for far less than a mile, when he told me to pull over to the side of the road. We got out, and made our way down a hill. There, under the roadway, was a heavy door with a strong lock on it, covered in graffiti. Durant went straight up to it, snapped off the lock, and then beckoned me over to the door.

"Welcome to the underworld…" he said in his deep, cavernous voice.

Inside, the concrete tunnels were quite dark, though once my eyes adjusted, I could see perfectly well. Again, the walls were covered with graffiti—suggesting that the officials in Cincinnati weren't quite accurate in their assessment that the tunnels were uninhabited.

"This is so freaky," I said, a little awed by the creepiness of the place.

"There is a series of tunnels much like this under the Thames," he replied, "abandoned for many of the same reasons. For a time, it served as a haunt for thieves, prostitutes, and vagrants. Now, it is home to something… quite worse…" He refused to elaborate any further, and I decided that I didn't really want him to.

We walked a bit deeper in, and he pulled a little glass bulb out of his bag and held it in his hand. As I watched, it slowly began to glow brighter and brighter, until it gave off enough cool, blue light that Durant could now see the tunnel in front of us as well.

"That's a neat little gizmo," I said.

"Hmm?" he replied, glancing down at his little light bulb. "Oh, yes. It was a gift from an old friend."

"But it doesn't give off much light, though, does it?" I continued. "I mean, I'm sure that it helps—don't get me wrong—but it's no flashlight."

"No," he said, stopping and letting out one of his sighs. "Indeed it is not. This bulb requires neither batteries nor electrical cords, nor any other external power source beyond the movement and warmth of my own body. Nor has it cracked or 'burnt out' in nearly a century of use."

"My mistake," I said, chuckling. "That's an impressive little gift, then."

"Tesla was an impressive man," he replied, and I think I saw the slightest smile cross his face. "Are you familiar with Nikola Tesla, Detective?"

"Not really, no."

"An engaging Serb, and an absolute genius," he said, with a genuine warmth in his voice as we began walking again. "I first met him at a fascinating exhibition in London in 1891, and we spent many hours over the next several years discussing his work, debating his obsession with Hinduism, and berating that bloody braggart, Edison."

"*Thomas* Edison?" I asked, surprised that he'd talk about him with such disdain.

"Indeed."

"You know," I interjected at this point, "I like and appreciate this little gadget that you've got yourself here, but I think that if you *invented* the light bulb, you should kind of *get* to be a little bit of a braggart."

"Perhaps," he said, stopping again and turning to me. "But then again, Edison did not invent the incandescent light bulb in the first place. I heard of a chap in Scotland who had demonstrated one nearly fifty years before Edison even began his work on it. And even when he *did* begin working on it, Edison was simply improving the existing designs of Sir Joseph Swan. Beyond using a better pump that created a truer vacuum within the glass, all that Edison really accomplished in the endeavor was to steal the credit for the invention."

There was a frustrated edge to his voice that took me by surprise. He must really, really not have liked Edison for some reason. But I couldn't help but think that his anger might have been clouding his recollection—or at least interpretation—of history.

"That's not what they told us in school," I said, a little skeptical.

"More's the pity then for your American educational system," he replied with a disapproving snort. "Edison was a showman and a businessman—the P.T. Barnum of the scientific world. He was the bane of Tesla's existence, and a blight on the history of the last century…" He turned away and continued walking down the tunnel.

"Well…" I ventured, trying to lighten the mood a bit. "Did Alexander Graham Bell actually invent the telephone?"

"By that, you mean the first working telephonic device to convey and receive intelligible words?" he asked, and I nodded. "Arguably so, though his race against a fellow from Chicago to apply for the patent was something of a draw, as I recall. Though I do seem to remember something about a fellow in Germany building a similar device a quarter century earlier…"

Talking with Durant was always a treasure trove of historical information, but he was destroying all of my cherished notions of classic inventors. I mean, I want to know my history accurately, but it's nice to think that you can trust what you've known since you were a kid. I'd had the same feeling of disappointment when they said that Pluto was never really a planet a few years ago.

"But Marconi did the radio, right?" trying to salvage something.

"No," he said, without missing a step. "That was Tesla as well…" And with that, the conversation was over.

*   *   *

We continued through the main tunnels for a while, then took an off-shoot that was clearly a rougher, later dig. It sloped downward sharply, and with all of the twists and turns, I could rarely see more than 30 yards ahead of us at best. This was no subway tunnel, I realized.

"It feels like we're going to the center of the Earth," I said.

"There is a monument to that very notion a few miles north of us in the city of Hamilton," he mentioned off-handedly.

"To what notion?" I asked.

"To John Cleves Symmes' conviction that the world is hollow and traversable," he replied. "The thing is in a park or somesuch place."

I was going to ask him more about that, but I was surprised instead by the sound of a loud, low growl. We stopped, and I pulled my pistol out of its holster by instinct. Durant turned back and smiled at me.

"This is no werewolf that assails us, Detective," he said. "But rather, the world's best guard dog." He whistled, and from around the next bend came a dog that looked—I'm not kidding—exactly like a kitchen mop with feet. The huge dog bounded up to us, barking, then stopped when it saw me. The thing hunched its back and growled fiercely at me.

"That's the way Flubber acted," I told Durant.

"The dog knows that you are not quite what you appear to be," he replied. "A werewolf may fool a man by his appearance, but never a dog." He stood there, motionless, with his hand outstretched, and the dog slowly moved toward him, very aware of me the whole time. After a few tense moments, it came close to him and began to lick his outstretched hand. He began to scratch it on its ears, and it whined in joyful satisfaction. "I do so love this breed…" he said.

"Is that your…" I began. "Is that Élénk?"

"Oh, no," he replied, giving the dog a little hug. The thing's head was almost at Durant's shoulder level. "I am sure that Élénk passed away decades ago, just as I am certain that this must be one of his descendants. They are a marvelous breed, you know. They were almost driven to extinction by the Nazis in the Second World War, because the Germans realized that the only way to get to the families which the dogs protected was to slaughter the dogs themselves."

I started to move toward the dog, but it bolted back, away from Durant, and began barking at me in fear. This thing was as big as a lion, and it was afraid of *me*. I tried to talk nicely to it, calm it down with a gentle tone of voice, but it just kept barking louder and louder.

"*Békadzet!*" I heard someone shout from down the tunnel, and the dog immediately quieted down. But it still stood there, watching me. After a few tense moments, we saw a very, very old man come down the tunnel toward us. He wore an old, cracked, brown leather jacket that reached down to his knees, and as he approached, I could tell that, old as he was, he still moved with confidence and strength. I glanced over at Durant, and I saw the biggest smile on his face that I'd ever seen.

"*Ahau, Nosamés,*" Durant called out to the man. Mkogisos stopped when he heard his voice, frowned, and then smiled back broadly when he recognized who he was.

"*Géte wénebozho éwabmenan…*" the old man said reverently, when he saw Durant.

"*Mno zhewébes ne?*" Durant asked, walking toward him.

"*Cho mno yési, Nmeshomes,*" the old man said with a dry chuckle. "*Cincinnati édayan…*" And Durant actually laughed in response. It really is no fun to hear people laughing about a joke when you have no idea what they just said—I assumed that they were speaking whatever it is that the Bodéwadmi spoke, but if anyone can figure out what they said, please let me know…

The two men embraced, and the dog came up and began licking Durant on the hand.

"*Ni je éshnekasyen?*" asked Durant, scratching the dog some more.

"I call him Nabésmo," the old man answered.

"Of course you do, my boy…" Durant replied with another smile, and the two men turned to go back into the tunnel. No one seemed to notice me or care that I was around, so I just followed behind them quietly.

*   *   *

Mkogisos refused to take us to the Lost Children themselves—well, he refused to take *me* to them. He said that he'd been protecting them from things like werewolves for too long to just bring one into their midst now. Instead, he brought us through a little side tunnel and into a larger chamber that I assumed was his home. It was cluttered but clean, filled with paintings, books, and memorabilia from a very, very long life. I saw a Nazi helmet, a line of silver bullets, a Japanese sword, a collection of African masks, an old-looking tomahawk, and a large, carved bust that looked a lot like what I expect Mkogisos looked like as a young man. It also looked a lot like the sort of work I'd seen Durant carve in the past. Nabésmo snorted at me as I came into the chamber, but then trotted over to a large, well-loved cushion and plopped down on it to watch us.

"Welcome to my home, Detective," the old man said to me. Even though he was cautious about me, he sounded genuinely sincere in his welcome.

"Nice to meet you," I replied. He looked down at my hands and smiled—though not with his eyes.

"I see that you are wearing my gloves," he said. There was an edge to his voice that I didn't understand until he added. "What do you hide on your palm with them, I wonder…?"

Durant turned to me and looked momentarily confused. Then he glanced at my hands and frowned deeply.

"Show me!" he barked. This time, it was my turn to sigh. I took off my right glove, and then, reluctantly, peeled off the left one. On my palm was the blistered pentacle. Mkogisos nodded, and Durant slammed his fist into the wall, cracking a chunk of rock off where he did so. "When were you planning to inform me of this?" he growled.

"We were kind of busy when I first noticed it," I said, recalling the combat at the time. "And later, it seemed… well… It was like I'd missed that window of opportunity where you can share that sort of thing, and it was too late to tell you later."

"Does this mark truly surprise you, *Nmeshomes*?" Mkogisos asked him. Durant glared at me for a moment more, then sighed and turned back to the old man.

"No," he admitted. "Not really. But I would think that common courtesy should have demanded that he tell me, rather than force me to find out in this manner from you."

"Takes one to know one?" I asked Mkogisos, more than just a little frustrated at this turn of events.

"What do you mean by that?" Durant responded.

"It means that I can smell the scent of the wolf on Mkogisos just as much as he can smell it on me," I replied, putting my gloves back on. "He's a werewolf. And I would've thought that a guy like you on a quest like yours—that there'd never be any way that you could have a 'truce' with one of these things."

"I should think," Durant said, his voice low and cold, "that you of all people would appreciate that I occasionally find it appropriate *not* to kill 'one of these things,' when I have the opportunity."

"*Kachi nitotamowiyin, tchoni ke kin kitakijuwenimasi kitch miketchiëwi nenni, kachi juweniminan...?*" Mkogisos commented, sitting down to pour a cup of coffee.

"What?" I asked.

"The Book of Matthew," Durant translated for me. "Chapter 18, verse 33. 'Shouldest not thou also have had compassion on thy fellow servant, even as I had pity on thee?'"

I realized that I had lashed out at this man, simply because he'd seen right through me. I guess a part of me felt a little jealous that Durant had such a long and obviously positive history with him, and I guess that I didn't appreciate that the first thing he did after inviting me into his home was to call me out. But he was absolutely right. How could I try to smear him in Durant's eyes when I was in the same situation myself?

"I'm sorry," I said to him. "You're absolutely right. I guess that I'm just—"

"All is forgotten, *Nshimé*," he said with a smile. "Would you like some coffee?" He just sat there, holding the cup toward me. I looked into his eyes, and I could see that he was telling the truth. In his mind, the entire matter was closed. I thanked him and took the coffee. It tasted terrible, and I drank every last drop.

Mkogisos explained that the Native Americans had independently developed the concept of skinwalkers, but that true werewolves had been brought over to the Americas by Europeans and used in what he referred to as the "Cherokee-Welsh War," whatever that was. Durant nodded and commented that the British had been using werewolves—foolishly, he added—as soldiers since the time of Cú Chulainn's *ríastrad,* whatever that was. They started firing tidbits of history back and forth so quickly and so esoterically that I felt lost almost immediately. Sitting there with the two of them, it was like talking with Durant, squared.

But the tone changed when Mkogisos finally got serious and asked Durant what we were doing there.

"I have not seen you in many years, *Nmeshomes*," he said. "You have respected my request, and I have respected you for it." I don't know what that part was about, but there was obviously a chunk of history that no one was going to talk about at that moment—at least, not with me sitting there to hear it. "But you come to me now for a reason. What can I do for you now? Is it about your pet *wendigo* here?" he asked, nodding toward me.

"You remember *La Société des Dragonistes,* do you not?" Durant asked him.

"Of course," Mkogisos answered. His face became very grave.

"A Russian contingent have come to Chicago," Durant explained. "We have exhausted our leads—but more to the point, they have infected my companion, and I..." he stopped himself in mid-sentence. "I decided it best to defer to your wisdom on this, as you are far more familiar with these sorts of matters than I..." Mkogisos looked at me, then back at Durant. Then he nodded.

"What sort of matters?" I asked them.

"Keeping the cursed alive," Mkogisos replied, and then he laughed deep and hard. The dog howled in unison with him, which just made Mkogisos laugh harder. In the end, I couldn't help but chuckle, too. It wasn't really that funny, but somehow, the old man's laugh was infectious.

"He reminds me of me, *Nmeshomes,*" he said at last, and Durant smiled in return.

"He does indeed," Durant replied. Mkogisos got up from where he was sitting and came over to me, sniffing me and looking me over carefully.

"Well, he has not yet gone through the change, yes?" he asked.

"He has not, no..." Durant answered.

"Then there is still a chance for him," the old man said, returning to his seat. And that seemed to be about all that he was going to say about that.

"What?" I asked, obviously wanting to hear more. "How is there still a chance for me?"

"You are from Rémy's pack," he said. "A very old and strong breed, yes. But because of that line and its beginning, there is a chance to break the curse."

"Who?" I asked him.

"Nicolas Rémy," Durant answered. "A magistrate back in France. He sired a bloodline that continues to this day."

"*Éhé,*" Mkogisos said with a nod. "Rémy was cursed by..." he paused, then frowned. Then he turned to Durant. "*Ni je gda kedyen 'méndowzet' Ingléshmon, Nmeshomes? Énéndeman ékedon i...*"

"The word you are searching for is 'witch,' my boy."

"*Migwéch, Nmeshomes...*" he said to Durant. Then he turned back to me. "I am an old man, Detective, and I forget simple things sometimes. Rémy was cursed by a witch. She was an old beggar woman whom he had passed in the street without helping, and when his son died a few days later, he assumed that she had cursed the young man out of spite. So he prosecuted her and convicted her for…?" He turned again to Durant.

"Witchcraft."

"*Éhé*," he nodded again, obviously embarrassed. "Witchcraft. In her last breaths, she cursed him to become a *wendigo*, like you. But unlike you and me, Rémy embraced his curse and his family has used its power in their crusade to rid the world of all witches. But the nature of the curse is where your chance comes from. If you can find and kill the one who bit you before you transform, then the curse should be broken, because you will have chosen a different path from that which Rémy chose."

"Just as I had hoped," Durant exclaimed. "Hearing of the pentacle, I thought that I had remembered the bloodline aright."

"Actually, we thought we'd done that," I explained to Mkogisos, "but it turned out to be the wrong werewolf. He said that he was from a pack started by a guy named Skorzeny." Mkogisos nodded in recognition when he heard the name. "He said that I'd been infected for a reason…" I didn't bother to tell him that I'd never actually been bitten.

"Skorzeny had been bitten by Rémy himself in Vienna in 1942," he explained to me. "I should know—I was there." He smiled at that, and it was a dark, unpleasant smile. I realized that there was a side to this old man that I don't think I'd ever like to be on the wrong end of. "But if they turned you for some purpose, then you will not have long to wait for answers. You will know the head of your bloodline when you meet him, do not fret," he said to me, leaning in close. "You will smell it on him."

"Is that the way it was with you?" I asked. Durant coughed, and Mkogisos leaned back again and sighed. He sounded just like Durant when he did.

"No…" he said darkly. "That is not the way it was with me at all…"

*   *   *

We stayed a bit longer, but we were also anxious to get back to Chicago. It was noon by this time, and I was ravenous. But I was also terrified by the thought of sundown coming before we found the head of the bloodline. He pulled some hard sausages out of a cabinet nearby and gave them to me to eat, and I couldn't help but gobble them down while we talked. They were delicious.

"Indian?" I asked him, finishing them off.

"Polish," he replied. He walked over to one of his shelves and picked up a single silver bullet, bringing it over to me. He handed it to me, and I could feel the heat of the silver, even through the gloves I was wearing. When I took hold of it, I saw that Mkogosis' fingers were blistered and burned. He hadn't even winced from the pain.

"Keep this, *Nshimé*," he said to me. "A present to you from me and from *Gímózábi*." I put it into the pocket of my coat—there were enough layers between it and me that I could barely feel it. "It will help you find your *wendigo*."

"How so?" I asked.

"It will burn bright the closer you are to him," he explained. "Or when he comes looking for you. Follow the trail of the pain."

With that, he walked us out, back into the tunnels. Nabésmo jumped up from his cushion and came with us. When we arrived at the same point that we'd originally met him, he stopped to say good-bye to us.

"It has been good to see you, *Nmeshomes*," he said, with tears welling up in his aged eyes. "My heart has been empty without you in my life."

"And mine without you in mine, *Nosamés*," Durant replied. He reached over and hugged Mkogisos, holding him tightly. I could see the tears streaming down the old man's face.

"Promise me that you will not return," he said finally, pushing Durant away from him. "I could not bear it if—"

"I promise you, *Nosamés*," Durant answered him, his voice hoarse with emotion. Nabésmo whined at their feet, and Durant gave him a good scratching. He leaned over and mumbled something to the dog that I couldn't hear in whatever language it was that they were speaking.

"*Bama pi, Nshimé*," Mkogisos said to me, wiping his eyes and smiling at me. "*Keshémnedo* is kind, and I wish you well."

"Thank you, Mkogisos," I said in return. "It's been a genuine pleasure meeting you."

"Now go," he told us both, and he turned to walk away. Durant just stood there for a moment, watching him leave. He didn't move until both Mkogisos and Nabésmo were again out of sight. Then he turned and began walking out of the tunnels again by the pale blue light of his little light bulb, snuffing a bit. We walked along in silence until we reached the opening where we'd originally come into the tunnels.

"He's a nice guy," I said, trying to break the tension.

"Indeed," he replied. We walked out into the daylight, and Durant carefully put his light bulb back into his *got uechan*. Just as carefully, he closed the door behind us and returned the lock, even though it was broken.

"He kept calling you '*Nmeshomes*'," I commented, not wanting to let this go. "What does that mean?"

"Hmm?" he replied, pretending not to hear the question. He began walking up the hill, back to the car.

"What does '*Nmeshomes*' mean?" I asked again.

"Oh, that…" he responded. He took a deep breath, then let it out as a sigh. "It means 'my Grandfather'…" He didn't look over at me. Instead, he just stood there in the cold air and the noonday sun. For the first time, I thought that he looked really, really old.

"I thought you told me that you didn't have any family left," I said at last.

"Did I?" he replied, shrugging his shoulders. "Then I must have lied…"

Background
From *Good Stories and Tall Tales of the American West* (Jack Hewlett, 1978)

There are countless legends surrounding the Colossal Cave system, located in the Rincon Mountains, only a few miles from downtown Tucson, Arizona. It's the largest "dry cave" in the United States—in fact, it's actually a huge labyrinth of intertwining cave systems, only a portion of which have been explored, even today.

The Hohokam Indians used the cave system for thousands of years before Columbus, mostly for ceremonial, religious purposes. According to some legends, their practice of burying their dead in the cave system attracted the attention of the "lizard people" who lived in the deep caves, which led to the Hohokam beginning to cremate their dead instead—and, ultimately, ceasing to use the caves altogether. Later tribes' (such as the Pima) use of horned lizards as fetishes for the sick and dying may reflect this legend (or, more likely, may have given rise to the legend in the first place).

The Apache and Sobaipuri Indians eventually took up use of the caves, but they weren't discovered by whites in the area until Solomon Lick stumbled into the system while looking for some stray cows. The *Arizona Daily Star* (January, 1879) reported that a group came out of Tucson to conduct a five-hour exploration of the cave system, discovering "a thousand varied beauties," and Lick himself began offering tours of the caves—for a price, of course.

By the 1880s, outlaws were using the caves as a hideout, including nine escaped prisoners from the Pima County Jail in 1882 and train robbers John Maier, George Green, and Josiah "Kid" Smith in 1887. But for some reason, no outlaw group felt comfortable staying in the caves for long, even though they would have been located close enough to Tucson to be accessible, but extensive enough to be a good place to hide. In fact, legend has it that at least some of the gold from these robberies is still hidden there, somewhere in the expanses of the deep caves.

One of the more colorful tall tales about the Colossal Cave system may explain at least part of the local concerns about the caves at the time. According to *Arizona Weekly Citizen* publisher Rollin C. Brown, a medicine man among the local Pima Indians began stirring up trouble, and may even have been behind the June 10, 1881 destruction of the *Citizen's* office by fire (though the paper was back up and running almost immediately, putting out their June 12 Sunday edition right on time).

As the story of this medicine man goes, he supposedly shed his skin as if it were a shirt and put on the skin of a lizard, calling up the *cimamag ki:li* (or *ciaḍag ki:li*), the "Old Man Lizard," who lived in the Colossal Cave system. The "Old Man Lizard" brought his followers, the Hohokam's "lizard people," who would then presumably be prepared to devour the white settlers in the region, returning the land to the Pima.

But the medicine man's plan was apparently thwarted by a group of do-gooders who happened to be coming through the area (or, depending on the story, came to the area specifically to stop the medicine man and/or the "lizard people"). There are different versions of the story to choose from, but in most versions, the group includes two Texans, two Indians, and a European (though at least one version of the story as told by James Buell included a half-breed Chinese priest as well). One of the Texans—either a Texas Ranger or an outlaw himself, depending on the accounts—traveled with an Indian renegade, possibly an Apache, as his scout. The other Texan was a tall sharpshooter who had made a name for himself overseas years before as a long-range rifleman. The European is a bit more of a mystery, since no two accounts provide the same country of origin, nor the same description of the man (some versions call him "well-appointed and unusually gentlemanly in his manner of dress," while others simply refer to him as "imposing").

But the other Apache who led them to the cave system was a well-known young brave named Samuel Sharp Nose, famous in the area as a crack shot and expert tracker. Why Sharp Nose would agree to lead the group to the medicine man's caves is uncertain, since he had always been adamant about not helping whites against his own people. Then again, there was little love lost between the Apache and the Pima at this time, so he may not have seen it as going up against his own, as much as going up against a mutual enemy. Whatever the case, after leading them to the cave entrance, Sharp Nose apparently washed his hands of the whole affair and left them.

As the story goes, on June 27, 1881, there was a huge fight between the two sides in the cave known as "Five Mile Cave," with the Ranger's Indian scout taking on the medicine man, the European grappling with the "Old Man Lizard" himself, and the two Texans thinning out the rest of the "lizard people," who were by then swarming the cave. In the end, the band was able to force the "lizard people" to retreat to a smaller tributary of the cave system, after which the sharpshooter set off a load of powder or gun cotton taken from the town's L. Zechendorf and Co.

store, which then sealed off the creatures' access to the main caves, never to be seen again. The blast was powerful enough that it left an entire acre pulverized and damaged most of the buildings in Tucson, blowing out almost all of the lights. In fact, the force of the explosion was even felt at Fort Grant, over one hundred miles to the east. Just outside of town, a small farmhouse caught fire when a lamp fell, but fortunately, the European was able to retrieve two small children who were trapped in the house at the time, so no one was seriously injured.

In a subsequent article in the *Arizona Weekly Citizen* by Rollin C. Brown, the cause of the explosion was attributed to "spontaneous combustion" of "poorly stored materials," so as not to unduly alarm the citizens. But on the plus side, between the fire at the newspaper office and the explosion in the caves, the city decided to create its own official fire department. On July 7, 1881, the *Arizona Daily Star* reported that "the members of the incipient Tucson hook and Ladder Company had a meeting last night at the club-rooms of the Gem saloon, about 20 of those who signed the roll being present."

Background
From *Nazi Assassination Conspiracies* (Candice Litchfield, 2010)

(NOTE: This background has been included in this book
because—almost impressively—nearly everything that
Litchfield asserts here about Nikola Tesla is inaccurate)

It is a well-known and established fact that Nikola Tesla, upon receiving radio signals from aliens,[1] created many spectacular devices and inventions, several of which are commonly misattributed to other inventors who were envious of Tesla's genius. The worst and most aggressive of these competitors was Thomas Edison, who fought against Tesla at almost every step of the inventor's life and career.[2]

Few people realize that Edison was also actually an early supporter of the Nazi government,[3] working through his associate and Nazi handler, Carl Laemmle.[4] This was why Edison refused to support

---

[1] *Actually, in 1899, Tesla did announce that he had identified extraterrestrial radio signals—though probably simply naturally occurring electromagnetic radiation. Tesla, however, was convinced that he was receiving messages from alien intelligences on the planet Mars. Whatever the case, his identification of these signals came mid-way through his career, and could hardly be said to be either the cause or the beginning of his creative output.*

[2] *Edison had employed Tesla at both the Continental Edison Company in France and the Edison Machine Works in America. They had a falling out in 1886 when Edison refused to pay Tesla the $50,000 that he had offered him to make his direct current system operable—as Edison famously remarked, "When you become a full-fledged American, you will appreciate an American joke." Tesla then went and created his own Tesla Electric Light and Manufacturing Company, developing his own, alternating current concept—later implemented by the Westinghouse Electric Corporation.*

[3] *Thomas Edison died in 1931, and German* Nationalsozialismus *(AKA "Nazism") did not come into governmental power until 1933. Though German sociologist Johann Plenge had discussed such socialism as early as 1914, there is no credible evidence that suggests that Edison had any connection to the movement at any point.*

[4] *Karl Lämmle emigrated to the United States at the age of 17, and was actually a competitor of Edison in the film business. In fact, the Edison Trust*

Tesla's early work in the field of radar research—because he was afraid that Tesla's efforts would help the Americans against the Germans in World War I,[5] since Edison had a vested interest in refusing to help the U.S. war effort against his German allies.[6] Laemmle, in turn, reported to the Abwehr[7] under Captain Conrad Patzig,[8] sending them coded messages on a regular basis about Tesla's whereabouts and most recent inventions.[9]

The most important of Tesla's extraterrestrial-inspired inventions was his death ray gun,[10] which he had perfected as early as 1937.[11] But after his rooms were ransacked by British spies,[12] Tesla backed off of his

---

[5] *attempted time and again to shut down Lämmle's efforts. The added fact that he was also a Jew makes Litchfield's allegation that Lämmle worked for the Nazis utterly ridiculous. Lämmle even financially enabled hundreds of Jews from Southern Germany to emigrate to the United States and thus avoid Nazi persecution.*

[5] *In 1917, Tesla did propose the use of electrical beams to find submarines in much the same way that radar would eventually be used—but he did not actually research or design anything. Edison correctly pointed out that Tesla's means of applying this proposed technology was inefficient at best.*

[6] *Again, this is simply unfounded. Edison actually worked quite closely with the United States government during World War I—particularly with Secretary of the Navy Josephus Daniels, who named Edison to the newly-created Naval Consulting Board. In this capacity, Edison worked diligently to provide the Navy with modern technology to fight the war, developing no less than 45 different new inventions for their use.*

[7] *The Third Reich's military intelligence agency.*

[8] *A decorated Naval officer who succeeded Lieutenant Colonel Ferdinand von Bredow as head of the Abwehr in 1932—nearly a full year after Edison's death. He was eventually transferred to the Oberkommando der Marine (High Command of the Navy), and served in the German Navy into the mid-1950s.*

[9] *There is no credible evidence that Lämmle and Tesla ever met—or even that they ever even lived in the same part of the country at the same time.*

[10] *Actually, though Tesla did claim to be working on such a weapon, this is a bit of a misnomer. Tesla once referred to the teleforce device he was working on as a "death* beam,*" which unfortunately led many to assume that it made use of deadly rays to destroy its target. But in fact, the beam itself was merely intended to be the conduit which would propel tiny, charged particles with tremendous velocity across vast distances—akin to the modern concept of a "rail gun." It was based not on any "extraterrestrial" inspiration, but on the work on electrostatic generators done by contemporary physicist Robert Van de Graaff.*

[11] *Indeed, Tesla proudly declared at a party celebrating his 81st birthday, "I have built, demonstrated and used it. Only a little time will pass before I can give it to the world."*

[12] *Tesla did not know who had gone through his notes during the break-in, and never claimed that it had been the British.*

plans to give the technology to British Prime Minister Neville Chamberlain, and instead focused on developing the death ray gun in secret.

In August of 1937, the Nazi assassin Otto Skorzeny[13] was sent to America to murder Tesla.[14] Stealing a New York City taxicab, he almost ran the inventor down when the elderly Tesla was crossing the street to feed some pigeons in the park. Tesla barely survived the encounter, and was left for dead[15] by Skorzeny, who then returned to Germany, wrongly assuming his mission to be a complete success.

But Tesla continued to work on his death ray gun in private, retreating to the relative safety of working at the hotel room he lived in at the New Yorker Hotel.[16] By the time Skorzeny found out that he was still alive, he was already back in Germany, and could not immediately return for another attempt. But the Nazis were desperate for Tesla's scientific genius, and the main reason that they were able to create such amazing weapons during this time was because they finally succeeded in stealing his notes.[17] In January of 1943, Skorzeny[18] and Nazi scientist

---

[13] *S.S. Obersturmbannführer Otto Skorzeny was an accomplished commando, whom General Dwight Eisenhower once described as "the most dangerous man in Europe." He went on to organize and/or to train several espionage units and agencies, such as the Nazi's Werwölfe units (the "Werewolves"), the post-war Spinne ("Spider") and ODESSA networks, and the Spanish neo-Nazi group known as CEDADE. The quintessential Nazi, the towering Skorzeny even boasted a dueling scar on his cheek.*

[14] *This is unlikely, since Skorzeny had just been assigned to lead the new S.S. Sonderlehrgang zbV (a commando unit designed for special missions) in Friedenthal two months prior to this, and would have been involved in the process of reorganizing them into the 502nd S.S. Jäger Battalion in August of 1937.*

[15] *Tesla reported that the accident "merely caused customary bruises and upset my digestion a bit," though he did remain bed-ridden for months afterwards.*

[16] *Primarily, he appeared to have been focused on feeding the local pigeons. As Tesla himself said near the end of his life, "I have been feeding pigeons, thousands of them, for years. But there was one, a beautiful bird, pure white with light grey tips on its wings, that was different. It was a female. I had only to wish and call her, and she would come flying to me. I loved that pigeon as a man loves a woman, and she loved me. As long as I had her, there was a purpose to my life." This relationship with the pigeon—which died in 1922—constituted the only love affair in Tesla's life.*

[17] *As Weinberg's* Mystische Zwangsvorstellung *(2008) clearly documents, the Nazis already had several brilliant scientists among their ranks—not the least of which was Laurenz Alfher, the director of the infamous Einheit Elf. It was more arguably Alfher's seminal work that under-girded many of Germany's scientific advancements than Tesla's.*

[18] *In January of 1943, Skorzeny was convalescing in a hospital in Vienna. He had been hospitalized since December of 1942, after being hit in the head*

Reinhard Gehlen[19] successfully made use of Gehlen and Tesla's "Rotating Field Amplifier" (more famously known as the "invisibility net")—used without Tesla's oversight with disastrous consequences in the Philadelphia Experiment[20] later on that year—to sneak into Tesla's hotel room, unseen.

After forcing him to open his safe and surrender his notes to them, the pair proceeded to smother him in his sleep,[21] placing a "do not disturb" sign on his door as a sick joke. They escaped back to Germany with the fervent hopes that Tesla's scientific knowledge would win the war for Hitler.[22]

If not for the daring intelligence work of American superstar Major Glenn Miller,[23] serving undercover in Europe as a musician, who

---

with shrapnel. Apparently, Skorzeny had originally just requested "a few aspirin, a bandage, and a glass of schnapps."

[19] *At this time, Generalmajor Reinhard Gehlen was overseeing the Nazi Fremde Heere Ost ("Foreign Armies East")—a military intelligence unit focused on the Eastern Front. He had no scientific expertise, per se, and no reason to be involved in any plot against Nikola Tesla, much less to be traveling in person to New York City.*

[20] *A classified military experiment which may or may not have been conducted in October of 1943. According to some theories, it was an attempt by the United States military to use electromagnetic radiation to render a ship invisible, both to enemy radar and to the naked eye. Supposedly, the U.S.S. Eldridge somehow instantly teleported from the Philadelphia Naval Yard to the Norfolk Naval Shipyard, well over 200 miles to the south, and then bounced back. Multiple witnesses in Philadelphia and Norfolk claimed to have witnessed this phenomenon, but the United States Navy officially dismisses the experiment as a hoax that never happened.*

[21] *The coroner actually ruled that Tesla had died from natural causes, of coronary thrombosis. Here, Litchfield appears to be basing her "research" on the highly dubious conspiracy theories of Eric Berman, who claimed to have heard this report from a dying Otto Skorzeny himself in Florida in 1999. Skorzeny actually died from lung cancer in 1975 in Madrid—though Weinberg (2008) does cite several theories pointing to the distinct possibility that Skorzeny had potentially faked his death.*

[22] *Far from being hopeful about the future of the Third Reich, Gehlen was so certain that the Nazi regime was about to fall that he agreed to participate in the failed assassination attempt on Adolf Hitler himself in July of 1944.*

[23] *Popular bandleader Glenn Miller actually did volunteer to join the war effort in 1942—but to modernize the U.S. Army Band, not to do intelligence work. Litchfield appears to be heavily leaning here on the similarly ridiculous "research" of Hunton Downs (2009), who claimed that Miller was a "super-spy" who had served under Hollywood movie star David Niven. Obviously, as an un-trained, easily-recognized, 40-year-old musician, Miller would hardly have been an ideal choice for espionage and field work. Interestingly, however, Niven really did muster out after the war as a Lt. Colonel, having commanded the special reconnaissance commando*

smuggled Tesla's notes from Germany to England in 1944, the world may very well have fallen before the Nazi war machine. Unfortunately, Miller was murdered by Skorzeny in a Paris bordello in early 1945,[24] and never saw the victory for the Allies that his selfless work had accomplished.

---

unit known as the GHQ Liaison Regiment.

[24] *Again, another baseless assertion by Downs. Glenn Miller actually disappeared when his plane inexplicably went down over the English Channel in December of 1944, perhaps due to its carburetor icing up in the cold. Skorzeny was solidly enmeshed in Operation Panzerfaust in Hungary at the time—well over 900 miles to the east of Paris.*

Chapter 18
Running Out of Time

The flight back home to Chicago was, in a word, awkward. I mean, that was all a lot to take in, and Durant seemed pretty down afterwards. He spent most of the time just looking out of the window of the plane, thinking. Every time that Victoria saw him, her face crinkled into a worried frown. On the plus side, it was a short flight, and, since it was over the noon hour, she made us a lunch of broiled white fish that was spectacular. I wouldn't have thought that you could use that word to describe white fish, but believe me, you can if it's as good as hers. Of course, the lobster cream sauce on top and the toasty Bâtard-Montrache chardonnay she poured us didn't hurt any. As I was finishing up my lunch, Durant finally spoke to me directly.

"You deceived me," he said, obviously still fairly frustrated about that.

"Whoa!" I replied, swallowing my last bite. "*That's* where you start up with me? I just met family that you swore to me you didn't have!"

"Neglecting to mention a grandson with whom I have not spoken in half a century is hardly equivalent to consciously hiding the clear evidence of your imminent transformation into a man-eating monster, would you not agree?"

He had a point.

"But I think I'm past the worst of it," I said, trying to mitigate things. "I haven't had any of those cravings or thoughts since early this morning. I made a decision, and I bounced my mind, just like you said." He just sighed, and his head drooped.

"How many addicts over how many centuries have declined further treatment because they were certain—*certain*—that they had beaten their addictions? You continue to misunderstand the nature of your lycanthropy." He turned and took a long sip of wine, savored it for a moment, then sighed again. "Primarily because you desire to misunderstand it."

"What are you saying?" I replied. "I'm desperate to understand what's going on!" He just snorted and ate his last bit of fish himself, sopping up the remaining sauce on his plate. "Seriously, I think that I have a handle on this now."

"'So sayeth the drunkard'," he said, lifting his glass and taking another sip. "People have ever been drawn to such self-deceptions, if doing so allows them to pretend that their weaknesses are actually somehow strengths. Humanity always desire to feel better about what and who they are within their foibles, when they would be better served to mend their foibles in order to become better people."

"But what if I really do have control over this?" I pressed him. "Couldn't this power be used to do some good in the world? What about Mkogisos?"

"My grandson is… unique…" he replied, setting his glass down. "As were the circumstances which allowed his present condition." He looked out the window again for the moment, lost in his memories. I wonder how many centuries back his thoughts were taking him.

"How so?" I asked, bringing him back. He turned around again, but didn't answer me directly.

"Infection with the Lycaon virus is progressive, Detective," he said. "Even if—and this itself is doubtful—but even if you were to 'have control' over yourself now, such control would necessarily fade and falter by this evening *because you shall desire it to falter.* You shall *desire* to give in to the beast within you, and thus shall it have free rein over you. It shall control you, in the end."

"But what about Mkogisos?" I asked again. "Can't there be some way to keep it in check? Can't we keep this on the side of the angels?"

"You yourself saw the prayer room in Bunin's home, yes?" he asked. "You heard Sydor's rants about following God's plan, about preferring the wilderness over Eden. These men—these animals—both assumed that they *were* on 'the side of the angels,' as you say." His words stung because I knew that he was right. No matter how hard I wanted to do the right thing, odds are, it would eventually devolve into thinking exactly like they did. And the scariest part would be that I'd never even see it happening, because I'd lose my ability to objectively evaluate myself at the same rate that I'd be thinking more and more warped thoughts. The more lost I became, the less I'd notice getting lost.

"One of the great ironies—" he continued, "or tragedies, if you choose—of evil is that though there are countless individuals in our world who follow Satan's paths, very few of them are aware of it, primarily because they do not wish to be. Ask most witches, and they will tell you that they serve ancient gods, or nature spirits, or ascended masters. Ask the *Société des Dragonistes*, and they will tell you that they hunt witches in order to serve God and embrace the natural tendencies which God created within each of us. Ask the common man on the street, and he will tell you that he serves no one but his own enlightened self-interest. But remember that the Devil has no cause of his own. He only wishes to draw humanity to paths which will lead us farther and farther away from God. And thus, all of these people—the witch, the werewolf, the oblivious—all of them may walk down Satan's paths, though none of them may realize or admit it."

"But doesn't that waste his resources?" I asked. "Isn't it at cross-purposes for the Devil to make his own witches fight his own werewolves?" He took one last sip of wine, then allowed the slightest hint of an unhappy smile to crease the corner of his mouth.

"Not if such combat makes both sides believe all the more that they are on the correct paths to begin with." He shook his head, disgusted at the ignorance of it all. "You must remember that Satan is a master tactician who cares nothing for the pawns whom he sacrifices for his goals. Thus, he is content to lose a battle here or there in order to achieve larger victories within the greater war at hand. If, for instance, receiving aid in capturing a murderer encourages the police to trust in the powers of 'psychics' and mediums all the more, then Satan is happy to sacrifice the one to bolster the growing respect for the other. In the end, both witches and werewolves are merely pawns on Satan's side—though both would vigorously deny it, to be sure."

"But if psychics work—" I started to argue.

"Werewolves '*work*,' Detective," he interrupted. "So would you place Bunin on your police force?"

*   *   *

We set back down at the same private airport outside of Chicago. The pilot came out to see us off as we gathered our things, and Victoria tried—completely professionally—to make small talk with Durant. He was courteous, if a bit brusque, and told them that he didn't know when he'd be back, but that they should keep the plane ready to fly at a moment's notice.

"As always, sir," Cliff replied.

"Of course, sir," Victoria chimed in.

He wished them well, then turned to go back to my waiting car. I saw Victoria watching him—noticed her breathing deepen, heard her heartbeat quicken, saw that look of worry crease her brow again. Was it like that for her every time that he left them? I decided that I really had to say something about her to Durant.

"So..." I began, once we were safely back in the car.

"Yes?"

"Victoria..."

"Yes?"

"She's..." As soon as started, I realized that I had no idea where I was going to go with that sentence. "She's very… nice…"

"Are you not happily married?" he asked.

"Yes," I answered, a little frustrated that that's where his mind went. "But *you're* not." He turned to look out the window, not responding to my comment. So I pressed the issue just a bit more. "Look, she obviously cares for you, and I was just—"

"I understand," he interrupted quietly, without turning toward me. "And I care for her as well. Quite a bit, in fact. I have cared for her since she was a little girl, and I shall continue to do so until long after she has aged, died, and turned to dust." He turned back to me, and I could see the pain etched on his face. "Is this really what you wished to hear?"

What could I possibly say in response to that? I couldn't begin to imagine what it must've been like, being Durant. He tried so very, very hard not to care about anyone—to just pass through people's fleeting lifetimes like a stone skipping across the surface of a lake. But inside of that really, really scary exterior, he still had the same heart that he'd always had. People still got in. He still cared. And it had to hurt him deeply, every time that he did.

"So is the Grail on the Raven?" I asked him, shifting subjects to spare him any more pain. I started the car, and he took a deep breath and visibly relaxed, obviously appreciating the change.

"Would one put so holy an object in so mundane a location as a mere conveyance?" he replied. It was hard to see the Raven as a "mere conveyance," but I could see his point, I guess.

"People have put important things in dumber places," I said, pulling away from the tarmac, figuring we'd check in on Tony. "Not too awful long ago, someone fished a copy of Action Comics #1 out of the ancient insulation of a decrepit old house." I looked behind us, and Cliff had already gone back into the plane. Victoria was still there, watching us drive away. She had her hand over her mouth.

"The first appearance of Superman…" he commented absent-mindedly. He hadn't seen a movie since 1934, but he knew about comic books. I really didn't get Durant sometimes. "In point of fact, a friend of mine once thought to hide the Stone of Scone on a golf course in Scotland."

"What's a 'Stone of Scone'?"

"Uneducated barbarian…" he snorted, sitting up in his seat. He seemed giddy to move the conversation from personal feelings to ancient history. "The Stone of Scone is the coronation stone of British monarchs, sent to Scotland by the Irish king Murtagh MacErc from its resting place in the Ráith na Ríogh at Tara when he loaned the Lia Fáil to his brother, Fergus, for his own coronation. For centuries, it has resided under the throne at Westminster, since Edward Longshanks stole it from the Scottish in 1296."

"Lia Fáil?" I asked. "Ráith na Ríogh?"

"The original coronation stone was essentially a large slab of marble infused with great quantities of orichalcum—vril—from the Atlantean city of Fálias—thus, the name, 'Lia Fáil,' which means, 'Stone of Fálias.' Because of this, the stone was naturally orientated toward the blood of true Atlanteans, and therefore recognized pureblood kings when it came in contact with them. At least it did, until Cú Chulainn impetuously hacked the stone into shards of its former self when it failed to recognize his foster son, Lugaid Riab nDerg, as king."

"How does a stone recognize a king?"

"With a roar."

Of course it did.

"Think of the Lia Fáil as a prehistoric version of a computer," he attempted to explain. "The orichalcum infusing it allowed the stone to process information, control the Atlanteans' technologies, and even provide instant communication—even extra-terrestrially—via a philotic stream directed through their *Asbrú*." Before you ask—no, I have no idea what any of that meant. "Thus, from the Ráith na Ríogh—the Fortress of Kings—Béothach and the descendents of the Tuatha Dé Danann could remain interconnected with their brothers, the other Atlantean refugees who had been scattered around the globe by the great catastrophe."

"The Vril War," I remembered, trying to latch on to at least *something* in all of that.

"Just so."

"So you're saying that British kings and queens have been sitting on an Atlantean stone all these years, huh?" I shook my head in disbelief.

"Well…" he said with a little twinkle in his eye. "Not exactly, no. After the stone was used by Mac Bethad mac Findlaích to crown himself at Dùnsinnan in 1054, I liberated it and buried it in a hill near the castle."

"You stole it."

"I *liberated* it from its *usurper*," he said—and rather emphatically at that. "When Mac Bethad was finally defeated by Máel Coluim mac Donnchada at Lann Fhìonain three years later, mortally wounded, he returned to Dùnsinnan to find the stone missing. He commissioned a 'new' Lia Fáil to be carved out of the plentiful red sandstone nearby, but then died before he could make use of it."

"So *that's* the stone that this Edward actually stole?"

"Indeed."

"But your friend tried to hide it on a golf course?" His eyes twinkled again.

"Truth be told," he said—and I could tell that he'd been waiting a long time to tell *someone* this story at *some* point, if nothing else just to share in the fun—"in 1950, three Scottish college students succeeded in absconding with the Stone of Scone."

"You mean, Mac Bethad's sandstone forgery," I interjected.

"Exactly. My friend, being the patriotic highlander that he was and believing it to be the genuine coronation stone of Scottish kings, hid the stone at the Royal Highlands Golf Club in Scotland so that it may never again be made use of by the hated English. Instead, he had a clever forgery created and returned to Westminster."

"He made a forgery of the forgery."

"Just so… though he believed that he was making a forgery of the original."

"So you're saying that since 1951, all of the kings and queens of England have been crowned on a fake *fake* Stone of Scone?"

"No, of course not," he replied, turning back to gaze out the window again. "Only Queen Elizabeth II…"

*   *   *

I called ahead, and Tony said that he'd be waiting for us at his place with some information. We drove in silence for a while, but I had to ask one more question before we picked up Tony.

"Can the Grail cure a werewolf?" I asked. It was kind of out of the blue, so I felt a little guilty just throwing it out there like that, but I had no idea how to lead up to it.

"Pardon me?" Durant asked, turning toward me again.

"You heard me," I said. "You've never offered the Grail to me, so I have to ask—*could* it potentially cure me?" He thought for a while before answering me.

"As I explained to you before, the Grail is not a 'miracle machine' that one simply trots out to work wonders, then returns to its shelf. Such is not its purpose."

"I get that," I replied. "But let's be honest here. Within the next five hours or so, I'm either going to be a monster or I'll be dead."

"Sunset is at 4:22 this afternoon," he corrected me. "So we actually have a little over three hours…"

"Lovely," I said, rolling my eyes. "Thank you. So in about three hours, things are going to get really ugly without some sort of miracle happening. But the Grail could provide just that sort of miracle, right? So why not even make the effort? Wouldn't it work?" He sighed and kept silent, looking out the window. I couldn't tell what he was thinking—if he was sad because it wouldn't work, or sad because it might work and he felt like he couldn't offer it to me for some reason, or just sad that I was even asking. After about a minute, he turned back, though he didn't try to make eye contact.

"The Grail is capable of curing a man of anything," he explained, but his voice sounded weary and uncertain. "But it only cures those maladies from which one might *wish* to be cured."

"Well, I wish to be cured of this!" I replied.

"But right now, the virus is merely incubating," he said. "It is not at its fullest strength. For the Grail to be effective in potentially curing one of lycanthropy, one must be nearly at the point of transformation—the disease must have fully infected the victim. And yet..." he let his voice trail off, and he sighed the deepest sigh that I'd ever heard from him so far.

"And yet what?" I asked him.

"And yet," he replied with another sigh, "by then, you shall no longer *wish* to be healed. By the time that the Lycaon virus has taken full effect, you shall no longer wish to be rid of it—and that is the great tragedy of the matter."

"So it's a Catch-22?"

"A what?" He knew about Action Comics and the Vril War, but he'd never read *Catch-22*...?

"Damned if you do and damned if you don't..." I explained.

"The technical term is a 'dilemma,' I believe," he said. "When there are only two logical options from which to choose, though both lead inexorably to the same conclusion."

"Thank you again," I said. "So what *would* the Grail do for a full-blown werewolf?"

"Perhaps nothing," he replied. "Perhaps something abominable. I would never wish to hand it over to them to find that out—would you?" That kind of put a damper on our conversation for a while. In fact, we drove the rest of the way in silence, until I finally parked the car at Tony's place. Durant never stopped looking out the window.

"So there's no hope?" I asked at last, shutting off the engine. That's when he turned back to look at me.

"There is always hope," he replied. "If this were not true, I would have put you down long ago..." And that's Durant's version of being all comforting.

We trotted up the stairs to Tony's apartment, but before I could even knock, Tony whipped open the door and shouted, "Where've you guys been all mornin'?"

"Cincinnati," Durant answered him with a matter-of-fact simplicity.

"O' course," Tony replied with a chuckle. "No, seriously..."

"You said that you had some info for us, Tony," I said, breaking them up. "Are we coming in or going out?"

"Goin' out," he replied, closing the door behind him and locking it. "We gotta get movin'..."

"Why?" I asked.

"'Cuz I just heard that they found Leah Wheaton!"

*   *   *

Apparently, at the same time that Lyn was toying with Tony back in that vacant building off of Addison, another group of *Obshchestvo Drakonisty* thugs had grabbed Wheaton and taken her off site. Without her weapon or phone, she'd had to play along until she could get a chance to turn the tables on them. She'd somehow gotten away mid-morning, but Tony had only heard about it just then. As we drove, I told him about meeting Mkogisos in the tunnels under Cincinnati, but I left out the parts about his relationship with Durant. The man had let himself get vulnerable with me, and I wasn't going to return that respect by blabbing about it to everyone else. He noticed what I'd skipped, and I could see in his face that he appreciated it.

Tony, however, thought that it was all a little too bizarre to be believed. That's when I pulled out the silver bullet and handed it to him. I felt it burning through the fingers of the glove—and it hurt worse than it did when Mkogisos had first given it to me.

"Yer kiddin' me!" he said, turning the bullet over in his hand. "This thing is, like, totally really silver?"

"Totally," Durant assured him.

"I didn't know ya could really make one outta silver," Tony said, looking at the bullet closer.

"Almost any metal should work," Durant explained. "And silver is only negligibly harder than lead, so it still works rather well, as would gold. Silver is, however, slightly less dense than lead, and thus, the decrease in mass provides slightly less penetration. But, since the benefit of using silver against werewolves lies in its composition rather than in its 'stopping power,' I should think that the trade-off would be worth its use, in the long run."

"Ever make a bullet outta gold?" Tony asked him.

"I never had any call to do so," he replied. "Though I am aware that certain undead species from the Orient—Egypt, India, China and the like—have an intense aversion to gold."

Interesting though all of that might've been, by then, we'd arrived at the hospital where Wheaton was being checked over. I wanted to make sure that we talked with her as soon as possible—any information that she had picked up might help me to figure out what to try next. So since we knew that she no longer had her cell phone on her, I wanted to catch her before she was released.

When we pulled into the parking deck, it was 2:05. I had a little over two hours before sunset.

*   *   *

She was still in the Emergency Room when we got there, but she was pulling on her coat.

"Hey!" she said, seeing Tony and me coming through the door. She came over and gave Tony a hug. "I was so worried when you got separated from me!"

"Naw," Tony said, giving her a quick pat on the back with his good arm. "It was you got separated from me…"

"What happened?" I asked her. All of the smells in the room started getting to me, and I was beginning to have a hard time focusing my attention. Disinfectant, latex, antibiotics, saline, old blood, medications of all sorts of different kinds—they all started jumbling up my senses. I could even smell *disease*. I had to try to shut it all down and push the scents away entirely.

"It was completely dark in there," she said, talking about the building that she went into with Tony. "I barely got through the door when someone knocked my flashlight and weapon out of my hands and grabbed me. In the dark, I couldn't see who it was or how many, so all I knew at the time was that a bunch of assailants—really, really strong assailants—had overpowered me and dragged me off to another part of the building."

"You say that they were unnaturally strong?" I asked.

"I don't know about 'unnaturally,' but yeah, they were tough," she answered.

"Were they…" I didn't know how to ask it without sounding like an idiot. "Were they… normal?"

"What do you mean?"

"I mean…"

"I presume that they took you elsewhere, where you were ultimately able to see them," Durant interrupted me. "Could you describe your attackers?"

"Yeah," she said, sitting back down on the examining table. "It turns out that there were three of them—which means that I don't feel quite so stupid getting caught, I guess." She and Tony shared a smile about that, but neither Durant nor I were in the mood. "Anyway, they were *Bratva* all right—you could tell from the tattoos. Two big guys, and one that looked like some sort of European underwear model. You know the type—slim hips, flat stomach, all muscle, greasy hair, ugly face. He had a tattoo of a spider on the back of his hand."

"A thief…" Durant muttered.

"Whatever," she said, and then she kept going. "They ended up tying my hands and throwing me into the back of a van, then taking me to a really creepy place off of Chicago Avenue."

That caught my attention.

"Tell me about the place," I said.

"It was an abandoned shop front, all boarded up. In the back, they had a Krokodil lab set up."

I probably ought to stop in the middle here and tell you a little bit about Krokodil, since she brought it up. It's a new drug that hit Illinois near the end of 2013, brought in by the Russians because it's simple to make using over-the-counter medications and easy to sell because it's so stinking cheap—and it's pretty much the most evil drug out there on the street today. Basically, you get a high much like you would from heroin, but it doesn't last anywhere near as long, and it's even harder to kick. It's ten times more powerful than morphine, so you become completely addicted within the first couple of times that you use it. Oh, and the drug itself is usually so dirty that shooting it up causes massive tissue damage, leading to really nasty abscesses and gangrene. Frequent users develop green, scaly lesions of dead tissue on their skin that look kind of like a crocodile's hide—thus, the name. Basically, you end up rotting from the inside-out. Personally, I've only ever seen one actual Krokodil user—a guy from Joliet being held in lock-up who smelled like he'd already been dead for a couple of days. The doctor who came in to examine him said that the gangrene had spread throughout his system, and that he had so much necrotic (read, "dead") tissue in him that he was already impossible to save. But even after he heard that, the guy was still begging for more. In fact, I've been told that the average life expectancy for a Krokodil user is something like two years—and those last several months are about the worst way to die. We've been having growing problems with heroin in the Chicagoland area for the past few years, but this Krokodil thing? That's just plain scary.

"They took me through the lab and then down into some basement set-up that reminded me a lot of what we'd seen at Bunin's house after coming for you and Agent Davidge," she continued. "There were half a dozen little rooms that they'd built down there with padded walls, all facing a big, open room." So Bunin had lied about there not being any other killing floors in Chicago. I could've sworn that he'd been telling us the truth about that.

"What was in the open room?" I asked.

"Nothing," she said. "Why?" The more I thought about it, the more I figured that if the main room was clean, then they may not have even killed anyone there yet. Maybe Bunin just didn't know about the place because it was so new?

"So how did you get away?"

"One of the big guys didn't seem too smart," she said. "In fact, I don't think that the guy even spoke English. The greasy guy gave him some sort of an order in Russian, then left the room to go back upstairs.

So the big guy took me over to one of the little soundproofed rooms—the only one that already had its door closed—and I guess he was planning to throw me into it. Though all of the other rooms were empty, he was dumb enough to open up the only room that already had a girl in it. Well, she jumped out and started screaming and clawing at the guy like crazy, and he freaked out. He sliced at her blindly with some sort of little, curved knife, and I used the confusion to kick him in the groin, then in the head. I realized that the girl was dead, so I used his knife to cut my hands free from the rope that they'd tied me with, got myself out of the building, and called 911 from the first phone I came to."

"You didn't see either of the other two guys on the way out?"

"Nope. I got very, very lucky." Then she added, "I did hear one of the guys talking about going back to a room at a motel in Lincolnwood to do some business. I don't know what motel it was, but I figure that we can check it out."

"Yer gonna get home and rest," Tony said.

"Actually, I'm going back to the office to write my report," she countered. "Then I'm going home and taking the longest, hottest shower my water heater can handle."

"I have one, last, really weird question," I said. Again, I didn't really know how to ask it without just asking it, so I just took a deep breath and went for it. "At any time, did any of these guys… *bite* you?"

"*Bite* me?" she replied, taken aback a bit. "No, no one bit me. I got out without a scratch."

"Do you mean that literally?" Durant asked her.

"What?"

"Do you mean that you did not receive even a single scratch throughout the entire abduction episode?"

"Yeah, no," she said, looking confused. "Only some light ligature abrasions on my wrists from wriggling out of the rope restraints. Why? What's all this about, guys?"

Durant spun a really believable-sounding story about these guys being into some sort of biting fetish, and said that it was distinctly possible that one of the guys was actually infected with rabies. We just wanted to make sure that she hadn't gotten similarly infected by a bite or other contaminating action, he explained. She seemed to buy it, but again, I was doing everything I could to focus on what she was saying and tune out all of the other inputs from my senses.

The nurse came in, so we let her get her stuff together and get going, and I pulled Tony to the side. There were still a bunch of cops milling around the E.R., and I didn't want them hearing what I was going to talk with him about.

"Tony," I said quietly, "I'm sure that someone's already on this, but I want you to check out that motel, figure out what room they might be talking about, and get us a warrant. And while you're at it, do me a favor and put in another call to Georgiy Chernomyrdin. Light a fire under him and let's see if he's got anything more that we can go on. And call Nate Kingery. Maybe he's dug up more on the leadership of the *Obshchestvo Drakonisty...*"

"I got it, I got it..." he said. "So this motel... Yer thinkin' it's the Patio?"

"That'd be my first guess," I agreed. "Or maybe River Park? Either one is sleazy enough for these guys to try to work out of. But whatever motel it is, we've got to jump on this, because if we can't get a warrant by, well, pretty much immediately, we're going to have to go in and check it out anyway."

"That ain't strictly legal," he said.

"I'm running out of time to keep things strictly legal..."

"Then yer gonna need this," Tony said, giving me back my silver bullet. "An' I'd suggest a little black mask ta go along with it..."

*   *   *

Durant and I left to go to the storefront that Wheaton had told us about, while Tony went off to Lincolnwood to check out that strip of motels along Lincoln Avenue.

"That has no effect on the passage of time," Durant commented as we drove down Chicago.

"What?" I asked. "What doesn't?"

"Looking at your watch repeatedly," he said. I hadn't even realized that I'd been doing it. "The time is what it is. Remember it and move on."

"It's a little after 2:30," I said. "Time's moving on a little faster than I want it to." We passed through the intersection with Spaulding, and I felt for the bullet in my pocket to see if it felt any warmer, but it hadn't changed since Tony gave it back to me at the hospital. Maybe you had to be fairly close to the head of the bloodline for it to work? I glanced at my watch... and then felt a little stupid. Out of the corner of my eye, I could see that Durant noticed me doing it.

"This place is in Ukrainian Village, not far from the cathedral," I said, trying not to think about the time.

"Is it?" he asked, not really asking. "And you think that we can find a substantial clue to the head of the bloodline there?"

"I have no idea," I answered him. "We're just out of good options, unless Tony finds something at the motel or with one of his phone calls. But I was thinking that maybe we could—"

Before I could finish that thought—right as we passed the U.S. Footwear on our right, but before we got to the Foot Locker on our left—I smelled almonds. Both of us sat bolt upright, and turned to one another.

"The Synod of Crows!" he growled.

"We need these guys alive!" I told him before he might jump out and start killing them. "They might just have the answers we need…" I slammed on the brakes and pulled over to the side of the road next to Kells Park, right across from Popeye's. The cars behind us leaned on their horns and whipped around us. One guy made an obscene gesture. But I pulled the LED light out and popped it onto the roof of my car, hit the hazards, and jumped out. Durant was already standing in the snow, looking out into the park.

"Where do you think they are?" I asked, looking across the street toward the Western Union across Kedzie. He didn't answer me. "Durant?" I asked, turning around to see what he was doing.

The wind was picking up, and the snow was beginning to blow all around us. Even as I was turning, I could tell that the sky was darkening—it happened that quickly. The trees in the park were swaying, but it looked like they were moving in all different directions—they weren't swaying in the wind. In the park itself, I could clearly see dozens of people, standing in formation, facing us with their arms outstretched. At the front of the pack was the Goth woman I'd seen across from the library on Wabansia, right after I'd first realized that I was changing. They were chanting something quietly, and the wind seemed to be reacting to their gestures. The stench of almonds was almost overpowering.

I immediately reached into the back seat of the car and grabbed the staff. Even through the gloves, it really hurt to hold onto it—far worse than it had before. When I stood back up, that's when I caught a completely different scent behind me. I turned, and perched on the roof of the Foot Locker were perhaps a dozen werewolves, facing the witches. In the lead was a large, caramel-colored one.

"Durant?" I called out again, looking around for him. I saw him standing by the open gate in the chain link fence surrounding the park.

He had his pocket watch out and was checking the time…

Background
From *Malleus Maleficarum* (Heinrich Kramer & Jakob Sprenger, 1486, trans. G.L. Burr)

From *Pars i, Quaestio 17*

So heinous are the crimes of witches that they even exceed the sins and the fall of the bad Angels;[1] and if this is true as to their guilt, how should it not also be true of their punishments in hell? And it is not difficult to prove this by various arguments with regard to their guilt. And first, although the sin of Satan is unpardonable, this is not on account of the greatness of his crime, having regard to the nature of the Angels, with particular attention to the opinion of those who say that the Angels were created only in a state of nature, and never in a state of grace. And since the good of grace exceeds the good of nature, therefore the sins of those who fall from a state of grace, as do the witches by denying the faith which they received in baptism, exceed the sins of the Angels. And even if we say that the Angels were created, but not confirmed, in grace; so also witches, though they are not created in grace, have yet of their own will fallen from grace; just as Satan sinned of his own will.

Secondly, it is granted that Satan's sin is unpardonable for various other reasons. For S. Augustine says that he sinned at the instigation of none,[2] therefore his sin is justly remediable by none. And S. John

---

[1] *Witchcraft has long been perceived as one of the worst sins possible in the Christian mindset—along with lascivious dancing, gluttony, sodomy, bestiality, etc. (see de Lancre's 1613* Tableau de l'Inconstance des Mauvais Anges et Démons*)—because in witchcraft, the practitioner is fully aware of the power of spiritual actions and personages, and has consciously and with forethought chosen to align themselves with God's enemy. Given that most if not all of the people in Europe would have been baptized into the Christian church at the time of the publication of the* Malleus Maleficarum, *then witchcraft would be—by definition—the worst form of apostasy from the faith.*

[2] *In his* Confessiones *(5th century)*

Damascene says[3] that he sinned in his understanding against the character of God; and that his sin was the greater by reason of the nobility of his understanding. For the servant who knows the will of his master, etc.[4] The same authority says that, since Satan is incapable of repentance, therefore he is incapable of pardon; and this is due to his very nature, which, being spiritual, could only be changed once, when he changed it for ever; but this is not so with men, in whom the flesh is always warring against the spirit...

But notwithstanding all this, his sin is in many respects small in comparison with the crimes of witches. First, as S. Anselm showed in one of his *Sermons*,[5] he sinned in his pride while there was yet no punishment for sin. But witches continue to sin after great punishments have been often inflicted upon many other witches, and after the punishments which the Church teaches them have been inflicted by reason of the devil and his fall; and they make light of all these, and hasten to commit, not the least deadly of sins, as do other sinners who sin through infirmity or wickedness yet not from habitual malice, but rather the most horrible crimes from the deep malice of their hearts.

Secondly, although the Bad Angel fell from innocence to guilt, and thence to misery and punishment; yet he fell from innocence once only, in such a way that he was never restored. But the sinner who is restored to innocence by baptism, and again falls from it, falls very deep.[6] And this is especially true of witches, as is proved by their crimes.

Thirdly, he sinned against the Creator; but we, and especially witches, sin against the Creator and the Redeemer.

Fourthly, he forsook God, who permitted him to sin but accorded him no pity; whereas we, and witches above all, withdraw ourselves from God by our sins, while, in spite of his permission of our sins, He continually pities us and prevents us with His countless benefits.

Fifthly, when he sinned, God rejected him without showing him any grace; whereas we wretches run into sin although God is continually calling us back.

---

[3] *John of Damascus, in his classic* Πηγή Γνωσεως *(8th century)*

[4] *Kramer and Sprenger allude here to the* Gospel of St. Luke, *xii, 47—"That servant, who knew the will of his lord and prepared not himself and did not according to his will, shall be beaten with many stripes."*

[5] *Specifically, in his* Dialogus de Casu Diaboli *(11th century)*

[6] *See also the Biblical* Book of Hebrews, *vi, 4-6 ("For it is impossible for those who were once enlightened, and have tasted of the heavenly gift, and were made partakers of the Holy Ghost, and have tasted the good word of God, and the powers of the world to come, if they shall fall away, to renew them again unto repentance; seeing they crucify to themselves the Son of God afresh, and put him to an open shame.")*

Sixthly, he keeps his heart hardened against a punisher;[7] but we against a merciful persuader. Both sin against God; but he against a commanding God, and we against One who dies for us, Whom, as we have said, wicked witches offend above all.

---

[7] *An argument echoed a century later and at greater length in Rémy's* Daemonolatreiae Libri Tres *(1595).*

Background
From *The Travels of Peer van Draeck*[1] (Randall MacMillan, 1997)

from *Volume II, Chapter 2*

And so it was that van Draeck found himself again cast from the sea onto an unknown shore. As he surveyed his surroundings, he saw wreckage from the *Mulher Infiel*[2] strewn around the beach; it appeared that his companions had not survived the storm, and that he was, once again, on his own.

His constitution was strong, so van Draeck commenced foraging for food. Finding what he first assumed to be bananas and then realised were the plantains known as *nayndra valay*, and recognising that his beach was facing westerly, he ascertained that he was either on a large, unknown island, or else the southwestern coast of India. As he made his way, the jungle became less dense, and he could see both hill rice nearby and the Ghats[3] in the distance, confirming that he had washed ashore on the latter rather than the former. That would place him within the Kingdom of Mysore, which was good. The Wadiyar Maharaja, Chamaraja V, was not an ally of the Dutch, but he was also certainly no friend to the Portuguese.

The plantains were far too tough to be eaten without being steamed or fried, but van Draeck was not starving. He saw a well-beaten path appear before him, and he followed it until he came to a little hut, nestled in the jungle near a small stream. Outside, a small child sat, weeping.

"Why do you weep, little one?" he asked her, but she didn't understand his words. He tried Portuguese, but that only seemed to upset her. Hearing a man's voice, her mother came out of the hut to see

---

[1] *Peer van Draeck was an actual, historical Dutch naturalist/mercenary, though his widespread travels have been the subject of folktales around the world. Unfortunately, little is known about the real van Draeck beyond these exaggerated stories about his exploits, and his own well-known book on supernatural creatures,* De Dødes Bog *(1642).*

[2] *The Portuguese ship which had captured van Draeck and his party earlier.*

[3] *The Western Ghats—a mountain range along the western coast of India.*

who was there. When she saw the white man, she was terrified, and pulled her daughter to her bosom.

"Please do not be afraid," he told the woman, speaking Portuguese. "I am Dutch, not Portuguese. I have survived a shipwreck in the storm last night." He knew just enough Hindi to try to at least repeat the main thought of his words to her.

The woman appeared to understand him, and she offered to cook the plantains that he held in his hands. He thanked her with a warm smile, and that seemed to put her more at ease. As she fried them, he attempted to speak with her.

"Why was the little girl weeping?" he asked.

She answered in a broken Portuguese, ""Father… he… taken… by Ḍāyana… yes?"

"Who is this 'Ḍāyana'? Why did the Ḍāyana take the girl's father?" he asked her, but she became agitated. She shook her head and tears began to form in her eyes as well. He stopped asking, not wanting to hurt the woman any more. When the food was ready, they all ate together quietly. It was simple fare, but it filled the belly and warmed the spirit. When they were finished, he tried talking with the woman again.

"Where is this Ḍāyana? Tell me, and I shall go find the girl's father," he said, again trying to repeat the thought in Hindi. Terrified, the woman pointed toward the Ghats.

"Follow… road to… darkest valley…" she told him in Portuguese. "Find mandira there…" He had heard the word "mandira" before; he knew that it meant "temple." He thanked the woman again, and reached into his purse, pulling out several gold coins to give to her. She looked shocked and fell at his feet, thanking him.

"No, do not thank me," he said. "You have fed me and shown me why my Lord has brought me here. I should be thanking you. Dhan'yavāda."[4]

As he walked back out of the hut, he found the little girl, sniffling outside by the little pen of goats which stood nearby. He squatted down beside her, reached into his purse, and pulled out a small doll for her. The girl's eyes lit up, and she stopped crying.

He tossled her hair and said, "I know that you cannot understand me, little one, but I promise to bring your father back to you. You must introduce him to your new little friend when I do."

With that, he made his way down the path toward the mountains. Soon, the green growth of the jungle began to disappear, and by the time he had walked only an hour or so, only dried grasses remained. In the distance, at the base of the mountains, he saw the ruins of a small,

---

[4]   *"Thank you" in Hindi.*

ancient temple. When he approached it, he could see that it had been abandoned long ago. The bricks were cracked and chipped, the paint had long since faded, and thick creepers had grown and died years before across the walls and through all of the openings. He prayed for God's strength, then stepped into the blackness of the entryway.

Within, he saw the orange-coloured glow of firelight in another room. Quietly, he crept closer to the doorway to see what was going on. Inside the chamber, he saw a man tied to a stone table, and above him, a beautiful woman was writhing and chanting an unholy song. In one hand, she held a knife, dripping with blood; in the other, she held a human finger. He looked back down at the man, and saw that she had indeed cut off the index finger of his right hand.

"Good Lord!" he exclaimed, and the woman heard him. She spun around and her face twisted as she hissed at him in surprise. But then, her aspect changed and she became beautiful again. For a moment, he thought her the most beautiful woman that he had ever seen.

"Come to me..." she purred, and he began to walk to her, even though he had no intention to do so consciously. By God's grace, he stumbled over a root which had grown across the floor, and the crucifix which he wore around his neck tumbled out of his blouse. Instinctively, he clutched at it, and immediately he came to his senses. He realized that he had understood her words, but somehow, he knew that she had not spoken in Dutch. He concluded that this Ḍāyana must be some form of a witch, who had cast her spell on him, much as she had obviously bewitched this poor man upon whom she had been working her foul magicks.

"By the holy name of Jesus, I shall not!" he exclaimed, and the woman hissed again in anger.

"The deed is done, nonetheless," she said, holding the bloodied finger up in her hands. She cackled, and thunder cracked above them.

"What have you done, witch?" he demanded, drawing his gleaming sword and making ready to fight.

"I have appeased the pretas[5] of this desecrated place!"

"What are you talking about, woman? What have you done to this poor wretch?" The Ḍāyana laughed again, and shouted something to the heavens in a guttural and unwholesome language which he did not recognise.

She spoke to van Draeck again, saying, "The sorcerers who once lived in this temple were great and dark and powerful, and they fought against the grey monks who live on top of the mountains and within the

---

5   *"Pretas" are hungry ghosts—the unquiet spirits of foul people who died in violence or in great sorrow. They have an insatiable hunger or thirst, and must be satisfied or else they will continue to bother the living, even to the point of taking their lives.*

mountains. They had not been able to defeat the monks in life, and one night, the grey devils swarmed over this place with their weapons of metal and light and slaughtered the sorcerers here in their sleep. The monks sliced off their fingers and took them back to Celambra so that even the corpses of the sorcerers could not work their magick against them."[6]

"But why torment this man and his family? Why take a finger from him as well?" van Draeck asked her.

"To appease the pretas! They hunger for fingers and flesh, seeking to replace their own, and so the prophecy stands that if one speaks the unholy words and performs the proscribed rites, offering an unwilling sacrifice of a living soul with nine fingers, then the pretas shall come and provide all of their power to the one who asks, dragging the soul of the nine-fingered sacrifice with them into Naraka[7] to pay for the empowerment." She licked the blood from the man's fingers, and he began to rouse himself from the stupour which had held him up to that point. Her captive began to scream and thrash about, but the Ḍāyana just laughed again in triumph.

Van Draeck realised that his sword would be useless against such enchantments, and he slid it back into its scabbard. The room around them began to thicken with smoke from the witch's firepots, but then the smoke began to coalesce into shapes, into human forms. But the forms were misshapen grotesques. Their bellies were distended, their necks were long, and their mouths were like a child's mouth, but filled with a hundred sharp needles as their teeth. While the rest kept back and appeared to be panting, waiting in great anticipation, one of the smoky shapes stepped forward to address the Ḍāyana, though its cloudy eyes did not appear to be able to actually see her.

"We come for what is ours, for the nine-fingered soul," it said in a voice that sounded like a nightmare. The witch screeched in reply.

"I have the sacrifice for you! I have the one with nine fingers! Now present the power for which I have sacrificed!"

The preta raised its hands, but van Draeck shouted for them to wait before they proceed any further. "You desire one with nine fingers, is this correct?" he asked the ghosts. They all nodded in unison in reply. "Well, then, this woman is the one whom you seek!"

"What insanity is this?" she laughed. "I have the man's tenth finger here in my own grasp!"

"No, you have the man's eighth finger, leaving him only seven in total. Only your hands now hold nine fingers in this chamber, besides

---

[6]   *It was commonly believed that a sorcerer must be able to gesticulate in order to work his magic.*

[7]   *That is, the underworld.*

your own two thumbs."[8]

The Ḍāyana's eyes grew wide in horror as the sightless smoky ghosts began to move toward her. "No!" she shrieked, but they no longer listened to the words of the living. "Ādi Śeṣa,[9] help me!" she cried out to her dark god, but no one came to her rescue. The cloudy shapes reached out to her, and van Draeck watched her own body twist and contort as if in labour, drawn away like paint being washed away by a rainstorm. It was a slow and painful-looking process, and the witch wept in agony and terror as her soul was stripped from her in bits and shreds. The hungry ghosts appeared to be devouring her spirit in a long succession of small bites, and van Draeck watched their pot-bellies swell. After several minutes, the deed was done, and one by one, the pretas dissolved again into the smoke from the fire pots. The last one to leave was the one which had spoken earlier.

"Do you wish to make a sacrifice to obtain our power as well?" the preta called to van Draeck.

"No. I serve the one, true God, and His is all the power that a man may ever need. Counterfeits such as yours serve only to bloat the belly while increasing the appetite, and they come at too high a cost. I shall have none of it, thank you."

"All power has a cost," the thing told him.

"Aye, and He has Himself paid that price in full." He pulled the crucifix up to his lips and kissed it, and the final preta dissipated into the air.

Van Draeck untied the man, bound his wounded hand, and returned him to his family with a stern warning that he must not trust strange women who beckon to him to follow…

---

8   *Just as in English, the Hindi words for "fingers" ("uṅgaliyōṁ") and thumbs ("aṅgūṭhē") are distinct.*

9   *The king of the serpent gods.*

Chapter 19
The Fury of Wolves and Crows

Witches on one side, werewolves on the other—I half expected the Vice Lords to swing by, since this was all going down in their territory, just so that we could try for the hat trick. I remember one time when Tony and I were doing surveillance outside of a Vice Lords house in Uptown, when we saw a bunch of Gangsta Disciples show up, armed to the teeth and looking for a fight. There we were, just two cops, caught there between rival, angry gangs. In retrospect, surrounded by monsters on the corner of Chicago and Kedzie, that evening in Uptown didn't look so bad in comparison.

"Any suggestions?" I asked Durant.

"We've still two hours until sunset," he said, returning his watch to his pocket. "So try not to die just yet." He reached into his *got uechan* and drew out that little silver dagger with his left hand, and then his sword with his right. I wrapped my hands around the Staff of Solomon until my palms burned—my left in particular.

"What do they want?" I asked.

"I—" he started to say something, but then obviously changed directions in mid-sentence. "I've no idea. But it would appear to be something decidedly unhealthy."

"Give us the pup, *Fánaidhe*," the Goth woman in the front of the witches called out to Durant. "An' we'll be callin' it a day..." Her voice had a decidedly Irish lilt to it, but was still harsh and cold. It took me a second, but then I realized that she was talking about me.

"Wait, why does she want me?" I asked. "What did I do?"

"I suspect that it has more to do with what you shall do in two hours' time," he replied. The sky grew darker as the clouds rolled in, and lightning began to flash back and forth. Did a werewolf have to wait until sunset if it's a cloudy day? How does that work? Then Durant turned and shouted back to the woman, "I'll not turn an innocent over to your hands, Morrígan! Your coven shall have to fight to take him from me." A bolt of lightning struck nearby, and the thunder was deafening. Durant's overcoat flapped in the wind like a dark cape, and I had a sudden flash of what it must have been like to face him on a medieval battlefield.

"Yer holdin' yuir stolen sword an' yuir holy righteousness as if they'll protect ye from me, *Fánaidhe*," she said with an evil grin. "But have ye not been seein' in the past few days that e'en *you* can be bested? Look around ye!" She gestured toward the witches behind her and the wolves behind us. "If we shan't be takin' him, then those whom me children call the *Mahwêwithowa* shall certainly be doin' so." She stepped forward and her voice got low—but both Durant and I could still hear her. "Jehovah's little pretty one, are ye?" she sneered. "The elder gods whom I serve are far older an' far darker than yuir pale Nazarene..."

"Jesus Christ was neither pale nor a recent addition to a pantheon of so-called gods," Durant snarled back. "He has been God since before the beginning of time, and through Him, all things were created." He glared at the witches, then at the werewolves behind us. "Your... *corruptions*... are thus neither elder nor gods—they are abominations, and I will *end* them..."

When she heard that, she threw back her head and laughed. "You? *You* shall end the Tchagal gods whose power was old when the earth was young?" The witches around her cackled in an echoing reply. "Do ye believe that Jehovah will watch o'er ye? Do ye truly believe that yuir safe?"

"No," he replied coldly. "I believe that I am *dangerous*..."

He darted at her in a blur, but she wasn't there when he got to her—she'd just disappeared. But that's when everything started happening, all at once. The rest of the witches started screeching, and I heard the werewolves howling behind us, and I knew that this was going to very quickly turn into the worst few minutes of my life.

I let Durant deal with the coven in the park, and I spun around to see the wolves leaping from the roof of the building. It was now almost completely dark, and the street lamps hadn't come on yet—something was keeping the sensors from activating—but I didn't feel more "wolfy" or anything. Apparently it's not the dark that does bring out the change, but the setting of the sun. Thank God for small favors.

A caramel-colored monster seemed about to pounce on me, then pivoted and jumped past me to the left, toward Durant. I tried to swing at it with the staff, but it was too fast and too far away. But a big black one jumped right into the arc of my swing by accident, and I struck it hard on the ribs. It howled in pain, then turned to face me, its fangs dripping with saliva. I thought of the fight in that horrible basement, and I couldn't imagine how we could possibly win this one.

There was no rain, but it was turning into the grandmother of all electrical storms, with lightning flashing across the black sky, and the wind whipping the snow around into near white-out conditions. But that's when I realized that I wasn't cold at all. I hadn't been cold in days. In fact, now that I was in the thick of battle, I suddenly felt very warm. The staff was still burning in my hands, but I no longer minded the pain. I found that it was exhilarating, and instead of waiting for the black wolf to attack me, I lunged first.

I rammed the carved cat's head of the staff into its belly as hard as I could, then swung it underhanded to smash it into the monster's groin. It may be a supernatural creature out of a European peasant's nightmares, but it was a *male* one, and there are certain commonalities that cross the barrier of species. The monster yelped and crumpled a bit, and that's when I swung the staff one more time and hit it across the side of its head. I felt the skull cave in, and the werewolf fell dead at my feet.

There was no time to celebrate, though, since two more wolves came at me just as fiercely as the black one had. The others seemed far more intent on whatever was going on behind me in the park. The first, reddish one slashed at me with its claws, raking three large gashes across my chest. It would have done far worse than that, but I realized that I was moving much faster than I had been even this morning, when I'd faced Sydor, and I'd dodged the worst of it here. I tried to focus on using my new speed and strength to my advantage.

The brown one limped a bit, and as it lunged for me clumsily, I leapt into the air over it, swinging the staff beneath me as I did, clipping the beast in the small of the back. It yelped, and the reddish one came after me with a vengeance, snarling and slashing. Again, I blocked the worst of it with the staff, but the thing was able to tear a great chunk out of my left leg with its claws. It was in too close for me to swing the staff, and my back was against my car, so I tried a different tactic and got in close, pressing the staff against it while I tore at its neck with my own hands. I couldn't tell if it was more surprised by the strategy or hurt by the staff's vril, but it reeled back onto its hind legs and stumbled backwards over the dead body of the fallen black werewolf, which now looked like a normal, naked human, wrapped in one of those hideous skin belts. It fell onto its back, and for a moment—only a moment—it was startled enough that it was vulnerable. So I pounced on top of it and rammed the Matteh ha Shelomoh down its throat with a level of violence that I never knew myself capable of. The thing twitched, and then it was still.

Behind me, the brown werewolf had recovered and was coming at me again. But seeing the corpses of the other two pack members, it was much more wary this time. It circled around me, limping, looking for an opening, and that gave me a moment to catch my breath. I could already feel my chest and leg healing, and I could smell the blood of the two werewolves I killed nearby. Across the street in the park, I could hear growling and howling and shrieks and lightning blasts and the smashing of great, heavy objects, but I also heard the telltale sound of Durant's sword slicing through the air and hacking through bone. But I dared not look away from the wolf in front of me to see what was happening.

The scent of blood and death began to work at me. I found myself breathing hard again, but not from exertion—it was from excitement. My stomach began to ache to be filled, and for a moment, all I could think about was sinking my teeth into raw flesh and ripping it from the bone. I tried to make my thoughts bounce to something else, but there was too much going on around me to reach for happier images. My left palm felt like it was on fire, even when I just held the staff with my right hand.

The wolf in front of me stopped and looked at me for a moment. Somehow, it recognized what was going on in me, and I recognized that it knew how close I was coming to giving into the gnawing hunger. For a moment, I stopped thinking about the monster as an opponent, and looked into its eyes. That's when I realized that it was Lyn Davidge.

Then I smelled something else. It was a musky odor—the same pheromone cocktail that I'd smelled on her the morning before, when she was surrounded by all of those cops at the scene of "Sticky Ike's" death. It had hit me hard that day, and it was hitting me even harder this time around. The blood was rushing through my veins, and I could feel my heart beating faster and faster. Sydor's words echoed in my skull— *To hunt, to kill, to feed, to mate—that is a man, yes?*

The wolf stood up on its hind legs, reached down, and undid the slim belt that I hadn't even noticed under its fur. The fur-covered body of the wolf melted into the lithe body of Lyn Davidge. Her face echoed the same hunger that I felt in my guts, and I suddenly felt dizzy, my mind was cloudy. With my last, stray, rational thought, I begged God to give me something else to bounce my thoughts to, because I was finding myself drowning in these.

I remembered that it was raining the day that I first met Joanna at college. She was moving her stuff into her dorm, and I was walking past on the sidewalk with a buddy of mine, since we'd already moved into our rooms that morning. But when I saw her trying to pull that heavy trunk out of the back seat of her car all by herself, with the rain coming down in sheets like that, I couldn't just walk on past and not do anything to help. I slapped Joe on the shoulder and the two of us trotted over and helped her drag her stuff inside. It was only after we had dragged that trunk and her boxes and a bunch of clothing bags inside that she finally came out from under that raincoat and I really saw her for the first time. Joe later agreed that he thought she was cute, but I knew that she was more than that. She may have looked a little like a drowned puppy at that moment, but when I saw her smile, when I saw those eyes—I only half-jokingly told Joe that I'd found the woman I was going to marry. It became a running joke with us until I finally had the guts to ask her out, and I've never wanted to date anyone else ever since.

So that's where my thoughts bounced—to that day when I first saw my wife in the rain. Little by little, I felt the wolf in me starve a bit, and I tried to focus on other things. I thought of the day that Chelsea was born, all wrinkled and screams and belly. I remembered that she'd opened her eyes and looked at me—made eye contact with me and held it, the way that nurses say newborns never do. And then I thought of the day that the twins took their first steps. They actually started walking on the very same day. It was amazing, and more than just a little bit freaky. One just saw the other one do it, and that was that. I thought of all the sweet, loving blessings that I'd been given, and I felt the hunger die away inside of me.

"You know," I said to her, gathering my wits as she glided toward me, "my Dad always used to say that there are three kinds of human beings in this world. And I've finally come to the conclusion that you're not one of them…" The look in her face changed from a sensual hunger to a fierce anger, and she squeezed the belt in her hand tightly. I'll be honest with you right here and now—she hadn't even begun to change when I brought the staff down onto her skull, and I don't feel the least bit guilty about killing her.

But I stood there for a moment over her body, trying to remember *Carolyn*—the woman who'd been hurt by someone as a girl, who'd pushed herself to become a top field agent with the FBI and committed herself to making sure that she saved as many other young girls from that sort of pain as she possibly could. I thought of the woundedness inside of her that she'd obviously never really dealt with, that had allowed her to fall so easily into becoming… well, the monster that she'd eventually become. Every bit of pain and suffering that she'd felt, that she'd seen, she then lashed back at humanity with, hurting as many men as she could in the time that she had. But I wanted to believe that that hatred was more *Lyn* than *Carolyn*. No, I didn't feel any remorse for killing Lyn—but I felt a great deal of sadness that Carolyn had gotten to the point that it had become necessary.

*   *   *

I looked up and saw what looked like hell on earth. The park was a scene of carnage—the white snow was drenched in bright, red blood everywhere. The werewolves were ripping through the witches, shredding their bodies as they went, gulping their flesh down in hot, gory chunks, and the witches were bashing the wolves with trees, garbage cans—three of them even held hands and flung a car at one of them, leaving it a furry, pulpy smear on the snow. And the Goth woman in black leather and fishnetting—the Irish one that Durant had called the

Morrígan—was standing on top of the playground equipment to get a better view of the battleground.

It actually took me a second to find Durant, but there he was in the center of it all. He was a blurred flurry of tattered coat and slicing silver, and wherever the blur moved, blood spattered and voices screamed. I took off my own coat and laid it over Carolyn's naked body—I no longer needed it to stay warm, and she didn't ask for what she'd become—and then I grabbed the staff in my hands and jumped the fence in order to join the fray. It was only later that I'd realized that it was a six-foot fence, and that I'd still cleared it with ease, like when I'd run the low hurdles in track in high school. I may not have been a wolf yet, but I was certainly no longer quite human.

But the witches were. As powerful as they'd become through whatever deals they'd made with whatever demons they'd conjured up, I remembered that they were still just human beings. I drew my pistol and started firing. When a werewolf came up toward me from the side, I swung the staff at it to keep it at bay. Out of the corner of my eye, I saw both Durant and the caramel-colored wolf make their way through the fight toward the Morrígan.

In front of me stood Manômini. Between her and Bunin, I was beginning to think of broken necks as a minor inconvenience for monsters.

"You killed my boy…" she rasped at me, a mad frown cracking her wrinkled face.

"And Durant killed you," I replied, glancing at the werewolf to keep track of both of them. "So that just means that I'm better at this than he is."

She howled in anger and screeched something that I couldn't understand. The werewolf at my side took a swipe at me, so I turned to swing the staff at it again. When I turned back toward the witch, she threw a little bag at me. I tried to dodge it, but with the werewolf right next to me, there was only so much that I could do. It struck me on the arm and broke open in a cloud of dust—and that was all. I'd expected it to explode like a hand grenade, or burst into fire like something that Durant would pull out of his *got uechan*. Instead, it just powdered my arm with dust. Just the same, I immediately brushed it off of me, just to be on the safe side.

"You have killed my boy…" Manômini whispered quietly, almost to herself. "And I shall kill you, mahwêwa, and then she shall give me the power…" She began to cackle—the classic, trite, crazy witch's cackle— and I pointed my pistol at her to finish her the same way I'd finished her son. But before I could fire, we were both surprised when a large, dark-colored wolf slammed into her from the side and began ripping her apart. Her screams lasted for a while, but I couldn't find it in my heart to feel bad for her.

But then I noticed that the werewolf at my side hadn't taken advantage of the opportunity to attack me. It was like the thing waited for me to be ready again for its attack. I turned to face it, and only then did it growl and try to slash at me again. It was clearly faster than I was, but I was still able to dodge it at least somewhat, even though it caught me by the right shoulder, forcing me to drop the staff into the snow. It reared back, roared, and then lunged again. Without the staff, all I could do was shoot it with my pistol. That didn't do much but knock it back a bit, but that was all the time that I needed to drop the sidearm, fall to the ground, grab the staff with my left hand, and then swipe at its head. I connected enough to stun the thing, but not to kill it. Within a second or two, it had shaken it off and prepared to attack me again. I braced myself for the impact.

But it never came. Instead, we heard a howl come from the direction of the playground, and we both turned to see the caramel-colored wolf leap for Durant, only to become impaled onto his sword. He spun and ripped through its side, then was going to come down again with the killing blow, when the Morrígan screamed and brought a massive tree crashing down onto him, knocking him down to the ground. The caramel-colored wolf slashed at the witch, but the Morrígan's body seemed to suddenly burst into a dozen flapping crows, and the wolf's claws only caught two of them. The other crows flew off into the stormy sky, cawing in terror.

The wolf in front of me ran as fast as it could to the wounded one's side, and together, they loped off into the snow-swirled distance, howling. I retrieved my pistol, picked myself up off of the snow, and began stumbling toward where Durant had fallen. I didn't realize until then just how much blood I'd lost in the fight, and I felt completely wasted. Almost immediately, the storm lightened up, and the clouds were beginning to thin, letting in the sunlight again. All around me were the torn and broken bodies of the slain—almost a dozen naked bodies that had been werewolves, and probably about three times that many slashed and torn bodies of those who had stood with the Morrígan. No one was left standing but me.

As I got close to the tree, I wondered how I'd ever get it off of him. I couldn't even begin to imagine how heavy the thing was, since it was such a huge old tree. But then, underneath it, I heard Durant growling in anger and pain, and the tree began to move. I'd known that he was strong, but even for him... With one long, rising roar and an impressive heave, he flung the tree to the side... and instinctively, I found myself taking a step back—not from the tree, but from *him*. I watched as he pulled himself up out of the snow, his clothes torn and caked with blood, his body covered in a dozen slowly-healing gashes. He stood there in the gory snow, gritting his bloody teeth, his eyes burning with a cold, gray fire. Thunder cracked behind him one last time, and I found myself trembling.

"Are..." I tried to ask, but my words choked my throat. "Are you okay?"

He was panting from exertion and the adrenaline rush of combat, and for a moment, I figured that he hadn't heard me. I was about to ask him again, when he let out a second roar even louder than the first. All the pain and anger in the world came out through that roar, and somehow, I dropped the staff. Durant pulled from his side a twisted piece of rebar that I hadn't even noticed, flinging it to the ground next to the body of a dead werewolf.

"This was a pointless slaughter!" he growled. "A pointless waste!" I thought that it was probably best not to respond, so I just stood there and watched him as he wiped the blood from his sword's blade on the relatively clean woolen coat of one of the fallen witches, then returned it to the *got uechan*. "And where's my bloody knife...?" he snarled, his accent thickening in his anger. I looked around in the snow, but I couldn't see it anywhere. But then I remembered that it was plated in silver, so instead of looking for it, I just tried to *feel* it. Within a few seconds, I sensed the silver under the body of one of the nearby werewolves. I pointed it out to him and walked over to it, but as I got closer, I felt myself getting weak. The world spun out from under me, and I fell face-first into the snow.

*   *   *

The next thing I knew, Durant was pouring something warm into my mouth. It tasted like cinnamon, and I began to cough.

"Good morning," he said with a smile—but his eyes were frowning.

"Wh-What happened?" I asked, trying to sit up. I felt as weak as a kitten, and I slumped back into the snow.

"Why don't you tell me?" he asked. "Precisely how were you attacked?" I told him about the caramel-colored werewolf who'd gone past me, and about the fight with the other two and Lyn. I told him about the werewolf that had run off to take care of the leader of the pack. And then I told him about Manômini coming back to life to smack me with her little bag. "Where was this?" he asked sharply. I pointed over to the fenceline, and Durant disappeared in another blur. A moment later, he returned with the shreds of the bag, a few grains of powder still clinging to the cloth.

"What is it?" I asked.

"It is *'ańt'į,*" he answered me. "And you shall die from it."

* * *

Now, that just didn't seem fair to me. All this time, I was worried that I'd turn into a monster, or that Durant would have to put me down—or, God forbid, Tony would. But now, this evil little old lady was going to be the one to take me out with a stupid little bag of powder?

"I thought…" I said, feeling my mind going a cloudy again. "I thought it took… longer…"

"You speak about your friend, Miss Gage," he replied. "But she was given a much smaller dose—and yours entered your bloodstream immediately, through your open wounds."

"You… You remembered her name…" I said weakly.

"Of course I did, Detective," he answered, pulling me to a sitting position and leaning me against the trunk of the tree that the Morrígan had thrown at him. "But I wanted to make certain that *you* did as well. Karen Annette Gage had not yet reached her thirtieth year before she was murdered by monsters such as the Morrígan and the wolf pack. I wished you to remind yourself that you were her friend, and thus to remind yourself upon which side of this conflict you ultimately desired to commit your loyalties."

I'd never heard her middle name before, so I *know* that Durant never did. I realized that he must have looked her up in the police personnel files after her death, and then remembered her name two years later. I couldn't remember if he'd ever even met her before she died.

"I know which side I'm on," I said, my mind getting clearer. "And I know why I'm on it."

"Good. And the draught seems to be doing its work."

"What *did* you give me to drink?" I asked.

"Something very, very old," he answered. But then he took a deep breath and added, "But it is only strengthening you for a time—it will not cure you." He sat there in the snow, looking at me for a long time, and I knew that he was thinking.

"Is there anything in that purse of yours that *can* cure me?" He sighed.

"No…"

I heard what he was saying, and I knew that I wasn't ready to die. Not yet. I wanted to see Joanna and the kids again. I thought of Tony, having to go through cancer all by himself once I was gone. Would Nita even sit with him in the hospital at the end? What are the rules for that sort of thing? Is a guy's ex-wife still morally obligated to be there and hold his hand so that he doesn't have to die all alone?

And I wanted to find the head of the bloodline. Even if I couldn't save myself, I wanted to end this horror. I wanted payback.

"So…" I said, seeing the pain in his face and wanting to give him something else to focus on. "You called that woman 'Morrígan'—I thought you said that she was probably a... whatchacallit... *wælcyrie...*?"

"The Morrígan has been used in that capacity by Odin at various times, though such was not her original purpose. That was more Macha's purview, as I recall..."

"So is this Morrígan any relation to a 'korrigan' like Rhiannon?"

"None whatsoever," he said, his face beginning to soften a bit. "Not even linguistically, though both are steeped in magicks."

"They sound the same."

"Vaguely, I suppose."

"Vaguely, nothing! They're off by, like, one letter..." He sighed and I could've sworn that I saw the tiniest smile twist the edges of his mouth.

"A korrigan is a water witch—a *nain rouge*," he reminded me. "The Morrígan is the Queen of Nightmares, the goddess of the crows. She is one of a trio of sisters who have served the dark powers since the Tuatha Dé Danann settled Ireland after Atlantis fell."

"You mean there are two others out there like her?"

"Not..." he took a deep breath, then let it out. "Not anymore, no. I destroyed her lascivious sister, Macha, quite some time ago, and later exiled Anann to the undying lands of Tír na nÓg. Badb is all that is left of the daughters of Partholón, and she has thus hated me for a long, long while. Of course, it hardly helps matters that we've now killed her Meshkwahkihaki daughter and grandson..."

Manômini and the tall man at Palmer Square... I thought to myself—generations of twisted evil, creating more generations after them.

"So what does '*Fánaidhe*' mean?" I asked him. "Nothing nice, I'd guess."

"It means 'Wanderer,'" he said, but then he scratched his beard and added. "Well, the nuance is more akin to 'Vagrant,' I suppose..." I couldn't help but laugh—and that time, I know that I saw a smile on his face.

"She said that you stole your sword. Is that another thing that you 'liberated' along the way?"

"Not quite," he said, standing up and stretching. "I found it on the wrecked ship of Solomon. But long before his father David was given it by God, the blade had belonged to the Atlantean Núada Airgetlám, the king of the Tuatha Dé Danann."

"Your sword is Atlantean...?" I shook my head that he could still surprise me like that.

"In point of fact, it predates Atlantis by a great many centuries," he answered. "Its grip is made from the trees of Eden, and its edge is tempered with orichalcum." He rested his hand on the *got uechan*, and I almost expected him to pull the sword out to show me again. "Only Excalibur has ever rivaled it in strength and craftsmanship."

I was feeling strong enough to stand as well, and I heard sirens coming toward us in the distance. There was no way that I wanted to be around here when they showed up.

"We need to get out of here," I told him, and headed toward the car. A crowd was beginning to gather on the other side of the fence, but the weather had luckily kept most people from really seeing much of what had been going on. Now that it was cleared up, the place was going to be a madhouse. Some big guy tried to stop me as I headed out of the gate, but I flashed him my badge and told him that back-up was on the way.

"Are you going to burn everything this time?" I asked Durant as he walked over to Carolyn's body.

"Not this time," he said, retrieving Mkogisos' silver bullet from my coat pocket. "With all of these witnesses, it would do but little good, and all that the police shall find is a pile of human corpses, just as they did this morning in the charnel house." He whispered something under his breath that I couldn't hear as he stood up from her body, but I heard him say, "Amen," at the end. Then he came and climbed into the car along with me.

*   *   *

I started driving down Chicago in the direction of where we were originally going—to the storefront that Wheaton had told us about. But somehow, it all seemed hollow now. I only went about another block or so, then turned off onto a side street and pulled to the side of the road.

"How long do I have, do you think?" I asked him. He sighed before responding.

"I've no idea. Between the draught I gave you and your lycanthropic constitution…" His voice trailed off, and he scratched his beard in thought before commenting further. "Without knowing the potency of the *'áńt'į*, it is simply impossible to say."

"So, you're saying it's like a race to see what I'll die from first …?" I snorted. Durant gritted his teeth, and I could see him clenching his fists in frustration. "It's okay," I told him. "Believe me, I want to get the monster who started all of this—but then again, I figured that you were going to kill me this morning, so I've been living on borrowed time already. I'm surprised that I've lived *this* long…"

That didn't seem much of a comfort for him, and I could tell that he was really wrestling with something. But the moment that I said that last bit, I started wrestling with a thought of my own. Why *had* I lived this long?

"That last werewolf I fought—he should've killed me," I said to Durant.

"It was distracted by my fight with the leader," he replied.

"No, before that," I said. "He had all the opportunity that he needed, but he didn't do it. Why is that?"

"Again, I have no idea," he said, rubbing the bridge of his nose. Can the Grail Knight even *get* a headache?

"Seriously," I continued. "The witches could've thrown a tree or a bus at me, but they didn't—they wanted me alive. Even Manômini chose a way to kill me that will take some time. I mean, they've been following me and watching me all this time, but they haven't finished me."

"They have tried, Detective," he said.

"Not really," I argued. "They've mostly tried to mess with *you*, up until now. Even Sydor seemed more interested in hurting me than in killing me."

"What is your point?" he asked me.

"And what about that first werewolf, the one in Bunin's house?" I continued. "Why didn't he kill me?"

"Because of your Neanderthal friend and my vril-cored staff, I should think," he said, turning back to me. "You did notice that he gutted Agent Davidge and sent you to the hospital, did you not?"

"But he didn't *kill* us—*either* of us."

"And this fact makes you unhappy why?"

"Because he was so fast, and yet he just stood there, like he was waiting for something. Tony had all of the time in the world to get to us. Why would he do that? For that matter, why would Lyn and the Russian wolf just play with Tony until you got there?"

"Sadism?"

"Maybe, or maybe it's something else." I scratched my head. "We've been so focused on stopping the monsters that we've been thinking about them as monsters."

"I fail to see your point," he said.

"I mean, yes, they're monsters, but they're also people. They have minds and motives and plans, but we've been hunting them like they're just gangbangers or animals. What if there's something more to all of it?" Something about that obviously made Durant uncomfortable.

"What are you suggesting, Detective?" he asked.

"I don't know yet," I replied. "But it's got to be something big. At first I thought that it was just a savage attack, you know? But then, why kill 'Sticky Ike' like that? If it was all about being a monster, why not eat him, like they have everyone else? When I found out about Sydor, I wondered if it was all about revenge, about his son's death. But then we found out that he hated Frank—that he'd killed Frank himself. So what's the motive here?"

"They are beasts, Detectives, in every worst sense of the term. There need be no 'motive' behind their form of evil."

"There's *always* a motive, Durant," I said. "There's always a why *behind* the what. I just don't know what it is yet."

He took another long, deep breath, and we just sat there in the car for a little while, silently watching the snow falling gently around us. It was so quiet and peaceful. I knew that we were almost out of time—that I was almost out of time—but I guess, it was just worth it to invest in just a little moment of peace before the end came.

"I can't even go home and see Joanna one last time, can I?" I asked. He closed his eyes.

"I have not spoken much of my time with Arthur, have I?" he asked at last. I realized that, with all of the history lessons he'd thrown my way, no, he hadn't really talked that much about the most important person he'd ever known.

"No," I answered him.

"After Arthur died at the Battle of Camlann, his bastard son, Medrawt, led an army of Picts against us from the north, and we met them at Camboglanna, an outpost along the wall. *Hadrian's* Wall. Camboglanna was on a high hill, overlooking the river Cambeck, and they came at us in waves, by the thousands. Medrawt thought that without Arthur to lead us, we would surely break and run against such odds. He had no idea what Arthur's example had birthed in us, you see.

"The night before that final battle, Myrddin reminded me that what Arthur had stood for—indeed, what he had created Caer Mallet to stand for after he was gone—was a different world than the one with which most of humanity was familiar. To the common man in Britain between the time that Rome receded and Arthur arose, life was hard and short and brutal. The average life of a Briton was filled with pain and sorrow, anguish and loss, and Medrawt wished to keep it that way, wielding sorrow as if it were another weapon in his arsenal to keep the people safely under the grind of his boot. Arthur saw the promise of a different sort of life, while the rest of us had grown up seeing only despair and societal decay. He called his knights together, and we rode side-by-side to give the world a new kind of kingdom—one based on law, order, and decency.

"Thus, when we stood on that wall, facing the Picts, we were painfully aware that what we guarded was not merely a construction of stone, nor even the boundary of our kingdom, but rather, nothing less than the edge of the world. To the south of us were homesteads and hamlets, books, families, children, and a civilization which Arthur had lived and died to build for posterity. To the north of us lay only madness, chaos, savagery, and death. How could we abandon our post, even in the face of an horrendous battle such as the one we faced that day at Camboglanna, and thus allow Medrawt and his blue-painted cannibals to destroy the hard-won peace for which so many had already bled and died?" His gaze was focused on something out the window, but I knew that his eyes weren't seeing the streets of Chicago, but a battlefield on the edge of the world. I saw tears well up in them as he thought about all of the friends and loved ones that he'd lost over the centuries.

"You tell me that one's motives are crucial, Detective," he said at last. "And you are, of course, quite right. Arthur's motives, Medrawt's motives, my own... yours..." He took a deep breath, and then turned back to face me. "Why we do what we do defines not only our actions and our destinies, but more importantly, our character. Thomas Chapel, we stand on Hadrian's Wall once again today, you and I. On one side of us is the world of light and joy and family. On the other side of us is the world of chaos and savagery. Evil is massing against us, Detective, and we must stand our ground to win the day."

"What happened at Camboglanna?" I asked. He sat for a moment, quietly, then sighed again.

"This shall be a near run thing, Detective," he said to me, ignoring the question. "And almost certainly an ultimately ineffective one. But I've little choice in the matter. If our motives do truly define us, then may God grant that mine be motives which honor my Creator and all those who have gone before me into Abraham's bosom."

"What are you *talking* about?"

"Detective," he told me quietly, his tone suddenly deadly serious. "You *must... not... turn...* Once you finally give in to the beast, there will be nothing for me to do but to hunt you down and destroy you myself. You do understand this, do you not?"

"I... Yes, of course I do. But—" He nodded, then opened the door of my car and stepped out. "Wait!" I shouted after him. "What's going on? Where are you going?" He gritted his teeth and took one, last, deep breath.

"I shall return as quickly as possible, and I pray that I am not already too late," he said. "But as God is my witness, I shall not let it end this way—not for you, and not for your family. I am off to hunt the wild goose in search of one, final, unlikely cure for you."

"What do you mean?"

"I go now to retrieve the Holy Grail..."

Background
From *Konungs Skuggsjá*[1] (1250, trans. L.M. Larson)

From *Chapter XI*

Irish Marvels Which Have Miraculous Origins

There is still another wonder in that country which must seem quite incredible; nevertheless, those who dwell in the land affirm the truth of it and ascribe it to the anger of a holy man. It is told that when the holy Patricius[2] preached Christianity in that country, there was one clan which opposed him more stubbornly than any other people in the land; and these people strove to do insult in many ways both to God and to the holy man. And when he was preaching the faith to them as to others and came to confer with them where they held their assemblies, they adopted the plan of howling at him like wolves. When he saw that he could do very little to promote his mission among these people, he grew very wroth and prayed God to send some form of affliction upon them to be shared by their posterity as a constant reminder of their disobedience. Later these clansmen did suffer a fitting and severe though very marvelous punishment, for it is told that all the members of that clan are changed into wolves for a period and roam through the woods feeding upon the same food as wolves; but they are worse than wolves, for in all their wiles they have the wit of men, though they are as eager to devour men as to destroy other creatures. It is reported that to some this affliction comes every seventh winter, while in the intervening years

---

[1] *An educational text written for the court of King Hákon Hákonarson of Norway, and structured as a dialogue between father and son—vicariously attributing the wisdom of the book to Hákon since it was intended to educate his son, Magnús Hákonarson (aka Magnús Lagabœtir or "Magnús the Law-Mender"), later King Magnus VI.*

[2] *That is, St. Patrick (missionary to and patron saint of Ireland). Born in Wales in 386 and christened Maewyn Succat, he later took the name "Patricius" ("born of a good father") when he devoted his life to God and returned to evangelize the Irish people who had kidnapped him as a youth. The Irish corrupted his Roman name as "Pádraig," from which we get the more common version of his name, "Patrick."*

they are men; others suffer it continuously for seven winters all told and are never stricken again.[3]

---

[3]   *See the poem on the "Wonders of Ireland" (an ancient Latin poem, collected in Thomas Wright's* Reliquiae Antiquae, *1843), which alludes to this transformation. Stories of men who have become wolves are also told in Giraldus (Giraldus Cambrensis, in his 1188 work,* Topographia Hibernica), *and in the "Irish Nennius" (the Irish edition of Nennius' 830 text,* Historia Brittonum); *but these differ widely from the account given above. Stories of lycanthropy and shapeshifters are found in folklore across the world, from the Polish* Baba Jaga *to the Malay legends of the* harimau jadian, *to the Native American* yee naaldlooshii.

Background
From *Topographia Hibernica* (Giraldus Cambrensis, 1188, trans. T. Forester)

From *Chapter XIX*

*Of the prodigies of our times,
and first of a wolf which conversed with a priest.*[1]

I now proceed to relate some wonderful occurrences which have happened within our times. About three years before the arrival of earl John[2] in Ireland, it chanced that a priest, who was journeying from Ulster towards Meath, was benighted in a certain wood on the borders of Meath. While, in company with only a young lad, he was watching by a fire which he had kindled under the branches of a spreading tree, lo! a wolf came up to them, and immediately addressed them to this effect: "Rest secure, and be not afraid, for there is no reason you should fear, where no fear is." The travellers being struck with astonishment and alarm, the wolf added some orthodox words referring to God. The priest then implored him, and adjured him by Almighty God and faith in the Trinity, not to hurt them, but to inform them what creature it was that in the shape of a beast uttered human words. The wolf, after giving Catholic replies to all questions, added at last: "There are two of us, a man and a woman, natives of Ossory, who, through the curse of one

---

[1]   *The belief in men who could transform themselves into wolves, was a very prevalent superstition, not only in the middle ages, but it continued in force to much more recent times, and formed part of the witchcraft superstitions, from which plenty of stories like this told by Giraldus might be collected. In England, where wolves have long disappeared, the witches of later times were said to have turned themselves into hares.*

[2]   *John Plantagenet (aka "John Lackland"), youngest son of King Henry II of England. John was made Lord of Ireland in 1177, after Pope Adrian IV issued his* Laudabiliter *papal bull which decreed that Henry had the legal and moral right to invade Ireland in order to "civilize" its savage people and reform their Celtic clergy to bring them more in line with the theology and ecclesiology of Rome. If this incident happened three years prior to John being made Lord of Ireland, then it would have taken place in 1174.*

Natalis,[3] saint and abbot, are compelled every seven years to put off the human form, and depart from the dwellings of men. Quitting entirely the human form, we assume that of wolves. At the end of the seven years, if they chance to survive, two others being substituted in their places, they return to their country and their former shape. And now, she who is my partner in this visitation lies dangerously sick not far from hence, and, as she is at the point of death, I beseech you, inspired by divine charity, to give her the consolations of your priestly office."

At this word the priest followed the wolf trembling, as he led the way to a tree at no great distance, in the hollow of which he beheld a she-wolf, who under that shape was pouring forth human sighs and groans. On seeing the priest, having saluted him with human courtesy, she gave thanks to God, who in this extremity had vouchsafed to visit her with such consolation. She then received from the priest all the rites of the church duly performed, as far as the last communion. This also she importunately demanded, earnestly supplicating him to complete his good offices by giving her the viaticum. The priest stoutly asserting that he was not provided with it, the he-wolf, who had withdrawn to a short distance, came back and pointed out a small missal-book, containing some consecrated wafers, which the priest carried on his journey, suspended from his neck, under his garment, after the fashion of the country. He then intreated [sic] him not to deny them the gift of God, and the aid destined for them by Divine Providence; and, to remove all doubt, using his claw for a hand, he tore off the skin of the she-wolf, from the head down to the navel, folding it back. Thus she immediately presented the form of an old woman. The priest, seeing this, and compelled by his fear more than his reason, gave the communion; the recipient having earnestly implored it, and devoutly partaking of it. Immediately afterwards, the he-wolf rolled back the skin, and fitted it to its original form.

These rites having been duly, rather than rightly, performed, the he-wolf gave them his company during the whole night at their little fire, behaving more like a man than a beast. When morning came, he led them out of the wood, and, leaving the priest to pursue his journey, pointed out to him the direct road for a long distance. At his departure,

---

3   *A 6th century Irish monk from Ulster, who eventually became the abbot of St Naul's Abbey in Donegal. Thus, the curse had been in effect for roughly six centuries, echoing an even earlier tradition of similar curses apparently levied by S. Patrick in the 4th century, toward unruly clansmen (see the 13th century* Konungs Skuggsjá) *and the Welsh King Vereticus (see Bernhardt-House's* The Legend of Vereticus: An Ancient Celtic Tale from the 1860s, *2006). Such lycanthropy was apparently common amongst the Scots as well (see the legend of Laignech Fáelad in Stokes' "Cóir Anmann," in* Irische Texte, mit Übersetzungen und Wörterbuch, *1891.)*

he also gave him many thanks for the benefit he had conferred, promising him still greater returns of gratitude, if the Lord should call him back from his present exile, two parts of which he had already completed. At the close of their conversation, the priest inquired of the wolf whether the hostile race which had now landed in the island would continue there for the time to come, and be long established in it. To which the wolf replied:—"For the sins of our nation, and their enormous vices, the anger of the Lord, falling on an evil generation, hath given them into the hands of their enemies. Therefore, as long as this foreign race shall keep the commandments of the Lord, and walk in his ways, it will be secure and invincible; but if, as the downward path to illicit pleasures is easy, and nature is prone to follow vicious examples, this people shall chance, from living among us, to adopt our depraved habits, doubtless they will provoke the divine vengeance on themselves also."

The like judgment is recorded in Leviticus:—"All these abominations have the inhabitants of the land done, which were before you, and the land is defiled. Beware, therefore, that the land spue *[sic]* not you out also, when ye defile it, as it spued *[sic]* out the nation which was before you."[4] All this was afterwards brought to pass, first by the Chaldeans, and then by the Romans. Likewise it is written in Ecclesiasticus:—"The kingdom is made over from one nation to another, by reason of their unjust and injurious deeds, their proud words, and divers *[sic]* deceits."[5]

I chanced, about two years afterwards, that I was passing through Meath, at the time when the bishop of that land had convoked a synod, having also invited the assistance of the neighbouring bishops and abbots, in order to have their joint counsels on what was to be done in the affair which had come to his knowledge by the priest's confession. The bishop, hearing that I was passing through those parts, sent me a message by two of his clerks, requesting me, if possible, to be personally present when a matter of so much importance was under consideration; but if I could not attend, he begged me at least to signify my opinion in writing. The clerks detailed to me all the circumstances, which indeed I had heard before from other persons; and, as I was prevented by urgent business from being present at the synod, I made up for my absence by giving them the benefit of my advice in a letter. The bishop and synod, yielding to it, ordered the priest to appear before the pope with letters from them, setting forth what had occurred, with the priest's confession, to which instrument the bishops and abbots who were present at the synod affixed their seals.

It cannot be disputed, but must be believed with the most assured

---

[4] The Book of Leviticus, *xviii, 27- 28.*

[5] The Wisdom of Jesus the Son of Sirach *(aka* "Ecclesiasticus"*), x, 8.*

faith, that the divine nature assumed human nature for the salvation of the world; while in the present case, by no less a miracle, we find that at God's bidding, to exhibit his power and righteous judgment, human nature assumed that of a wolf. But is such an animal to be called a brute or a man? A rational animal appears to be far above the level of a brute; but who will venture to assign a quadruped, which inclines to the earth, and is not a laughing animal, to the species of man? Again, if any one should slay this animal, would he be called a homicide? We reply, that divine miracles are not to be made the subjects of disputation by human reason, but to be admired. However, Augustine, in the 16th book of his *Civit. Dei*,[6] chapter 8, in speaking of some monsters of the human race, born in the East, some of which had the heads of dogs, others had no heads at all, their eyes being placed in their breasts, and others had various deformities, raises the question whether these were really men, descended from the first parents of mankind. At last, he concludes, "We must think the same of them as we do of those monstrous births in the human species of which we often hear; and true reason declares that whatever answers to the definition of man, as a rational and mortal animal, whatever be its form, is to be considered a man." The same author, in the 18th book of the *Civit. Dei*, chapter 18, refers to the Arcadians, who, chosen by lot, swam across a lake and were there changed into wolves, living with wild beasts of the same species in the deserts of that country.[7] If, however, they did not devour human flesh, after nine years they swam back across the lake, and re-assumed the human form. Having thus further treated of various transformations of man into the shape of wolves, he at length adds, "I myself, at the time I was in Italy, heard it said of some district in those parts, that there the stable-women, who had learnt magical arts, were wont to give something to travellers in their cheese which transformed them into beasts of burden, so that they carried all sorts of burdens, and after they had performed their tasks resumed their own forms. Meanwhile, their minds did not become bestial, but remained human and rational." So in the Book which Apuleius wrote, with the title of the *Golden Ass*,[8] he tells us that it happened to himself, on taking some potion, to be changed into an ass, retaining his human mind.[9]

---

[6] De Civitate Dei Contra Paganos *(5th century).*

[7] *Augustine was citing a lost work by Marcus Terentius Varro (written in the 1st century BC)—a story discussed in more detail by Pliny the Elder in his 1st century AD work,* Naturalis Historia.

[8] *The book's title was actually* Metamorphoses, *by Lucius Apuleius (2nd century), though Augustine had referred to it as* "Asinus Aureus" *(i.e.; "The Golden Ass"), and Giraldus follows his lead here.*

[9] *Similar stories are told by other old writers; see William of Malmesbury's* Gesta Regum Anglorum *(1125), book ii. ch. 10. However, Giraldus appears*

In our own time, also, we have seen persons who, by magical arts, turned any substance about them into fat pigs, as they appeared (but they were always red), and sold them in the markets. However, they disappeared as soon as they crossed any water, returning to their real nature; and with whatever care they were kept, their assumed form did not last beyond three days. It has also been a frequent complaint, from old times as well as in the present, that certain hags in Wales, as well as in Ireland and Scotland, changed themselves into the shape of hares, that, sucking teats under this counterfeit form, they might stealthily rob other people's milk. We agree, then, with Augustine, that neither demons nor wicked men can either create or really change their natures; but those whom God has created can, to outward appearance, by his permission, become transformed, so that they appear to be what they are not; the senses of men being deceived and laid asleep by a strange illusion, so that things are not seen as they actually exist, but are strangely drawn by the power of some phantom or magical incantation to rest their eyes on unreal and fictitious forms.

It is, however, believed as an undoubted truth, that the Almighty God, who is the Creator of natures, can, when he pleases, change one into another, either for vindicating his judgments, or exhibiting his divine power; as in the case of Lot's wife, who, looking back contrary to her lord's command, was turned into a pillar of salt;[10] and as the water was changed into wine;[11] or that, the nature within remaining the same, he can transform the exterior only, as is plain from the examples before given.

Of that apparent change of the bread into the body of Christ (which I ought not to call apparent only, but with more truth transubstantial, because, while the outward appearance remains the same, the substance only is changed), I have thought it safest not to treat; its comprehension being far beyond the powers of the human intellect.

---

to believe that here, Apuleius was giving a bona fide relation of what had happened to himself, when Apuleius was clearly attempting to write a piece of fiction, as Augustine even admitted.

[10] *in the* The Book of Genesis, *xix, 23-26.*

[11] *in the* The Gospel of St. John, *ii, 1-11.*

Chapter 20
Illuminations

In an instant, Durant was gone. I looked for him in the rearview mirror, but all I saw was my own reflection—and I have to admit that I was more than just a little bit shocked at what I saw there. My face was gaunt and pale, and there were dark circles underneath my bloodshot eyes. My first thought was that the fight in the park had taken more out of me than I'd realized, and that I really ought to get myself something to eat. But as my stomach began to growl at that plan, it struck me that my face reminded me more of how Karen had looked when we'd found her body in the lobby of her building. This wasn't blood loss—this was the *'áńt'į*. Even if Durant's cinnamon potion might have been keeping me from feeling the effects, the *'áńt'į* was still taking its toll on my body nonetheless. How long did I have until I just withered away, like Karen did?

Luckily, before I could waste too much of what little time I had left feeling sorry for myself, I got a phone call from Tony.

The first words out of his mouth were, "Ya want the bad news, the good news, or the other bad news?"

"I guess the bad news first."

"Okay," he said. "The bad news is I can't find a single motel in all o' Lincolnwood that's rented a room out ta guys what match the description o' any Bratva-type guys."

"Well, put the screws to them!" I barked at him. "We have to find that motel!"

"I *did*, Tom," he snapped back. "I'm tellin' ya, it ain't no good. Maybe they was playin' her or somethin', or maybe she was jus' confused, 'cuz there ain't no Russians rentin' a room nowhere in Lincolnwood. Without a warrant ta make sure, it's lookin' like a wild goose chase."

I seemed to be dealing with a lot of those that day.

"Okay, so what's the good news?" I asked him.

"I talked with Kingery, an' one o' them bodies the police found in the basement this mornin'? Ya won't believe who it turned out ta be."

"Who?"

"Isador Vissarionovich Postyshev!" he said. "All naked an' chopped in half..." I remembered seeing his body on the ground after Durant had finished him off, but I hadn't recognized him as Postyshev at the time.

"That's great!" I said. "I wanted him in custody, but I'll take good news where we can find it right now."

"Yeah, well, not so good," Tony replied. "'Cuz th' other bad news is that, without Postyshev, th' judge denied us th' warrants we wanted ta get. We got nothin'..."

"You're kidding me!"

"Wish I was," he said. "He said that Wheaton said that we should go downtown an' talk to the judge all in-person, but I think it's a waste o' time."

None of this made any sense, and I didn't have time for any of it. All of our leads were drying up again, and I had maybe an hour and a half left until sunset—that is, if I even lasted that long anyway, thanks to the *'áńt'j*. But just because Postyshev was dead, that didn't mean that the murder investigation was over. And surely, with Wheaton's report on that third killing floor down on Chicago, there had to be more than enough evidence to justify a warrant to follow up on all of it, wasn't there?

Even if I didn't make it—*especially* if I didn't make it—I had to make sure that Tony and the others had enough to follow up on.

"*What* judge?" I growled.

"Delacroix," he replied. "An' he's a tough one ta try an' budge."

"Well, we're going to budge him pretty hard," I said. "Meet me over there. *Now...*"

*   *   *

So Henry Delacroix was a hard-nose, okay. So he knew the law and wasn't famous for bending once he'd made up his mind, fine. But there was no way that I was letting this drop. I had Tony call Nate Kingery back and get him to try another judge, just in case I couldn't get Delacroix to give us the warrant. But I still couldn't see why the old man would hold us up on this one.

By the time I got down to the Daley Center, it was around 3:30. I left my car on the street with the LED light on—I figured that within an hour, where I parked was not really going to matter much. Besides, if I lived long enough to have to worry about paying a ticket, I'd happily pay the ticket. Walking in past the Picasso, I started thinking about why I was wasting time on this. Couldn't I just have been storming all of the motels in Lincolnwood? Couldn't I have been scouring the scene at that shopfront on Chicago for some sort of clue that the CSI guys might have missed? I had the senses for it now. Why was I heading upstairs to growl at a little Cajun judge?

I'm not sure that I really have an answer for you—at least, not one that I could put into words very well, even if I understood it completely myself. I guess you could say that, with time clicking down and my aggressive nature kicking in more and more, Wheaton's suggestion of putting pressure on Delacroix seemed at least like doing something pro-active, instead of just running around like an idiot, hoping against hope that something, somewhere, might accidentally turn up. I knew who Delacroix was, where he was, and what I wanted out of him, and I wanted my pound of flesh from *somebody* before my time was up on this earth.

Stepping out into the cold, mid-afternoon Chicago air, I was bombarded again by smells and sounds from all around me. I could smell hot dogs and mustard, perfumes, old coffee, salt on the streets, *everything*—and I had to stop and focus to try to shut all of that out. Horns honked, people's voices carried, a garbage truck was driving down a nearby block. My head was *aching* from all of the sounds, and I just wanted it over. And somewhere, deep inside of me, it was like I could almost hear a voice saying, *If you become the beast, then you can control the beast...*

"No!" I shouted, clapping my hands over my ears. Some woman walking past me into the building looked at me like I was nuts, and she picked up her pace to get inside. My left hand was throbbing, so I started trying to orient myself by focusing on the pain. Only the pain. That was all that there was in the world—the pain shooting through my left palm. What did it *feel* like? Was it a sharp pain? Was it throbbing with the beat of my heart? Little by little, all of the other sounds began to die away, and I stopped smelling anything. When I opened my eyes, the world was even more super-saturated with color, but there was nothing I could do about that.

I walked inside the building, flashed my badge to security, checked the directory, and went up to Delacroix's office, up on the 11th floor. To be honest with you, I don't even remember if he had a secretary or anything—the world was becoming a blur around me, and I just kept walking until I was in his office, looking over his desk at the man. For a guy who was causing me so much frustration here at the end of my life, he was thoroughly under-impressive-looking. He was short, pudgy, and round-faced, with wisps of faded blonde color here and there amongst his thinning white hair.

"It's all right," he said to somebody behind me. "What can I do for you, young man?" he asked me, that light French accent making his words sound warm and comforting at the same time that it made him sound alien and effete. I showed him my badge.

"Tom Chapel," I told him. "Detective with Area 5, currently on loan to Operation Cross Country. And I want to know why you denied us the warrants we were looking for to complete our investigation!"

"You do not look very healthy, Detective Chapel," he said, frowning. "Perhaps you need to take a rest for a bit, no?"

"I don't have a bit," I replied. "And because of you, I don't have my warrants." His frown deepened, and he took a deep, angry breath in through his nose.

"Watch your tone, Detective," he said quietly. "I can have your badge by the end of the day…"

"You can *have* it at the end of *this* day," I replied. "Why did you refuse us the warrants?"

He looked like he might have boiled over for a moment, then seemed to take a left turn in his brain. Taking off his glasses and setting them on his desk, he took another deep breath and calmed down.

"What investigation is this in regards to, Detective Chapel?" he asked me.

"The *Obshchestvo Drakonisty*," I told him. "Isador Postyshev, Nikodim Bunin, and the abduction of Detective Leah Wheaton! Why are you shutting us down?"

"Hmm…" he replied, grabbing his glasses again. "I seem to know those names." He rifled through a few file folders on his desk and found the one he was looking for. Opening the folder, he began looking over it through his lenses, but without actually putting the glasses on. "Yes, those were two of the men found this morning in a mass execution by the Russian mafia, were they not?"

"Something like that," I answered him. "But the investigation surrounding them is still ongoing. There's apparently another killing floor like the one they were found on up on Chicago Avenue, where Detective Wheaton was taken to."

"Yes," he said, closing the file and setting his glasses down again. "That would be the second time that you've mentioned her. You say that she was abducted?"

"Yes, blast it!" I growled. "She filed the report this afternoon, so it may not be in the system yet, but yes, they took her to the storefront on Chicago that the cops found."

"One of your colleagues mentioned that when he chatted with me, Detective Chapel," he said, looking a little confused. "But when we followed up on that, we found no report of such a—what did you call it?—a 'killing floor' on Chicago, nor was any report made by Detective Wheaton today."

"Like I said, maybe it's just not in the system yet."

"No," he replied, quite intensely. "Believe me when I tell you that no such reports exist. A Lt.—" he glanced down at a note on his desk.

"A Lt. Chacon reported back to me that no such activity had occurred today at all." He sat back in his chair, and his old, watery eyes seemed to soften a bit. "Detective, I am hardly in a position to issue warrants based on shoddy evidence, particularly when your two key suspects are now dead—the victims of the same level of gangland violence which had elicited your investigations of them in the first place."

"That's... That's not possible..." I said, finding myself slumping into one of the chairs in front of his desk. "Wheaton... they must have killed...?" I was losing focus again, and I just felt so incredibly tired, exhausted by life. Part of me thought it was the *'áńt'į*, but part of me also knew that I was just finally hitting my breaking point. It was all too much, and I just wanted it all to stop. *The wolf can beat the 'áńt'į,* I felt the voice inside me telling me. *Free the beast and save yourself!*

"Are you all right, son?" Delacroix asked me again. "Do you have someone whom you could call to come to help you?"

Tony was on his way, but the first person that popped into my mind was Durant. He was coming, and he was bringing the Grail. What did that even mean? Would he get here in time? And, if he did, what would the Grail be able to do for me? If I wasn't bad enough off, my curse would still be on me—but if I was already on the brink of succumbing, then would it be able to work at all? Why had I just spent the last week getting beaten up by life over and over and over?

"Detective Chapel?" he called out to me, though his voice sounded like it was coming from a mile away. "Did you hear me?"

Somebody down the hall came in with a pastrami sandwich, and I was so tired that I felt my senses kicking in again. Even through a series of closed doors, I lost myself in the scent of the meat and the sauerkraut. The deli had used a warm, recently-baked rye bread, and they'd smothered the sandwich with a coarse-ground, spicy brown mustard. What kind of melted cheese was that? It wasn't Swiss or mozzarella. I was betting that it was Provolone. It smelled so good, and I was so hungry...

And that's when I smelled something else—something I hadn't noticed earlier, when I'd first walked into the office. I smelled a scent that reminded me of Bunin and Sydor, of Lyn, of that middle-aged man sitting calmly behind the counter at the shop between Hamlin Park and Roscoe Village, and even of Mkogisos. It was a scent that I'd come to recognize as the scent of a werewolf.

I looked back at Delacroix in silent disbelief. His pale, blue eyes looked back at mine, and—as if in slow-motion—I watched his face melt from a feigned concern to a knowing smile.

"What is it that has roused you from your malaise, Detective Chapel?" he asked. He stood up from his chair with a small grunt of pain, instinctively clutching at his side as he did so.

"You're one of them..." I said, watching him. Now that I was paying attention, I saw that he didn't move quite right. For an older, overweight man in obvious pain, he still glided with a grace and a strength that didn't seem to match his appearance. He hid it well—I don't know that I would've been able to see it a week earlier—but to my new eyes, it was there nonetheless.

"Or *you* are one of *us*," he countered, leaning against the corner of his desk. "Does that seem such an horrific possibility to you?"

No, the voice in my head said. *Give in and become one of the pack...*

"It's..." I tried to answer, but my mind was becoming cloudy again. "It's not over yet..." He smiled kindly, chuckling softly.

"Do you put your faith in the *Chevalier du Graal*?" he asked me. "That he might yet bring the cup in time to save you?" He leaned forward and took a strangely intimate tone with me. "To be honest with you, I hope in something very similar..."

"H—How do you know Durant?" I asked, trying to pull myself back into the moment.

"Oh, I have known of him by many names, of course" he replied. "We have never met, but his reputation precedes him throughout the ages. But where are my manners?" He stood up again with a wince and another painful grunt, formally extending his hand to me. "My own name is Nicolas Rémy," he said by way of introduction. "And I have been around for quite some time myself..."

*   *   *

"I was never bitten, you know," he said to me as I tried to clear my mind and focus. "I was cursed—and, foolishly, I believed for some time that it truly was a curse, that the old *gitane* who had killed my son had succeeded in separating me from the God whom I had served so fervently up until that point. As she burned at the stake, she shouted her curses at me to outwardly become the beast that she had perceived me to be inwardly, but I dismissed her ravings. But then, at the next full moon, the first pentacle appeared." He pointed to his left palm. It was clear and unmarred, but somehow, I could still see the lingering afterglow of thousands of upraised pentacles that had branded him over the centuries. "Of course, I saw it as the devil's mark, and the next morning, after remembering how I had transformed and slaughtered sheep in the moonlight, I was certain that I had been damned.

"But this was not true, Detective Chapel. I was given an epiphany by God one morning while reading an old copy of the *Quaestiones* of Johannes Duns, who argued that the powers of the Devil could and should be used back against him. As I pondered that thought, I was struck by the notion that if God truly were omnipotent, then surely he *allows* the Devil to use his powers—in truth, he must *plan* for him to do so. Was this not the case with Job? Did the Devil not have to ask for God's permission before working his curses upon the body of a righteous man? And did those seeming curses not finally serve to honor God, in the end?" He shifted his weight and winced again, holding his side.

"I was shown that what I had erroneously believed to be a malediction was, in fact, ultimately, the work of the Divine!" His eyes sparkled in excitement while he was sharing this with me. Strangely, I was of two minds on the subject. Part of me was becoming clear-minded again, and I saw him to be obviously insane—and yet, part of me resonated with his words and wanted desperately to believe that someone like us could still be something other than a monster.

"You think God did this to you?" I asked.

"I know that God allowed it to happen, yes," he answered. *"Dieu sait qui a tort et a péché...* God knows his children, and he knows when their sins are not of their own making. Did God himself not change the Babylonian king into a beast? Did he himself not give command over the lions as to whom they should not devour—and whom they *should?* Did he himself not speak to Saint Pierre on the rooftop and to all of us who followed him, commanding us, *'Surge et occide et manduca!'*— 'Rise, kill, and eat!'? How can it be a sin for us to act upon that which comes naturally to us, if our God is the *Grande Auteur* of all Nature?"

I knew that he was wrong—I *knew* that he was wrong—and yet, his words sounded so compelling to me. My stomach growled, and for the first time, the pain in my palm felt *good*, felt *right*. It felt like being born again.

"I realized then that we had been given a gift," he continued, "and that it is the gift of strength and of freedom. *'Libertate nos Christus liberavit,'* Detective Chapel—'It is for freedom's sake that Christ has set us free!' So why ought we to shackle ourselves once again to those weaknesses which had held us all in bondage before? One must feed the beast which God has given you, my boy, to make it strong." He held his side again, but I could hear a growl begin to enter the background of his voice.

"I was once a devout Prométhéen—a man who considered every possibility and every ramification before deciding upon my actions. But with this revelation from God, I came to realize that it was not tortured Prométhée whom we should emulate, but rather, his brother, Épiméthée. Only the hubris of man makes him believe that he could possibly know the will of an infinite God. To plan, to assume that one even *can* meaningfully plan—this is blasphemy of the most subtle and heinous kind. We are not called to *evaluate* God's will with our questions and our catechisms and our logics, but rather to have faith enough to step out in his will and to do what we would never contemplate doing on our own. Our world had become choked and stunted by those who believed that reason should outweigh appetite, and that intellect was worth more than passion. But we were created to be passionate beings, and we do a grave disservice to our Creator when we deny ourselves what we truly are within us. If one has passions, then one must *indulge* those passions, rather than imprison the heart and emasculate the spirit with thought and self-recrimination. We must strive to be the obedient-yet-chaotic beasts which God created us to be in Eden, not this domesticated and diluted bastardization that our science and civilization have twisted us into becoming. Thus, while the Prométhéen man sees the wild and beautiful world around him and perceives nothing but plans and schedules and problems and solutions, the Épiméthéen man is better equipped to actually savor the world, consume it, and thus find succor and hope beyond what he can merely comprehend. It was hope which the classical Épiméthée received from his Pandore, and it is that hope which we bring back to the world today."

"What kind of hope are you bringing?" I snapped back. "What kind of hope did your monsters bring to the children that they slaughtered down on that killing floor? What kind of hope is your *Obshchestvo Drakonisty* bringing to all of the people that they'd abducted, sold into slavery, murdered…? That's not hope, Mr. Rémy—that's predation."

He just smiled pleasantly and shook his head.

"You misapprehend our purposes, Detective Chapel. *La Société des Dragonistes* has always been tasked with being a modern Saint Georges, standing against the dragons of this world, such as the *sorcières* and the vampires and the dark dealers of evil. In any war, there are casualties, yes, but such is the nature of these things. God has given us power, but that power has its cost, and that power must be fed. If an Allied army must burn a town to stop the evil of the Nazis, we would applaud them, would we not? If my *Société* must take a life here or there to stop *Le Maître de Tous les Maux*, then should we not similarly applaud them nonetheless?"

"But you're doing the same things that they do," I argued, clearing my mind again. "You're no better than the vampires, treating the rest of humanity like cattle!" If I could just last until Tony got here, maybe we could stop these guys. I kicked myself for leaving the Matteh ha Shelomoh in the car—though how could I have explained carrying that thing into the Daley Center to security?

"Ach!" he snorted, looking thoroughly disgusted by my comment. "We are nothing alike. The Magus and his Covenant are parasites, leeches, maggots, hiding in the dark and sucking at the living in a pretense, a mockery of life. We *are* life, young man, in its rawest and most God-honoring form. Does any other man run so fast or live so fully or love so freely or fight so fiercely as those who have given themselves over to *La Bête de la Lune*? The Covenant follow their *Danse* and their pretty, petty rules, marking their steps in a decayed and decadent promenade. They are fallen demons, wearing the corpses of their victims as an artifice to hide their true natures. It is an abomination! But we—we are the strong who are strengthened in our holy cause by the sacrifices of those too weak to fight for that cause themselves. They give of their lives so that our fight against darkness may continue. And then, we sometimes share that strength with others so that our pack may grow, that we might better serve God. An evangelism by blood, if you will."

"You're talking about Carolyn and me," I said.

"And others," he replied. "The first whom I brought over to our cause was my own daughter, but then together, we blessed others in Angers, Châlons—wherever we perceived the growth of evil, needing to be kept in check by the power which God had allowed us to wield."

"And what keeps your werewolves in check? Even if I believed any of this, you can't all be in it to serve God…"

"Oh, no," he sighed. "There are always counterfeits and rival packs, such as the ones which spawned fiends such as Gilles Garnier, or Satanists such as Petrone de Armentières or Jean Grenier or Joannes Malrisius or Pierre Gandillon. But not in *my* pack, no. No, all of my children are servants of Heaven, I assure you."

"They're all murderers and monsters!" I shouted. "And that Skorzeny guy was a Nazi! You're crazy if you think that your pack has anything to do with serving Heaven!"

For the first time, I saw Rémy get angry. "I will not be questioned by a mere pup!" he growled, and I saw his teeth begin to sharpen. "My children are neither angels nor gods, but rather men who have been touched by God's hand. Are we perfect? No. But we serve a purpose, and now, so do you as well. Very soon, I pray, you shall serve that purpose and bring us the blessings which we so desperately need."

"What are you talking about?" I asked. "Why did you turn Carolyn and me? This has never been about just adding us to your pack. What's going on here?" His face softened again, and he leaned down closer to me.

"You do not know?" he asked. "You have not guessed? And this *Chevalier* in whom you have placed your faith, he has not told you?"

"Told me what?"

"He has not told you why Ruthven had come to Chicago? Why *Le Synode des Corbeaux* and *La Société des Dragonistes* are both here, now, to meet the Covenant?"

"No," I admitted in frustration. "Why?" I realized that, in my anger, my own voice was becoming more and more of a growl as well.

"*Très intéressant…*" he said, scratching his chin. "He must not trust you very much."

"*Why?*" I growled again.

"If the *Chevalier du Graal* has not told you, then who am I to do so?" he answered me, smiling. "Besides, you will certainly know everything, soon enough…"

"Why have you done this to me?" I shouted, jumping from my chair to grab Rémy by the collar. A minute before, I was feeling so weak, but now, filled with rage, I felt stronger than I've ever felt in my whole life. Seeing that in me, Rémy just smiled.

"Yes, feed the beast which God has given you, Detective Chapel," he said to me quietly. "Let it out and let it sing. But not just yet. He has not yet come."

"*Who* hasn't?" I asked again, but then it struck me—he wants Durant here. But why would any werewolf *ever* want Durant in the same room with him? And wouldn't he want me to transform, to change into a monster and be part of his "army" for if and when Durant ever *did* show up? What benefit was he hoping to gain from me still being human when the Grail Knight came along to kick his furry butt all the way down Washington Street and into the Chicago River?

Because that's the whole point… I realized. *Because he wants the Grail. From the beginning, this has always been about getting the Grail…*

I dropped him and spun around, intending to get out of there as fast as I could to warn Tony, to warn Durant somehow not to bring the Grail with him, that all of this had been a huge trap. Imagine my surprise when, there in the doorway stood Detective Leah Wheaton.

"Wheaton!" I yelled. "Get out of here! Call Tony and tell him—"

"Whoa…" she interrupted me. "Calm down, Tom. What's going on? You look horrible."

"You have to get out of here," I told her again. "You don't understand what's going on here, and I don't have the time to explain it all to you."

Leah just shook her head and chuckled, and I heard Rémy beginning to do the same behind me. I turned back to see him coming toward her in the doorway.

"Get out, Leah!" I barked back at her, trying to put myself between them.

"Come in," he said quietly, and she brushed past me, into the office. They met right next to me, and she embraced him warmly, giving him a soft nuzzle and a series of gentle kisses. She turned back to me and smiled again, cradled in his arms.

"I would introduce you, of course," he said to me. "But I believe that you have already met my lovely daughter, Alleia…"

Background
From *De Vervloekte Leven en Dood van Stubbe Peeter* (George Bores, 1590, trans. D.L. Ashliman)

A most true discourse, declaring the life and death of one Stubbe Peeter,[1] *being a most wicked sorcerer.*

Those whom the Lord doth leave to follow the imagination of their own hearts, despising his proffered grace, in the end through the hardness of heart and contempt of his fatherly mercy, they enter the right path to perdition and destruction of body and soul for ever: as in this present history in perfect sort may be seen, the strangeness whereof, together with the cruelties committed, and the long time therein continued, may drive many in doubt whether the same be truth or no, and the rather fore that sundry false and fabulous matters have heretofore passed in print, which hath wrought much incredulity in the hearts of all men generally, insomuch that now of days few things do escape be it never so certain, but that it is embased[2] by the term of a lie or false report.

In the reading of this story, therefore, I do first request reformation of opinion, next patience to peruse it, because it is published for example's sake, and lastly to censure thereof as reason and wisdom doth think convenient, considering the subtlety that Satan useth to work the soul's destruction, and the great matters which the accursed practice of sorcery doth effect, the fruits whereof is death and destruction for ever, and yet in all ages practiced by the reprobate and wicked of the earth, some in one sort and some in another even as the Devil giveth promise to perform. But of all other that ever lived, none was comparable unto this Hell hound, whose tyranny and cruelty did well declare he was of his father the devil, who was a murderer from the beginning, whose life and death and most bloody practices the discourse doth make just report.

---

[1] *Or "Peter Stübbe" or "Peter Stump," since his left hand had been chopped off by a woodsman when he had been found—in wolf form—attacking a young child, years before he was finally apprehended.*

[2] *That is, "brought."*

In the towns of Cperadt[3] and Bedbur[4] near Collin[5] in high Germany, there was continually brought up and nourished one Stubbe Peeter, who from his youth was greatly inclined to evil and the practicing of wicked arts even from twelve years of age 'til twenty, and so forwards 'til his dying day, insomuch that surfeiting in the damnable desire of magic, necromancy, and sorcery, acquainting himself with many infernal spirits and fiends, insomuch that forgetting the God that made him, and that Savior that shed his blood for man's redemption. In the end, careless of salvation, he gave both soul and body to the Devil for ever, for small carnal pleasure in this life, that he might be famous and spoken of on earth, though he lost heaven thereby.

The Devil, who hath a ready ear to listen to the lewd motions of cursed men, promised to give him whatsoever his heart desired during his mortal life: whereupon this vile wretch neither desired riches nor promotion, nor was his fancy satisfied with any external or outward pleasure, but having a tyrannous heart and a most cruel bloody mind, requested that at his pleasure he might work his malice on men, women, and children, in the shape of some beast, whereby he might live without dread or danger of life, and unknown to be the executor of any bloody enterprise which he meant to commit.

The Devil, who saw him a fit instrument to perform mischief as a wicked fiend pleased with the desire of wrong and destruction, gave unto him a girdle which, being put around him, he was straight transformed into the likeness of a greedy, devouring wolf, strong and mighty, with eyes great and large, which in the night sparkled like unto brands of fire, a mouth great and wide, with most sharp and cruel teeth, a huge body and mighty paws. And no sooner should he put off the same girdle, but presently he should appear in his former shape, according to the proportion of a man, as if he had never been changed.

Stubbe Peeter herewith was exceedingly well pleased, and the shape fitted his fancy and agreed best with his nature, being inclined to blood and cruelty. Therefore, satisfied with this strange and devilish gift, for that it was not troublesome nor great in carriage, but that it might be hidden in a small room, he proceeded to the execution of sundry most heinous and vile murders; for if any person displeased him, he would incontinent[6] thirst for revenge, and no sooner should they or any of theirs walk abroad in the fields or about the city, but in the shape of a wolf he would presently encounter them, and never rest 'til he had plucked out their throats and tear their joints asunder. And after he had gotten a taste hereof, he took such pleasure and delight in shedding of blood, that he

---

[3]   *Kerpen.*
[4]   *Bedburg.*
[5]   *Cologne.*
[6]   *That is, "unrestrained."*

would night and day walk the fields and work extreme cruelties. And sundry times he would go through the streets of Collin, Bedbur, and Cperadt, in comely habit, and very civilly, as one well known to all the inhabitants thereabout, and oftentimes was he saluted of those whose friends and children he had butchered, though nothing suspected for the same. In these places, I say, he would walk up and down, and if he could spy either maid, wife, or child that his eyes liked or his heart lusted after, he would await their issuing out of the city or town. If he could by any means get them alone, he would in the fields ravish them, and after in his wolfish likeness, cruelly murder them.

Yea, often it came to pass that as he walked abroad in the fields, if he chanced to spy a company of maidens playing together or else a milking their kine,[7] in his wolfish shape he would incontinent run among them, and while the rest escaped by flight, he would be sure to lay hold of one, and after his filthy lust fulfilled, he would murder her presently. Beside, if he had liked or known any of them, look who he had a mind unto, her he would pursue, whether she were before or behind, and take her from the rest, for such was his swiftness of foot while he continued a wolf that he would outrun the swiftest greyhound in that country; and so much he had practiced this wickedness that the whole province was feared by the cruelty of this bloody and devouring wolf.

Thus continuing his devilish and damnable deeds within the compass of a few years, he had murdered thirteen young children, and two goodly young women big with child, tearing the children out of their wombs, in most bloody and savage sort, and after ate their hearts panting hot and raw, which he accounted dainty morsels and best agreeing to his appetite.

Moreover, he used many times to kill lambs and kids and such like beasts, feeding on the same most usually raw and bloody, as if he had been a natural wolf indeed, so that all men mistrusted nothing less than this his devilish sorcery.

He had at that time living a fair young damsel to his daughter, after whom he also lusted must unnaturally, and cruelly committed most wicked incest with her, a most gross and vile sin, far surmounting adultery or fornication, though the least of the three doth drive the soul into hell fire, except hearty repentance, and the great mercy of God. This daughter of his he begot when he was not altogether so wickedly given, who was called by the name of Stubbe Beell, whose beauty and good grace was such as deserved commendations of all those that knew her. And such was his inordinate lust and filthy desire toward her, that he begat a child by her, daily using her as his concubine; but as an insatiate and filthy beast, given over to work evil, with greediness he

---

⁷   *That is, their cows.*

also lay by his own sister, frequenting her company long time, even according as the wickedness of his heart led him...

Thus this damnable Stubbe Peeter lived the term of five and twenty years, unsuspected to be author of so many cruel and unnatural murders, in which time he had destroyed and spoiled an unknown number of men, women, and children, sheep, lambs, and goats, and other cattle; for, when he could not through the wariness of people draw men, women, or children in his danger, then, like a cruel and tyrannous beast, he would work his cruelty on brute beasts in most savage sort, and did act more mischief and cruelty than would be credible, although high Germany hath been forced to taste the truth thereof.

By which means the inhabitants of Collin, Bedbur, and Cperadt, seeing themselves so grievously endangered, plagued, and molested by this greedy and cruel wolf, who wrought continual harm and mischief, insomuch that few or none durst[8] travel to or from those places without good provision of defense, and all for fear of this devouring and fierce wolf, for oftentimes the inhabitants found the arms and legs of dead men, women, and children scattered up and down the fields, to their great grief and vexation of heart, knowing the same to be done by that strange and cruel wolf, whom by no means they could take or overcome, so that if any man or woman missed their child, they were out of hope ever to see it again alive, mistrusting straight that the wolf had destroyed it.

And here is to be noted a most strange thing which setteth forth the great power and merciful providence of God to the comfort of each Christian heart. There were not long ago certain small children playing in a meadow together hard by the town, where also some store of kine were feeding, many of them having young calves sucking upon them. And suddenly among these children comes this vile wolf running and caught a pretty fine girl by the collar, with intent to pull out her throat; but such was the will of God, that the wolf could not pierce the collar of the child's coat, being high and very well stiffened and close clasped about her neck; and therewithal the sudden great cry of the rest of the children which escaped so amazed the cattle feeding by, that being fearful to be robbed of their young, they altogether came running against the wolf with such force that he was presently compelled to let go his hold and to run away to escape the danger of their horns; by which means the child was preserved from death, and, God be thanked, remains living at this day...

Likewise in the town of Germany aforesaid continual prayer was used unto God that it would please Him to deliver them from the danger of this greedy wolf.

---

[8]   *That is, "dared."*

And, although they had practiced all the means that men could devise to take this ravenous beast, yet until the Lord had determined his fall, they could not in any wise prevail: notwithstanding, they daily continued their purpose, and daily sought to entrap him, and for that intent continually maintained great mastiffs and dogs of much strength to hunt and chase the beast. In the end, it pleased God, as they were in readiness and provided to meet with him, that they should espy him in his wolfish likeness at what time they beset him round about, and most circumspectly set their dogs upon him, in such sort that there was no means of escape, at which advantage they never could get him before; but as the Lord delivered Goliath into the hands of David,[9] so was this wolf brought in danger of these men, who seeing, as I said before, no way to escape the imminent danger, being hardly pursued at the heels, presently slipped his girdle from about him, whereby the shape of a wolf clean avoided, and he appeared presently in his true shape and likeness, having in his hand a staff as one walking toward the city. But the hunters, whose eyes were steadfastly bent upon the beast, and seeing him in the same place metamorphosed contrary to their expectation, it wrought a wonderful amazement to their minds; and, had it not been that they knew the man so soon as they saw him, they had surely taken the same to have been some Devil in a man's likeness; but for as much as they knew him to be an ancient dweller in the town, they came unto him, and talking with him, they brought him by communication home to his own house, and finding him to be the man indeed, and no delusion or fantastical motion, they had him incontinent before the magistrates to be examined.[10]

Thus being apprehended, he was shortly after put to the rack in the town of Bedbur, but fearing the torture, he voluntarily confessed his whole life, and made known the villainies which he had committed for the space of 25 years; also he confessed how by sorcery he procured of the Devil a girdle, which being put on, he forthwith became a wolf, which girdle at his apprehension he confessed he cast it off in a certain valley and there left it, which, when the magistrates heard, they sent to the valley for it, but at their coming found nothing at all, for it may be supposed that it was gone to the Devil from whence it came, so that it was not to be found. For the Devil having brought the wretch to all the shame he could, left him to endure the torments which his deeds

---

[9] *Here, Bores alludes to the Biblical story found in the book of* 1 Samuel, *xvii, 1-ff.*

[10] *Feher claims that the magistrates of Cologne sent word to Nicolas Rémy, the magistrate of Nancy, to seek his expertise in trying the case (see his* Das Gesetz und die Rechtsstreitigkeiten im Mittelalter, *1932), but this is unlikely, as Rémy rarely if ever left the duchy of Lorraine until the fear of the plague finally drove him to the countryside in 1592.*

deserved…

Stubbe Peeter was condemned, and their several judgments pronounced the 28th of October 1589, in this manner, that is to say: Stubbe Peeter as principal malefactor, was judged first to have his body laid on a wheel, and with red hot burning pincers in ten several places to have the flesh pulled off from the bones, after that, his legs and arms to be broken with a wooden ax or hatchet, afterward to have his head struck from his body, then to have his carcass burned to ashes…

This, Gentle Reader, have I set down the true discourse of this wicked man Stub Peeter, which I desire to be a warning to all sorcerers and witches, which unlawfully follow their own devilish imagination to the utter ruin and destruction of their souls eternally, from which wicked and damnable practice, I beseech God keep all good men, and from the cruelty of their wicked hearts.

Amen…

Witnesses that this is true:
       Tyse Artyne.
       William Brewar.
       Adolf Staedt.
       George Bores.
       With divers others that have seen the same.

Chapter 21
The One That You Feed

Actually, it made total sense. I started thinking back, and all of the pieces lined up perfectly. Why did we go to Bunin's house in the first place? Because Wheaton said that she'd recognized him and passed the case on to us. It was Wheaton who had first turned me on to hunting down the Synod of Crows. It was Wheaton who'd been disgusted by Lyn's actions once she'd finally given into the change—why? Because she thought she'd disgraced her pack? It was under Wheaton's watch that Lyn had stalked and killed her first victims, and then she'd supposedly "lost" her. It was Wheaton who'd tried to get Tony to leave the staff of Solomon in the car when Lyn and the Russian trapped him in that building off of Addison—and then got herself conveniently "abducted," only to show up later, unharmed. It was Wheaton whose text would have sent us into that ambush on Chicago Avenue. In fact, I realized that *every* fight that I'd walked into over the past couple of days had been because I'd followed a lead or a suggestion that had been given to me by Leah Wheaton. But why tell us about that storefront where she'd supposedly been taken? Just so that we'd get caught in that crossfire between the wolves and the crows? Why come up with a phony story that she'd never be able to back up in a police report? Is that why she'd never written her report? But wouldn't that come out at some point?

But what if she didn't care if it ever came out or not? What if the *Société des Dragonistes* was coming down to their endgame, and none of that would matter soon? Is that why Wheaton told Tony to get me to come down and meet Rémy in person—to get me right where they wanted me for the end?

They wanted the Grail. Durant was bringing it to me—and now, that also meant that he was bringing it right to them.

"My daughter has been orchestrating all of this for quite some time," Rémy told me. "This is why I pulled some strings to get her on the police force, and to have her assigned to Detective Kingery after she had eliminated Detective Schroeder. To get close to *you*."

Jim Schroeder was a friend of mine, and a good cop. We'd worked in the same office for years. I glared at Wheaton, and she shook her head again.

"Don't worry, Tom," she purred. "I made it quick and relatively painless for him."

I really, really wanted to kill her a lot.

"That sounds a lot like a plan," I growled, "and I thought that you didn't like plans, Rémy. They're some sort of blasphemy, right? Doesn't that make you a hypocrite?"

His smile faded and a frown creased his brow. Leah—or Alleia or whatever—just chuckled and kissed him again, then stepped away from him, back toward the door.

"You are a little man trying for little victories now, Detective Chapel," he said in reply. "I will only indulge you until the *Chevalier* returns… and then I will take great pleasure in gutting you myself."

"It's a legitimate question," I countered, taking a step back myself. Wheaton was between me and the door, but I thought that maybe I could get past her. Surely they wouldn't try to chase me into the public hallway, right? "I mean, you talk a good talk about following God, but then your pack tortures and slaughters innocent kids in a charnel house hidden in a basement. You rail against making plans and thinking ahead, and yet, your daughter here works for months to set me up."

"Not just my daughter," he corrected me, gazing at her hungrily. "My *queen*…"

"Yeah, and that's not creepy at all," I replied. "So, basically, if you put it all together, I'm thinking that you're just full of hot air here, Nick. You just seem to be trying to justify the fact that you just like eating people…" I kept angling toward the door, but Wheaton was on to me and blocked the doorway with her body.

"Tom," she said to me, "you're not getting the big picture here. My father is a great man, and he's got a great vision of the way that the world should be."

"With you guys at the top of the food chain, right?"

"As it *should* be, yes," she replied. Rémy suddenly seemed tired, and moved back behind his desk again, clutching his side and wincing. Wheaton obviously hurt along with him, her face wrinkled in sympathetic pain. "Look what he's done to you…" she whispered.

"Why did you target me?" I asked her, seeing if I could get her to lose track of why she'd moved to the door in the first place. "Why did your father say that all of this was to get to me?"

"Because the *Chevalier* seems to like you for some reason," she answered me. "We watched what happened with Ruthven two years ago—we saw what he was willing to do for you and for your mate and whelps."

"My family."

"Whatever," she said, rolling her eyes. "Fine. Your *family*. As you can imagine, he's not an easy creature to get to, but *you*…? You're just a man, and there are all sorts of ways that we could get to you and hurt him through you. But then, the more I thought about it, the more I saw you as an even bigger opportunity—not just to hurt him, but to *use* his compassion for our own gain."

"You're talking about the Grail," I said. And she smiled.

"I knew that you were a good Detective, Tom," she replied, taking a step toward me… and away from the door. "The *Chevalier* never stays in one place very long, never opens himself up to anyone around him. And he never—*never*—has the Grail with him. None of us have ever even seen the thing. So how do we get him to bring it out and bring it to us? We just have to hurt him—or someone he cares about—and make that hurt deep enough to get him all warm and sloppy inside. To get him to make a mistake and bring the Grail out for us. He's done it before, and I was betting that we could make him do it again. I was betting on *you*, Tom."

I stepped up toward her, but I made sure that I went around a chair to do it—getting myself just that much closer to the door. As I did, she turned a bit to face me—taking another step *away* from the door in the process.

"Do you even care about the Synod of Crows?" I asked her. "Or is all of that just window dressing, just a cover for the real, big play for the Grail?"

"Of course I care," she said, glancing back at Rémy, who was now slumped in his chair and not paying attention to us. "Look what they've done to him. Between them and your friend, they've almost finished him off. I want the Grail to make him strong again—young again. And I want to feast on the guts of everyone who's ever hurt him."

"But for revenge, right? Not for some pretended sense of the glory of God." She glanced back at Rémy one more time before moving in and speaking quietly to me. As she got close, I could see the gray roots of her hair. She still looked young—maybe in her thirties—but the years still took their toll, even on a strong werewolf like Alleia Rémy.

"We are the reason why mankind hid themselves in caves, fearing the dark of the night," she said, whispering so that her father couldn't hear her. "We are the reason why children tremble when their parents leave them alone in their beds. Because deep down inside, humanity knows—they have always known—that their betters are hunting in the deep woods, and that we will always be stronger than they." Her eyes turned sultry for a moment as she sucked in a deep breath, and I could tell that, in her own way, she was as turned on by the power as Lyn had been. "You ask me if I see myself as a servant of God? Sure. But to be honest? I mainly just see myself as a kid in a candy store, a drunk at an open bar. The sheep out there are afraid of us, and they *should* be. There's just not enough blood and flesh in the world to ever satisfy my hunger—but I'm looking forward to finding out if I'm wrong..." She licked her lips instinctively.

Part of me now realized that I had a decent shot at the door, but part of me really, really wanted to rip her to pieces. I felt my blood rushing through my veins, and I heard my own breaths coming in rich, panting waves. The *'áṅt'į* was still eating at my strength, but not as quickly as the Lycaon virus was revving it up. *The wolf can beat the 'áṅt'į,* I heard my inner voice say again. *Free the beast and save yourself!* And I realized that the only way that I was going to survive any of this was to do exactly that—to give in and let the wolf come out. But I knew that I had to be strong enough to control it, instead of letting it control me.

"Give me the strength..." I whispered a small prayer, taking off my gloves.

"That's exactly what I've done, Tom..." Leah whispered back, smiling. She reached out for me, but all that I felt toward her was anger and loathing. I knew that, for all of Rémy's posturing about following God, his daughter was the epitome of everything vile and horrible that the werewolves represented. I have no idea what Alleia had been like before her father changed her into this, but the centuries had not been kind. Sure, she could cover it better than monsters like Bunin or Sydor or even Lyn could, but did that make her more of a human inside, or even more of a monster? At least you could see it on them, smell it on them. With her, it was all hidden. She could sit and play with your children and seem all warm and caring, and then eat them afterwards without a second thought. I pictured her keeping that lunch date that Joanna had wanted to have with her, and my blood boiled. Strength and power began to surge through me, and I forgot all about the door. All I wanted to do was to rip her to shreds and then gulp her blood down my throat.

"No!" I roared, and I lunged for her. At least, I think that it ended up coming out as a word, but I'm not sure. All I know is that the hands that reached out for her soft neck flesh had claws, and that dark fur was beginning to cover them. I felt my teeth ache, and the world began to spin around me.

Wheaton spun with my attack. Even though I'd surprised her, she was still so *fast*, so horribly, horribly fast. Instead, my claws ripped open her blouse, exposing the skin of her chest and shoulder... and I fell backwards in shock. Her whole torso and upper arm were covered in pentacles—puffy and pink and bleeding at the points. I looked down at my own palm, and saw that the same thing was happening to my own pentacle. The sight and smell of her blood—and, to be honest, my own—was beginning to drive me into a frenzy.

"Not yet!" I heard Rémy shout as he leapt over his desk at me. His body tore through his clothing, elongating and twisting into the shape of a large, caramel-colored wolf. I could still see the healing wound of a gash in his side, recognizing it as the damage that Durant's sword had done to him just a little over an hour earlier. That was why he was still hurting so badly, and that was part of why they wanted the Grail so much. He was getting old, and he wasn't what he used to be. But he still gained strength from the transformation, and by the time he got to me, I was no match for him.

At least, Tom Chapel would have been no match for him, but I knew that I was more than just Tom Chapel now. I had the power of the wolf in me now, and I could control it, *direct* it. These monsters had degenerated into beasts that only knew murder in their hearts, but I knew that I could use it to do *good*, to *stop* the evil. I could use it to kill Rémy and to take his queen and to take his pack and to do whatever I wanted to do with them. Together, we could find the witches and make them pay—finish off Durant's Morrígan once and for all. We could hunt down Simon Magus and his Covenant of vampires and rip them apart. Every foul creature of the night would take notice that the werewolves were a force to be reckoned with, a force for good, and we could rule this place, like Durant said that Arthur had back in the day. A modern Camelot, with the pack as my knights.

"Give me that strength..." I prayed, but I think that it was really only a growl.

Rémy lunged toward me, but I side-stepped and raked his wound open again with my claws. He howled in pain and smashed against one of his bookshelves, knocking it over onto himself. Out of the corner of my eye, I saw Wheaton ripping off her clothes and beginning to change herself—but I saw a wild gleam in her eyes that looked to me more like excitement than anger.

Quickly, I jumped at Rémy before he could get up. The sun hadn't gone down yet, so I hadn't fully transformed yet—but I did have the claws and the teeth and the ferocity that I needed, and he was still weakened from Durant's earlier attack. As he twisted under the bookcase to get free, I pounced on him, slicing and ripping at his neck with my claws. He sliced back toward me with his own, but he was too weak now to do much damage. With my right hand, I flung the heavy bookcase to the side, and with my left, I swiped at him one more time, ripping through his neck, all the way to the spinal column. I was about to lean down to bite through the rest when I turned to look at Wheaton.

She had fully transformed into a large, gray wolf with bright, blue eyes—the same wolf that I had seen kill "Sticky Ike" in the alleyway, and the same wolf that had attacked Carolyn Davidge and me back at Nikodim Bunin's house.

And I thought that she looked beautiful…

I was prepared for her to attack me again, but instead, she cocked her head to the side and sniffed at the air. I had wondered why no one had come to see what was going on in the judge's office, why security wasn't up here already, but then I saw that she had pulled down another of the huge bookcases and shoved it back against the door. Nothing was getting in here until we *decided* that they could come in.

The she-wolf padded over to me slowly, sniffing. She gave no indication of aggression, but when she got to Rémy's body, she leaned down and nuzzled his face. Amazingly, somehow, he was still barely alive. She licked at his muzzle, then down his jowls, then at his neck. But as she got to the growing pool of blood there, her licking increased into more of a gulping, and I could hear her panting with excitement. It made me excited, too, and I was so very, horribly thirsty…

Rémy raised a paw weakly to stop her, but then she snapped at him and bit through his spine with one sharp bite. His paw dropped to the ground, and his head rolled to the side. As he began to shrink back into a human form, she continued ripping at his flesh with her teeth and claws, devouring him with an infectious enthusiasm. I leaned down myself to join in the feast.

But that's when the door burst open, smashing the bookcase back against the wall. And into the room strode Pieter Durant.

*   *   *

Several security guards were running up behind Durant in the hallway, but he grabbed the bookcase and flung it back against the door again, shutting us all back into the room. When he saw me, his face contorted into a mask of sadness and concern.

And the gray wolf took advantage of the opportunity that Durant's momentary shock gave her, and she leapt for him. He only barely got to the side in time, and her claws took a chunk out of his thigh as she passed by him. That's when I noticed that Durant hadn't taken the time to change since I'd last seen him.

Pieter Durant hadn't cleaned up. That meant something, but I couldn't quite put the pieces together to decide what that was.

She turned and pounced at him again, and he only just had time to fling one of the large, leather chairs in the room at her, knocking her back against the wall. Then, with one, fluid motion, he reached into his *got uechan* and drew an old revolver. Wheaton saw that she'd lost the initiative, so she tried out a different strategy—in less than a second, she'd melted back into her human form and climbed out from behind the wreckage of the chair.

"Wait!" she said, holding her arms out in front of her. Durant simply cocked his pistol.

"I have a gift for you," he said to her.

"What?" she asked, cocking her head in confusion.

"From my grandson…" he replied coldly and pulled the trigger. Even from where I was standing, I could feel the heat from the silver bullet as it crossed the room and blew a hole through Alleia Rémy's forehead. She fell to the ground, and I felt a strange combination of relief and sadness. But more importantly, I still felt the power of the wolf coursing through me.

Durant turned toward me and set the pistol down onto a table that was somehow still standing through all of this. He watched me for some time, and I watched him in return. Part of me wanted to say something, but I didn't have any words in my head. Another part of me wanted to leap past him into the hallway and find a place to hide until the sun could go down and I could finally, *finally* turn into what I'd always wanted to be—the wolf inside of me. I pictured myself running through the woods, bringing down a deer and feasting upon it. I pictured myself ripping through criminals and gorging myself on their soft, warm flesh. I pictured myself going home…

As we stood there, I saw the pain in his face, and there was the quickest flash in the failing afternoon light of something silver under his chin. It was that crucifix that he always wore. His clothes were still in tatters, and I could see that crucifix around his neck, stuck to his chest by all of the caked and drying blood that was covering him.

I'd never really thought about what a crucifix was until that point. It wasn't just a cross—it was like a little statuette of Jesus crucified on his cross. His moment of weakness, when he'd allowed evil to conquer him. I found myself staring at it, lost in it. There was Jesus, whom I'd always admired, and whom I'd recently begun to take far more seriously. But there was Jesus, nailed to a piece of wood by evil people whom he could've easily taken out, easily killed. He let himself get murdered, when there was still so much that he could've done. He could've been a king, with a queen at his side, ruling the planet and making it a golden place. We wouldn't even have *needed* an Arthur, if Jesus had just had the strength to do what he *should* have done, when those soldiers had come to arrest him.

At that moment, I knew what I would have done. I would have torn through those soldiers and killed them all. I would have brought my disciples into my pack and taken them to the palace and feasted on the Romans, on Pilate, on everyone there. I would've set up my kingdom there in Jerusalem and then spread it to the whole world. I imagined legions of Roman werewolves, growing my empire toward the ends of the earth, and the planet would be bathed in blood. I'd have been a far better Messiah than Jesus ever was…

"Thomas Chapel…" I heard Durant say quietly. The sound of his voice snapped me back to reality, and the horror of what I'd just been thinking suddenly sunk in.

"God help me…" I prayed, but again, I think that it was probably more like a whimper by the time it came out of my mouth. "God forgive me…"

"Detective," he continued. "You must come back to us."

I fell to my knees, and I thought of how I'd just pictured Jesus, and I was ashamed. I'd given myself over to the Lycaon virus, even though I knew what would happen. I'd done what every addict before me had always done—I'd found a justification for doing exactly what my addiction was screaming for me to do, and I'd given in to it. God help me, there was nothing left for me now.

Durant took a deep breath and reached into his *got uechan*, drawing out his sword. I could feel the heat from it where I was kneeling, and I knew that the only way to stop my curse—the only way to protect my family, Tony, everyone—was for Durant to end me now. I just hoped he would do it cleanly and quickly. I never wanted Joanna to know what I'd become—what I'd *almost* become.

But then he transferred the sword to his left hand, and reached into his bag again with his right, keeping his eyes and his blade on me the whole time. Slowly, he pulled out a small, earthenware cup, really almost more like a little bowl. It was old, it was scuffed, and it wasn't at all what I thought that the Holy Grail would look like. But somehow, I could feel that it was—I could feel… I dunno… the power of God, I guess, coming off of it in waves. From the pocket of his torn overcoat, he then pulled a simple bottle of water, twisted off the plastic cap, and poured a small amount into the cup.

He dropped the bottle and then transferred the sword back to his right hand.

And he just stood there.

"You must *wish* this, Detective," he said at last, his voice as cold and dark and deep as I'd ever heard it in all the time that I'd known him. "The cup of Christ will only heal what you *wish* to be healed of. You must renounce the beast. Now." I saw him clench his sword tightly— and I smelled something on him that I never thought could even exist. I smelled *fear*…

That gave me a sudden and unexpected jolt of exhilaration, even in the midst of my shame.

The great Pieter Durant was afraid of *me*. I realized that, for the first time, I might actually be powerful enough to take him down—fast enough to get to him and tear his flesh before he could swing that sword of his. That's why he'd shot Alleia Rémy, because she was so powerful. He'd been afraid of her. He knew that he wasn't fast enough to kill her with his blade, and he was afraid to get close enough to her to find out. I felt the sun going down, and I knew that it wasn't too late for me to kill Durant and claim the Grail for myself and… and to…

In every man, there are always two wolves fighting for control, the words came to me in my mind. *But which one is the strongest one? The one that you feed…*

Why hadn't Durant taken the time to change his clothes?

Why had he allowed Sydor to tear at his flesh for my sake?

Why had Jesus Christ allowed the Romans to nail him to that cross?

I realized that I was wrong before, because it hadn't been out of weakness. Jesus Christ was never weak. Letting someone hurt you when it's in your power to stop them takes something a lot stronger than weakness—it takes a very strong kind of commitment. Let's be honest—it takes a strong kind of love. But don't misunderstand and get all "that's so lame" on me—I don't mean the namby-pamby, emotional crap that people write songs about on the radio, or the twisted feelings that Rémy'd had for his daughter, or that Lyn had been living out once she'd changed, or, for that matter, even the purer kind of romantic love that I had for Joanna and she had for me. I'm talking about something much simpler and deeper and more powerful than any of those gushy, emotional feelings. I'm talking about the simple, profound decision to make the needs of someone else more important in your mind than your own needs, even if it kills you.

I thought of the disciple (who was it…? Peter…?) chopping off the ear of one of the men who came to take Jesus away that night in the garden, and how Jesus had stopped to heal the guy before he went off with them. Unlike me, he hadn't wanted to conquer humanity—he'd wanted to *win* them.

And then I thought about Flubber and that whole "alpha dog" concept that I talked about before. He finally accepted me because he knew that I was obviously the strongest one in our home, and that gave him a sense of security, because he'd learned that he could trust me, and he'd decided that it was kind of cool to know that the toughest guy around was also the most trustworthy. As I thought about it, I realized that God was basically the ultimate "alpha dog" in the room—not because he'd growled and barked and snapped back when he was attacked, but because he'd had the strength *not* to. And I guess knowing that gave me a sense of security, too.

"God, give me strength…" I prayed again, but then I stopped when I realized that I'd been praying for the wrong thing all this time. The truth was, the Lycaon virus was stronger than I was, and it was just going to keep getting stronger, no matter what. There was no way that I was going to win that fight, so fighting against it was actually the dumbest way to try to fight it. That was just playing into exactly the sort of mindset that the curse wanted me to have, making me more and more like the wolf the more I tried to muscle my way against it. With those two wolves striving inside of every man, you don't wrestle for control—the only way to win is to *starve* the thing out.

"God, help me accept just how *weak* I am…" I prayed again, and I think that my growls finally began to sound more like words. "I can't beat this thing, but I keep trying to, and that's just what it wants—that's what my addiction wants. It wants me to wrestle with it, when what I need to do is kill it and walk away." I felt hot tears streaming down my face, and I couldn't seem to hear or see anything else around me. "Take this away from me, God. Please just take it, and take it away from me…"

I felt something cool against my lips, and I realized that Durant was holding the cup there for me. I knew that my palm still burned, and that I could still feel my claws and my fangs, and that being this close to his crucifix was still physically painful. I knew that I was still a monster, and yet here he was, the greatest monster-killer that the world had ever known, holding the cup that had once caught the blood of Christ in it to my lips. I didn't want to be a monster any more, but the more I thought about it, the more I realized that I didn't want to be cured anywhere near as much as I wanted my brain to be washed clean and *forgiven* for the thoughts that I'd been letting go through it for the past few days.

I leaned my head down and took a sip, and that's the last thing that I remember.

Background
From *Memoiren eines Soldaten des Deutsch-Französischer Krieg* (Günther Adalbert Felix von Wächter, 1883, trans. K. Schultz)

It was in the aftermath of that battle at Noisseville[1] under Prince Friedrich Karl[2] that the following exchange was overheard by me while recuperating in hospital, not far from where I fell. On 1 September, I found myself under the care of a stocky Dutch physician who was attending the Second Army there, as his ambulance corps fought to save as many of our wounded as possible. Indeed, the world had lost nearly as many Prussians as French that day, though our boys prevented Marshal Bazaine from breaking out of our siege. The exchange was between a young orderly with a thick moustache in the hospital called Friedrich, and a large man with an exotic accent who was called Vordenburg. I was impressed by the philosophy of both men, and I took notes as I listened to them. I was also reminded of this interaction when, in this past year, I had the good fortune to hear this young man once again during a lecture tour on his book, *The Joyous Wisdom.*[3] I have not seen the older man since that Thursday morning outside of Metz, but I noted that he held himself with the bearing of a soldier, even as he exercised the mind of a philosopher. I have endeavoured to reproduce here their argument to the fullest of my ability, using my old notes as a guide…

FRIEDRICH - All men are naturally willful. Such is the way of humanity since the beginning.

VORDENBURG - But that only proves that one should direct one's energies toward serving the Lord.

FRIEDRICH - I fear that I do not follow your line of reasoning.

---

[1] *A battle in the Franco-Prussian War, fought in France on August 21, 1870.*

[2] *Prince Friedrich Karl Nikolaus of Prussia, nephew of King Wilhelm I—who was soon to become the first emperor of the new German Empire.*

[3] Die Fröhliche Wissenschaft (*better known in English as* "The Gay Science")*, written by Friedrich Nietzsche and published in 1882. The young orderly may very well have been Nietzche, as von Wächter claims, since the writer did serve in this capacity during the Franco-Prussian War.*

VORDENBURG - Tell me, have you read John Duns Scotus?[4]

FRIEDRICH - Of course.

VORDENBURG - He was a brilliant Irishman. In fact, he was a Franciscan whose uncle, Elias Duns, was the first Scottish Vicar General of the order, and whose writings;—though sadly minimal, due to his unfortunately early death;—were nonetheless formative in;—

FRIEDRICH - As I said, I am familiar with the man… But we were speaking about willfulness.

VORDENBURG - Yes, of course, forgive me. As I was saying, Duns Scotus argued that infinite will naturally inclines toward infinite good. Thus, the stronger the will, the greater the propensity to do good. *'Est inclinatio naturalis ad summe amandum bonum infinitum;—'*[5]

FRIEDRICH - I find that idea laughable, and ultimately morally reprehensible.

VORDENBURG - Ah, but consider how he continued. 'There seems to be a natural inclination to love an infinite good to the greatest degree possible, because the free will of itself and without the aid of any habit promptly and delightfully loves this good, so that we seem to experience an act of love for an infinite good. Indeed it seems that the will is not perfectly satisfied with anything else. And if such an infinite good were really opposed to the natural object of the will, why is it that the will does not naturally hate an infinite good?' Do you understand?

FRIEDRICH - I thoroughly understand, though I do not in the least bit agree.

VORDENBURG - And why is that?

FRIEDRICH - Duns Scotus says that the stronger the will, the more it will desire to do good, but never has this been true in the history of mankind. I would argue that a 'will to power'[6] is nature's primary motivational force, not the quest for an 'infinite good,' if such a thing could even exist. Great men of will are born to be great, and greatness is their destiny. To deny them that destiny is a travesty against nature, a 'slave morality' designed to drag all men down to an equally low footing, so that the few cannot rise to the excellence that is their birthright. Some are born to be sheep, and to press them to become leaders of men should be a bastardization of their purpose in life. Others

---

4   *An influential Celtic Catholic theologian at the turn of the 13th to 14th centuries. It is historically uncertain whether he was in fact Irish or Scottish.*

5   *"There seems to be a natural inclination to love an infinite good to the greatest degree possible."*

6   *"Machtgelüst," (later "Wille zur Macht") a concept which Nietsche arguably developed from Schopenhauer's earlier "Wille zum Leben" ("desire to live") and which he first expressed in his* Der Wanderer und Sein Schatten *(1880).*

are born to be wolves, and to force them to chew cud should be just as much a bastardization of their purposes in life. Does not your own long experience in life teach you this? Are you not, by your own nature, more knight than peasant, more wolf than sheep? Is this not the reason that Providence gave the wolf fangs, that he might feast upon the sheep, who were made for that very purpose? Thus, men of great will are drawn not toward an infinite good, but rather toward the pursuit of personal excellence and self-affirmation. The highest morality must be that which perpetuates and strengthens such men. I suppose one could perceive that as an infinite good in and of itself;—to breed superior men in order to improve the species;—though I hardly think that you would agree with this.

VORDENBURG - Hardly. As always, falsity is specked with truth. True, God desires that Man improve himself, continually learning and bettering the circumstances of both his life and the lives of those around him, but the obsessive pursuit of personal glory and self-aggrandizement is nothing less than the root of all sin. It was this very desire to 'become superior' that brought Adam and Eve low in the Garden. Man is Man, and God is God; thus, all men are Man, but no man is God;—do you see? To view one man or a few men as naturally superior to their fellow men is to miss an essential truth: not all men are equal in every facet of their being, but all men are equal in the sight of God;—and that is, of course, the critical point. 'God is no respecter of persons,'[7] but rather, He loves all of His children indiscriminately. To further your own analogy, where you see some great men born to be wolves, I see great men born to be *wolfhounds*, bred to be strong enough and dominant enough to effectively protect the Shepherd's sheep. Yes, they have been given fangs, but to fight off their enemies, not to devour those under their watch. Their sustenance is provided by the Shepherd, not by their own innate and self-serving savagery, and so it should be with Man as well. Consider this: if God, whose will is infinitely strong, chooses to seek only an infinite good for His children; if God, whose power is infinitely great, was willing to lay down His pride and His life to achieve that infinite good; and if God, whose wisdom is infinitely vast, views all of mankind as spiritually;—though not forensically;—equal, ought not we, who have been created in the *imago dei*,[8] follow His divine example and do the same when interacting with our fellow man?

FRIEDRICH - Perhaps, if I were to accept what you say about God;—but I have abandoned that path, though you may continue to believe in it, if it brings you some peace to do so. Nonetheless, in my experience, the human will seems not drawn so much to the good as it is

---

[7]   *From the Biblical* Book of Acts, *x, 34.*
[8]   *The "image of God."*

to the extreme, and nothing you have argued thus far suggests otherwise. The more powerful the will, the more powerful the pull toward infinite goodness or infinite evil, dependent solely upon the basic inclination of the person involved. The peasant, whose will is weak, seems drawn to neither extreme, and thus he achieves little in his life save a consistent service to mediocrity;—a true 'slave moralist.' Whereas the conqueror, the over-man such as yourself, whose will is strong, seems inexorably drawn to either pole;—evil or good;—his life bespeaking either a growing commitment toward good or a spiraling seduction into evil. Thus God as you describe Him, for example, has committed His formidable will toward helping His 'children' because that is His nature. On the other hand, the Turk, whose will is iron, revels in dissipation and in his absolute power over his slaves; thus, his strength of will has driven him to become swallowed whole by his own evil.[9]

VORDENBURG - But do you not see? Your very words themselves prove Duns Scotus to be correct. The will is an agent of self-discipline, not discipline over others. Power over one's subjects can be many things;—physical superiority, force of presence, whatever;—but it is not necessarily the will. The will is the strength with which one controls one's self, disciplining one's mind and focusing one's purpose toward a specific, unselfish end. Strength of will is forcing one's own self to do what the weak-willed man would not force himself to do. Strength of will is marshalling one's energies to act contrary to one's own desires. Those who are truly strong in their will are not necessarily those who can command vast armies, but rather those who can have dominion over the immense vastness of their own desires. The Proverbs teach us that 'he who is slow to anger is better than the mighty, and he who rules his spirit than he who takes a city.'[10] Thus, the strong-willed conqueror is successful because he can commit his will to the infinite good, whereas the weak-willed conqueror may be successful only in spite of his malleability by evil. Do you see?

FRIEDRICH - But surely the superior man does have self-discipline; in fact, he must needs see that ability as paramount. One could not be an Alexander or a Napoleon without the requisite ability to live a life of consummate discipline.

VORDENBURG - Ah, but in this, your perception of self-discipline is flawed. Regimenting one's life is not the same as true self-discipline. Curbing one's passions;—denying one's own heart those things which seem all-important at the time;—this is true self-discipline. To limit one's life only to the gratification of one's own desires, to limit one's efforts only to the pursuit of personal excellence, to limit one's focus

---

9   *His viewpoint reflects how bad relations between Europe and the Turkish Ottoman Empire were, at this point in history.*

10 *In the Biblical* Book of Proverbs, *xvi, 32.*

only to self-aggrandizement;—this is not self-discipline. This is simply focusing one's worldly desires and then prioritizing one's time and energy in order to achieve them in an orderly fashion. It is an act of bureaucracy, not an act of the will. Remember your own words, young Friedrich: the Lord 'has committed Himself toward helping His children';—an act of the will;—but the Turk was 'swallowed whole by evil,' you said;—'*swallowed*.' Does this sound like a strong will?

FRIEDRICH - No, but;—

VORDENBURG - He revels in his dissipation because he hasn't the strength of character or of will to fight it, to master it. He revels in his power over his slaves because he knows, somewhere, deep inside of himself, that he has no such power over himself. He has made himself powerful in this world because it is the only way which he knows to combat the weakness which resides within himself. Lao-Tzu once wrote, 'To conquer others is to have strength; to conquer yourself is to be strong.'[11] Again I submit to you that the stronger the will;—the stronger the man;—the greater the propensity to do good. Can you not feel, even within yourself, an infinite yearning toward an infinite good? Does your heart not yearn to make a positive difference in this world? Nothing less than such perfection should ever truly satisfy you.

FRIEDRICH - Perhaps, yet is that not still a selfish lust for perfection? Are you not still suggesting that I seek perfection to satisfy my yearnings, to strengthen myself all the more, so long as those yearnings point me in the direction of the Christian God, or so long as that strength is used in altruistic endeavours? In this, are you not still suggesting a life of perpetual striving that drives one toward achieving personal goals? And is this not precisely the mindset which you are attempting to debate against? Forget for a moment the presumed 'positivity' of the goal;—is the attitude of personal improvement and self-satisfaction that one is achieving one's personal goals not the same? I thought that God demanded contentment in His servants, a peaceful subservience in which they accept their lot and do not presume to ask for more? Did not the Apostle say that he had learned to be content whatever the circumstances?[12]

VORDENBURG - Ah, but you are confusing a desire for the world with a desire for God. We must not lust for worldly things, but rather we ought to lust after God.

FRIEDRICH - How is this any different than the lustful sacrifices yielded in the worship of pagan deities in darkest Africa? Or the effeminate rituals of the ancient Hellenist? Wouldn't all of this constitute a lust for one's god?

---

[11]   *Quoted from the philosopher's* Tào Té Chīng, *written in the 6th century BC.*

[12]   *He alludes here to the Apostle Paul, writing in the Biblical* Letter to the Philippians, *iv, 10-13.*

VORDENBURG - The lust is different, just as the object is different. With false gods, the lust is a carnal one, and the object is;—in truth;—not the worship of the gods in question, but rather the gratification of the worshipper. When one joins with a pagan priestess, one is lusting only after the gratification of one's own corrupted desires, and this is;—as I have said;—the true root of all sin. All sin flows from the desire to pleasure ourselves, to gain more and more power as we crave more and more gratification. A lust for God is a strong, spiritual desire, not a carnal one, and the object of this desire is to know Him more, to grow closer to Him and to be changed into His image. But perhaps 'lust' is a misleading term. From now on, shall we say that one should strongly desire the Lord?

FRIEDRICH - Ah, a shoddy semantic trick to hide your shifting ground! Is this 'strong desire' not simply another way of saying that one might desire more to gratify one's own needs as well?

VORDENBURG - No, because you wish it not for your own personal gain nor for your own empowerment nor for your own gratification, but rather to honor your Father, to be more and more pleasing in His sight;—to be more and more the son whom He created you to be. It is the difference between the wolf who is aggressive because he wishes to fill his own belly and the wolfhound who is aggressive because he wishes to protect his charge and to make his Shepherd proud, hearing his voice cry, 'Well done!' at the end of the day.[13] It is at the core of the fundamental difference between the Kingdom of God and the battleground of this world;—the wholehearted yearning after the Lord versus the utter hopelessness of self-gratification. The grand irony of our lives is that to choose the former is to find increasing fulfillment, while to choose the latter is to find increasing emptiness of spirit. Which of these should the logical man thus choose?

---

[13]   *Here, Vordenburg appears to allude to the words of Christ from a parable found in the Biblical* Gospel of Matthew, *xxv.*

Chapter 22
Gift Fish

I awoke the next morning in my own home, lying on the couch with an afghan pulled up over me and Flubber lying across my legs, fast asleep. I looked up and saw Durant in the chair across from me—also fast asleep, but now cleaned up and wearing an extremely well-tailored gray suit. I pictured Victoria picking it out for him, and it made me smile. Come to think of it, I'd sometimes wondered if Durant even *needed* to sleep any more. Now I know.

Personally, I felt like I'd been asleep for about a week. Every bone in my body ached, but it was a *good* ache, like after you have a really strong workout. I didn't feel the withering weakness of the *'áńt'į,* but I also didn't feel the gnawing hunger of the wolf inside of me. Looking across the room at Joanna's hutch, I saw my face reflected in the glass— neither gaunt nor furry. I whispered a quiet "Thank you..." and Durant bolted up from his chair with a start. In a weird sort of way, it was comforting that his movements were a blur to me again.

Then again, I still wasn't quite myself, either. As soon as Durant moved, Flubber jumped in response, and I could smell his scent change from relaxed to alert. And I could both hear and smell the fact that Joanna was taking a shower, even though she was on the other side of the house. My senses were no longer what they'd been at the height of my infection with the Lycaon virus... but they were no longer entirely human, either. As I would find, that fact was going to be far more important than I could ever realize at that moment, lying there on the couch in my living room with my dog on my lap.

At the Thanksgiving service that we'd gone to a few weeks before, I'd heard the story about Jonah and the whale, clearing up a bunch of my misconceptions about the story. For instance, I guess the Bible never calls it a whale—it was a great big *fish* that swallowed him up. Whatever. But more to the point, contrary to what I always thought growing up, the fish swallowing Jonah wasn't intended as a punishment from God or something—in fact, God sent the fish to save Jonah's life, since he was drowning at the time. Now, I know that no one in their right mind would ever say, "Hmm, I'd like to be swallowed by a fish later on today..." but that doesn't change the fact that the fish was a *gift*—something that you'd never ask for, but something that turned out to be exactly what you really needed.

You could say that the Lycaon virus ultimately became a "gift fish" to me. There's no way that I would have ever asked for what I'd gone through over the past week—no way that anyone should ever wish to be attacked by werewolves! And yet, I'd somehow gotten through it all and come out the other side... *changed*... And when that Christmas rolled around, that change was going to make all of the difference, though I couldn't have foreseen that at the time. But I'm getting ahead of myself.

Durant was standing over me, watching me intently. He wasn't quite on guard, but he did have his hand instinctively on his *got uechan*, ready for anything.

"I'm okay..." I told him. He frowned for a moment, then nodded and sat back down in his chair. Flubber watched him for a second, then turned to look at me for another second, snorted, and then went back to sleep.

"Then praise be to God," Durant said. *"Non nobis, non nobis, Domine—sed nomini tuo da gloriam..."*

"Yep," I agreed, though I didn't know exactly what he'd said. But the tone of it seemed just about right. "And thank you, too." He shook his head and shrugged.

"I did very little this week," he said. "You were the one who destroyed Rémy and ended that particular bloodline."

I thought back to what had been going through my head when I'd killed him, and I was ashamed. I never wanted to think those thoughts again—not because they'd been so alien to me, but because they'd obviously been at least a dark part of me walking into the infection, just like Carolyn's brokenness had already been a part of her. I never wanted to go there again.

"I'm not proud of that," I said quietly. "But I think, by the end, that Alleia was actually the 'alpha' of that pack. And you shot her."

"And it gives me great joy to have done so, yes," he replied. I began stroking Flubber's fur, and he twisted so that I could scratch him on his belly.

"So why did you use the gun?" I asked him.

"It was the proper caliber for the bullet," he replied. I could never tell when he was trying to be funny or when he'd just missed my point.

"Okay, smart guy—why use the bullet instead of your sword?"

"It seemed the most expedient weapon to use at the time," he answered me. And then he took one of those deep breaths that he always seemed to use to try to work through his stronger emotions. "And I did not wish to have a sword in my hand when I faced you in the heat of the battle..."

He'd used the old six-shooter—probably the same one that he'd worn on his hip back when he'd met Wyatt Earp and Bat Masterson, I figured—*because* he'd only had the one silver bullet. That meant that after he'd killed Alleia Rémy, he'd been left standing there, facing me, with an empty gun—and that he'd *planned* it that way. Yes, he did eventually draw his sword, but thinking back, I remembered that he'd done so only after I was already on my knees, only after I had already past by the most dangerous point inside of me. Had he drawn the sword to cover me, as I'd originally thought? Or had he drawn it so that I would keep feeling the pain from the orichalcum on his blade, and get shocked back to myself? I dunno... but that's when I realized that the fear I'd smelled on him wasn't that he'd been afraid of me—it was that he'd been afraid *for* me. He was genuinely scared that he might have to kill me, and he'd decided that he'd rather face a werewolf unarmed than to be tempted to have to do that. But there was no way that he was ever going to say any of that outright.

"Y'know..." I said, helping him save face a bit. "Mkogisos gave me that bullet for a reason."

"Then why did you keep mislaying it?" he asked.

"That bullet was supposed to point me to Rémy," I replied, ignoring him. "It was going to burn hotter the closer I got to him. That really could've helped at the end, there..." I saw just the barest crack of a smile break on his face.

"He lied," was all he said.

"What?"

"Mkogisos lied to you," he repeated. "It was obvious that you needed something in which to place a sense of hope, so he handed you one of his silver bullets. Of course the thing would become more uncomfortable as the day wore on, since the Lycaon virus would be taking a greater and greater hold on you. But he surmised—and quite correctly, it appears—that the further into darkness you fell, the more you would need to be reminded of the presence and purity of light."

That sneaky old Indian. Part of me wanted to smack him, and part of me wanted to shake his hand. I really wished that I could've met him when he was in his prime.

"I don't think that I like you people," I told him, and he actually chuckled a bit. I heard Joanna's shower turn off, and that's when I smelled that she'd taken out some breakfast sausage from the freezer and left it on the counter to thaw. Sausages and eggs on a Saturday morning. Throw in a bagel, and that sounded just about like Heaven to me.

"You cut it awfully close there with the Grail, you know," I told him. "Another minute or so, and I would've been a lost cause."

"We are all in God's timing," he said, "and not our own. The infected person must needs be at the brink of damnation, and yet still have the strength remaining to potentially choose salvation, else the

Grail could not help. There was no guarantee of success, even then." Far more quietly, he then added, "In all the long centuries of my life, using the Grail in this manner has worked on only one other occasion, and I had not expected that blessing to be repeated here."

"Mkogisos..." I said, putting the pieces together.

"Mkogisos..." he replied, his voice soft and low.

*   *   *

Joanna made Durant stick around for breakfast. You had to know that she was going to. About halfway through, Chelsea even conned him into letting her sit on his lap for a minute and whisper something that she thought was incredibly important in his ear. I had to strain to make sure that I didn't hear it—some things are only precious because they're shared between just you and a loving child, and I would never dare to take that from them.

I did appreciate that Durant never told Joanna just how far gone I'd become. Oh, she and I talked about it later—I always make it a point to be very honest with her about everything, since that helps me from making the same sorts of mistakes that Tony made to end his marriage with Juanita—but there's a big difference between me telling her that I'd almost lost it and Durant telling her that I'd almost lost it. From me, it comes off as an openness and honest confession that gives her confidence in the future. From Durant, I'd be afraid that it would just scared her.

But right then, surrounded by my family, eating sausages, eggs, and a toasted bagel smeared with cream cheese and chives, life seemed just about perfect to me. Flubber sat under my chair, waiting for me to "accidentally" drop something for him to eat, and the twins were busy getting more egg on their faces than into their mouths, and my wife? My wife was *radiant*.

"You know," I said to Durant, taking a sip of orange juice to cleanse my pallet. "A couple of days ago, I was actually wondering what, if anything, made you any different than the *Société des Dragonistes*."

"Indeed?" he replied, trying not to sound as shocked as he obviously was. "And what, if anything, did you decide?"

"Watching you with Chelsea there reminded me of something that I read a while back. Something that reminded me of you."

"Not more research for another one of your books, was it?"

"Absolutely not," I lied—I'd already promised Joanna that I'd write this and try to do it right. "But it's kind of a metaphor that I think sums the difference between the two of you in a nutshell. When it comes down to it, you're at least as dangerous as they are, but to think of Chelsea being around one of them is a terrifying thought, while seeing her with you just makes me confident that she's well-protected. The *Société des Dragonistes* are a pack of wolves—but you? You're a wolfhound."

"What'th a woofhound?" Chelsea asked Durant through the gap in her front teeth.

"A very large hound, bred to hunt wolves to protect the herd," he answered her.

"They tend to be big, shaggy, scary-looking, gray dogs," I told her. "But with their families, they're just soft-hearted puppies, like Flubber."

"You're a woofhound, Uncle Pieter!" she giggled, grabbing him by the beard. That seemed to cross a line with him, and he politely placed her back in her own chair.

"I seem to remember arguing something to that effect at one point myself," he said, smoothing out his beard.

"Like I said, it reminded me of you."

"In point of fact, Friedrich Nietzsche and I disagreed upon a great many things," he said, obviously remembering precisely the episode that I was talking about. "I met him while he was serving as an orderly for Van Helsing at the Siege of Metz, and we argued long into the night on several occasions about his misguided views about God and the nature of the *Übermensch*. But years later, he wrote something with which I could not agree more. He argued, '*Was mich nicht umbringt, macht mich stärker*'— 'What does not kill me, makes me stronger.'" He let his eyes rest on me for a moment. "Have you not yourself found this to be the case, Detective?"

"I do believe that I have," I answered, smiling. "I guess that Nietzsche was pretty wise after all, wasn't he?"

"The man contracted syphilis and died drooling and mindless..." he replied, brushing some crumbs off of his lapel. That's when I decided that it might be better to finish this conversation somewhere else.

*   *   *

We went outside and sat in the backyard, watching the snow as it drifted down. Neither one of us really seemed to feel the cold any more, but I loved seeing the world blanketed in the unsullied whiteness of it all. Somehow, it just always felt like the snow was washing the world clean again, even though I knew that it was really just a whitewash, and that everything was still just as dirty and grungy underneath the drifts. But at least for that moment, the world around you just seems so spotless and peaceful. We sat in silence for a bit, just drinking it all in. But then, I had to speak up.

"So, is the Grail back... wherever it is that you keep it?"

"It is indeed," he replied. I waited a beat before I spoke again.

"You should've let Tony take a sip while it was here," I said. I tried really hard to make it sound more like an observation and less like an indictment, but I'm not sure how well I succeeded. Durant sat for a bit, just watching the snow. I wasn't sure if he was going to respond at all, but after a few moments, he took a deep breath and answered me.

"He refused to drink from it," he said.

"What?" He sighed, and then turned to me.

"Apparently, Detective de Tullio overheard our conversation about the Grail whilst we assumed that he was asleep, and he refused to drink from it." Durant had the oddest look on his face when he told me that— a combination of surprise, sadness, and maybe even respect. "He said— " and here, Durant did such a spot-on impression of Tony that I could totally picture him saying it— "'I figger if God wants me healed, he'll heal me, an' if he wants me dead, he'll take me home. But healin' everbody all th' time ain't what ya was given that thing for, an' ya got better things ta do...' Though he knew that it might save his life, he nonetheless rebuffed me and refused to drink from it." Durant shook his head and looked back at the falling snow. "He is a much more profound thinker than I believe that I had given him credit for..."

I sat and watched him for a moment, watching the snow. He seemed saddened that he wasn't able to help Tony, but like I said, that sadness was tinged with a whole lot of newfound respect. A week ago, these guys couldn't stand one another. But now, I could see that, at least on some levels, they had begun to understand one another. They'd never admit it to one another, of course, but that's okay. They'd both admit it to me—at least as much as they could—and that's enough.

"Wait a minute," I interjected, suddenly picking up on something. "You said that Tony 'refused' to take a drink from the Grail?" Durant sighed one of his patented sighs.

"We have been through this already, have we not?"

"If he 'refused' the drink," I kept going, "then that means that you must have *offered* it to him, right?" He suddenly looked uncomfortable. "Even with all of your 'high and mighty duty' talk, you still offered to let him take a drink for the Grail, didn't you ...?"

"I should never have brought the cup of Christ to Chicago," he said, trying very hard to shift the focus of the conversation. "I should have let you change, then promptly decapitated you. It would have made my life quite simpler."

"Uh-huh..." I replied.

"One less werewolf in the world..." he muttered, stiffening and *actively* now watching the snow instead of talking to me. I began to chuckle, but then was struck with an unpleasant thought that kind of ruined the moment for me.

"You realize that they're still out there...?" I told him.

"To whom are you referring?"

"The *Obshchestvo Drakonisty*. There are still more of them out there. There's a whole organization that's still kidnapping and killing, that's still muscling into the Bratva and trying to push out the local gangs here in town. There's still human trafficking going on that has nothing to do with any of that. And there's at least one more brown-furred werewolf that I remember seeing at Kells Park—the one that helped Rémy get away after you almost sliced him in half."

"Of course," he replied. "We have taken out their leadership and blunted their fangs, but yes, there are always more of them out there. And other packs as well."

"And the Covenant, and the Morrígan and her Synod of Crows."

"And other things, far more foul than they."

I looked back at the snow, and thought of the dirt and grease and everything hidden beneath it. Humanity just sees the surface of the world, and we never really want to imagine the filth that we can't immediately see in front of us.

"It never stops, does it?" I asked him.

"In a millennium and a half, it never has, no," he said. "But then again, neither do I."

I watched him again, thinking of how long he's been at this. I know how much I love my Sundays with the family, or going to see a Cubs game, or those two weeks of vacation that I really do at least try to take each year. When was the last time that Durant just *rested*—just took the time to sit back, take a few days off, and *rest*? I couldn't picture him doing that, knowing that every day that he sat back and did nothing was another day that innocents would be lost, and it made me appreciate his dedication to his little one-man war all the more. It made me think of a quote that my Dad always appreciated from one of Tolkien's *Lord of the Rings* books: "War must be, while we defend our lives against a destroyer who would devour all; but I do not love the bright sword for its sharpness, nor the arrow for its swiftness, nor the warrior for his glory. I love only that which they defend." I don't find Durant's war a pleasant or particularly glorious struggle, and every fight I've ever been in personally has been bloody and scary and ugly. But thinking about the "why" behind the "what" of his long, unending fight, it just made me appreciate Pieter Durant all the more. He was never, ever going to stop, until one of these monsters finally killed him, or God himself took him home.

"If you will recall, when I arrived here three days ago," Durant said, bringing me back into the conversation by turning back to face me, "I confessed that I had not come back to see you, as such, but rather because I had been on the trail of the Queen of the Vampyri. I had found that Lamashtu has apparently made Chicago her home for the past several decades."

"You're kidding me!" I replied. "She's been here the whole time?"

"Evidently," he replied.   "Apparently, the Covenant is calling together a great gathering of the various species of night-fiends at the close of Saturnalia, and they have resolved for this to happen this year— indeed, a week from now—in this very city. Ruthven had obviously been tasked with creating some sort of power base in preparation for the convocation, but we were able to stop him before he could finalize his plans."

"But why Chicago? And why now?" I asked him.

"I have no idea," he answered me. "But this city appears to be something of a magnet for arcane creatures—they love Chicago, though I do not know why."

"I wish they didn't..."

"Indeed."

"So why are you only telling me this now?" I asked. "Why didn't you tell me that at the very beginning?"

"Well," he answered me, "I was about to do precisely that when your vicious guard dog attacked me." He almost smiled at that, but then his face turned much darker. "After that, in truth, by the time we next had the opportunity to speak of it, I had no idea which way you would end up turning—which side you would ultimately find yourself serving. If you had indeed given in to the wolf, then I would not want *La Société des Dragonistes* to learn that I was aware of the gathering."

I had to admit that he made a good point. I mean, I was *that close* to playing for the other team, and it could've gone either way. I couldn't blame him for keeping something like that from me. But then, that led me to another question.

"But if you knew that something that big was going down, then why did you waste three days with me and this whole *Obshchestvo Drakonisty* thing, when there were so many bigger fish to fry?"

He almost smiled again, then let out one of those great, big, deep sighs that you know is going to lead into telling another one of his stories.

"There was a young man in the court at Caer Mallot," he said, launching into it.   "A Scandian prince whose name was Hraustir— meaning 'Courageous'—and he served Gawain as his squire for a time. Gawain could not wrap his tongue around the boy's Scandian name, so he just called him by an English equivalent. I sarcastically called the lad 'Fearless,' and Kay simply referred to him as 'Wooden Head.' The youth was infamous at court for throwing himself into one adventure after another, week after week. It would have been comical, had the situations not been so regularly dire.

"On one occasion, Fearless received word from his homeland that

Scandian warriors were needed in Denmark to lend their aid to a friendly king called Hróarr Halfdan, one of the Skjöldungar, who was apparently dealing with some sort of swamp creature or other who was attacking his hart's hall each night. Always ready for an adventure, Fearless leapt for the opportunity to both serve his father's wishes and prove his mettle in battle. When Gawain heard of this, he temporarily abandoned his own quest for the Green Castle and caught Fearless at the docks, preparing to leave.

"'And would you be abandoning my employ without so much as a by-your-leave, varlet?' he bellowed at the youth.

"'I am only obeying my father's call for warriors,' Fearless answered him.

"'Aye, and was it that, or your own heart's call to be a hero?' Gawain asked him. 'You've responsibilities here, lad, and I haven't invested so much time in you these past years, just to stand idly by and watch you feed yourself to a bog monster in Hleiðra today.'"

"'But it's my choice,' Fearless countered.

"'Nay!' the knight bellowed back, pulling at his moustache as he often did when riled. 'As my squire, 'tis not your decision to make, without my own leave—and I choose not to give it!'

"Fearless was crestfallen, but he had to admit that his father's call was a general one, not specifically to him directly, and that Gawain's direct orders thus took precedence. He had learnt the hard way before what it cost to break faith with his knight. Thus, in sadness, he agreed to return with Gawain to Caer Mallot and allow the adventure to pass him by.

"'But Sir Gawain,' he said as they rode along the path toward home, 'Why did you interrupt your search for the Green Castle over this? Why abandon something so important over something so trivial?'

"'Because, lad,' the knight replied, 'there's nothing trivial about you. When at last I find the castle, that's my head to be lost to the Green Knight in proper payment for my own pride. And when I'm gone, who is it that will wear my armor and serve Arthur in my stead? I'm not training you to be a squire, my boy—I'm training you to be a knight.' And that was the last that they spoke of it."

"And what happened with the bog monster?"

"Hmm?" he replied. "Oh, a small band of the Gautar led by a chap named Böðvar Bjarki—called the 'Bee Hunter' by his comrades—dealt with that rightly enough. Gawain was quite right to keep Fearless safely home at Caer Mallot."

After that, Durant just quietly sat and stared out at the falling snow again, content with the answer that his story had given me to my question. As I thought about it, I guess it did answer me pretty well. Why waste three days on solving my problem, when there was a much larger issue at hand to deal with? Because Durant didn't see my problem as small at all—and, more importantly, I guess he saw me as kind of like his squire, his protégé, that he was grooming to take over his job, if anything should ever happen to him.

The more I thought about that, the more profound it became to me. He wasn't just telling me that he liked me—he was telling me that he *trusted* me, that he was more or less training me to become the next Grail Knight, if things should ever come to that, just like Sir Gawain had trained this Hraustir guy to take over his own place at the Round Table, if the Green Knight had succeeded in killing him. So, in both cases, taking a step away from the "bigger" quest wasn't just sentimentality or a waste of time—it was an investment in the future by making sure that someone was always standing on the wall, building a better world.

"I'll try to live up to that," I said quietly. But I guess I sounded serious enough that Durant turned back to me and nodded in affirmation.

"Then it is time," he said, with a sense of finality to his tone.

"Time for what?" I asked him. And then he *smiled* a cold, scary smile.

"It is time that we reminded the monsters why it is that they fear the light…"

**If you are being trafficked, or know someone who is,
help is only a phone call away.
Please call the National Human Trafficking Resource Center
1-888-373-7888**

For Further Reading

Abraham of Worms (1458) הקסם הקדוש של אבר-מלן *("Die Heilige Magie des Abramelin," published in English as "The Book of the Sacred Magic of Abramelin the Mage")*

Acosta, Joseph (1835) *Recueil de Voyages et de Mémoires Publié de la Société de Geographie ("Collection of Voyages and Published Memoirs of the Society of Geography")*

Agrippa, Heinrich Cornelius (1510) *De Occulta Philosophia Libri Tres ("Three Books on Occult Philosophy")*

—— (1565) *Quarto Libro de Occulta Philosophia ("Fourth Book on Occult Philosophy")*

Albritton, Claude (1989) *Catastrophic Episodes in Earth History*

Alexander, Hartley Burr (1920) *Latin American Mythology*

Altomare, Donato Antonio (1553) *De Medendis Humani Corporis Malis ars Medica ("Medicines for Medical Maladies of the Human Body")*

Apuleius, Lucius (2nd century) *Metamorphoses*

Anselm of Canterbury (11th century) *Dialogus de Casu Diaboli ("Dialogue on the Downfall of the Devil")*

Antoine, Michel (1989) *Louis XV*

Aquinas, Thomas (13th century) *Summa Theologiæ ("Complete Theology")*

Artemyeva, Tatiana, & Mikeshin, Mikhail (1998) *"Иван Иванович Шувалов (1727–1797), Просвещённая личность в российской истории"* (*"Ivan Ivanovich Shuvalov (1727-1797), an Enlightened Person in Russian History"*) in *The Philosophical Age: Almanac*.

Augustine (4th century) *Confessiones* (*"Confessions"*)

—— (4th century) *De Moribus Ecclesiae Catholicae et de Moribus Manichaeorum* (*"On the Morals of the Catholic Church and on the Morals of the Manichaeans"*)

—— (5th century) *De Civitate Dei Contra Paganos* (*"The City of God Against the Pagans"*)

[Author Unknown] (1250) *Konungs Skuggsjá* (*"The King's Mirror"*)

[Author Unknown] (13th century) *"Þrymskviða"* (*"The Lay of Thrym"*) in *The Poetic Edda*

[Author Unknown] (13th century) *Völsungasaga* (*"The Tale of the Völsung Family"*)

[Author Unknown] (1755) *Официальные Отчеты для Императорского Двора Летнего Сезона* (*"Official Reports of the Summer Season for the Imperial Court"*)

[Author Unknown] (1889) *Ophiolatreia: An Account of the Rites and Mysteries Connected with the Origin, Rise, and Development of Serpent Worship in Parts of the World*

Bailey, Lloyd (1968) *Noah: The Person and the Story in History and Tradition*

Barber, Malcolm (1994) *The New Knighthood: A History of the Order of the Temple*

Barber, Paul (1988) *Vampires, Burial and Death: Folklore and Reality*

Barère, Bertrand (1844) *Mémoires de Bertrand Barère* (*"Memoirs of Bertrand Barère"*)

Baring-Gould, Sabine (1865) *The Book of Werewolves*

Bernhardt-House, Phillip A. (2006) *The Legend of Vereticus: An Ancient*

Celtic Tale from the 1860s

Bores, George (1590) *De Vervloekte Leven en Dood van Stubbe Peeter* (*"The Damnable Life and Death of Stubbe Peeter"*)

Bossu, Jean-Bernard (1777) *Nouveaux Voyages dans l'Amerique Septentrionale: Contenant Un Collection De Lettres Ecrites Sur Les Lieur, Par L'auteur, al Son Ami M. Douin, chevalier, Capitaine Dans Les Troupes Du Roi, Ce Devant Son Comarade Dans Le Nouveau Monde* (*"New Voyages in North America: Containing a Collection Of Letters Written On the Binder, By the author, Via His Friend Mr. Douin, Knight, Captain in the Troops Of the King, In Front of His Comarade in the New World"*)

Boguet, Henri (1602) *An Examen of Witches*

Bourke, John Gregory (1887) *Witch-Songs of the Navajo Medicine Chiefs*

—— (1891) *Scatalogic Rites of All Nations. A Dissertation Upon the Employment of Excrementicious Remedial Agents in Religion, Therapeutics, Divination, Witch-Craft, Love-Philters, etc. in All Parts of the Globe*

—— (1892) *The Medicine-Men of the Apache*

Bremen, Gerhardt (1896) *Offizielle Dokumente und Papiere der Russischen Zaren* (*"Official Documents and Papers of the Russian Tsars"*)

Brightman, Robert A. (1988) *"The Windigo in the Material World"* in *Ethnohistory*

Cædmon (7th century) *Codex Junius* (*"Junius Manuscript"*)

Cambrensis, Giraldus (1188) *Topographia Hibernica* (*"Topography of Ireland"*)

Casanova, Giacomo (1798) *Mémoires de Jacques Casanova* (*"The Memoirs of Jacques [Giacomo] Casanova"*)

Claraevallensis, Bernardus (12th century) *"Sermo de Aquaeductu"* (*"The Sermon at the Aqueduct"*) in *Sancti Bernardi Opera Genuina* (*"The Genuine Works of Saint Bernard"*) (1854)

Copeland, Harold Hadley (1907) *The Ponape Scripture—A New Translation*

—— (1911) *The Prehistoric Pacific in Light of the "Ponape Scripture"*

Copway, George (1847) *The Life, History and Travels of Kah-ge-ga-gah-Bowh*

Cord, Alex (1993) *To Dream of Wolves* (unpublished doctoral thesis)

Crumlin-Pedersen, Ole (1997) *Viking Age Ships and Shipbuilding in Hedeby/Haithabu and Schleswig*

Cushing, Frank Hamilton (1896) *Outlines of Zuñi Creation Myths*

D'Amboise, Michel-Paul (1453) *Tractatus Artibus Diabolicis, Quae Europam et Seducunt Iuvenes Mulieres in Peccatum Diluvium ("A Treatise on the Devilish Arts Which Flood Europe and Seduce Young Women into Sin")*

Da Casale, Ubertino (1305) *Arbor Vitae Crucifixae Christi ("The Tree of the Crucified Life of Jesus")*

De Acosta, José (1590) *Historia Natural y Moral de las Indias ("Natural and Moral History of the Indians")*

De Born, Bertran (1184) *La Tragèdia de Perseval, lo Cavalièr Que Pòt Pas Morir ("The Tragedy of Perseval, the Knight Who Cannot Die")*

De Lancre, Pierre (1613) *Tableau de l'Inconstance des Mauvais Anges et Démons ("Portrait of the Inconstancy of Evil Angels and Demons")*

De Liguori, Alphonsus Maria (18th century) *Le Glorie di Maria ("The Glories of Mary")*

De Troyes, Chrétien (1181) *Perceval, le Conte du Graal ("Perceval, the Tale of the Grail")*

Downs, Hunton (2009) *The Glenn Miller Conspiracy: The Never-Before-Told Story of His Life—and Death*

Duerr, Hans Peter (1978) *Traumzeit: Über die Grenze zwischen Wildnis und Zivilisation ("Dreamtime: Concerning the Boundary between*

Wilderness and Civilization")

Dumas, Alexandre (1853) *Isaac Laquedem*

Duns Scotus, John (1297) *Quaestiones super Libros Metaphysicorum Aristotelis ("Questions on Aristotle's Book of Metaphysics")*

Eusebius (c. 324) *Historia Ecclesiastica ("History of the Church")*

Feher, Friedrich (1932) *Das Gesetz und die Rechtsstreitigkeiten im Mittelalter ("The Law and Legal Disputes in the Middle Ages")*

Fischer, Walter A. (1999) *The Early Empire: The Reign of Augustus*

Fontini, Kelly (2013) *The Cracked Mirror: An Ethnographic Examination of Abnormal Psychology*

Foxe, John (1563) *Actes and Monuments of these Latter and Perillous Days, Touching Matters of the Church* (AKA *Foxe's Book of Martyrs*)

Gettius, Aulus (2nd century) *Noctes Atticae ("Attic Nights")*

Ginzburg, Carlo (1966) *I Benandanti: Stregoneria e Culti Agrari tra Cinquecento e Seicento ("The Good Witches: Witchcraft and Agrarian Cults in the Sixteenth and Seventeenth Centuries")*

Glanville, Ernest (1903) *In Search of the Okapi: A Story of Adventure in Central Africa*

Gundersson, Jens (1999) *Odin: Myter og Sagn av Allfader ("Odin: Myths and Sagas of the All-Father")*

Hamberger, Klaus (1992) *Mortuus non Mordet. Dokumente zum Vampirismus 1689–1791 ("The Dead Do Not Bite: Documents about Vampirism, 1689-1791)*

Hegesippus (c. 180) *Ὑπομνήματα ("Memoirs")*

Heidenberg, Johann (1499) *Steganographia ("Stenography")*

—— (1514) *Annales Hirsaugiensis ("The Annals of Hirsau")*

Herodotus (5th century BC) *Ἡροδότου Ἁλικαρνησσέος ἱστορίης ("The*

Histories of Herodotus of Halicarnassus")

Hewlett, Jack (1978) *Good Stories and Tall Tales of the American West*

Hippolytus (c. 220) *Refutatio Omnium Hæresium ("Refutation of All Heresies")*

Hornklofi, Þórbiörn (9th century) *Haraldskvæði ("Harald's Saga")*

Hostiensis (13th century) *Summa super Titulis Decretalium ("Commentary on the Titles of the Decretals")*

Irenaeus (c. 180) *Adversus Hæreses ("Against Heresies")*

Isocrates (5th century BC) *Τέχνη της Ρητορικής ("The Art of Rhetoric")*

James I, [Rex] (1597) *Dæmonolgie, In Forme of a Dialogie, Divided into Three Bookes*

James, Edwin (1830) *Outline of the Paradigma of a Chippeway Vocabulary*

—— (1833) *Essay on the Chippeway Language*

John of Damascus (8th century) *Πηγή Γνωσεως ("Fountain of Wisdom")*

Jones, James Athearn (1830) *Traditions of the North American Indians*

Kane, Anthony (2008) *"Horror Movies and the American Psyche"* in *The Journal of American Film*

Keck, Paul & Pope, Harrison & Hudson, James & McElroy, Susan & Kulick, Aaron (1988) *"Lycanthropy: Alive and Well in the Twentieth Century"* in *Psychological Medicine*

Kelley, David H. (1990) *"Proto-Tifinagh and Proto-Ogham in the Americas: Review of Fell; Fell and Farley; Fell and Reinert; Johannessen, et al.; McGlone and Leonard; Totten"* in *The Review of Archaeology*

Konchalovsky, Evgeny (1830) *Краткая История Склады на Протяжении Веков ("A Concise History of Storehouses Throughout the Centuries")*

Kramer, Heinrich, & Sprenger, Jakob (1486) *Malleus Maleficarum* (*"Hammer of the Witches"*)

Lagerkvist, Pär (1960) *Ahasverus Död* (*"The Death of Ahasuerus"*)

Lao Tsu (6th century BC) *Tào Té Chīng* (*"The Great Book of the Path of Virtue"*)

Lavanter, Lewes (1572) *Of Ghosts and Spirits Walking by Night*

Leighton, Alexander H. & Dorothea C. (1945) *The Navaho Door: An Introduction to Navaho Life*

Litchfield, Candice (2010) *Nazi Assassination Conspiracies*

Lombard, Peter (1150) *Libri Quattuor Sententiarum* (*"The Four Books of Sentences"*)

Löns, Hermann (1910) *Der Wehrwolf* (*"The Warwolf"*)

Lucian of Samosata (2nd century) *Ἀληθῆ διηγήματα* (*"True Stories"*)

Lycophron of Chalcis (3rd century BC) *Ἀλεξάνδρα* (*"Alexandra"*)

MacKenzie, Alexander (1801) *A General History of the Fur Trade from Canada to the North-west*

MacMillan, Randall (1997) *The Voyages of Peer van Draeck*

Magnus, Olaus (1555) *Historia de Gentibus Septentrionalibus* (*"History of the Northern Nations"*)

Majoli, Simone (1612) *Dies Caniculares* (*"Dog Days"*)

Mech, L. David (1970) *The Wolf*

—— (1999) *"Alpha Status, Dominance, and Division of Labor in Wolf Packs"* in *Canadian Journal of Zoology*

Melendez, Juan (1682) *Tesoros Verdaderos De Las Yndias En la Historia de la gran Provincia De San Juan Bautista Del Peru De el Orden de Predicadores* (*"True Treasures of The Indies in the History of the Great Province of San Juan Bautista, Peru, from the Order of Preachers"*)

Meyboom, Paul G.P. (1995) *The Nile Mosaic of Palestrina: Early Evidence of Egyptian Religion in Italy*

Mitford, Nancy, & Foreman, Amanda (2001) *Madame de Pompadour*

Morgan, William (1936) *Human-Wolves Among the Navaho*

Müllenhoff, Karl (1845) *Sagen, Märchen und Lieder der Herzogthümer Schleswig, Holstein und Lauenburg ("Legends, Fairy Tales and Songs of the Duchies of Schleswig, Holstein and Lauenburg")*

Nennius (830) *Historia Brittonum ("History of the Britons")*

Nietzsche, Friedrich (1880) *Der Wanderer und Sein Schatten ("The Wanderer and His Shadow")*

—— (1882) *Die Fröhliche Wissenschaft ("The Gay Science")*

Norton, John (1816) *Iroquois Creation Myth*

Nutini, Hugo, & Roberts, John (1993) *Bloodsucking Witchcraft: An Epistemological Study of Anthropomorphic Supernaturalism in Rural Tlaxcala*

Ovid (8) *Metamorphoseon Libri ("Book of Transformations")*

Oviedo y Valdés, Gonzalo Fernández de (1526) *General y Natural Historia de las Indias ("General and Natural History of the Indies")*

Pausanias (2nd century) *Ἑλλάδος Περιήγησις ("Description of Greece")*

Pavón, Teresa (1994) *Nuevos Descubrimientos en la Historia de los Mayas ("New Finds in Mayan History")*

Petronius, Gaius (1st century) *Satyricon Liber ("The Book of Satyr-like Adventures")*

Peucer, Caspar (1553) *Commentarius de Praecipuis Divinationum Generibus ("Commentary on the Principal Forms of Divination")*

Phillips, Heather (2010) *"The Great Library of Alexandria?"* in *Library Philosophy and Practice*

Plato (4th century BC) *Platonic Dialogues: Τίμαιος, Κριτίας, Ἑρμοκράτης (The Timaeus, the Critias, and the Hermocrates)*

Pliny the Elder (77) *Naturalis Historia ("Natural History")*

Prinn, Ludwig (1503) *De Vermis Mysteriis ("Mysteries of the Worm")*

Punt, William (1548) *A New Dialoge Called the Endightment Agaynste Mother Messe*

—— (1551) *A Cataloge of Secret Abhominations*

Quinet, Jean Louis Edgar (1834) *Ahasvérus ("Ahasuerus")*

Rémy, Nicolas (1595) *Dæmonolatreiæ Libri Tres ("Demonolatry in Three Books")*

Rosenberg, Donna (1989) *World Mythology*

Schenkel, Rudolf (1947) *Ausdrucks-Studien an Wölfen: Gefangenschafts-Beobachtungen ("Expression Studies of Wolves: Captivity Observations")*

Scheretzius, Sigismund (1621) *Libellus Consolatorius de Spectris ("Consoling Little Book of Spectres")*

Schoolcraft, Henry Rowe (1884) *The Indian Tribes of the United States: Their History, Antiquities, Customs, Religion, Arts, Language, Traditions, Oral Legends, and Myths*

Sigebert of Gembloux (11th century) *Chronicon sive Chronographia ("Universal Chronicle")*

Solinus, Gaius Julius (3rd century) *De Mirabilibus Mundi ("The Wonders of the World")*—also known as *Collectanea Rerum Memorabilium ("Collection of Curiosities")* and *Polyhistor ("Much Learning")*

Spence, Lewis (1908) *The Popol Vuh: The Mythic and Heroic Sagas of the Kichés of Central America*

—— (1914) *The Myths of the North American Indians*

Spencer, Herbert (1886) *Ecclesiastical Institutions: Being Part VI of the Principles of Sociology*

Spina, Bartolomeo (1523) *Questio de strigibus, una cum Tractatu de praeeminentia sacrae theologiae & quadruplici Apologia de Lamiis contra Ponzinibium* (*"The Question of Witches, Together with a Treatise on the Preeminence of Sacred Theology and Four Apologies about the Witches Against [Gianfrancesco] Ponzinibio"*)

Sprod, Dan (1977) *Alexander Pearce of Macquarie Harbour*

St. Martin, M. & Boyle, Henry (1825) *The Universal Chronology*

Stokes, Whitley (1891) *"Cóir Anmann"* (*"The Fitness of Names"*) in *Irische Texte, mit Übersetzungen und Wörterbuch* (*"Irish Texts with Translations and Dictionary"*)

Stratmeyer, Dennis & Jean (1977) *"The Jacaltec Nawal and the Soul Bearer in Concepcion Huista,"* in *Cognitive Studies of Southern Mesoamerica*

Stuhlinger, Ernst (2001) *Völkerschlacht* (*"The Battle of Leipzig"*)

Sturluson, Snorri (1225) *Ynglinga Sögu* (*"Yngling Saga"*) in the *Heimskringla* (*"The Chronicle of the Kings of Norway"*)

Summers, Montague (1927) *Geography of Witchcraft*

——— (1928) *The Vampire, His Kith and Kin*

Temme, Jodocus Deodatus Hubertus (1839) *Die Volkssagen der Altmark* (*"The Folktales of the Altmark"*)

——— (1840) *Die Volkssagen von Pommern und Rügen* (*"The Folktales of Pomerania and Rügen"*)

Torquemada, Antonio de (1584) *Hexameron, ou Six journées contenans plusieurs doctes discours sus aucuns poincts difficiles en diverses sciences, avec maintes histoires notables et non encores ouyes* (*"Hexameron, or six days containing several learned discourses on some difficult points in various sciences, with many notable stories and things unheard of"*)—also known as *"The Spanish Mandevile of Miracles, or the Garden of Curious Flowers"*

Trintignant, Jean-Éric (1956) *La Vie Exquise de la Marquise de Pompadour* (*"The Exquisite Life of the Marquise de Pompadour"*)

Turnbull, Stephen (2004) *The Walls of Constantinople, AD 324–1453*

Van Swieten, Gerard (1768) *Abhandlung des Daseyns der Gespenster ("Discourse on the Existence of Ghosts")*

Verstegen, Richard (1605) *A Restitution of Decayed Intelligence in Antiquities Concerning the Most Noble and Renowned English Nation*

Vincent of Beauvais (11th century) *Speculum Historiale ("Mirror of History")*

Voltaire (1764) *Dictionnaire Philosophique ("Philosophical Dictionary")*

Von Wächter, Günther A. F. (1883) *Memoiren eines Soldaten des Deutsch-Französischer Krieg ("A Soldier's Memoirs of the Franco-Prussian War")*

Walker, Barbara (1983) *The Women's Encyclopedia of Myths and Secrets*

Walker, Ernest (1964) *Mammals of the World*

Walpole, Horace (1745) *Letters of Horace Walpole*

Weinberg, Avner (2008) *Mystische Zwangsvorstellung: Die Jagd durch die Nationalsozialistische Deutsche Arbeiterpartei für Übernatürliche Macht ("Mystical Obsession: The Nazi Hunt for Supernatural Power")*

Wharton James, George (1920) *Indian Blankets and Their Makers*

William of Malmesbury (1125) *Gesta Regum Anglorum ("The Deeds of the English Kings")*

Williams, John (1791) *An Enquiry into the Truth of the Tradition, Concerning the Discovery of America, by Prince Madog ab Owen Gwynedd, about the Year, 1170*

Winstanley, William (1881) *A Visit to Abyssinia: An Account of Travel in Modern Ethiopia*

Witherspoon, Gary (1974) *Language and Art in the Navajo Universe*

Woodward, Ian (1979) *The Werewolf Delusion*

Ximénez, Francisco (1715) *Empiezan las historias del origen de los Indios de esta provincia de Guatemala, traduzido de la lengua quiché en la castellana para más comodidad de los Ministros del Sto. Evangelio, por el R.P.F. Franzisco Ximénez, Cura doctrinero por el Real Patronato del Pueblo de Sto. Thomás Chuilá ("Beginning of the histories of the origin of the Indians of this province of Guatemala, translated from the Quiché language to Spanish for the greater convenience of the Ministries of the Holy Gospel, by the Reverend Father Francisco Ximénez, Parish Priest for the Royal Patronage of the Town of Santo Tomás Chuilá")*

Yarrow, Henry Crecy (1881) *A Further Contribution to the Study of the Mortuary Customs of the North American Indians*

Young, Davis (1977) *Creation and the Flood*

Something large and menacing stood in the shadows, watching. I knew that it wasn't a werewolf—it smelled more like… well, like death. Like dead flesh. But not like a vampire—I couldn't smell that scent of old blood on its breath, or that ichor that the vampires have sludging through their veins. Besides, it was too big for a vampire, or any other man, for that matter. Its eyes seemed to gleam yellow-green in the dim light.

"Tell Herr Peregrinus, der *Tageslichtwanderer*," it said in a voice as dark and deep as a mountain cavern. "Tell him, *'Der Teufel wird Sie bald zu finden'*…"